About the Author

Stanislav Sevelski is a Russian-American linguist and translator. Born in Moscow, Russia to a family of Jewish, Russian and Romani origin, he relocated to the States as an adolescent and has been dedicating his life to traveling, teaching languages in different countries and writing ever since. Due to his mixed origin and lifestyle, Stanislav is deeply interested in cosmopolitanism, as well as intermixing of cultures and languages. For several years the object of his scholarly focus has been the Holocaust and the Porajmos (the Romani genocide) in Nazi German concentration camps - namely, the mutual penetration of languages and customs in the conditions of extreme stress. 'Requiem for Brünnhilde' is fictional work based on this research, and his first large-scale literary project in English (Stanislav has previously published two novels and an academic study in comparative linguistics in Russian).

Requiem for Brünnhilde

Stanislav Sevelski

Requiem for Brünnhilde

Olympia Publishers
London

www.olympiapublishers.com
OLYMPIA PAPERBACK EDITION

Copyright © Stanislav Sevelski 2025

The right of Stanislav Sevelski to be identified as author of
this work has been asserted in accordance with sections 77 and 78 of the
Copyright, Designs and Patents Act 1988.

All Rights Reserved

No reproduction, copy or transmission of this publication
may be made without written permission.
No paragraph of this publication may be reproduced,
copied or transmitted save with the written permission of the publisher, or in
accordance with the provisions
of the Copyright Act 1956 (as amended).

Any person who commits any unauthorised act in relation to
this publication may be liable to criminal
prosecution and civil claims for damage.

A CIP catalogue record for this title is
available from the British Library.

ISBN: 978-1-83543-190-0

This is a work of fiction.
Names, characters, places and incidents originate from the writer's imagination.
Any resemblance to actual persons, living or dead, is purely coincidental.

First Published in 2025

**Olympia Publishers
Tallis House
2 Tallis Street
London
EC4Y 0AB**

Printed in Great Britain

Contents

I 1st Violin 11
II 2nd Violin 33
III 1st Violin 51
IV 2nd Violin 76
V 1st Violin 103
VI 2nd Violin 125
VII 1st Violin 147
VIII 2nd Violin 163
IX 1st Violin 179
X 2nd Violin 196
XI 1st Violin 215
XII 2nd Violin 229
XIII 1st Violin 243
XIV 2nd Violin 258
XV 1st Violin 273
XVI 2nd Violin 287
XVII 1st Violin 301
XVIII 2nd Violin 313
XIX 1st Violin 325
XX 2nd Violin 338
Coda 358

*А только вышло по-другому,
Вышло вовсе и не так.*
Egor Letov (Pryg-skok)

I
1st Violin

Intro

Not that I object to routine work.

Not that I question the sacred premise that any labor is, ultimately, an ennobling activity.

Not that I, for a second, doubt the shrewdness of Angel's insight.

It is not doing certain things but being placed in charge of those I inwardly revolt against.

I might have been happily running on the bureaucratic wheel, under someone else's supervision, should Angel explicitly advise me that doing so is by his order and for the good of "The Cause". I could have forgotten sleeping, eating—even reflecting on my own research and my music—the two things that keep my sanity intact among the wretchedness. I could have given my all to the treadmill without a second thought.

It is being appointed ringmaster of the rat race that poisons my existence.

Another thing gnawing at me is the suspicion that the entire knavery is not in concord with Angel's academic conscience either. One can hardly perceive it as anything less than demeaning to his genius.

Are financial considerations so pressing he should place them above his scientific integrity?

They probably are, and it is certainly not my place to cast aspersions on Angel's motives.

If only someone else could be tasked to control the process; if only this particular cup could be taken away from me!

Farben want their copy typewritten on Remington. Pharma-Ko want theirs handwritten, always in one and the same hand, no capitals. The Hygiene Institute want theirs signed and stamped at every new entry. Then, finally, the Reichsführer wants it all retyped for him on Olympia Elite, to be delivered daily to his desk, with a special envoy.

And then, of course, all the talk about the friendship and hearty collaboration between the doctors is a sentimental myth.

We should at all times remember we are AU, not BU.

It is in BU that they let Hoven and Ding run riot with their abominations. Hoven—with his fake thesis, which he's had written for him by the inmates, his sleazy ways, and his filthy intrigues—becoming deputy director of the institute! Ding—with his unscrupulous grabbiness—heading the entire rabbit lungs Giroud vaccine affair! Unheard of!

No, we here at AU do not allow such outrage to take place. We here at AU are all impeccable in our professionalism. Our hands are clean, our heads cold, and our consciences stainless.

No doubt.

Only financial considerations are still there to be reckoned with. Along with diplomatic ones.

Farben and Pharma-Ko cannot stand each other, but they both must love us. So must the Hygiene Institute and the Reichsführer. We cannot let any of these important players down. By no means can we afford to disappoint them.

And so it falls to me to make sure the right field be left blank every now and then, in all their respective copies. A different field in each copy of course. Just like we do in the twin study under the "Cause of Death" heading. Only here, the job has a lot more amusing diversity to it: it is a new column every time, according to what exactly the receiving party wishes to emphasize at a particular moment.

And so it is that, on my instructions, they omit "vomiting" here, "diarrhea" there, "constipation" now, and "tinnitus" then.

What have I done to bring upon my head the curse of this position? Is there, perhaps, another way to placate the karma rather than fishing socks out of dirty laundry?

Pointless wondering.

*

Anton burst in on me like a comet into the gray Polish skies—headlong, dapper, and agitated to the point that the air around him sparked. Sparking, too, was his Lucky Strike (Anton—ever the Yankee admirer!) on which he dragged energetically.

'Bet you don't know the news!' he started, parking half his butt on the edge of my desk in the bon-vivant manner he employs when preparing to deliver an especially tickling piece of witticism.

'Farben have ordered another batch of thirty for Rutenol, with nine control. And, guess what, Pharma-Ko want a new batch too—for this new celebrated concoction of theirs…'

'Yes, Anton, I know the news,' I replied, staring past him into emptiness.

Sometimes I find his inexhaustible sense of humor slightly annoying.

'Come, Maestro, don't look so glum.' He reached across the desk and lifted my chin with the back of his long left index finger. 'We are doing a good job here. Akridin may be a bit of a quack potion, but Rutenol stands a chance. All we need is a little more control time…'

'All we need is that they keep it down long enough for it to be able to start taking this chance. And not die of side effects before it does so,' I interrupted.

'True.' He extinguished his cigarette in my ashtray. 'Our problem is we only get one trial, which either works or it doesn't. We act on the core, so to say. You administer it, then you get the swollen lips, then vomit all over the place, then myocardial weakness or toxic cachexy—and that's it; no possibility of a second take. We lack what those lucky bastards in Hohenlychen wound infection study had galore. Peripheral territories. You take a prisoner with perfectly healthy legs, gash those legs, infect the wound with wood or glass shards, place the injured limbs in traction, destroy muscles and nerve fibers, inject them with pus and blood-poisoning bacteria and whatnot. A leg gets gangrened, you chop it—or part of it—off and voilà! Start all the same anew on the other leg, or another spot on the same one. No wonder our miserable efforts here pale in comparison with those sulphonamides giants'…How helpful it would be to have the legroom they had!'

'It would, wouldn't it?' I intoned, mocking him and his ever-so-graceful puns.

Anton jumped to his feet, swiftly turned to face me, leaning forward and resting both his hands, wide apart, on the edge of my desk.

'Anyway. Have you decided on our setlist for The Evening, Maestro?'

'Oh… I thought we were doing… Beethoven, definitely?'

He caught me off guard. I'd completely forgotten about the damned evening.

'Well, *Romance No. 2* is your pièce de résistance. I mean, what else? Shall we do Bartók?'

'Probably. We might as well.'

'The autumn-leaf-haired Undine promised to help me out with the vocals on "The Nightingale" should you not mind including Alabieff in our modest repertoire'—he winked with meaning—'in Italian, no less.'

'I do not doubt Birgitte's talents'—I smiled—'but isn't Alabieff exactly what our famous one-of-a-kind AU girl orchestra covered the other day? Wouldn't it look a little plagiarized now if you and Birgitte did it?'

Anton let my jealousy wash over him. 'Not at all. It is just a romance, not *The* entire goddamn "Charge of the Light Brigade" we are going to plagiarize. Our girl band covered that too, with deplorable results. Angel seemed to hate it. Rumor has it, he left the room almost at the first bar.'

'Why don't you just go ahead and finalize the list yourself?' I suggested. 'You've always been better at pleasing those smug Pharma-Ko types without losing your dignity.'

'There's nothing I would not do to please YOU, Maestro. And God knows this has never been anything less than protein to my dignity.'

For all his sniggering mannerisms, I always feel better after talking to Anton, my own personal Peter Kreuder. Better and somewhat lighter. Must be on account of him so effortlessly possessing the one skill I have never mastered—the blessed art of not giving a damn.

*

It was dank outside—so much for the syrupy idyll of the Małopolska May. The wet space of the playground looked vast and unreal, like in one of these messy dreams that occur just before dawn.

The kids were scampering about, unaffected by the gloomy skies. Two bedraggled madcaps were pushing around the ball Angel had brought them the other day—mostly, it seemed, for the sake of stepping into squelchy pools of dirt—disturbing the swampy lull, crushing into it with their feet.

A pouting Sinti girl was shoving a Kalderash boy in the chest. '*Zigeuner, zigeuner! Gehe weg, weg! Ich bin eine fräulein, und du bist ein zigeuner!*'

I could not but once again admire Angel's talent, so wisely applied to organizing the children's leisure: their propensity for savage freedom so tactfully channeled into sports and games; their puppyish attachment to their parents so sensitively provided for. He could think of the tiniest detail and see the complex picture from so many different angles at once.

Take the twin project, for instance. What exquisite intellect, what divine inspiration one must be blessed with to devise something so simple and yet so brilliant! The Dionne quintuplets are born—the vigor of a life raised to the power of five ignites a spark which ten years later, collides with the dynamite of a mind that explodes into research amounting to a revolution in modern medical science. We infect one twin with typhus and then transfuse his blood into the other. We change the eye color of one and see if it stays, or changes back to what it was, to match his brother's. We sow two twins together and observe God's purposes in their billow-like, awe-inspiring actions. Such a respectful application of these little lives as to turn their benighted existence into powerful tools of progress—how else can it be described other than incarnate grace glowing with the light of an absolute and unquestionable genius!

The very fact of something like this becoming a reality proves the ultimate righteousness of "The Cause", the unparalleled privilege bestowed on our generation. Our generation that has produced giants of Angel's caliber.

And who am I to complain? Drawing up some papers, overseeing some formalities, and arranging an evening for Pharma-Ko once in a couple of months. Isn't it a laughable price to pay for being part of the very building force of "The Cause"? Especially when one has willing helpers like Anton at one's disposal.

Reminding myself of The Evening, I reasoned something *Allegro di Bravura* was probably in order, to honor Pharma-Ko's new development. Or something solemn and celebratory. Come to think of it, "The Charge of the Light Brigade" would not be such a bad idea. Or *Entrance of the Gods,* for that matter... Both of which would sound inexcusably enfeebled, of course, on our modest premises and without the brass section...

*

Incongruously, I thought of the unforgettable evening ten years ago.

My first university year.

My first evening at the Schwarzes.

Professor Schwarz and I were discussing the upcoming Friedrich Wilhelm event, and I suggested that Franz, Oliver, and I should do Wagner. I said I could orchestrate.

Then this tall, lean, olive-skinned, but pale adolescent entered the living room.

She was wearing a tight black dress and black stockings, which made her legs look unnaturally long, like an ostrich's. Her dark, auburn hair was disheveled. Her eyes were thickly lined and gave an eerie impression of two black swamps on a long-nosed face. If anything, she was the opposite of canonically pretty.

She reminded one of a very young, misguided witch.

In her stockinged feet, she made her way across the room, flaunting her movements—she manifestly perceived them as feline grace. Approaching the professor, she entwined her arms around his neck and pressed her long-lipped mouth to his cheek. Then she turned to me and smiled—a smile that was meant to be playful but came across as sad—the melancholy grin of a pierrot attempting at naughtiness.

'You are a musician, aren't you?'

The girlish voice was comically striving for huskiness.

'Do not do Wagner then; do Weill instead. The "Alabama Song." That's a lot more in the mood of the times. Do you like Brecht?'

'Pray, don't mind my daughter, Christian,' said the professor, giving her a kiss on the forehead. 'She becomes a little silly when she sees a handsome young man.'

This is how I met Indigo. The love of her father. The likeness of her mother. The child of the system.

A late and only child, she was adored and pampered. Her father, the professor, made sure she attended the best humanities school in Berlin.

At sixteen, she was fluent in English and French, and making inroads into Italian and Spanish.

She was a positive bookworm. Swallowing volumes of French and English decadents, she worshipped Wilde and Huysmans, learned Diderot and La Rochefoucauld by heart, and put expensive portraits of Keats and Shelley up on her purple bedroom wall. She saw herself as an amateur philosopher. She applauded Heidegger, pitied Nietzsche, and derided

Baeumler. She avidly soaked up art, music, theater, and cinema; appreciated the classics, but was especially fascinated by the morbid forms to which the System served as such fertile soil. That particular predilection had a genetic basis.

Indigo's mother was an American cabaret singer of Italian descent. Ginevra Bellardi, stage-named Gina Belle, had been the wonder of a Manhattan cabaret called Indigo Blue until she contracted a mild form of tuberculosis, which urged her to seek help from a then already famous German doctor, Professor Albert Schwarz.

'She was terribly concerned that the disease might affect her vocal chords. And I had just published my work on the laryngeal complications, which happened to catch the eye of the owner of Indigo Blue. In the States, they hunt up information like true scouts should,' the professor reminisced affectionately.

Recommending Doctor Schwartz to his best singer proved not such a wise move on the part of the cabaret owner. It was to lose him the star of the show, for not only did the professor fall in love with his transatlantic patient and go on to marry her, but the war-bled Berlin, too, embraced the American diva and took her to its bosom like an ointment for its wounds. The former New York singer now sang in the German capital and was so dearly loved that the proprietor of the new venue, which she graced with her presence, agreed to rename his cabaret Indigo Blue on her request, in the memory of the place which had opened Gina Belle a window into stardom.

It was, however, neither tuberculosis nor loss of voice that, years later, killed Frau Schwarz. Indigo's decadent mother threw herself under a streetcar in Friedrichstrasse, succumbing to the influence of a substantial dose of cocaine to heavy abuse of which she had taken toward the end of her earthly existence. Little Indigo was ten years old when she became half-orphaned.

The professor never quite got over the loss of his wife, whom he adored despite (or perhaps, for) her truly primadonna-like spending habits, daily tantrums, gross neglect of parental duties, and dementia tendencies, which aggravated after their first and only child was born.

'Gina was too delicate, too exotic, a songbird for this rough world. The weight of mundanity bore too heavily on her wings and eventually crushed them. Even my love, no matter how great, was helpless to save her…'

Indigo, too, seemed to admire and lament her late mother, notwithstanding that the intemperate Gina had been so chary of normal motherly care.

'What little girl needs a mother when there is a creature like Gina Belle around to instruct one in fabulous womanhood? Even if one is only eight years old!' She laughed.

In fact, apart from herself, her mother was the only female, dead or alive, for whom Indigo felt affection. All other women in the world she uncompromisingly and ostentatiously despised.

'She wouldn't let another girl approach, let alone touch me, when I came to collect her in the kindergarten'—the professor sighed—'and, as bad luck would have it, children generally adore me. Every time, a flock of curious little things would come up and start flirting, making eyes at me, and showing their toys. Once, I was imprudent enough to pick one up and toss her into the air. This girl seemed friendly with Indigo, and she smiled especially invitingly at me every time I came. Well, my jealous daughter burst into tears. She whimpered all night, refused to eat or talk to me, and even ran a temperature. I patiently tried to talk sense into her, pointing out that Berta—the girl at the kindergarten—looked like a good friend, and, to my mind, Indigo's resentment was irrational. To which she, through tears, gave me a look a mature woman could've given an overly optimistic youth, and passed her sentence:

"Papa, oh papa, you are so NAIVE! She and the others, they are only nice to me on a whim, or when you are around. As soon as I start trusting them, they turn on me, refuse to play with me, push me, and call me "crow" because they say I have a nose like one!"

I would simply flee from other little girls who made an attempt at contact with me ever since.' He chuckled. 'Lest I break my child's heart.'

What really did break her heart was the professor's sudden death of an infarction three years after I first met her. She nearly died herself of mere grief. Her love for her father was overwhelming—so intense that it eventually turned into a weapon that wounded her all but lethally.

Just like her other, less worthy loves wounded her later on.

*

Back in the office, I started on the paperwork. Getting it over and done with is gratifying enough to spark off a dose of inspiration for an evening session. The inspiration I so badly want in this inflamed appendix of Europe.

But it was not to be.

It was the ubiquitous Guido Karp to interrupt me this time.

Just like Anton, Guido broke in uninvited and without knocking. Only, unlike Anton, Guido is not blessed with the redeeming qualities of wit and elegance. Nor does his presence ever make me feel lighter. If anything, his boorish manners cause me to sense the unworthiness of my position all the more, in no small measure because I know the lout wants my job. He craves it more than anything else in his mediocre life.

'So. Forty for Farben, and forty for Pharma-Ko. Sounds like we have our work cut out for us. How are you coming along there?'

Every time Guido has me within eyeshot, he just can't help playing the boss. His undernourished self-esteem cries out loud to be fed, the poor fellow.

'I'm telling you,' he droned on, not bothering to wait for an answer. 'If it hadn't been for those three Belgian *Mischlinge* last month, we'd be filled to the brim; we'd be bloating like toads, brother. Two hundred and thirty-six fresh and ready objects escaped. Two hundred and thirty-six, man! The stinking Belgian swine!'

Guido snorted in exasperation.

'Well, the Warsaw Ghetto had thirteen thousand potential objects up in flames, on the same day,' I observed.

But Guido waved away my attempt at philosophical attitude.

'Those thirteen thousand were not ours. The Belgian two hundred and thirty-six bugger me a damn sight worse. These were headed straight into our lab, man. And slip through our damn fingers; they did all right, thanks to their slinking Belgian resistance scum.'

He was tiring me out. I sighed and offered, 'Look. Do you want to draw up the batch lists? I'm sure you'll have it all up and running in no time. Anton and I could vouch for you with Angel. He'd understand. He'd see that a stickler for neat bookkeeping like yourself is a lot better fitted for the job than a slowpoke with his head in the clouds like me. And I'd feel much more in my element executing your instructions than giving you any.'

I found myself speaking sincerely.

Guido squinted, his watery eyes sinking into his cheeks.

'I would take you up on that one, brother, if I cared any less for you. But, as it is, how can I ever part you with this desk when I know you cherish it so much? What other bureau would make a better place for the portrait of your black-eyed Carmen? Where would you feel more comfortable sitting and staring at her for hours? Do you know if she still smokes, by the way, your rebellious gitane? Or has she quitted?'

Ever since he spotted on my desk the photograph of Indigo holding a cigarette in between her slender fingers, Guido hasn't missed a chance to needle me about her exotic appearance and my obsession with her, sermoning me at every opportunity on how unnatural it is for a German woman to smoke, especially flaunt this habit.

As I coolly ignored his taunts, Guido continued, 'Actually, come to think of it... Come to think of it, old chap, you have enough on your plate observing this revolting noma, the Gypsy plague... No? I reckon, if you really switched on those bright brains of yours and conjured up some truly Nobel prize piece of medical science there, and then, perhaps, put in a word for me with old Josef...' He rolled his eyes and shrugged his shoulders in mock wondering. 'Then, who knows if he might not just lend an ear and allow me to rid you of the neat bookkeeping... Eh? Especially now, that we are short of material, and Pharma-Ko are pressing with their tall order? Perhaps he'd have you get on with noma alone, and I'd sweat my guts with Rutenol and the new Pharma-Ko job for you?'

His cheeks flushed, taking on a decidedly beetroot color; he perspired and puffed, unable to contain his excitement at the thought.

'I'd even let you keep the portrait of your smoking Esmeralda on my desk, mind you!'

Winking and chortling, Guido left me, pleased with himself for having brought the conversation so masterly round to the only subject that really mattered in his greedy Guido Karp world: the possibility of him heading the Farben-Pharma-Ko project.

*

I spent an hour raking my brains over the batch lists, practically in vain.

Much as I hated to admit it, Guido was right. The notorious April attack on the twentieth convoy between Boortmeerbeek and Haacht did set us back. Left the labs in dire need of material just when the two new typhus orders struck.

And so, suppressing the urge to look in on Epstein and Bendel in the experimental barracks, I took another bumpy ride to AU2, crossed the playground again, and headed for the main family camp to do the impossible and find potential objects.

Every time I enter those barracks, I just cannot stop admiring their dwellers' paradoxical attitude toward life. Their roving habits restricted by the confinement, they, nevertheless, seem always in motion. They wonder from corner to corner, chat endlessly, twang their instruments, bet, argue, quarrel, and reconcile. They daydream so intently you can almost hear the bell-ringing of their thoughts. The daily discomforts inherent in the camp's quotidian reality, like limited food rations and poor hygiene, do not appear to trouble them much—thanks to nomadic existence, they are accustomed to taking inconveniences in their stride. Yet they cling to certain rituals which, in their minds, are associated with cleanliness. They become bitterly upset in case observing those is hindered by circumstances. Not regarding serious disease or high mortality as particularly tragic, they are, at the same time, terrified of death and the dead. Infinitely good-natured and habitually cheerful, they may show true viciousness at a trifle gesture, or even a mere glance from a member of another clan, if they by some reason interpret it as a slight (their criteria of what manifestations should be regarded as offensive and what as innocent are still beyond my comprehension, for all the long time I have spent studying their rules of cohabitation). They are mercurial while being almost pathologically indolent, naive and trusting like children, and, simultaneously, sly and deceitful—not alien at times to committing acts of downright heinousness, like betraying a close friend.

Little Damira slid off the bunk and ran up to me, grinning broadly.

'Onkel Heidert!'

She put her scabies-ridden arms round my thigh; pressed her face to my hipbone.

'I knew you'd come today, the voices in my head told me!'

I felt a hot wave of shame flood my neck and cheeks; I did not bring her anything. Over and over again I had to kick myself for not being Angel—neither intellectually, nor morally. He could think of everything—sweets, little toys, and the right words. I hopelessly and dumbly forgot.

For want of a friendlier gesture, I patted Damira's bony skull and proceeded to greet her mother, Marusya—a still young Gypsy who looked more like her daughter's sibling rather than parent.

'Hope the day rewards you for your hard work, Doctor Heidert.'

She did not look up at me—she was nursing. The wrinkly-faced baby, Damira's brother, lay on her bent elbow, while she slightly rocked him.

All of a sudden it became clear to me I was wasting my time in this barrack. I knew everybody here too well. Their names, faces, and medical histories. I knew that, for different reasons, none of them suited. Either the age, or the physicality, was not right. Or else, they were needed—and way too good—for other purposes.

Damira, for instance. No considerations in the world—political or financial—would ever persuade me to sacrifice her to Pharma-Ko. Not now, that she is starting to show a tiny, but promising ulcer in the area of her left cheek, just above the upper lip.

I was about to leave when, out of the corner of my eye, I noticed this lad whose name I can never remember. A young, tall, and moody fellow. Always quiet, always with a violin I haven't yet heard him play. Long-limbed. Healthy.

Him, perhaps?

Something about this Gypsy inevitably reminds me of a picture on Indigo's wall—an illustration of a work by an obscure Russian Romantic poet called "Tamara and Daemon."

Indigo spent hours contemplating this daemon figure—the dark, aquiline profile, the reclining position, and the naked shoulders. Muscular yet fragile. The eyes full of Weltschmerz, with a glint of perversion and perfidy lurking in their dusky depth. How fascinated she was with the sickly image!

Many a time she took my face in her hands, turned it so she could see the left side of it, and exclaimed, 'Oh, you do look like him! That's what I like the most about you. You ARE like him! If only you would grow your hair a little longer…'

Once I, jokingly, took her own face in my hands, turned it slightly sideways and gasped with exaggerated horror. 'Good Lord! Indigo! It is not me, it is you who looks like him. You are metamorphosing into him through sheer contemplation—you are stigmatic, do you know this?'

Though I was speaking in jest, this observation was not entirely untrue. With her messy dark hair, chiseled features, and twilight eyes, she might as well have been the sitter for that particular painting, where the daemon was all marble profile and dazzling shoulders, while the weeping Tamara beside him—just a pair of black braids (in Indigo's album, I had seen other images of the daemon by the same artist, where the Fallen Spirit looked less effeminate).

Quite unexpectedly, she threw her arms around my neck and kissed me on the lips. She said it was the best compliment someone had ever given her.

Far from associating herself with the heroine Tamara—the daemon's defenseless victim—she wanted to resemble Tamara's abductor—the disturbed creature, whose soul, she said, was the reflection of her own.

She sought his features—both outward and inward—in others too, and was magnetized by those in whom she thought she found them.

As to myself, Guido Karp did not hit too wide off the mark, pointing out that my attraction to Indigo was of an unwholesome nature.

For how else to explain the fact that this confounded daemon of hers started haunting me too? Sometimes I did indeed see him in the mirror, looking, with a certain lighting and at a particular angle, at my own face.

Those moments gave me strange, triumphant shots of pleasure. But he never tormented me more than when I saw him coming through in other men, predominantly strangers—their features, facial expressions, bodies, and postures.

Those appearances had a morbid appeal. I was, in spite of myself, drawn to them, though the more they attracted me, the more they poisoned my nervous system with a corroding jealousy.

Same dull ache along with burning explosions under the ribs occurs every time I catch a glimpse of the somber Gypsy with his violin.

And this time too, instead of deciding if he would be good for Pharma-Ko's tests, I ended up wondering whether Indigo would see in this dark profile her adored daemon as vividly as I saw him there myself.

*

Singularly flustered after my visit to the Gypsy camp, I couldn't face returning to the office. It would have been in vain, and exercises in futility always made me sick to my stomach.

I drove home instead.

I stood for a while, resting my forehead against the windowpane, torpidly staring into the purplish dusk which was thickening over the Rynek Główny market square.

I was trying to collect my thoughts.

It was music of all things I suddenly craved after saying hello to the residents of the barrack. It was playing, not writing the goddamn lists I wanted to do.

Nearly two weeks had passed since the last time I took Cosima out of her mahogany case.

Ever so timid. Always procrastinating. Wary of another failure and the sheer discomfort of a disappointment. Like a child tearfully scared of having a splinter removed out of his foot with a needle.

What I love about Cosima, however, is that she is patient with me. Forgiving my faintheartedness, she reflects calm persistence in her replete, layered browns. There is a hidden reserve of strength—a restrained glint of passion—in her hazelly shimmer.

Away with diffidence!

Siegfried struck—brave—rushing headlong into the main theme.

For an hour, I bowed détaché d' ravenously on open strings, chasing tempo and character. Siegfried burned the hand, tearing forward. Cosima clung to the shoulder, her habitual composure giving in to the thrill of the hunt.

I know it every time it comes near.

I can feel its heat on my fingers and its pulsation in my veins.

I can hear it, smell it, and taste it when it is within my grasp.

The dazzling creation, the intoxicating ecstasy of sound which might ensure that my name be scribed in the Annals of Music alongside the großen meister.'

Yet every time I stretch out my hand, trembling with anticipation, it disintegrates. Leaves me groping around, stuggling to snatch a single mood, a thread, or a molecule.

All in vain. All not right.

Nothing much has changed since my Bayreuth fever.

Is it any wonder Indigo Schwarz had such a grip on me if she was virtually the only person in the world who understood. Immediately and perfectly.

We did continue the conversation about Wagner. About music in general. About art and literature, our respective studies, and everything. The professor, who, with his characteristic well-roundness and gentle humor, participated in the discussion at first, presently excused himself and retired into his study, choosing to leave us tête-à-tête, as he sensed that the two young people—his beloved daughter and his favorite student—were obviously drawn to each other.

I cannot quite explain what I saw in her from the start that prompted me to decide to tell her about the most significant, the most intimate thing in my life, my greatest dream—all on the day of our very first meeting.

Was it her outlandish allure that bordered on grotesquerie? Did it, perhaps, help me lose the natural bashfulness I would certainly have felt in the company of any other young, intelligent creature in favorable circumstances, the daughter of one of my mentors?

Or could it be her straightforward manner combined with astonishing judgments?

Or might the poignant sense of melancholy and strangely endearing defenselessness which did, counter to all the other, militant constituents of her nature, permeate her entire being, somehow make me feel I was safe confiding in her?

Even to this day, I cannot stop wondering.

I told her about Bayreuth—the four unforgettable nights when my father had taken me, a promising twelve-year-old violinist, to see Der Ring as a reward for my exemplary studies. I told her about the impact those four nights had on me. On my entire life.

I told her how overwhelmed I was by the grandeur, the splendidness of the performance, and the sheer scale of the meister's most sublime creation.

How deeply, how indelibly, the character of Brünnhilde impressed me—the embodied paradox of a compassionately loving, womanly nature wedded with recalcitrance, vengefulness, cruelty, even…

I recounted to her how, back in Berlin, I had come down with a fever, probably the gravest in my adolescent life, which terrified my parents as it almost killed me. For over two weeks I was thrashing in delirium, my lungs torn with a violent cough, my blood and brain ablaze.

And in the merciless flames that raged within my head, I could see my defiant Valkyrie burning, clinging to the back of her noble horse Grane—agonizing, yet undaunted—broken, yet unbent. And, as her released spirit ascended toward Valhalla, which was to share her fate, I suddenly saw it—perceived Brünnhilde's soul in all its unresolved complexity. All its facets were momentarily revealed to me; its contradictions comprehended and embraced by my own enflamed consciousness.

Then, before I had a chance to fathom the tremendous vision, sight transformed into sound. I could not see it anymore, but I could hear it. The Valkyrie's soul was now music playing in my head—the most stunning, painful, mesmerizing music I had ever known.

That night proved the critical point in my illness, for by the morning my temperature dropped and I started on a slow, enfeebled, coughing and sweating way to recovery.

When, however, I finally accumulated enough strength to crawl out of bed and on weak legs made my staggering way to the violin (my unforgettable Isolde), I could not reproduce a single note of the sonic magic I had heard in my delirious state.

That was when I attempted suicide—only to be saved, half my body dangling from the window—by a horrified maidservant.

Luckily, my desperate deed was attributed to my yet uncured physical infirmity, and I was spared my parents' attempts to seek psychiatric assistance, which would have likely occurred, should the overall state of my health have been different.

There is barely a means I have not applied to recover my uncreated creation ever since.

I spent sleepless nights striving to notate it and restless days struggling to play it.

I tried describing it verbally and writing the descriptions down to read them subsequently to my meisters, hoping their experience and musical intuition might work a miracle for me.

I sought to recall it in my sleep.

I even passed winterly hours outdoors, with my coat off, in a pitiful attempt to contract a fever again and, through it, return into the delirious state which had kindled the divine spark in me.

And although some deceitful moments did communicate to me the ephemeral impression that I almost gained on it—nearly held it in my hands, in my head, and in the strings of my instrument—all the more bitter was my disappointment afterward—an hour, day, or several nights later, when, trying to play it again, I realized I was not and never had been, even close to capturing the magic.

So immediate and intense was my rapport with Indigo, that,

inadvertently, I began describing it to her in technical terms.

'A violin concerto, not romantic, baroque rather…' I was explaining in a confused manner, for want of clearer verbal means and yet arduously desiring to convey to her what had become my life's goal.

'Nothing Wagnerian of course, none of that grandiosity—strictly chamber and elitist… Ostinato rhythmic pattern in sixteenths as the core element, non-stop motion… Energetic tempo, allegro or allegro molto, but not too fast, probably allegro ma non troppo… And the mood—the mood is paramount—furioso or feroce…'

She insisted that I play my drafts to her. Despite my reservations, I complied.

She said she could feel exactly what I wanted to express, that she wished she were a composer herself—or, better, a psychoanalyst—to be able to help me.

'Have you read the theory of the unconscious mind? It is not so much Wagner inspiring you, as your own innermost self rushing to the surface and demanding to be heard,' she was enlightening me in the Jewish intricacies of her much-admired Freud. 'Brünnhilde's moods are nothing but your own states of mind, which you may not always be aware of. You are, yourself, your Brünnhilde.'

Over time, as our friendship grew, I came to associate my unborn sonic child with her rather than the heroine of "Der Ring."

Thus Brünnhilde's moods became Indigo Mind. Nothing spelled *ostinato* for me more than Indigo Schwarz's personality.

*

A gentle knock on the door brought me out of my stupor.

'Yes, Birgitte. Come on in!'

In the whole of AU, there is only one hand that can knock this way—a breezy, volant *tah-tahmn*, as though the bones were as light as a bird's.

This wonderful lightness—of figure, touch, gait, voice, and manner—just about sums up Birgitte. Not counting, of course, the spellbinding shock of autumnal hair. It is not for nothing that in the family camp they call her "Loli Tschai"—"red girl." For the red hair and the girlishness makes Birgitte what she is—a creature, able, at times, to distract me from my twilight-blue thoughts about Indigo.

'No rest for the wicked, laborer?' She brushed her lips against my cheek lightly—like everything else she does.

'Alas!' I returned the kiss.

'Bet you now wish Guido for your deputy!'

'Won't deny it. Just made him an offer, as a matter of fact.'

'Not surprisingly! Oh…'

Her glance fell on Cosima, spent and placated after the hunt, lying in her characteristic serenity on my bed, Siegfried beside her, guarding her rest.

'You've been playing? Preparing for The Evening?'

'Yes—no—well, yes! Preparing for The Evening too.'

'Will you play one of your own pieces? My favorite? That… wait, don't tell me!'

She shut her eyes, striving to recall, then brought her hands to her cheeks, ashamed of her forgetfulness.

'I can't believe it; my memory is becoming a positive sieve.'

'I know which one you mean,' I hurried to reassure her, for the flaming blush—the attribute of all gingerheads—was flooding her cheeks too instantaneously and too enticingly for me to endure.

'I hope you do, dear. I'd love to hear you play it. It would make this entire evening ordeal so much more bearable!'

Birgitte is a born anthropologist, even in the literal sense of the word. She knows, understands, and feels other human beings deeper than anyone else I've ever met. Her attention to detail is only perhaps surpassed by Angel's, while her tact and delicacy are unparalleled. To say nothing of her being a brilliant scholar. Not surprisingly, everyone who is lucky enough to be in her orbit falls under the spell.

The children cling to her. She spends hours talking to them. Without an exaggeration, their interacting—the little scruffy bunch gathered around her while she labors away at her research—the notebook on the dainty lap, the fragile wrist fluttering incessantly, the sharpened pencil flying across the paper—is one of the most endearing sights I have ever been blessed to contemplate.

Can then anyone blame Anton, or even Guido-the-boor (for nothing human is alien to him) that they, too, fall at the feet of the irresistible being and, each in their own fashion, express their delight?

I ought to learn to control my ever-gnawing jealousy.

'I hear Anton and yourself are considering "The Nightingale" for The Evening? A duet?'

She squinted and shook her head, bringing the riches of her hair in a wavy stir.

'Anton is overoptimistic about my humble abilities. He would like me to sing in Italian. I'll disgrace him, but then…' She winked playfully. 'He has been warned.'

I put my hand on hers.

'You two will make a sensation.'

She lowered her eyes and smiled bashfully.

'As long as the meister approves…'

'He does.'

Her voice, though lacking in strength, is not, it has to be admitted, devoid of pleasantness. Airy and clear, it does attractively set off Anton's confident piano.

She turned her face sharply to me.

'I'll do it on one condition. You play Tongues of Flame.'

She knitted her eyebrows and pursed her lips, childishly smug—proud of having recalled the name of my piece without a reminder.

I sighed resignedly.

'I will if you ask me to. Although you know I have forsworn playing my own compositions at such events.'

'I know it should feel a bit like casting pearls to you in that society, but for me personally?'

I sighed again and nodded.

'For you—yes. All right.'

All her coy blushing is a façade, of course. She is a flirt all right, this Birgitte. And she does exactly what has always rendered me defenseless before a woman—encourages my work, appreciates my creativity.

Precisely the means which Indigo, consciously or unconsciously, employed. The tactic infallibly disarmed me, making me forgive any mischievous stunts she pulled.

Indeed, I had probably been the only artist to whom my Indigo was a faithful muse until, after her father's sudden demise, she moved into her aunt's house to start sharing a roof with the venerable lady and her son. Indigo's sojourn with her father's sister and her cousin Bernie marked the beginning of the bane of my life—Indigo's "berniemania."

Bernie was not a daemon—he was a pierrot. Another of the sickly types that never failed to enchant my susceptible decadent, for it reflected another facet of her own complex personality—or so she thought.

And cousin Bernie, forsooth, had all the attributes—the emaciated thinness, the alabaster paleness, the black eyebrows, the hollow cheeks, and the never-ending hypochondria. He was also a self-proclaimed painter and, just like Indigo's late mother, suffered from a mild form of tuberculosis—both of which made him irresistible for Indigo.

The latter circumstance proved especially effective in signing my death warrant, for I have always been blessed (or, in this case, cursed) with good health.

Nothing could go a longer way in lowering a man's chances with Gina Belle's daughter than wholesomeness.

Thus Indigo became what I, in my frustration, called "a berniemaniac." Henceforth it was, predictably, not mine, but Bernie's art (at least the form of activity he had the effrontery to call his "art") she took to encouraging. She even managed to drag me into the process—against my esthetic sensibility, male pride, human integrity, and better judgment.

But did I have a choice, really?

'Promise?'

Once again, it was Birgitte's clear voice that brought me out of my reverie.

'Promise what?'

'Will you play Tongues of Flame at The Evening? Please?'

'Ah! Yes. If you want me to. Promise.'

*

All women are flirts. Flirts and attention seekers. Regardless of being, by their disposition, serious or light-minded, sophisticated or simple, somber or cheerful. Regardless also, it seems, of whom the attention comes from.

Look at Birgitte, for instance.

Pretty, educated, refined, and angelic character.

Well, I could understand her making eyes at Anton Lauer. For Anton's merits cannot be denied. Anton is handsome and stylish, with a sense of irony to put Schaub-the-jester to shame.

But her partiality to Guido beats me.

As soon as we said our goodbyes and Birgitte fluttered out of my flat, I saw from the window her lavishing smiles at the boor who happened to be loitering just outside my building (what business did he have tarrying there, I wonder?). He intercepted her just as she was making her way out of the front gate—all bearish grace and lustful smiles cracking his simpleton's face!

It was no small effort to keep myself from rushing out and putting my fist through that dumb, sniggering muzzle.

What can an autumnal Freia like herself find in that Fafner?

I mean, the vulgarity of his very mind!

The pig refers to noma as "the revolting Gypsy plague" and, at that, has the temerity to call himself a medical scientist.

If we assume noma is a Gypsy plague, what is ignobility of mind then? The plague of all lowly souls?

It was in this exasperated state that The Idea hit me.

Hardly can we predict to whom we will owe our next spark of divine inspiration—a nymph or an ogre!

Force vitale!

Of course!

How simple, how elegant the explanation is!

In the circulatory systems of the vertebrates, blood leaves and returns to the heart due to this indefatigable muscle's work against both the viscous resistance of the system and gravity; lymph flow, too, although without a central pump and in conditions of low pressure, defies gravity thanks to smooth muscles'—namely valves—and adjacent skeletal muscles' action.

Yet there are processes that still haven't found a rational explanation, such as the ascent of sap in Tracheophyta plants.

What is, indeed, the force that brings the sap in motion? Capillary action? Transpirational pull? Root pressure?

Nonsense!

Oversimplified, unprovable flimflam.

The only plausible theory that has ever been put forward is the one proposed by the vitalists, who rightly emphasized the fundamental difference between living organisms and non-living entities, asserting the obvious truth that the mysteries of life could not be reduced to a mechanistic process.

Force vitale!

Even the vitalists, however, largerly underestimated the **intelligence** of the force of life. The force that is evidently not just some uniform motion but a conscious, self-recognizing, and wise will.

Plants are living things; so are humans.

The same vital force that explains the vertical transport of fluids in vascular plants via xylem is, therefore, behind the development of noma in asocial representatives of the Hominina subtribe.

Without the participation of a vital function, it would be simply impossible for pathogens to begin interacting with other bacterial organisms so intensely as to produce necrotizing ulcerative reactions in the young of a particular kind of subhumans, within a strictly limited period of time, and on an epidemic scale.

What can it be other than nature taking its course in the most glorious way!

The cleansing *exitium sui* mechanism gets activated in a specific cluster of organisms when the time comes for them to clear the way for a loftier and a more viable kind. When the natural order of things demands it. And, obediently, the inferior physiology complies—and this submissive act of self-destruction is the most noble deed in the course of its ignoble existence. The one that redeems the very fact of it having been created in the first place!

Sensing that in my head—in my hands now—I was holding invaluable material for both the Institute for Anthropology and the Hygiene Institute, I sat down and started writing. I had to nail The Idea while it proffered itself so lavishly, so distinctly—to be captured.

My head was humming, attacked with a tremendous rush of blood.

My heart was beating out a triumphant rhythm.

Since my Bayreuth fever, now was the first time I was feeling alive again—thinking, generating, and accomplishing at the top of my abilities.

I do not resent AU anymore.

I do not despise Guido-the-boor.

Nothing—absolutely nothing—comes our way without a reason. And now I know why AU and Guido have marched into my life so boldly, forcing their importunate presence on me.

They have done so in order to bring out the scientist in me. To prove to all of the civilized world that Christian Heidert is one.

II
2nd Violin

Not that I object to routine work.

Not that I don't regard the political education of Mihai as a worthy task to undertake.

Not that I don't at times even enjoy our little clashes.

The trouble is, the old man is a veritable *baro godi*. The more we squabble, the more the big soul takes to me. Like a warm-hearted father to a wayward son.

Look at today, for instance.

There lies Mihai, sprawled out on his bunk, languorous like your Adam on the Sistine Chapel's ceiling. There sit I, having a peaceful conversation with Lavuta, giving her an innocent afternoon caress. And, suddenly, something starts tick-tick-ticking, most obnoxiously offsetting Lavuta's rhythm. Well, I tune in, and what should I hear other than Mihai's mind working, preparing to go on the offensive. And what am I left to do? I lazily start fortifying my garrisons.

'What you said about Tito the other day…'

He stirs and coughs. That prickly cough of his, for want of a gauntlet, Mihai employs as a challenge to combat.

I man my battle stations while never letting go of Lavuta, who is conspiratorially clinging to my shoulder.

'Yes, Babbo. What was it I said?'

Mihai doesn't bother to remind me the details of the particular debate he is referring to. He lunges straight forward.

'What you said is all wrong. Wrong and weak.'

'Weak? Pray, what is it you mean, Babbo?'

He bursts into an angry cough and bangs his parchment-dry fist on the bunk.

'You know exactly what I mean, boy, and you can wipe that smirk off your face! I'm telling you it is WEAK to disparage a man just because he is more brave and talented than you.'

'Why, I didn't disparage anyone, Babbo.'

'No? You didn't?' Mihai is seething by now. 'You didn't say Tito was a— what was this ugly name you called him?'

'He said Tito was a pelican,' Vano, the little sycophant, chimes in from the floor where he is sitting, shuffling his greasy card pack.

'Exactly, a pelican.' Mihai is relieved to be prompted the ingenious invective. 'Vano, that's a good lad—always there with his young memory to help the old man out. A pelican! You should be ashamed of yourself and your weakness!'

'A politican.' I sigh wearily. 'Vano ought to spend less time picking his nose and more doing the grammar exercises I give him.'

'And here you go again with your snottiness,' Mihai launches on a new round. 'What difference does it make—"pelican" or "politican"? How dare you call the greatest *ataman* in the world bad names?'

'Well, I said he was a future politican, Babbo, not a current one. I am forecasting a probable scenario, not calling names. No one denies the greatness of his role in the here and now. He certainly serves his purpose.'

'Serves? And why would Tito serve anyone? Tell me! He doesn't serve, he is a true rebel and a leader—not like you, a smart-assed layabout! Now, that's what you envy him, eh? That's what you wish you had!'

At this point the wisest tactic for me is continuing on the mild defensive, as my cantankerous opponent has largely quenched his thirst for argument, and, should I play my cards right, it is all going to be gently sloping to an idyllic denouement from here on.

'I'm saying he serves a *purpose*, Babbo,' I explain softly. 'It means he is the right man for the moment. It's not belittling him in any way, just the opposite.'

'Always you think you are smarter than everyone else with these long words of yours!'

And here an idea of an elegant comparison occurs to me—one that will ensure a favorable truce.

'See, Babbo, I like to think of Tito in a way like I think of our Baba Tanya.'

A spark of curiosity flashes in the old man's eyes—and that curiosity is not of a disapproving kind.

'How so?'

'You see how many patients she has. They all come to her; they all need her. Not that she cures them, truly, no. But she helps them forget about what *really* hurts.'

I nod at Baba Tanya, who is occupying her favorite corner—big, dark, and imperious—giving young Marusya instructions on how to treat her mastopatia and make her new baby's colics go away—Marusya at her short, chubby feet, all attention and reverence.

Mihai's eyes turn yet another shade warmer.

'Why, you are right there, son. See, where you're right, you're right; I will never say you're not. Tito is a little like our Baba Tanya; this is so. What is it you say about her?'

'A charlatan is a malingerer's best friend…' I whisper, lest the ever-alert Baba Tanya hear and sound alarm at being verbally disrespected.

'Yes, yes… a shar… whatever. Not sure what these clever words of yours mean, son, but they ring true to me.'

*

A malingerer is a charlatan's best friend, that's how the original went.

Shandor's voice—cozy like crackling of logs on the hearth, yet biting like carbolic soap—comes alive in my ears, dragging behind itself a chain of other sounds, smells, and visions.

The air of the marquee is damp and saturated with sawdust. The woody scent fills the nostrils, nestles in the throat, and clings to the skin. Businka is neighing in the stable—an impatient, capricious, girly "yyyiiiiihhh." Flame the Mad is galloping in circles round and round, his charcoal mane cascading about the ebony neck (why do they only insist on crimping it? It is so much more vibrant and, indeed—a lot wildly wavier like this, the natural way).

Yoska is standing in front of Shandor—skinny, pale, one leg bent, and face frozen in the ultimate expression of a plaintive plea. Shandor is sitting down, his back against Danior-the-Drummer's giant drum. Shandor is all lordly, knowing, and right. Yoska is all childish, pleading, and miserable—and at such moments I honestly start to wonder what it is I find in the boy.

'Please. I am not joking, Shandor. It's my knee, and it's squeezing the life out of me. You know it is. You know she can help me. People say she's worked wonders for them and raised them from the dead. Please, Shandor, can I go to her?'

'Of course,' sneers Shandor, beating out a mocking rhythm on Danior's drum with his shapely fingers. 'Go the way of all the other morons, child. Convince yourself your knee is the end of the world. Indulge the impostor lady. Indeed, a malingerer is a quack's best friend, so go—what are you waiting for?'

The little contretemps are over Yoska's old injury—his dislocated kneecap, which has long since healed but apparently keeps reminding of itself whenever there occurs a streak of damp weather. And when it does, Yoska feels it is his inalienable right to make sure the entire world is aware of his suffering, and, preferably suffers with him. He does amaze me sometimes, the unruly love of my life. A dashing horseman, intrepid like a feline predator, irrepressible like a wild mustang, irreverent like a young satyr. One that wouldn't let out a groan when a burning log fell on his bare back; when Flame the Mad nearly crushed his thigh with his five hundred kilogram Arabian bulk; when a Transylvanian gambler's blade went through his neck, missing the carotid by half an inch. All chivalrous exploits, to be mentioned with indifference and proudly worn the scars of on his lithe frame. But should a slight fever, a mild cold, or the dreaded knee bother him, and he will literally pull all the nerves out of your body with his whining.

The healer that Yoska seeks to consult is a local celebrity—the buxom wife of the top communist leader of the Soviet town of N. Her name, ironically, coincides with Baba Tanya's. It is Tatiana, the full Russian version of "Tanya" (do all middle-aged women bearing this name suffer from a superiority complex?). Unlike Baba Tanya, however, this lady is well-groomed and an officially trained oncologist, complete with a dissertation and a membership in the Academy of Sciences. Or so they say. Nobody really knows what is true in Soviet Russia and what is not. Especially when it concerns communist leaders' next of kin. Some things become true only because it is inappropriate to call them in question. Or because they are repeated a sufficient number of times. This phenomenon is, to my mind, the most mysterious Soviet state secret, darker than the whole underbelly of the NKVD.

Just like Baba Tanya, this Tatiana miracle doctor is rumored to prepare solutions for people—those that supposedly cure all their ailments—existent as well as imaginary. Her little business is, naturally, kept under a thick veil of secrecy (like most things in the USSR), as the practice is not exactly in correspondence with the general line of the party, or, for that matter, the Academy of Sciences.

The real reason why my Yoska-the-malingerer so badly longs to see the dubious creature is, I suspect, his unquenchable curiosity paired with a rather infantile weakness for plump female bosoms. Shandor suspects the same, hence his sternness and sarcasm.

Otherwise, Shandor has a heart of gold. He did not for a second hesitate about putting an end to my lone wanderer's existence when he spotted me in Camden Town, where I had gathered a sizable crowd doing orders ("I will guess and play to you the music of your heart, madam." "Bring your young lady over, my friend—I'll compose a tune for her which will make her love you till the end of her days." "I'll fiddle a little song to you, sir—it will give you an idea that will rescue your business." We were quite a sensation, Lavuta and I, but our fame was beginning to develop side effects, as our most devoted admirers were seriously starting to wonder if we couldn't, perhaps, charm the stock market as well, with our music).

Shandor assured me my act was exactly the one their show was wanting. He invited me to visit the marquee and, if I liked it, join the *kumpania* and the show.

I agreed and followed him to Surrey, where his circus was making a stop.

I did like it. It reminded me of my own, to which I had, over a year ago, bid the last farewell.

But it was not nostalgia or Shandor's generosity that determined my decision. It was the beautiful vision that greeted me as I entered the marquee: a youth standing upright on a black stallion's back—tall (about my height), razor-blade slim. He was rehearsing a juggling act—quick, agile—lightning in his limbs.

'Yoska, my nephew,' Shandor introduced him. 'And Flame, our best artist, though a skittish one as hell.'

The youth jumped off Flame's back on the saw-dusted floor; our eyes met. From that moment on, wild horses would not have dragged us away from each other.

*

'Jaaas, Jaaas!'

Boiko is tugging at my sleeve, demanding attention.

I'm back in the present—namely, the AU Gypsy family camp.

'Come, quick!'

I surmise it is about one of the nuisance jobs Boiko has a talent of bringing upon his own head as well as those of others, unreasonable enough to associate with him.

The trouble with the family camp is, we are not normally included in labor commandos outside the camp. This means we get all the aimless tasks inside, which our self-proclaimed bosses, due to the lack of imagination and sense of irony, invent for us off the top of their heads. For those of us who "ask" for it, that is. And Boiko is certainly one "asking" for it—permanently and desperately.

Carrying logs from block to block without a reason or digging improvised trenches "from the fence to lights out," as the Russians joke, can surely be as boring, dumbing, and cheerless as Dante's purgatory. Can anyone really blame Boiko and the likes of him that they weary of it at some point and start getting up to all kinds of stunts like feigning swoons, succumbing to skin and lung diseases on purpose, or staging their own deaths? Can anyone judge them, too, for sometimes living the part too fiercely and translating the act into reality? I, for one, wouldn't.

Boiko, as a matter of fact, is not as artful as all that. His stunts are usually simpler; he just comes and begins moaning and demanding help until he gets it. The good thing about Boiko is, he is perfectly aware that help comes at a cost. The good thing about the cost is, it is agreed upon, and no one is better at procuring what's required than Boiko. For not only does he have our valiant Sonders at his service, but actually manages to bum a smoke off Doc Josef Angel himself.

As I know Mihai is running out of his snuff and I am the only one who takes care of the quarrelsome Tito supporter (Vano is there exclusively when something immaterial, like toadying, comes in demand), I promptly voice a top-up order for the old man and follow Boiko outside.

Only this time, counter to my expectations, it is not about giving a hand in a pointless task.

It is Rosa having a seizure. Arched back, she is sprawled across the walkway, foaming at the mouth, crooked fingers digging into the wet ground; her handsome, slightly mustached face distorted into a gruesome mask.

'Can you put something in her mouth? I'm afraid she'll bite my finger off if I try to…'

'No need.' I lean forward to turn Rosa's stiffened body on its side. 'You'll hurt her teeth. It'll be over in a minute, don't worry. Just make sure she rests afterward.'

He wants me to play something to make her epilepsy go away. He explains that doctor Epstein has examined her and said she might be of interest for the "study." He now fears if they find out about the seizures, they may turn her down.

'Dina the painter drew her portrait the other day. Just look at her, Jass,' he continues dreamily as he contemplates the recumbent Rosa slowly regaining her senses. 'She is beautiful, isn't she? She deserves something good. The best. Doesn't she?'

I agree, and I would have happily played something to have the two of them die in each other's arms instead of what is to happen. But therein lies the rub: Boiko is the only one to die within the confines of AU in less than a year's time. Rosa is to live—a long, inebriating life which will end loudly in a Parisian jolly quarter, not old Yosef's lab. And I am not here to interfere with such glorious turns of fate, though I do sympathize with Boiko's tender feelings for the sultry epileptic.

*

I leave Boiko to his lovey-dovey business of bringing Rosa round and enter the hut, only to be accosted by Damira. Crying and shaking, she throws her intangible weight against my solar plexus, buries her face in the burlap of my overalls, and sobs unrestrainedly.

'What is it, child?' I lift her chin and wipe the liquid off the cheek, in which the gangrene has already started drilling a tiny hole.

'Vano is at it again!'

I knit my eyebrows in exaggerated strictness.

'What is it Vano has done again?'

Vano jumps up and scurries off to hide behind Mihai's back.

'I've done nothing!'

'Yes, you have!' Damira's eyes, the little charcoals, burn with indignation. She clutches at my hands; her palms are cold and clammy.

'He is telling the *shilmulo* stories again!'

'*Di-niiii-liii!*' *V*ano screeches from under Mihai's arm. 'It is no *shilmulo* stories! It is history stories! Tell her, Babbo Mihai!'

'He is telling stories about that Danubian voivode who had many Roma slaves, and he pierced them with a long stick and drank their blood.' Damira snuffles. 'He is saying that his *mulo* will come for me soon, to put his stick through me and all my family and all the Roma, and suck all our blood out!'

'Isn't he coming for Vano, too, then?' I ask. 'If he comes for all the Roma? Vano is also a Rom, isn't he?'

Damira's sobs die down, the logical contradiction drying her tears more effectively than my comforting hand. She stared at me, puzzled and suddenly calmed. Her grip loosens. I release myself from her embrace and make my way to Mihai's bunk, enjoying the show of Vano diving under Babbo's armpit for more safety.

'They are no *shilmulo* stories,' Vano twangs petulantly. 'Tell her, Jass, you know all things in the world. Voivode Dracula really lived. If a man really lived, then it is neither *shilmulo* stories nor *mulani* stories—it is history stories.'

'Your acquaintance with the story of Count Țepeș does you credit,' I commend him. 'But how about the new portion of German irregular verbs I assigned you? Have you learned those?'

'Sein-war-gewesen,' Damira cuts in readily, leaping on the chance to one-up the sneaky storyteller.

Vano looks down and mutters something akin to sulky excuses.

'So do me a favor and set yourself to the task instead of freaking girls out with macabre tales,' I admonish him.

Even Mihai doesn't seem willing to play Vano's advocate this time, and the little upstart begins intoning his "singen-sang-gesungen."

*

In a few moments, however, Vano is jolted out of his routine by a comically relevant call.

The door of the hut swings open—and on the cracked threshold there springs up Petko, one of our revered *Prominenz*.

Petko is short statured, slouchy, and pockmarked, with a clownishly squeaky voice. I cannot fathom what magic he uses to inspire the mere mortals to stand at attention at the sight of his mothy countenance. They do, however, and Petko happily crows his announcement, 'Obersturmführer Karp is on his way, so clean yourselves up, gyps. He would like to know how many of you can actually speak German. Good German, that is. Those who can will be invited to take part in a new research.'

Petko stumbles upon the clever word but makes as if to have coughed. His voice cracks and momentarily turns a pitch higher, thus becoming even more cockadoodledoo.

'But I'm probably wasting my breath on you, scum; none of you qualify anyway. You're all dumb illiterates, now aren't you?'

Petko's teeth show in all their rotting splendor as he stretches his mouth into a self-congratulatory grin. His eyes rove about, avidly taking in the effect his message has produced on the mere mortals. While at this, he makes quite an amusing spectacle. I would've even enjoyed it a couple of minutes longer, had I not had enough of Petko by now. The information he brings poses an interest. It has a caressing jingle of a laugh and material reward to it, and I sure have a taste for this type of adventure.

I now need to concentrate, and Petko's presence is distracting.

So I pinch Lavuta's a string. The 440 Hz standard pitch is barely audible in the breathing, steaming vastness of the barrack. Yet the hypersensitive Petko immediately clutches at his temples and screws up his eyes.

'The stench in this place!' he hisses. 'You are all perfect swine, gyps, now, aren't you? You never wash. Always your filthy barrack makes me sick, every single time. You watch out when Obersturmführer Karp arrives here; he will...'

Petko swings his arm as if attempting to strike at the entire population of the hut, but, never finding a concrete target and more annoyed at himself than anybody else, he storms out—just in time for me to tune in.

*

Replacing Petko in the doorway is Guido Karp, aka Guido "The Cabbagehead."

This one truly is a remarkable character. A red-faced, loud-mouthed, touchingly stupid bully—too good to be true.

'*Stillgestanden...*' barks Guido.

His piglike eyes roam the cowered barrack dwellers. Those still reeling from the prominent's recent visit are now completely starstruck by Obersturmführer Cabbagehead's proximity.

'...*Abschaum*...' he adds somewhat uncertainly after a pause.

Guido borrowed this word from Petko (Petko is an avid collector of fancy German vituperation), no doubt, and is now wondering if it adds him enough weight in the given context. For, not able to boast of an advanced education in humanities, Cabbagehead normally goes for the more traditional "*Schweine*..."

'*Also... Wer kann normal Deutsch sprechen?*'

The gist of the speech to follow is that there is help needed in the lab for Obersturmführer Karp personally, that the helpers will be granted certain privileges, and that the works will be largely conducted after lights-out; most importantly, this is a matter of utmost secrecy, and under no circumstances is one to discuss it with anyone else.

What becomes clear to me as I tune in is that Guido is up to monkey business. And, this being the case, there are fun times ahead. Guido is the ever-running gravy train, and it would be an inexcusable waste not to make the most of the sweet fellow.

The one answering Guido's call is not Vano with his freshly learned irregulars. It is Boiko, our love-tormented Romeo, who jumps up from his bunk.

'*Ich glaube das kann ich Deutsch gut sprechen, Herr Obersturmführer...*'

This saddens me, as I have a genuine liking for the dexterous admirer of Rosa's charms. Guido's practice is to drive the poor devil into his grave even sooner than I expected. But, like I said, Rosa has far more enticing prospects ahead of her, and it is not my place to interfere.

And, though with an aching heart, I do leave Boiko to his fate.

*

The visiting day does not seem to be over yet.

Next to pay his respects is Doctor Christian Heidert, aka, "Young Werther."

As is his habit, Doctor Heidert arrives unannounced.

One could probably call Christian a pretty face if he didn't incessantly strive to please everybody. As it is, his delicate features bear the stamp of eternal preoccupation and perpetual guilt.

This time, however, there is something else to his manner. A new kind of spiritedness. It almost feels as if Young Werther were in line for what Shandor would have called *"kintala"* (not sure our philosophical ringmaster employed the word in its traditional sense, but he used to smack his lips, relishing the three syllables every time Yoska performed some unimaginable new somersault off Flame's back).

It is obvious, anyhow, that there are sorrows in store for Young Werther before he reaches the blissful balance. Also *after* he reaches it. I can see this as clearly as the silver pips and stripes on his black collar patch.

Nevertheless, I am almost endeared by the sight of doctor Heidert today, as I watch him humoring Damira—the object of his special interest. There is this radiant question mark in the back of his mind. Always a pleasure to observe someone whose questions are about to find answers, even if it should come at a high cost.

My tender feelings do not seem to be shared by Vano, my student of German. The little punk takes advantage of the good doctor's absent-mindedness. Vano slips a hand into the doctor's pocket and renders it a cigarette pack lighter, while the unsuspecting Young Werther is giving Damira a parting hug.

Vano's nefarious deed is watched by Boiko, who is making all manner of gleeful faces to express his approval. Boiko has it in for Heidert, as the beautiful Rosa is known to throw an occasional languid glance the pretty doc's way.

Oh, well, *à l'amour comme à la guerre*, so once again, I refrain from judgment.

*

Karma doesn't take long to lash back at Vano for his pettiness and at Boiko for his gloating.

In the face of Bushalo[1] Karl, it crashes in, grabs the two by the collars, and drags them out, growling abuse. The log-stacking job has not been finished (or properly done), and Boiko, as the habitual scapegoat, is the first

---

[1] bushalo – sour (Romani)

to get it in the neck. The second is Vano, as he happens to be sitting next to Boiko (the two are stopped midway through exchanging mirthful comments on Vano's recent act of *choribe* from the naive Doctor Heidert).

I follow them out.

A big, knotty log lies across the yard, just where Boiko and his luckless assistants dropped it, like the proverbial beam in the eye. This means Bushalo will have a field day.

As an overseer, Bushalo has been granted the right to carry a whip. And carry it he does, with all the panache his sour soul is capable of. In action, however, he leans toward using his fists, rather.

He is certainly strong, Bushalo; one has to give him that.

Boiko is doubled with a punch in the groin. The puny Vano is sent spinning with a thwack on the side of the jaw.

Both have their faces rubbed against the knotty surface of the log—their noses and mouths instantly torn and bleeding.

'I'll teach you, Kalderash *khul*...'

Now that the punished both lie at his feet, Bushalo is ready to make use of the whip as well.

Normally I would've left a case like this alone. Vano has, after all, to be taught some decency, and Boiko has to learn to keep his *gajengi baxt* in check.

But "normally" applies to nothing that has to do with Bushalo Karl. With him, I have my own account to square.

Like many of our proud Sinti *chiavalei*, Bushalo does no work to speak of but is commissioned to policy the Jewish camp. So am I. Thus, I often find myself side by side with Sour One, which, while far from being a pleasurable position, does make for an interesting study from time to time.

So, the other day, I am distracted by an especially productive dialogue with Lavuta and arrive later than usual, only to see my David's ivory fingers—the most exquisite fingers I have known in this world—clutched and bruised in Bushalo's stubby paws.

'Snap-snap-snap,' Sour One roars. 'I'm going to break these scrawny sticks of yours, one by one. How will you play your piano again then, little Jewish queenie?'

As *bibaxt* would have it, I've left Lavuta behind, which means I'm restricted to using my two bare hands. It also means I have a split second to act, as Lavuta alone has the faculty of slowing down time.

I acted, and it was quick enough to rescue David's lovely upper extremities and dislocate Sour One's jaw. Only, it did not feel remotely sufficient to me. Not even in the ballpark, as they say across the Atlantic.

Every time I see Bushalo since that day, I get an itchy soul.

Today's no exception. And today Lavuta is within reach, so all I have to do is take her on my shoulder, leisurely walk back outside, and start playing a lazy tune.

And this slow melody of ours takes Bushalo's guts in such a fierce grip that he fouls his burlap trousers, clutches at his belly, and whimpers like a beaten cur. Off to the latrine he runs—pronto—leaving the two hapless victims by the log, forgetting they even exist, as his intestines are currently giving him a lot more urgent matters to worry about.

I take pleasure in the sight of Bushalo Karl's running. Just as I will one day take pleasure in being the cause of his death.

*

As a matter of fact, I owe Bushalo.

It is thanks to him I found David.

The ivory-skinned, slender-waisted grace is everything Bushalo is not, so Sour One was wont to make the boy his pet victim. He singled him out so blatantly and tormented him so elaborately that at some point David became physically impossible to overlook.

But it was not his suffering at the hands of Bushalo that caught my attention. It was the naughty spark that flickered in the corner of the green, whimsically speckled eyes every time Sour One caused him pain. The instant I saw that defiant little light flash from under the long eyelashes, I knew what the inexplicable urge that had driven me to AU in the first place was. I knew it by name, face, and body.

This was not long before we had our first heart-to-heart.

He was a musician, a pianist from Kraków. Lost the meager remnants of his family to the recent Warsaw Ghetto clash. He had delicious freckles which looked like diced almond sprinkles on the creaminess of the skin, a humorous way of knitting his eyebrows, and a playful smile.

At some point I called Bushalo to one side and spelled it out that should I, by any unfortunate accident, see his sourness anywhere near my porcelain minstrel again, then his, Bushalo's, would be a long, painful, and shameful death. Fiddled him a convincing tune to reinforce my statement.

And for a while Karl was on his best behavior.

Until once David happened to be summoned before Josef the Angel, no less, with orders to play Schumann's *Träumerei* to a small off-the-record medical gathering.

That set Bushalo off.

Like most of his kind, Bushalo holds superior authority in stifling, overpowering reverence. As for old *Onkel* Mengele, that one is Karl's undisputed idol.

And here was this skinny Jewish worm, brazenly stealing the approval of the venerated *ray baro*—actually sung the praises of, afterward!

Surely my modest warnings were dwarfed against the jealousy that engulfed Bushalo's soul.

And Karl snapped.

It was then that I caught him in the act of threatening to break my pretty pianist's fingers.

Therefore, I had to sentence Bushalo.

*

While Bushalo is awaiting his sentence and I—the day to execute him—Lavuta still has plenty of opportunity to hone her punitive powers on Sour One. Which she does, with my assistance, every time our convicted felon decides to go sour on someone else within our sight.

She's always come to the rescue of my insane, irresistible loves, Lavuta has.

Like in the Soviet town of N, where Yoska managed eventually to run into trouble…

Shandor's circus surely made the most of the place.

We stayed there, performing, week after week, under the auspices of the *Rajispolkom,* whose leaders kept us on the pretext of inculcating communist political literacy in the "Gypsy" youths and converting us into *Komsomol.*

The real reason was far from politics, of course. It was not even the local young *komsomolkas*' lively interest in the agile "Gypsy" performers. It was their communist dads and grandpas' unquenchable love for the "Gypsy" music. The bon vivant Russian *pomezhiks* had successfully passed their affection for Tsyganochka and the collared bears down to their post-revolution communist successors.

Night and night again, after the show, we—Shandor, Yoska, Danior, Tomka, Laila, and I—headed for the red-brick building where Georgyi Mikhailovich, the Chairman (or *Predsedatel*) of the *Rajispolkom,* dwelt in his three-bedroom flat full of garish carpets, crystal vases, and chandeliers. With him in this Soviet luxury abode resided his wife, Tatiana Gavrilovna, the plump-bosomed doctor. It was to her, Yoska at some point yearned to show his ailing knee.

Georgyi Mikhailovich was a hospitable host; he loved to entertain his guests. Being the *Rajispolkom* top authority, he was visited by important officials on a daily basis, so entertain he had to a lot, and he went about it with gusto.

We wore red silky shirts and wide belts and brought plenty of eye-flashing into play, especially when there were women among Georgyi's guests. The girls shook their upper torsos, clanged their bracelets, and jingled their *galbi.*

The *Predsedatel* was, indeed, a worthy successor of the glorious Russian merchants. There was black caviar, whole smoked sturgeons, champagne, cognac, and vodka on his table galore, and he would wine and dine us without end. He also paid handsomely.

So once, as we, by popular demand, were going through the umpteenth rendition of Ochi Chernyiyeh, Tatiana Gavrilovna, the host's wife, rose from the table in her velvet gown. She came up to Yoska and me.

She put her plump arm around my shoulders, snapped her fingers loudly in Yoska's nose, and shook her full bosom, imitating Tomka's sultry gesture.

'I have Gypsy blood flowing in my veins too, you know,' she declared. 'My great-grandmother was a Gypsy. It is not for nothing that I have always been so drawn to your music, culture, and lifestyle. I am a vagabond by nature, you know! Ah, if only I could once go wandering freely, like you do!'

The lady was visibly in her cups, and her outpourings were not to be shaken off easily. Yoska had no better idea than to get down on one knee, look Tatiana Gavrilovna passionately in the eye, and start vocalizing yet another Ochi.

"Eyes as black as night

Full of gypsy fire,
How you can ignite
Torment and desire!
Now you promise love
Now you flash with hate.
You have seared my soul
You have sealed my fate…"

On the last line about "fate," Yoska, our mellifluous tenor, pressed Tatiana Gavrilovna's proffered chubby hand to his lips dramatically.

At this, I had a queasy feeling that "fate" was closing its ranks on us and that something must be done to stop it without delay.

But the *ray baro*, including Georgyi, seemed all happily drunk, safely engrossed in their party bragging, clamoring for more Ochi, and paying zero attention to what was going on. The caviar was enticingly on display, and the vodka was calling.

And, for once, I stupidly chose to ignore the inner voice.

The hostess, meanwhile, began tugging first at mine, then at Yoska's sleeve, insisting that we follow her in the direction of the bedroom. I cheerfully declined on the pretext I was too much under the influence of the choicest liquor offered by the host to make entertaining company. Yoska complied, however, and melted with Tatiana Gavrilovna into the lascivious darkness of the hallway.

Soon he reappeared—a little flushed, hair messed-up, simpering and pulling at his shirt.

The host and the guests, lost in their bacchanalia, were still incognizant of what was happening beyond the lush table. I tried to calm myself; though a close call it was, we successfully got away with Yoska's little prank.

Alas, it was only the beginning of the hassle to follow…

*

I take the boys, Vano and Boiko, back into the barracks. Neither is badly injured, but both make a sorry sight—beaten, bruised, aching, and bleeding.

I accompany them to the far right corner where Baba Tanya is queening it, authoritatively explaining to Mihai the difference between the terms *drabarni* and *gicisvara*.

'*Drabarni*—that I'm not, old man,' she booms, uncompromisingly hewing the air with her pudgy arm. 'Don't you ever call me *drabarni*. Vedoma, that old hag, she's a *drabarni*. I am a *gicisvara*; I know what I'm doing.'

The lecture on the distinction between the two words, sacredly observed by Vlax Romani, according to whom a *drabarni* is a hustler, while a *gicisvara*—a proud professional—produces a visible effect on Mihai. If he has always held Baba Tanya in esteem, now he is positively in awe of her. With his eyelids down, he takes a pensive snuff and nods solemnly.

By the hand, like children, I lead the sniveling Vano and Boiko up to Baba Tanya, for verily no one knows how to talk children through all kinds of children's hurt better than she does.

But upon approaching the revered *gicisvara*, Boiko is fast in forgetting his own pain. Quickly does he turn Baba Tanya's compassionate lip-smacking round to his beloved epileptic's plight.

'You know how she suffers, Baba Tanya,' he talks plaintively as she dabs, in turn, at his and Vano's scars. 'I wish I could help, do something for her.'

'That girl is in a bad way, indeed.'

Baba Tanya frowns and shakes her round, heavy head. Her voice thickens.

'Yes, in a bad way indeed,' she repeats slowly, and Boiko's eyes fill with despair.

'But she can be helped. You listen to me, boy!'

Boiko jerks his chin, trying to turn his face so that he could show her full concentration. He immediately squeals with pain, for Baba Tanya's dabbing stick slides abruptly across his torn cheek. She takes his head firmly in both hands and returns it in the initial position.

'You sit still,' Baba Tanya commands. 'You don't want me to pierce that cheek of yours through, do you? I'd say it's had its share for today—wouldn't you?'

With a blood-dripping grin, Boiko obeys.

'You listen to me! I will make medicine. She will take it thrice a day—you will give it to her. It will help keep the dropsy at bay for a while. But then she will need more of the medicine. And then more, for the rest of her life.'

'*Nais Tuke*,' Boiko whispers. 'I will do as you say. If you prepare this medicine, I will make sure she takes it as often as you tell me she must.'

'You know,' he ventures diffidently after a pause. 'Doctor Epstein has looked at Rosa. He says she is "an interesting case." He doesn't know about the dropsy yet. But I thought, if he took her to his lab for his studies, then maybe he could cure her... I mean... make it go away... forever?'

At this, Baba Tanya interrupts him with a peremptory swing of her arm, which sends the flab on its backside into a fierce ripple.

'*Shesti*!' she explodes, screwing up her face. 'What does Epstein, this Jew, know! What can he do? He is a slave here; they all are. You listen to me, boy. You pray that Baba Tanya stay in good health. I know what your Rosa needs. I can cure her. Your Epstein cannot. He doesn't know the first thing.'

Intimidated, Boiko attempts a nod, which causes him to groan with pain once more.

Baba Tanya purses her lips and puffs, calming down.

Vano, whose cheek and nose have been smeared in ointment and bandaged with a rag from Baba Tanya's inexhaustible supply, cautiously slips from under the healer's arm and sits down next to Mihai, in whose proximity he feels securest.

The old man pats him on the head, takes another snuff, and winks at me.

'A shar... what's that word, son?'

'Never mind, Babbo.' I wave a hand. 'A *gicisvara* is good enough.'

III
1st Violin

'All right, Dr. Heidert, I promise. Your secret is safe with me.'

Angel's voice sounded vigorous as he labored away at the operating table.

'Angel?'

I handed him a pean, and he swiftly clamped the hepatoduodenal ligament.

'Come, Christian. You've been wearing a thoroughly mysterious look of late. One could think you've unearthed treasure and are pondering where to rebury it.'

I said nothing, just admired the precise movements of his hands.

'Your treasure hiding would be fine by me—indeed, I wouldn't be nosing around if it weren't also for the constant signs of exhaustion you've been displaying the past few days. You are undersleeping, and your nerves are on edge.'

Nothing escaped him.

His observation was in fact an understatement, for not only had sleep been the last thing on my mind those several nights, but my *Force Vitale* had been, oxymoronically, all but draining me of my life juices, while at the same time fanning the divine flame within me to the point that I could barely stand the heat. I spent the night time writing and rewriting the draft; then the morning hours reading through the result, loathing it, tearing it up, and burning the shreds; then the day going through my motions in the office; then the night writing and rewriting the draft again.

'You are burning your candle at both ends, while you can hardly afford to do so. It is telling on your concentration. And badly.'

He was now manually compressing the ligament, but the bleeding continued.

'The hepatic vein's traumatized, and this has completely passed you by, hasn't it?'

I lowered my eyes.

'I apologize, Angel.'

I have to admit I was desperately looking for an opportunity to tell him about my discovery—just waiting for a good moment and selecting the right words. But there and then was obviously not the former nor had I yet chosen the latter.

'No need for apologies.'

Completing the hepatectomy—a procedure which certainly showed his proficiency at its most immaculate—Angel adroitly extracted the liver and placed it into the proffered kidney dish.

'I'm just saying you've got to rest. Your body and mind are crying out for a good unwinding.'

At his signal, I passed him the 20 cc hypodermic with a long needle.

'How about coming out for a hunt with us next weekend? *Hütte Soletal*? No civilization, no gloomy thoughts. A river in the woods. All rusticity and nature. What say you?'

He administered a neat phenol injection into the object's heart and laughed warmly.

'Pray do not tense up; I'm joking, of course! I'm well aware that you abhor hunting. Why, it is not the season anyway. But the idea of simple and animal-friendly basking on deckchairs in the company of charming ladies, desserts, and good whiskey wouldn't seem entirely repulsive to you, would it? Your friend Lauer is coming. Give it a thought.'

Having instructed the new Jewish assistant that the object's and his twin's bodies were to be sent to the dissecting room, Angel ordered to prepare their livers for the lab and winked at me.

'You never know where you might eventually decide to rebury that treasure of yours, and in the woods is always more secure.'

Now that he suggested it, I am debating between Solahütte and The Evening. I was actually considering the latter for an unofficial announcement. With everybody of importance having to be there, their attention would be ensured. But Angel has put me in two minds. Perhaps I should not let anyone know just yet? Especially in the presence of the Pharma-Ko people.

Maybe Solahütte, with its closer circle of colleagues and friends, would really be a better setting?

Yet the atmosphere at these leisurely gatherings never seems right—

one can hardly discuss something serious.

Should I then not put anyone in the know for a while? Not until I have committed it to paper, in some proper form, at least...

Or only tell Anton? Him, and Birgitte too?

I'm feeling even more at a loss now that Angel has so transparently given me to understand my work on The Idea is no secret—not for his lancet of a mind, anyway.

*

Much as I delight in everything Angel does, I must confess it was purely out of a wish to make amends for my distractedness during the hepatectomy that I volunteered to deliver the freshly obtained material to the lab and personally monitor the tests. The effect of acute toxic dystrophy of the liver during standard antituberculosis therapy does not interest me, not genuinely.

Too predictable.

What I would delve into with utmost passion are other aspects of tuberculosis—mostly experiments aimed at finding a preventive vaccine. This, I guess, is the principle difference between Angel's approach and mine. He is crazy about details, manifestations, complications, and side effects. Always the process, never the result. I, to the contrary, aim at solutions. Comprehensive ones.

What would I not give to have the degenerate disease go away? Be cured. Completely. Forever.

Few things have caused me so much suffering as the existence of this faux-intellectual plague. The one Indigo exalted so. The one I never stood a chance of contracting.

Professor Schwarz's death proved to have a direct and indulgent influence on the life of his consumptive nephew Bernard (or Bernie "the artist"). If before, Frau Treder only had the financial powers to send her son to a relatively modest sanatorium once in two years, then after, the love-stricken Indigo insisted on sponsoring her adored cousin's seasonly sojourns in the finest Alpine clinics. Out of the inheritance her father had left her, of course.

Is it any surprise Bernie started developing a complication after a complication?

Soon Indigo's benevolence came to be perceived as a solemn duty, which my soft-hearted decadent was only too happy to perform.

Of all the sanatoria where he underwent treatment, Bernie favored Bad Wörishofen most. A small Bavarian spa town west of Munich, combining peaceful monastical allure and, allegedly, the most effective water cure in Europe.

God knows what particular charm Bernie found in the respectable settlement (logically thinking, a quaint place like that should have bored someone like him senseless). As it happened, Bernie claimed that only in Wörishofen he was able to create unselfconsciously, for the town "had a way of revealing one to oneself and helping embrace oneself as one was, without embellishment." Whatever he meant by this.

Bernie's favored subject in painting was, predictably, self portrait. Every time Indigo and I came to visit, he proudly demonstrated to us some new auto shoulder-lengths in twisted pauses and varied degrees of completion. Bernie so hysterically strove to be seen as the reincarnation of the demented pornographer Schiele he all but shouted it on a loudspeaker.

Only Schiele, degenerate though he was, possessed a kind of talent—which was precisely what Bernie wished he could boast of too.

Bernie's pieces did have the degenerateness, the lewdness, the sickliness—all in due measure. Everything except the divine spark.

This would have been obvious to anyone with the eyes to see. But Indigo was blind to all that testified against Bernie, no matter how loud it screamed. She melted over his nondescript doodling—the umpteenth angular shoulders, unnaturally tilted heads, disproportionate features. She plainly refused to see him as anything less than a tortured genius—a delicate body lacerated by ailment; a vulnerable soul torn apart by its own complexity and the world's crassness. She got drunk on such a vision of him.

Sometimes it was portraits of Indigo or Bernie's mother executed in the same grotesque style that he showed us alongside countless depictions of himself. Once even my turn came to be rendered on paper with a crooked, semitic nose and unevenly placed, wildly staring eyes.

On another occasion yet, we saw a portrait of an unknown youth—about our age, sandy-colored hair, sensuous lips.

'Looks like the young Rimbaud!' Indigo exclaimed in rapture. 'What's the name? Is he an absinthe drinker? Does he write poetry?'

'His name's Ernst. He's a patient here, like me. I suppose you will meet him soon. And he sure would not say no to a glass of the green potion.'

Soon enough, Ernst came in to introduce himself. Green eyes, a slightly turned-up nose, a pouty mouth.

I immediately knew there was a perverse mischief going on.

I only wish I hadn't been so cruelly, so mercilessly right.

*

I waylaid Guido by the entrance to the lab. Somehow I sensed he'd be there. That, too, in part, explained why I so readily offered Angel my services as a delivery agent.

I expected to find Guido at the door, for I assumed he would be hanging around, waiting for Schlöhm, the new Jewish assistant, to arrive, in the hope of tailing him back to Angel's office and running his Farben-Pharma-Ko obsession by the top authority figure again.

Well, I had other ideas for Guido.

Beholden though I am to Guido and his grossness for having accidentally inspired The Idea, I have been, for the past two days, fuming at him for other things.

First and foremost, he won't leave Birgitte alone. He pesters her with his vulgar attention at every opportunity.

Then, there is an unpleasant task I have been saddled with, due in no small part to the boor's efforts. It was initially Guido's own responsibility, but he didn't hesitate to shift the job onto me by turning down his own candidature and putting forward mine. Explained to Angel and to Weber, I was a "more skillful diplomat" and, thus, perfectly suited for the delicate mission in question, unlike himself, with his "less-than-popular straightforwardness."

Angel took the advice without hesitation, not so much for the ludicrous reasons the boor adduced, but mostly because Angel is used to being able to count on my reliability.

But if Guido thought he could put an Augean stables mess on me and then snatch my position while I was busy cleaning it, then he had another thought coming.

'So, how are we coming along in Raisko?' I confronted him, employing his own preferred manner.

Choked by the outrightness of which he never supposed me capable, Guido made a rather pitiable attempt at saving his face.

'Why, our little test laboratory there is known as "cornucopia," brother.' He giggled with poorly faked mirth. 'Weber is in clover with his poisons. Demands fat capos to be bled, and the soldiers get him some daily. He needs a lot of blood, Weber, to serve his boss Mrugowsky. Mrugowsky's man at AU; that's what he is. And where else would the two find such a selection of thighs to shoot their aconite-filled bullets into if not in our Block ten, under Angel's protective wing, I ask you? The young Münch might not be so happy, poor Hans—not enough elbow room to follow his ideas through, but…'

While listening to the drivel he was spouting, I couldn't help but smile and congratulate myself inwardly.

If nothing else, at least I made the shiftless bastard maximally exert his powers of fast-talking. The latter were, frankly, mediocre, but now he was trying to make the best of them in order to pretend he had no clue what the hell I was talking about.

This little distraction could not go on forever, though, no matter how much it amused me.

'I'm well aware what kind of work is done in Raisko, brother.'

I felt no remorse about blatantly mocking his favorite style once again—I was too furious to be my usual tactful self.

'I'm talking about the Bayer request. Our delicate mission, remember? What steps have been taken so far?'

At this, Guido's face fell. Not so good at prevarication to begin with, now he had completely exhausted his modest per-day potential.

'Eh… actually, I thought maybe I'd ask you to…'—he bleated, but I interrupted him again, with more resolution.

'I am sorry, my friend. Like you justly pointed out the other day, I have my hands full as it is, with Farben-Pharma-Ko and "the Gypsy Plague." Circumstances force me to put the Bayer-Raisko thing completely in your charge, and I do hope you will rise to the occasion. May I?'

Leaving the tomato-red, puffing Guido in the hallway, I brushed passed him into the lab.

Still no compunction whatsoever. Sometimes a man has got to find his voice, and sometimes he's got to make it heard.

*

Pleased at myself for having cut Guido-the-boor down to size, I left the lab to venture out into the family camp.

The Idea requires material to come to fruition, and no one except for me is going to provide any. Especially now, while I still have not decided when and how it is best to reveal *Force Vitale* to the colleagues and the world.

I know I must take my project entirely into my own hands.

I found the block in its usual self-contradictory state: a kind of intermediary between perpetual slumbering and easily ignited commotion.

The youths were lounging on the bunks—semi-drowsy, but getting into a loud argument at the slightest noise or stirring from the side. The old were rocking slightly to the motley tunes of their own or their neighbors' low humming. The children, as was their wont, were running about, whimpering and giggling incongruously.

A corpulent, dark-faced elder female (they respectfully address her as Baba Tanya) was sulkily bending over Marusya, examining her inflamed right breast. A short while ago, this Marusya delivered a baby male and immediately broke into acute mastitis, followed by a cluster of more peculiar mammary complications. While Baba Tanya, apparently seen by her fellow tribesmen as some sort of healer, muttered spells into the taut, painfully glistening redness of the younger female's flesh, Marusya's baby was squalling blue murder in his sister Damira's lap.

As I many times explicitly told the block dwellers not to stand at attention on my arrivals, now they all but fail to notice my visits at all. Which is precisely what I want. I love to observe them in their naturalness. Indeed, when allowed to go, unhindered, about their daily routines, they present invaluable material for study.

I touched Damira, the main focus of my attention, lightly on the shoulder. She raised her eyes.

'Onkel Heidert!'

Her long mouth stretched even more into a weary smile, giving her the appearance of a sad little frog.

'Oh, forgive us!' she exclaimed, covering the baby's face with the palm of her hand. 'My brother won't go to sleep. He has a tummy ache, and he wants mamma back. He's hungry. But mamma—she is not feeling so good at all…'

Then, seeing that I wanted to talk, she suddenly made a swift decision.

'Jass!'

This name, it turned out, belonged to my bête noire—the "daemon" with the violin, for it was he who emerged out of the blue with his inevitable instrument.

Damira touched the lad's hand and nodded at the baby. Whispered something which sounded like a request.

The male barely glanced at her or the screaming bundle on her lap. Staring bluntly into the wall, he raised the bow.

What he went on to play was an unidentifiable tune executed in the blurry manner so characteristic of Gypsy violinists. Impressive, however, was the fact that not only was the baby calm, quiet, and asleep in about twenty seconds of the melody, but that it immediately immersed me, too, into a state of drowsy stupor.

*

All of a sudden I felt so sleepy I almost could not stand. I certainly could not talk or collect my thoughts enough to formulate a coherent sentence. Even recalling the purpose of my visit to the block was a struggle.

I remember mumbling to Damira the first thing that popped in my head (was it some manner of apology?) and staggering, semi-comatose, out of the barrack.

I stood in the yard for some time, thirstily sucking in the damp air, in the hope of clearing my head.

That helped, to a degree. At least I felt I was again able to think and act consistently.

The inexplicable somnolence was, however, not so easy to shake off. The pestering idea in the front of my mind remained to escape into the relative safety of my office, lock the door from the inside, plunge into the chair, fold my arms on my desk, drop my head on them, and allow myself some minutes of cleansing, revitalizing, and sanity-saving sleep.

I actually did set about fulfilling the intention, for I still feared I might collapse in the middle of the playground and become lethargic in full view. At that moment, like never before, I was thankful for the amenity of a chauffeur. I was definitely not in a fit state to drive myself back to AU1.

But the stars decided against my plan, for just as I was approaching the office in anticipation of a nap, I bumped into Anton.

'Heil, Maestro!' He grabbed me by the shoulders. 'How lucky is it you should be deposited here in my arms the second I as much as conceive the thought it would be good to swap words with you? It has to be for a reason I conjure you up easily like that.'

He snapped his fingers with a jaunty click.

'I have a marvelous idea. We absolutely must do Träume. For The Evening, I mean. I reckoned where there's you, there's got to be Wagner. Right?'

'And how can I say no to that?' I smiled, trying as hard as I could to hide my abnormal sleepiness.

Anton noticed nevertheless.

'Hey, are you all right? You look like death warmed up.'

'No, no, I'm fine. Just a bit under the weather, that's all. Have been feeling somewhat woolly-headed since morning today. Embarrassed myself in the operating room, in front of Angel, even.'

To my amazement, I almost didn't tell any lies.

'You have, haven't you?' The momentary expression of concern on Anton's face instantly changed back to the habitual gregariousness. 'Then I know exactly what you need. Come with me.'

He pulled me by the hand like a parent does a child, inducing to follow.

We went to the canteen and asked for strong coffees with cognac. Took them with Anton's Lindt chocolate bar, which we shared somewhat unevenly, as he let me eat most of it. I could not find my cigarettes (I vaguely remembered I'd had a whole pack in my pocket, but it was nowhere to be found), so we smoked two of Anton's Lucky Strikes each.

The remedy worked; the fog in my head lifted. I woke up enough to start sounding Anton out regarding Solahütte.

'There's something tremendous I'm onto. A kind of revelation. Working on a paper right now, mostly at night… partly explains my wooziness during the day, perhaps.'

Anton threw back his head in amazement; excitedly clasped his hands on one knee. His eyes glistened.

'Goodness, Chris! Cannot wait to hear the details. Or read… will you be giving a report?'

'That's precisely what I wanted to seek your council for,' I was immensely enjoying his reaction.

'I'm your man.'

'I've been wondering if an official report is in order just yet. The hypothesis is so striking it may come as a shock to some. Should I try and parcel the effect out a bit? Make a simple announcement first? In a laid-back atmosphere? Angel suggested the next Solahütte gathering. Or shall The Evening be more fitting, do you think?'

Anton advised against Solahütte.

'Not this particular gathering—I'd vote no. Höss is coming. It will be all about him lamenting the Reihsführer's pesky obsession with putting every moldy stump to good use. You will not get a word in edgeways.'

How only does Anton manage to always keep abreast of things while also impeccably doing his job?

'Really? And what is it we are failing to put to good use this time?'

'You'll never guess. The Jews.'

'The Jews?'

'That's right. You see, the Jews, especially the young and able-bodied, are wily. Our simple-minded Gypsy pets have nothing on them. The Jews are lazy too. They tend to shirk in a typically Jewish fashion—by bribing their fellow prisoners into doing tasks for them. Even if you strip them of all their money and possessions, they still find the means; isn't that mind-boggling? So apparently the Reichsfürer wants us to put an end to the outrage, and the Commandant is, naturally, at a loss what to do, 'cause we have already done every thing possible and impossible, all to no avail.'

'Of course the Jews will always outsmart us, the Teutons.' I smirked. 'This has been on since the mighty Goliath of our kin challenged his puny opponent to a fair combat and was slain by the treacherous sling instead.'

'Nail on the head! I've been observing a specimen for my fatigue study here for a while—a pianist, by the way, so a twice as interesting case for me, as you can imagine. Now you've got to see him. The very picture of the dodgy Shepherd King—same subtle ways and foxy eyes. You wouldn't be surprised his name's David!'

Anton chuckled and ordered more coffee.

Thanks to him—my good, faithful, lighthearted friend—I was for the first time in a few days feeling calm and confident.

*

'Are you in touch with her, at all? I mean, does she even write?'

Having sated our caffeine lust, we proceeded to my office. It was decided I would withhold the *Force Vitale* presentation some more—even from Anton—until the right occasion arose, and we switched to worldlier topics, such as our love lives.

Anton was admiring Indigo's photograph on my desk.

'She is a striking girl.'

'She is that.' I nodded slowly, lighting a Lucky. "And no. She doesn't write.'

'So chances are she may be happily married to a prompter suitor than your sweet self by now, with two kids toddling about and one on the way?'

'For all I know, she may not even be in the Reich anymore. I last saw her when she stormed out of her aunt's place with the intention to relocate back into her late father's flat in Prenzlauer Berg, and from there—straight to America.'

'Holy crap, Maestro!' Anton comically reworked his straight features into an expression of indignation. 'How like you to be holding out on a friend for months, not sharing the intel that he's got a charming kindred spirit out there!'

'Yes.' I rolled my eyes. 'Another Yankee admirer.'

'Time to start a club.'

'In her case, there may be something akin to a return-to-the-roots call underlying that attraction. Her mother was American.'

'It's getting more exciting with every word you say.'

'Married with kids, I doubt, however, knowing her.'

'Of course not; I was joking. One glance is enough to see she is no marrying type.'

'Nor, sadly, a child-bearing type. Used to say she could only love children for money.'

'That's a witty one.'

'I don't know about witty. Sounded rather appalling to me, coming from a young woman. She coined the phrase when she was giving private classes of French and English to the neighbors' ten-year-olds to make some cash on the side.'

'Well, then I expect they were highly "industrious" and "obedient" pupils.'

'To the best of my knowledge, they were a handful, yes.'

'In which case yours truly is wholeheartedly on the side of the enchanting teacher. Will you allow me?'

Carefully picking up the portrait, he took a closer look at it.

'This face is extraordinary. Could she by any chance be of sapphic disposition, with such strong features, do you think?'

'Not likely. She could not bear as much as being around other women. Never had a girlfriend I knew of... She did take pleasure in being admired or flattered by females. But except for such cases—and they were few—she had no use for members of her own sex.'

While I was saying this, I actually remembered Indigo's one clash with lesbianism, which once for all shattered whatever slight doubts I might've had regarding her sexuality.

During one of the interim periods that Bernie twiddled his thumbs in the capital while awaiting another treatment season in an expensive clinic, he once insisted that he, Indigo, and I visit a couple of his friends, "two charming girls, in love with creativity and each other."

Indigo was not thrilled about the idea—she much preferred being the only female in a male company. Needless to say, I was even less enthused with the prospect of wasting an evening in the society of two sloppy Dada *émancipées*, listening to their nonsense and looking at their daub.

Indigo, however, was used to doing anything to please Bernie, while I was in the unfortunate habit of indulging Indigo at all costs. Which meant whatever plan Bernie suggested got unanimously accepted by the three of us.

So we went.

The "creativity-loving" couple resided in the garish monstrosity of the glorified Hufeisensiedlung, and was predictably proud of it. Their entire union was founded on the cult of the elder one, Antonia. All the creativity was Antonia's, all the love was channeled toward her.

Taller and thinner even than Indigo, with even more angular features, Antonia sported an uncompromisingly short crewcut, wore baggy suspender overalls, and spoke with a nasal twang, somnambulantly stretching her syllables.

Antonia was a cripple. As a consequence of childhood osteomyelitis, she was afflicted with severe limping. She almost didn't move without crutches and complained of periods of acute pain. Antonia's health and her art were the pivot of hers and her partner Lotte's lives. The young women hardly discussed anything else except the said two topics, but those two they discussed incessantly.

As for the art, Antonia took her cue from Hannah Höch—her worshipped role model and, ostensibly, personal teacher. Just like Hannah's, Antonia's sphere of artistic interests lay in photomontage. Just like Fräulein Höch's, the main issue of her struggle was the misperception of the celebrated concept of the "New Woman."

The loud blue walls of the room were covered with Antonia's work—flashy collages featuring men's and women's faces expressing a motley of emotions; all manner of cogs, wheels, crooks, steps, and ladders; an odd body part—usually an arm or a leg—turned upside down; whole random words, as well as single letters.

The younger girl—the blonde Lotte—a petite, plump-cheeked, surprisingly feminine creature hung on her companion's every word, and attended to her every wish. Lotte waited on Antonia; packed her long pipe, on which Antonia took protracted, dramatic sips. Never taking the adoring eyes off her friend, Lotte even reached out now and again to stroke the prickly stubble on the back of Antonia's head and the nape of her neck.

As our hostesses rattled on and Bernie lavished praise on Antonia's art and the overall harmony of the two partners' relationship, I started noticing a thinly-veiled irritation in Indigo's gestures, a vexed tension in her limbs.

When speaking about her maladies, Antonia had a way of combining apocalyptical terms with a humorous tone, ostentatiously making light of her suffering while at the same time letting everybody know how severe it was. The meek Lotte's eyes filled with tears every time her adored friend wittily contemplated another grim health scenario. Indigo wouldn't stop grinding her teeth at that. I was sensing an imminent explosion.

When, to my relief, we finally said our goodbyes and made our way out, Bernie and I were treated to a parody show. At the central staircase, Indigo abruptly stopped, collapsed on the stony surface overlooking the little pond, bent her right leg, hiding it under her backside as if it were amputated, half-closed her eyes in an affected display of anguish, and, unnaturally stretching her vowels, delivered a nasalized potpourri.

'Yeeeahh, you knooow... mon kidneys are giving out... yes, they are... aaaand, ohhh, mon heart's virtually a deadbeat... yeeess, oh, and mon legs are falling off so I'm probably going to end up in a wheelchair...'

Bringing her two fingers and thumb halfway to her face and pursing her lips to mime a drag on a long pipe, she concluded with a rueful smile.

"Ohhh, you knoow, thaaht's cool; we'll muddle through…'

Then, abruptly breaking character, she scorched us with fierce black eyes and shouted.

'I wanted to tell her: Let me just strangle you and put you out of your misery—then there'll be no need to muddle through—or pile on the agony!'

We were still so close to their windows, and Indigo made it so loud, I assumed Antonia and Lotte could hear every word of that contumely.

To my astonishment, however, Bernie was amused by her outburst. It cracked him up.

'Come on, Indie,' he said when he was done laughing, 'you won't deny that Antonia's art is great, will you?'

'Why, I admit it. I'm even grateful to her. She gave me an idea of how to keep the kids I tutor busy in the breaks. They too enjoy cutting things out of newspapers, and if I tell them they can glue the cuttings together into one farrago, and this will be called "art"—oh, I imagine they'll oink with excitement!'

Never before had I heard Indigo openly deride Bernie's views—she hardly ever expressed as much as mild disagreement with her beloved pierrot. But this time she positively flew off the handle.

Still, Bernie did not seem affected by Indigo's scoffs and continued laughing together with her.

'Hey, ingrate, show more respect. You ought to realize the people you've been honored to hang out with are the cream of German liberated womanhood. You want to be a liberated woman yourself, now don't you, Cuz? You care about women's rights, no?'

She gave him a look of mocking bewilderment.

'Me? The only woman whose rights I care about is yours truly. And I feel liberated enough to do as I please, without having to make a fuss about it. I can study anything I want, learn any profession I choose, travel any place I'm drawn to, take any lover I desire. And although I may despise marriage, recoil from cooking, regard maternal instinct as an atavism, and never set foot in a church, I still take pleasure in a man's opening a door for me, lighting my cigarette, or giving me flowers. It is a gesture of gallantry, and there is nothing about it that might infringe my rights—if anything, I'd say it augments them. What has made a woman liberated in all ages is being intelligent. Only, this is a rare case, so, for want of intelligence, some women feel the need to give themselves ugly haircuts, wear clownish clothes, reject masculine help with lifting a heavy suitcase, or produce shoddy "art" to imagine they are on par with the stronger sex. Well, I do not suppose transforming themselves into the travesty of an ugly man makes them a freer woman.'

That declaration had Bernie in stitches once again. Shrieking with laughter, he grabbed Indigo's both hands and helped her off the ground.

'I say you could not have made yourself any clearer, unrivaled, Cuz! We sure as hell get your meaning. Don't we, Chris? She doesn't need to be a feminist who gets to be a Cleopatra! So you will not reject my humble attentions? Or Chris's? Not like these hoi polloi womanists do? Will you, oh incomparable queen?'

'With all my heart I shall always accept and welcome your noble wooing, my dear knights!' Indigo played along, now also laughing, cheerful, and relaxed. Her anger was gone.

For once I was grateful to Bernie—all of a sudden he knew better than I how to dissolve her tension and make her happy again.

*

'Did she sing?' Anton interrupted my train of thought. 'Such a compelling appearance calls for a suitably charismatic voice, or am I wrong?'

'She had some voice, a charming one in fact. Her mother was a cabaret singer, so there must've been some genetic predisposition there too. She enjoyed singing but never wanted to take classes or develop it in any way. Never believed her voice was her forte. Said the world didn't need another sparrow striving to be a nightingale and that she'd rather be a good writer than a mediocre singer. She was convinced writing was her vocation.'

'So she wrote then? I say, Maestro, I'd be more than curious to take a look at a sample of her *belles-lettres*, should you happen to have some in your possession.'

I dismissed that with a weary wave of a hand.

I do keep some copies of her manuscripts, but those evoke too many sad memories to even pull out of the drawer, let alone reread or show someone else.

Fortunately, Anton didn't press the matter.

'Speaking of nightingales!' he exclaimed gaily. 'Did I tell you Undine wanted a word? About The Evening?'

'No, as a matter of fact, you didn't.'

I was glad to change the topic.

'Well, she plainly refuses to do the Italian version of the romance with me, unless you personally monitor our rehearsals and give your full approval. You are the only one whose judgment she seems to trust when it comes to music.'

I sighed resignedly. Anton winked.

'What did you expect? Being a genius carries responsibilities. Why don't you pay an early visit? She must be home by now—trying hard to lose herself in her article writing, our indefatigable anthropologist. Or maybe even rehearsing—solo, by her aging Förster. Your call could come as a much-needed diversion.'

I wanted to suggest that, with rehearsing purposes, it would probably be more expedient if we went together, since Anton was meant to be a voice and I—only a humble stage director.

I did not.

All of a sudden I clung to the opportunity of seeing Birgitte alone.

'Go,' Anton egged me on. 'She'll be happy to see you. It'll cheer you both up.'

*

I like to believe there is some symbolism, some imperceptible meaning in the fact that Birgitte and I are neighbors in this ghost town. We live vis-à-vis. She rents a place on the opposite side of the main square. Her landlady, like mine, is a stout, mustached spinster of a pole. This unromantic coincidence inexplicably stirs sensual strings within me every time I think of it.

A man's soul is a dark well, even if the man is your own, relatively familiar self. Sometimes only more so, for this circumstance.

When crossing the Rynek Główny, on my way to the faceless brick block, which Birgitte graced with her tenancy, my ears were accosted with plaintive whines and insistent whelping.

A dog!

I looked around for the source of the noise.

My search could not have been shorter. Sensing friendly human presence, a puppy—barely two months old—emerged from under an upset potato cart the moment I turned my head. Whimpering for attention as sorrowfully as only dogs know how to, it waddled straight at me on unsteady paws, wagging its tail and demanding cuddles.

I bent down and patted the smooth little head. My hand was immediately slobbered all over, and the boots smeared in slushy, tiny paw prints.

I picked the creature up and held it in front of my face to examine. An apricot spaniel mix breed. A male. A soft, warm, dirty bundle of unconditional love.

I unbuttoned my overcoat and slipped the silky intruder underneath, pressing him to my chest and completely giving up hope of turning up at Birgitte's like any semblance of a neat and trim swain.

I decided I'd be turning up with a little present instead.

Light steps behind the door with a worn-out sign: "**Dzwonek nie działa. Proszę zapukaj do drzwi**" announced Birgitte's presence to me and to my sniffling live load. The puppy stirred when the sound of the turning door handle reached his keen ears.

There she was standing—a svelte silhouette against the brownish dusk of the stingily lit corridor; autumnal hair in slight disarray.

'Chris!' She slapped her long thigh softly. 'I wasn't…'

'I know. I'm sorry. But do not blame me—the responsibility is entirely Anton's. He sent me here practically by force. Said you were demanding to be given voice instructions at once, otherwise threatening to sabotage the treasured evening performance.'

I garnished the tirade with a disarming smile for which there was no real need—she was glad to see me and not trying to hide it.

'Anton, and you will never grow up, will you? Two naughty schoolboys. Well, I do need a voice coach, Maestro. And I won't deny I envisaged you for the role.'

She shook her head and looked down at her long silk bathrobe in sham embarrassment.

'But you will have to forgive my homey attire—your advent has not exactly been annunciated.'

'Your attire could not be more suitable to receive the gift I bring.'

I unbuttoned my coat, revealing the little market-square dweller nuzzled up against the left breast pocket of my tunic.

Birgitte gasped, clasping her hands together.

The stream of tenderness in which my stray find and myself were being bathed in the following minutes exceeded my most optimistic expectations.

She took the puppy from my hands and buried her face in his plush tan belly.

'Oh my God, Chris, it must be for a reason you've always reminded me of the conjurer who came to my birthday parties when I was a kid and pulled tiny fluffy beasts out of his hat. Where did you dig up this adorable waif? Boy, does he need a bath?'

Scooping up the little animal from the floor where she had landed him a moment before to have a sniff around, she made a decisive movement toward the bathroom but stopped midway and took a sharp turn in the direction of the kitchen.

'No, a bowl of soup first. He must be starving, the poor mite; he's skin and bones.'

There turned out to be no soup, so Birgitte poured a bowlful of milk, soaked some bread crumbs in it, and placed her new four-legged charge on the floor in front of it. The grateful creature didn't even bother to take a token sniff but rushed straight into noisy lapping.

For just a few seconds, Birgitte watched him with adoration. Then she became restless again.

'He is terribly thirsty too. I should've given him some water first; that was stupid of me. And we are going to need to get him some meat; he's grown enough for it...'

'Do you really think you can adopt him then?' I asked.

She bit her lip and gave me a long look.

'Well, we cannot abandon him now, can we? Let's see... Will I be able to quietly smuggle him out and back in every time he needs to be walked? Keep him, invisibly and inaudibly, in my room? Probably not. When Pittypat One finds out, she will murder me and then demand I and the little mongrel clear the premises that very minute.'

Suddenly she stopped and laughed—the clear, crystal-clinking laughter of hers I like most.

'And then I will threaten her I will actually leave if she doesn't allow me to keep my puppy. It's either me with him or no me at all. She will relent; she likes me. I'm a good tenant! Besides, she is not that mean, really,

Pittypat One. She hides a good heart behind the intimidating mustache. They both do, our Pittypats, don't they?'

At that, I laughed too. Pittypat One and Pittypat Two, as we have jocosely christened our respective landladies, indeed are like two peas in a pod.

'Besides, I reckon an offer of a slight bonus to your monthly rent might add some heart-softening magic,' I suggested. 'I could help you out a little.'

'Oh, that will come as a panacea; no two ways about it!'

She carefully picked up the puppy, who had successfully put away the milk and was now enthusiastically polishing the bowl with his tongue.

'Just look at him. A healthy, happy child! In need of a bath!'

He licked her face, and she giggled—merrily, now herself like a naughty schoolgirl.

There sure is a lot I can thank the pooch for. He has lighted up the life of a charming creature and apparently secured me a piece of her heart.

There was once another four-legged being who had a similar effect on the heart of a beloved, unattainable girl. One that won me her—if only short-lived—favor over a generally much preferred rival.

Tino the Black Beast.

When Indigo moved into her Aunt Magde's place, lost her head for Bernie, and started dedicating the best time of her life emphatically and exclusively to him, the only little opening that still remained for me was to take her out on long walks in the evening—after she finished work and I— my studies.

Bernie, with his tubercular disposition, was wary of nocturnal strolls (or, plain lazy to get off his derrière), so there was never any need for me to worry that he might feel inclined to join us on our little sorties.

As Frau Treder lived in the vicinity of Treptow, we (or, mostly I—as it was always me who planned the route) made the most of the park.

Dreamily did we saunter along the dark horse-chestnut alleys, talking.

We talked endlessly, just like in the good old times—of her late father, her work, her love for Bernie; my studies, art, the meaning of life. She was so wise, so profoundly understanding. Yet at other times she was stubborn, subversive, and argumentative.

How I cherished those short, elusive, Bernie-free moments of mystical intimacy! The bodies only touched lightly, but the souls mutually penetrated and mingled in a transcendent communion which no earthly hand, no sordid thought might touch!

After a while, we were familiar with every farthest corner of the park, it seemed—every nook and cranny.

Once she was in the middle of firing her worldview at me.

'You do not owe the truth to anyone. Only tell the truth to people who deserve it—and those are few. In fact, people deserve the measure of truth directly proportionate to their intelligence. Otherwise, tell them exactly what is optimal, according to the circumstances. Give them the amount of truth they are able to healthily digest—that is, the amount that will not harm them or, through them, you, or others…'

It was then that we heard a heart-rending "meow."

Indigo forgot to finish the lecture.

'We must find the little one! He is somewhere very close, under one of these bushes, or on a tree, for sure! He's suffering. We must save him.'

A tree it was to be, and I was to devise a salvation scheme involving Indigo sitting (oh, the blessed minutes!) on my shoulders and pulling herself up to reach a knotty branch where the little black fluff ball had apparently been chased to by a local loose canine pack.

When it was over and everyone was safely down, all I remember was Indigo's disheveled curls hanging down over a pair of wildly staring yellow flashes whose furry owner kept producing harrowing cries.

'He is so fluffy! He is so black! Tino, he will be my little Tino… My little own Rodolfo Valentino…'

No amount of exhortations on my part could convince Indigo the idea was utopian. I tried to remind her that Frau Treder was—or, at least, firmly believed she was—allergic to feline fur and, generally, never counted among great pet enthusiasts. I tried to explain that her precious Bernie, in his ultimate egotism, cared about nothing except himself, his "art" and his "malady," so would probably consider adopting a stray, wet, dirty kitten as reprehensible a folly as his mother would.

I almost shouted that it was *their*, not her own house, she meant to take the foundling to.

Indigo virtually repeated Birgitte's resolution, 'Then I will tell them it is either me with the kitten, or I take the kitten and move back into my father's place. I do not for a second doubt it will be keeping me and Tino they will choose.'

The scenario that followed was as accurately predicted by me as it was augmented by Indigo.

Auntie Mag was none too pleased. Bernie was on his mother's side. Indigo stood her ground. Eventually, it was Indigo who won the battle.

Not that Frau Treder so much cherished her niece's presence under her roof. Mostly, she wanted her brother-the professor's generous death pension to continue to go toward her only son's wellbeing. She was even prepared to lay aside her ostensible allergy and consent to keeping a cat, lest she and Bernie should part with that benefit. Money does things to people.

Tino the kitten was to grow into an imposing beast with a luxurious black coat and mesmerizing amber eyes. He became the creature Indigo loved more than any other living being, including even Bernie. Much later, when she wearied of Bernie and lost all respect for her aunt, it was Tino, of course, who followed her back to Prenzlauer Berg in a deluxe velvet pet valise…

*

Contrary to the initial purpose of my visit, Birgitte and I did not even attempt to start rehearsing Alabieff. I'm not sure whether it was the puppy with his distracting sweetness or no work had inwardly been meant to take place anyway.

While the puppy napped on Birgitte's bed in between us, I was happily holding forth on my own composing instead of coaching his new mistress in vocal techniques. Birgitte had a thousand questions.

What was the mysterious piece I had been laboring away on all the time? On what stage of readiness was it? Why did I never play it in public? Why would I not play it to her personally?

I was apprehensive about telling her the story of my musical obsession. Birgitte is a gentle, sensitive, wise, and understanding creature. But she is not an Indigo. She doesn't possess that unconventionally irreverent turn of mind.

Birgitte is all about moderation, reasonableness, and goodness. I feared that, though she would probably never allow herself a word of criticism, she might see my decade-long chasing after one elusive piece as an unacceptable form of self-indulgence, even an abnormality.

So I honestly told her it was a violin concerto I worked on when the mood took me. I emphasized, however, that, contrary to what she might think, it was only in the germinal stage—so much so in fact, I hadn't even quite decided on the structure yet.

I dwelt on supposed technical details, saying that roundedness of form in such a piece was all important, which explained my unwillingness to perform it to anyone (especially someone like her, whose opinion I valued) before it was finished and polished.

What I chose to completely withhold was my emotional tie with Indigo Mind—the story of how it had been conceived as Brünnhilde's Moods, coming out of the flames of my childhood fever; how then, for many years, it was slipping away from me, and how, the more it was doing so, the greater its hold on me grew.

'The entire piece is planned in a minor key, but I envisage it flat rather than sharp. Flats impart a dark, matted coloration to sound,' I expatiated. 'D or G. Just remember all these glorious Bach Double, *Paganini No.4*, *Vieuxtemps No.4*, and Sibelius in D Minor; *Bruch and Prokofiev No.2* in G Minor.'

Eventually Birgitte stopped me with a smile and a touch on the arm.

'All right, Maestro, I can see you are doing your homework. Whenever the grand vision is cast in a tangible shape, I call dibs on the first hearing.'

'You can count on it.'

Then a delightful idea struck me.

All the while I had been looking past Birgitte into the opposite wall. Now I turned sharply to face her.

'Tell me.' I placed my hands on her forearms. 'Have you ever tried composing yourself?'

She looked abashed; even blushed a little.

'No, to be honest, I have never tried... I don't believe I'm able to. Why?'

'What would you say if I suggested we compose something together?'

She shook her hair in a humorous protest, blushing even more.

'Are you making fun of me?'

'A small piece,' I urged. 'A romance. In F, or G major. Like *Beethoven's No. 2*, or *No. 1*.'

'Chris, you must be joking. I barely know how to notate.'

'Nothing of the kind will be required of you. That shall all be my part of the work.'

'What part do you want to be mine then?'

'Yours will be the inspiration part. You will be in charge of mentally leading me from one note to the next. All you will have to do is be around, talk to me, and be radiating as much light as you are today.'

Now her face was perfectly ablaze.

'Oh, Maestro...' There was a catch in her voice. 'What a romantic you are...'

Flustered as much as she was, she then got a grip on herself and attempted irony.

'And what a flatterer!'

I could barely hear her by then.

A warm wave of inspiration, which started coming in moments before, now completely swept me over.

Sitting before me, with a tiny living being at her thigh, was not Birgitte anymore—it was Freia, the golden-curled Freia, the cat-driven, the boar-accompanied goddess of fertility, love, the mystical seiðr, the sacred gold.

The music of the romance was delightfully flowing through my head as I was talking to her.

Freia's reverie.

I could already see the entire score.

I knew I had to run home and put it down immediately, while it was still playing within me. Birgitte knew too—she caught on at once.

We stood up simultaneously. Feeling the sudden absence of the two human bodies which had been warming him from two sides, the puppy gave a single saddened yelp.

Birgitte handed me my coat and kissed me on the cheek as I started clumsily making my way toward the door. I embraced her and promised to serenade her with the new-born romance by the time we saw each other again.

*

It proved easier said than done, however.

For no sooner did I, trembling with anticipation, lean over the notepaper, than did the clean-cut, ripe, and mellow sound of the romance inexplicably lose its clarity.

I could still hear the main theme, but the accompaniment blurred. Other musical pieces—all the many ones I had learned, played, or composed—were importunately cutting in, unsettling me, and blotting out the target.

After hours of an unnerving struggle, I did pin it down, after all.

I reworked the initial idea completely.

It was not to be F or G major. It came out in E minor. And, instead of scoring it for a violin solo and an orchestra of strings, oboes, bassoons, horns, and flutes, I reduced it to simply piano and violin. Andante 12/8. 4 bars of introduction by piano; a violin movement; the same intro by piano inducing violin again; then a climax repeated twice; then return to the first violin theme; double stops of violin tying it all up and tailing off to the end.

I played it.

Well, I could rightfully claim I had captured and embodied Freia's reverie. It had NOT escaped from me, not like Indigo Mind.

That much was true.

But!

But.

God Almighty, how flat and shallow, how simplistic and saccharine it sounded compared to what I, hypothetically, could have composed. Compared to that same unattainable, adored, and accursed Indigo Mind, for instance!

How mediocre.

I could not complain; the result fell short of my initial idea. I had played around with the arrangement and key, true. But the theme, the mood, and the essence remained intact.

Only, *that* theme, mood, and essence, which had been richly flowing through my system like a stream of linden honey before I returned from Birgitte's, now struck me as nothing more than a naive and syrupy little song. An almost vulgar one even. One worthy of a begging fiddler in a back alley.

I thought of the violin-playing Gypsy in the family camp. Could I give the new romance to him, perhaps? Could he rearrange it in some circus manner and use it to lull babies to sleep?

In short, I despised myself. Once again.

It was almost dawn—I had spent the night working on the romance. I felt as limp as a dishrag, but vexed and restless. The thought of sleep somehow seemed entirely absurd.

In a last desperate attempt to regain a modicum of self-respect, I put music aside and tried to add some paragraphs to the *Force Vitale* draft.

All to no avail. My words sounded just as hollow as my notes did.

After two more miserable hours (it was broad daylight when I finally gave up), I did not manage to construct a single sentence for which I could give myself any credit.

What, in the name of divinity, is happening to me?

IV
2nd Violin

'He is like a little wolf cub when he won't sleep. He howls like one, and I think he can eat me alive like one. He can swallow me up whole.'

Immediately Damira gets a slap on the back of her head from Marusya.

'Don't you talk of your own brother like this.'

Damira is not offended. She never resents her mother for slapping her.

'When he sleeps too deep, though…' she continues unperturbed, 'when he sleeps too deep, I'd rather he howled again, because I start thinking he may be dead.'

Marusya scowls at her daughter but neglects to slap her this time.

'And when does he ever sleep as deep as that, I'd like to know.' Mihai chuckles. 'I only ever remember him howling.'

'Sometimes he sleeps like that,' Damira insists gravely. 'He does when Jass plays him to sleep.'

Baby Dando, Damira's brother, was delivered in the truck, under the burlap. His birth caused his father's death.

Initially, it had been supposed to be the other way around. Marusya, Damira, and the newborn were probably not even going to reach the traditional communal bath. They would have been put down on the way there, so feeble and useless for any practical purpose they looked.

Lasho, the head of the family, was, to the contrary, wiry, albeit on the short-statured side. He was nimble and fidgety, with singularly sharp features, all of which gave him a semblance to a curious little rodent. He had a prickly black mat of poodle-fur hair on his head (the shave-off of which he was spared, due to his premature demise), and he struck me as the most unquenchable chatterbox I had ever met. Lasho also happened to be the most infamous liar in the world, as well as definitely the worst (meaning, the most unskillful) one. It was this particular quality, along with his little son's birth, that signed his death sentence.

When I think of Lasho, I remember what Shandor used to say when he chided his nephew Yoska for the fibs the boy often told (it has to be mentioned that, after Lasho, Yoska was the second most willing and least skillful liar I've known).

'Now if there is a type I genuinely loathe,' Shandor would boom, making sure Yoska blushed for shame, 'it is a lame liar. One who gets caught. Especially one who, after getting caught, will blunder into the same lame lying again and again be punished with having his lameness exposed.'

Shandor-the-wise!

Every time he said that, I found myself wholeheartedly agreeing. This is probably because I so appreciate good lying. I will applaud a good actor who will put on a quality show for me. One who will know people in general and me in particular well enough to crack what I might fall for. Bite on what makes me tick. Like anyone who does something well, a good liar will have my attention. I might do what he wants and not regret it, even knowing I've been duped. I'd take it as due payment for a good performance—professionalism, after all, must be rewarded.

Only a good liar, like a good anything, is not very often encountered. The late Lasho certainly did not belong to the rare category.

'My wife is having a fit of the Gypsy disease called "noisy sleep," Herr Obersturmführer!' He was passionately convincing Guido Karp, who had arrived to inspect the new transport, and was more than a little puzzled by the groans and screams coming from under the messy tarpaulins in the hindmost corner of the truck's bodywork.

'It is not contagious, I swear you. She is only having some bad gypsy dreams… We'd do well not to wake her up now—she'll sleep them off, and by the time she wakes up, the disease will be all gone!'

The sight that revealed itself to Obersturmführer Cabbagehead when he tore off the rough covers was of a shrieking young woman with legs splayed apart and a shivering little girl cowering beside her while trying to pull a baby out of her mother's gaping womb.

The effect the apparition produced was an unexpected one.

Instead of shooting the useless, filthy creatures on sight, Guido actually gave orders to provide medical assistance to the woman in childbirth. Immediately following this, he recalled about Lasho and commanded that the lying Gypsy bastard who'd had the effrontery to jeer at a German officer be thrown into a ditch which a small squad of Jews had just dug to serve as their own grave. He ruled that the swine be put a bullet in the head, alongside the ditchdiggers.

As Marusya was being collected and carried away on a stretcher with the terrified Damira in tow, their husband and father came to face the freshly disturbed, steaming soil under which he was to be buried.

Still Lasho persisted in his ravings, now babbling that the "noisy sleep" disease sometimes produced a kind of hallucinations in those who happened to look at the sick person in the active phase, and so what Herr Obersturmführer had just seen in the truck was an illusion, and his wife was not delivering a baby, but only "noisily sleeping."

Even lying in the ditch, shot through but still alive, the poor man wouldn't calm down and patiently wait for the definitive head bullet, like his Jewish fellow-sufferers did. Instead, he rolled back his eyes and held his breath, pretending he was already dead.

That perimortem act of Lasho's became a standing joke with the Kapos, who would relish it for months afterward, retelling the details to each other for countless times, bleating with laughter.

*

Baby Dando was named so for his teeth. Teeth he didn't have, of course, but when, against all odds, he managed to survive his hapless father, it was unanimously admitted the baby had a lockjaw grip on life.

Damira, an adoring sister though she is, often fatalistically reproaches the little creature for having proved his viability at Lasho's expense. When I try to explain to her she is not being fair, she stubbornly whispers, 'It is easy for you to say. Your own little son did not gnaw your life out for himself to live, he was not born a little wolf cub.'

My own little son did not.

He did, however, while still unborn, claim the life of my dearest friend.

Damira knows the story. I told it to her many times to entertain her. She seems to take my life as a fairytale, and always asks for more.

*

After the revelry at *Predsedatel* Georgyi's, I could not go to sleep, though I was tired and drunk. I kept waking up from Businka's tearful neighing in the stable, and every time, just before waking, I saw Yoska standing on all fours, tearing forth and giving those heart-rending neighs.

When I opened my eyes, however, I inevitably saw that same Yoska lying beside me, deep in his nervous, twitchy sleep. Somehow it made me even more apprehensive than his neighing in my dreams. And, if I might have had doubts before, now they were peremptorily ousted by the grim clarity.

We were in for a thunderbolt, and it was only a question of *when* it would strike.

We didn't have to wait long.

The clammy Russian morning came, bringing in its tow a hangover and a militia raid on the marquee.

What was the matter?

We were accused of theft. Or, more specifically, Yoska was.

The stumpy men in long, heavy coats refused to give explanations. Silently, they handcuffed my sleepy, confused, mumbling love, led him out, and pushed him into the *voronok,* which drove off into the early spring grayness as swiftly and nonchalantly as its handlers acted.

Shandor insisted on following me to the *uchastok,* which I expected would throw in additional complications.

It did.

Shandor, in his misplaced intelligentsia manner, tried to reason with the gray-eyed commissars. Said he was not asking to see his nephew but would appreciate being, at least with some approximation, enlightened regarding the circumstances of the crime for which the boy had been arrested.

In response, Shandor was called "a tramp with no notion of active citizenship." He was told that he'd better forget about his nephew and move his circus out of the town in twenty four hours, unless he wanted to lose track of his other tramp companions along with his nephew and have his horses processed in a sausage factory.

This got me angry.

As Shandor clutched at his heart and gasped for air (that strong, composed, sarcastic Shandor turned into a prince Myshkin every time a next of kin or a loved one was in danger), I pulled myself together. I willed away my headache and the tremor in my hungover extremities.

I took Lavuta out.

In the bile-color corridor I started fiddling their favored Ochi

Chernyiyeh—offhandedly, cheekily, Gypsy tramp style.

The *Starshina* was a portly man in his late fifties.

Instantaneously overcome with a feeling he was going to have an apoplectic attack, he sounded alarm. Pressing a hidden button under his oak desk, he summoned the runty sergeant. The latter had just given Shandor the vociferous brush-off and now vacantly stared at me playing in the corridor, wind taken out of his sails. He made an awkward movement toward the door in an attempt to answer the *Starshina's* summons but was paralyzed.

Moreover, on the sergeant, Lavuta seemed to also have some kind of thought-arresting effect (not that there was much to arrest, of course). Whatever primal inner dialogue might have been crawling behind that low forehead came to full stop. The kid froze halfway between the unbelieving indignation at my playing in the corridor and the servile "at attention" he was going to present to the *Starshina*. His gray eyes mindlessly bulged, and saliva trickled out of the corner of his mouth.

Leaving the young sergeant in Shandor's care, I went, still playing, behind the reinforced metal door, to attend to the *Starshina*.

In the best traditions of Gypsy Feast performers, I came before his eyes—in a red silk shirt, a wide grin across my face, Lavuta at my chin—fiddling a romance.

The man did not look good. His cheeks, forehead, neck, and bald spot turned the color of raw meet. There were tears in his bloodshot eyes. He was scratching at his throat and wheezing.

No one in this world had ever been so defenseless against Lavuta's onslaughts, so crushed in her grip as those gray-eyed militia types. She turned them inside out and tied them in knots.

I played a few more bars, then lowered the baton and said I wished to see my companion, who had been taken into custody.

Still wheezing, spasmodically opening his mouth like a fish, the *Starshina* pressed his secret button and called the sergeant.

It took some seconds for the kid to unfreeze. Then he stepped in and unconfidently saluted—dazed as if brought round out of a swoon. Saliva glistened on his chin.

Orders were given.

Minutes later, the manacled Yoska was brought out of the entrails of the gloomy institution and led down the hollow-sounding corridor to meet us.

This time, much as Shandor was eager to, I did not let him do the talking. I determinedly took Yoska to one side.

Yoska looked more astonished and upset than angered by his gaolers' conduct.

I asked what the charges against him were.

Apparently, *Predsedatel* Georgyi's wife Tatiana Gavrilovna's diamond brooch had gone missing, and Yoska was suspected of having stolen it.

Well, given that he was the only one who had entered her bedroom the previous night and spent there awhile; that the good lady had not been quite sober; and that Yoska was, on the whole, not at all averse to *choribe*, there was every possibility of that being the case.

I asked if he had done it.

Though looking lost, he shook his head with a great deal of resolution. Absolutely not. He had not. He swore.

Now, like I said, Yoska was known as a shameless liar, but by no means a good one. Most people could see through his substandard tall tales, while with me he never even attempted any.

And this time I knew he was telling the truth. He had not done it.

I asked if everything else had gone well between him and Tatiana Gavrilovna the night before.

He lowered his eyes and grinned lopsidedly.

I was not surprised. For, much as he thought he admired puffy female breasts, it had always really been taut, velvety, bronze-skinned male flesh that perked my Yoska up. My flesh, first and foremost. Now, for better or worse, there was a world of difference between the pasty Tatiana Gavrilovna and me. Obviously, my drunk love's performance in her chambers had not quite lived up to the lustful lady's expectations.

This gave me a thread—a good and thick one. I tuned in.

What revealed itself to me was that Tatiana Gavrilovna did not in fact bear Yoska as much malice as to actually perjure him. She did, however, resent his non-consummation enough to have sincerely convinced herself he was the cause of her brooch's disappearance.

The brooch, meanwhile, was peacefully hiding itself under the thick Persian rug on the floor of Tatiana Gavrilovna's bedroom, having been inadvertently pushed there with the owner's oblivious foot. The troublemaking jewelry piece had come unfastened and slipped off the lady's blouse when she and Yoska were hastily undressing each other the night before.

I went back into the *Starshina*'s office and said that the main witness, Tatiana Gavrilovna, was to be put on the phone to me without delay.

Georgyi's number was dialed, and his wife was asked to the receiver.

Following my instructions, she retrieved her missing property.

After completing formalities (which were made as brief as it was physically possible), Yoska walked free.

*

But, although we were now clear of all the charges, and *Predsedatel* Georgyi personally came into the marquee to apologize for his wife's wrongly made accusations, the hassle was yet far from over.

For, along with the apologies, *Predsedatel* voiced an urgent demand; the circus must, after all, leave the town in the nearest prospect.

He realized that since we were completely unprepared, it was hardly feasible to have all our props collected and moved out in twenty-four hours.

He was ready to allow us forty-eight hours.

He actually granted us the permission for a goodbye performance. But, as he hoped we understood (he added in an embarrassed voice), after his wife had been compromised in connection with our presence, it was no longer possible for the town to give us shelter.

We had to go.

That development was no tragedy for me personally. I was by then bored stiff with the town and its dwellers, and, if anything, would've been happy to clear away. But it meant serious complications for Shandor. Shandor had debts to cover and counted on the remaining month of stable work—sold-out circus shows and, first and foremost, our overbooked soirées for the fat party cats—as a financial salvation (we had been positively raking it in all the while in N). So I promised Shandor if I didn't think of a less drastic method by the time of our "goodbye performance," then I would use Lavuta to win us back the favor of Georgyi and his Party mates.

Use Lavuta this time, however, I was loath to. Like I said, my heart was not in it.

As things turned out in the end, I did not have to waste my violin's powers on the paltry matter.

For in the evening of that day, a new character entered the picture.

The character was of a skinny—almost emaciated physique, porcelain complexion, well-sculpted cheekbones, two ashen braids, and huge, moist eyes which stared across with the expression of a horrified gazelle. Though, generally, Shandor did not allow strangers backstage, she somehow managed to slip through, unhindered, right after the show. She made her way straight at me.

I was helping Yanoro, our tightrope walker, roll up his ropes.

She stopped in front of us and stood still until, giving in to her insistent gaze, I dropped what I was doing and returned the look.

'Is it true that this was your last show? Is it true you are leaving?'

Shandor had announced in the beginning that "due to unforeseen circumstances," the circus, sadly, had to close the tour sooner than the posters indicated.

Her cheeks, though naturally pale, were ablaze; the narrow, almost flat chest was heaving under the drab schoolgirl's uniform.

'You were supposed to stay till the end of spring. Did something happen? Does somebody want you gone?'

There was no need to tune in—one glance at her sufficed to see she was agonizingly in love with me. I now faintly recalled having observed those translucent features in the audience, in the front row, probably at every single one of the recent performances.

Any attempt at professional taciturnity would be ridiculous—she read me, and she knew that I knew she did.

I nodded slowly and conspiratorially whispered, 'That's right. *Predsedatel'* of the *Rajispolkom* wants us gone.'

'You did something that displeased him.'

There was not a shadow of interrogative intonation in the utterance.

I shrugged.

'So he says.'

She lowered her eyelids and shook her head, at which her thick braids came into a slight rustling motion.

'*Predsedatel'*'s niece is my best friend. I will talk to her. I will talk to him myself if needed.'

Then, bestowing upon me one of those cosmic looks only her eyes were capable of, abruptly changing the tone, she concluded with, 'Please, stay some more.'

This was no plea—she was not begging. Nor was it a stubborn little girl's capricious demand. It was a very strong, very sincere request. One that I now felt I would not be reluctant to grant.

I could also rest assured that from this moment on, no further steps were required from Lavuta or me in regard to getting Georgyi to retract his decision. Lyuba (so was the girl's name) would take care of the matter.

It was a relief.

The following afternoon, the expected call from Georgyi came. He said he and his wife had "discussed the situation," and it was decided that our further sojourn in the town would not after all imply any embarrassment for his family. Therefore, he "invited" us to stay and continue our tour in N.

At the following show (which had been supposed to be our farewell), Shandor elicited a delighted applause from our admirers by informing them that "the unforeseen complications" had been happily removed and the circus would continue its nightly performances.

Our young mediator Lyuba was in the audience, of course. And of course, as soon as we finished, she came backstage to see me.

I hugged her and thanked her for having stepped in. Shandor heartily squeezed and shook the palm of her pale hand—narrow and bony like a sparrow's foot. Yanoro, Danior, the girls, everybody came up to express their gratitude.

So did Yoska.

I watched them as they took stock of each other.

They sure made a great match, the two most exquisite creatures I had known. They sure appreciated each other's loveliness. And they sure as hell immediately knew what role the other played, or would play, in my, or their own, past, present, and future lives.

So did I, naturally.

For, as soon as their hands touched, the ominous vision of Yoska standing on all fours and neighing in Businka's voice I'd had two nights before flashed through my mind again, like a lightning through stormy skies. And, although that lightning ignited a flame which engulfed my heart in a scorching sadness, I realized there was no way I could stop the imminent disaster.

Alas—just as efficiently as I can, when I must, influence the feelings of others, so incapacitated I become when my own heart plays a trick on me.

Here they were, standing before me holding hands, the two living beings for each of whom I could have laid down my life without a moment's hesitation. And here was I—seeing that the presence of one of them in my world would cause me a painful loss of the other—and knowing myself completely helpless to ward off the fate.

Jealousy.

The accursed emotion which in its ability to poison the soul and prompt self-humiliating decisions, is only second to pure fear. An emotion which, if one were to analyze it rationally, even makes no sense at all.

For, come to think of it, how can feelings for different objects conflict? How can they mimic, or oust, or replace each other any more than a splendid painting can a breathtaking book? Yet, just like fear, it remains one of the hardest emotional states to break out of.

I have once had one of those dear to me fall prey to jealousy. I am most certainly making sure this never happens again. And I'm well aware I must not drop my guard, because beautiful David is almost as suspicious as he is charming; ergo, he is in a risk zone.

Should I sense another potential object on the horizon, I will know exactly what precautions to take lest they have any, direct or indirect, possibility to harm each other.

Not that I am much wiser now than I was then, but experience does, after all, count for something. It should, at least.

With David, I turn on my gentle irony-poking mode—this seems to work best on him.

And I start from afar.

In fact, it is usually himself who starts. He may, for instance, smile wistfully and say, 'You know, my uncle always passionately argued it was because we had turned away from Eretz Israel that this new plague in the face of the maniacs Hitler and Himmler befell our people."

Yet, however rueful his smile may be, there will be the naughty spark twinkling in the corner of his eye.

'This is because Yahweh, our God, is a jealous God.'

'Correct,' I pick up. 'So what's the conclusion? Do not be like Yahweh. Do not hurt innocent living beings out of ill-grounded rancor.'

He wags his graceful finger at me.

'You should not say such things, really. It was Yahweh after all who willed the miraculous salvation of Jerusalem from Sennacherib, as had been prophesied. In 702 B.C.? Have you read of this?'

'702 B.C., was it? The date when, the Nazis maintain, Jew was born... Of course, my devout darling, I've read of this. And tell you what? The story smacks of a lucky coincidence, almost like our prominent Petko stinks of sour Polish beer and unkosher pork sausages. But this only goes to prove that your people are remarkable. You may not be "the people of God," but you are certainly a people of luck, which, considering what a sadistic arsehole your God is described to be, is a preferable option.'

At that, my coltish David is usually not able to pull a serious face anymore. He cracks up. He laughs—openly, lightly, irreverently. And I most willingly join in his jollity.

*

'*Stillgestanden*!'

Guido.

Who else to press on a violinist's eardrums as obnoxiously as Obersturmführer Cabbagehead?

Guido pops up unannounced, and in a somewhat quieter fashion than is his usual style. This means he has come to collect Boiko.

Boiko is ready.

He has been waiting since morning. In preparation for lights-out, he has been restlessly pacing the barrack, endlessly checking on Rosa until she rolled her eyes and asked him to leave her alone, picking up unnecessary tasks, chain-smoking out of his bottomless stash, and getting into everyone's way.

For the entire day he has not been once bothered by the yard jobs. Unofficial word has been sent to the overseers that their pet scapegoat poses a specific interest for Obersturmführer Karp, so is, for the time being, not to be beaten, kicked, pushed, or otherwise subjected to potential physical damage.

In between other things, Boiko has been talking to Baba Tanya.

Since the recent run-in with Bushalo, he has enjoyed the *gicisvara*'s motherly attention. She checks on his healing cheek regularly, applies more ointment, and changes the bandage. But, first and foremost, she gives him copious instructions: on how to treat Rosa, secure her favorable disposition, and how, for his own and Rosa's sake, benefit from the arrangement with Guido best.

'You listen to your Baba Tanya, boy. This Karp, he is a puppet. He is a nobody. He reports to the main doctor here, like everyone else.'

'To Doctor Angel, Baba Tanya? To him?'

'Right, boy. That is the only one here whose word counts for something. So what do you do? You watch well what Karp the puppet will be doing to you. And then you go to that Angel doctor, and you report it all to him. Hear what I'm saying? You report it all to him.'

At this, Boiko expresses polite uncertainty, 'But... how will I get to talk to him, Baba Tanya? A high-up person like this? I only ever said two words to him once, when I asked him for a smoke... when it comes to asking for a smoke, I'm afraid of no one! But—report to him? Why would he listen to me? How will I...'

The *gicisvara* dismisses his doubts with a hewing move of her puffy hand. 'You will find a way! You are a smart boy; otherwise, your Baba Tanya wouldn't be wasting her time on you!'

She straightens her back, and her pendulous breasts come in formidable swinging under the stained blouse. Then she resumes her lecture, 'That Doctor Angel will go far, I'm telling you. A long and wide path he has before him. I can see this as clear as I can see you. Such a bright head—and such a *bakalo* too! The lucky one!'

'Lucky indeed; this is what I always thought he was, *gicisvara*,' Mihai puts in his two pennies with a respectful nod. 'Although in what way, I cannot really say. Just feel it. You are right, as always.'

Baba Tanya smoothes out her floral skirt and purses her lips.

'In what way! It is easy to say in what way, old man! Know how many times he was wounded? Heard from how many scraps he got out alive?'

'I heard in Russia? Near Rostock? Or what's the place called?'

'There,' the *gicisvara* pensively nods. 'And not only there. In many other places too. But that's not the point. The point is... look at him. That face is the face of a warrior. The face of a winner. The face of a *bakalo*.'

'*Onkel* Mengele looks like a prince!' Damira readily agrees.

'Doctor Heidert is more handsome than him,' Rosa dreamily interposes.

Luckily, Boiko is spared from hearing Rosa's judgment, as right at that moment the *gicisvara* grabs him by the chin and turns his face so he looks her in the eye.

'You heard me, boy? Come on, say what Baba Tanya wants you to do!'

'I should report to Doctor Angel all the things Obersturmführer Karp and I will be doing in the laboratory,' Boiko obediently repeats.

'That's my good boy!' She contentedly chuckles, pinching him on his healthy cheek.

And now Boiko is ready. He springs to attention ecstatically when he sees Guido's face, stretched out with a complacent grin.

Guido gives Boiko a conspiratorial wink as he approaches. The straightforward officer can hide no emotion whatsoever. The entire mixture of fear and excitement he is feeling in connection with his planned prank is splashed across his debonair mug.

I feel a new scorching stab of sadness as he leads Boiko away. The point is, we shall not see our good-natured tobacco procurer again.

Guido's plan is simple (like everything else Guido-related is). In secret from everyone, he intends to try hard and please a major pharmaceutical conglomerate by single-handedly providing "proof" that their new development is a good thing (which it doesn't really happen to be). Then he hopes to rush a substantial lot of the stuff to the market—the frontline, in other words—with the profit going, undivided, into his pocket. With this end in mind, he will conduct some token trials—on Boiko and a number of other wretched guinea pigs. Then he will draw up papers which will state that the amount of experiments conducted on the subject has been at least threefold and that every single one has gone off with a bang. While, in actuality, the few objects he is going to use will all meet their respective *Del/Adonai* in rash, sweat, puke, and photophobia in block 32. The luckier—meaning, the least resistant—ones (our Boiko included) will slip into a coma early on.

Boiko actually will find himself close to Mengele "the Angel" a number of times. Only, contrary to Baba Tanya's instructions, he will not be able to utter a word about Guido's mischief. The only two syllables his parched lips will, in his delirious throws, be able to articulate are the ones of his cherished epileptic's name. And, regrettably, the voluptuous Rosa is not going to hear that febrile, palatal-dental declaration of love made on deathbed—otherwise even her lukewarm heart might've been touched.

But, for better or worse, Rosa is to make her way out and travel to Paris cool and unperturbed, as she was born to be. I am the only one in this barrack who is going to know of the entire affair. And, while it is not up to me to save Boiko from the typhus injection for which he has volunteered, I will sure be able to make Guido-the-schemer pay for his little stunt. In hard cash—to begin with.

*

Not long before Guido, Doctor Heidert stopped by.

This one is circling Damira. He is also circling me, though he doesn't quite realize it yet.

Unlike Guido's, Christian's intentions are entirely free from pecuniary interests. A Young Werther that he is, he seeks elevated delights—sublime love, creative self-realization, scientific truth.

A boy after my own heart.

Although it is little Damira's fate to die at Heidert's hands, her death will not technically be of his making. The task he sets himself is mere observation. His firm belief that nature is on his side will prevent him from causing additional suffering. Damira and other similar objects he is going to use already carry the evidence of something he looks to prove—there is no need to infect them deliberately.

Nevertheless, Doctor Heidert will cause his measure of pain. As a matter of fact, he will cause a lot. And for this he will be punished. Only, differently from Guido's, in Christian's case there will also be a reward apart from punishment. A dubious one—but a prize, all the same. It is a gift to have one's questions answered, even if subsequently you find the answers too much to deal with.

Damira clings to Christian. On her list of princes, he is probably only second to me and Mengele, " Angel."

At this stage, it is a father figure the cuddly creature mostly looks for. Never quite got over the loss of Lasho; lacking tenderness from the distracted Marusya; saddled with nannying little Dando. Her childish desire for an older male company is everything one would expect. Yet behind the angular gestures of infantile affection, a careful observer can easily discern the unselfconscious graces of a budding coquette. She knows exactly how to approach each particular "daddy" best, her instinct for subtle distinction is unerring. She is a respectfully obedient little pupil to "Onkel" Mengele;

a wide-eyed admirer to "Onkel" Heidert; a delighted listener to me.

It is painful to think she will not live to see herself in her prime when she could have easily made up with keen female intuition for whatever she might lack in exterior. The exterior too, by the way, though showing no promises of perfection, might have, if allowed to apex, blossomed into a flower of unconventional charm. She could never have become Rosa, but she may have been something more intriguing—a flawed seducer, a scarred enchantress. The tadpole would have turned into a striking pin—a high-cheekboned head on a slight, narrow-hipped body. The frog-like mouth would have been transformed into long, sensuously curving lips; the solicitous eyes of a frightened mousekin—into moist vastnesses full of unobtrusive understanding many a man would've longed to drown in.

All a potentiality to be reduced to nothingness by Doctor Heidert and his colleagues.

But, as things stand now, Christian is a welcome distraction for his victim. He pats her on the head, gives her the much wanted hugs, and humors her. She looks forward to his visits and their little chats. He is by no means chary of these attentions, and, by bringing into the hut a breath of fresh, *outside* air—that of refined intelligence, encouraged talent, unrestrained humor and proud elegance—he probably adds more color to her existence than even I am able to. For this, I am infinitely grateful to our exalted Young Werther. Damira will not last, so every second of her short life counts.

To praise him for making Damira happier, I give Christian some moments of carefree somnolence (a byproduct of lulling baby Dando to sleep, as a matter of fact). As to his punishment for murdering her, this he will administer to himself. All in good time.

*

So what do we have here?

We have Obersturmführer Cabbagehead who struggles to reconcile his patriotism with practicality and fob off some defective pills on his own kin while convincing himself that he is doing a lot of good for the motherland and just a little good for his own pocket.

We have Young Werther who spiritedly tries to serve the science and his country by proving that malnutrition-induced gangrene is brought about by a congenital inferiority.

We have Angel, hell-bent on reinforcing Arian blood with newly-obtained, sensational ways of changing the odious brown eye color to the much sought-after cobalt blue.

Bleak indeed.

The only comfort is to remember the global medicine has not yet completely gone to the dogs; not the entire world is Germany. The US Army Medical Corps are clearing the release of penicillin for use in all military hospitals, for instance. To think how much good this miraculous mold could have done here, in our sickly parts.

Boiko's prompt departure with Guido leaves an air of euphoria in the barrack—everyone seems livened-up. The famous German efficiency is being discussed in ecstatic tones.

Baba Tanya cannot stop extolling the talents and supernatural luck of Mengele. Mihai stares at her, wide-eyed in pure admiration. He fidgets, nods, yes—yeses, politely grunts. He is visibly running out of means of expressing enthusiasm. He is nervously trying to think of new ones.

After Mihai leapt to the conclusion that it was Baba Tanya who, with her wise council, somehow "arranged" it for Boiko to work with Guido and Josef the Angel, her status in his eyes has risen to the level of goddess. He doesn't hide it, and Baba Tanya is pleased.

'Those Americans and Englishers, they have nothing on the *Deutsches*, I'm saying to you,' the *gicisvara* trumpets exasperatedly. 'And why is this, you tell me?'

The question is addressed to Mihai, and the poor man is dismayed, for he knows he will never guess the right answer. So he resorts to the tried-and-true tactics of nodding and grunting, which he feels is getting hopelessly stale.

But Mihai's fears are unfounded, for his is just the reaction Baba Tanya wants to see. The *gicisvara* needs no answers. Those she has herself—and is impatient to voice.

'This, old man, is because them Yankees and Englishers do not have the likes of the Doctor Angel in their ranks!'

Mihai bends his head and moos.

Then there is a silence during which Baba Tanya proudly puffs, and he scours his mind for fresh ways of showing full agreement.

I take pity on the old man and help him out. I softly clear my throat.

This reminds him of my existence, and Mihai hits on a brilliant idea. As Baba Tanya's attitude toward me is tacitly disapproving, he decides to challenge me to a loud verbal combat where my position will be guaranteed to appear against—and his—for her.

And in this complex tactical move, Mihai's instinct does not misfire.

'Hear this boy?' he starts scrappily. 'Those favorite Englishers of yours, they are good for nothing! They are children against the *Deutches*! They will never win the war.'

I should not let Mihai down now, and I briskly return the ball to his court.

'Why, Babbo, I beg to differ. The British have actually done pretty well so far. Cracked some big codes. Are sinking German submarines as we speak?'

Barely a split second passes before Mihai and Baba Tanya start hissing at me in unison, like two indignant snakes.

'You are talking heresy, boy!' Baba Tanya condemns my judgment.

'Right! Even a hare would see you are talking crap!' Mihai charges on, in the name of his corpulent Dulcinea.

'Well, Babbo, Baba Tanya, with all due respect—I have arguments to prove my point.'

Nothing today has yet given me so much gratification as playing the windmill for Mihai to tilt at. The old man deserves his little pleasures. He receives them even more gratefully than Damira does hers. It is this inimitable triumphant look on his wrinkled face I want to see. And I am rewarded with it in full measure.

*

I especially treasure Mihai's manifestations of joy, as they so poignantly remind me of Shandor's. The two men are poles apart in about everything but their expression of gratitude. This hot-breathing, eye-glistening, silent triumph—a trembly but inextinguishable candle light emanating from within.

Last time I remember Shandor thus lit inside was when, owing to Lyuba's intercession, Georgyi apologized to us for the second time in two days and "allowed" us to continue performing in N.

For myself and Lyuba, it marked the beginning of our short-lived idyll.

Every evening after the show, light, invisible like vapor, she penetrated backstage to spirit me away. And every time I was happy to elope with my limpid abductor.

Like two fugitives, we hid in the dark entrances of brick apartment blocks. Like two shadows, we mingled with leafless, early spring trees of N's iron-fenced parks and gardens.

We talked, telling one another things each understood the other already knew. Or, sometimes we did not even say any words at all, just joined eyes, arms, and lips to deeper penetrate into those evident and inexhaustible truths.

She was the typical daughter of post-revolutionary Russian intelligentsia parents. Her mother descended from patriotic gentry who, having lost their estate to the Bolsheviks victory of October 1917, still chose not to flee abroad and stayed in the motherland at their own risk. Her father, an art and museum scholar, belonged to the relatively widespread category of intellectual commoners.

Lyuba spent most of her young life studying and reading. Her parents wanted her to become a doctor. She wanted to become a traveler. She spent nights losing herself in her adored Verne, London, Cooper, and Mayne Reid, breaking the darkness of her room with just the light of a single candle, lest the exacting Mama and Papa notice the post-bedtime violation.

She was a studious recluse and a reckless adventure-seeker; a loving daughter and an indomitable rebel. She was a headlong still and a silent cry.

It was Lyuba's best friend Zhenya, *Predsedatel*'s niece, to whom I owed both Lavuta's spared effort in mollifying her uncle, and the acquaintance with my new love.

When Shandor's circus had stopped in N, and our shows gained the standing of a local sensation, this assertive ginger-braided wench dragged her reclusive classmate out of the peace and quiet of the book-filled bedroom and brought her into the marquee for our Saturday night performance.

And then it was me in my red-lined black cape Lyuba saw during our "Flying Horses" number.

After that, she did not miss a single show.

She was concerned about the possibility of her parents finding out about our meetings. I reassured her, explaining that as long as she did not wish them to know, the mildest mental interference on my part was sufficient to reduce chances of this to almost zero.

She believed and trusted me unconditionally. She insisted, though, that at some point she would like to tell them. She was just waiting for a good time.

I did not particularly look forward to meeting the Mama and Papa, as, unlike Lyuba, I had no illusions anything good might come out of it. I told her, however, I would be ready to do so the moment she deemed it right to introduce me. I said so partly because I did not want to sadden her (she had utmost respect for her old people) and partly because I knew it was never going to happen anyway.

This, and Lyuba's lower marks at school (our late night dates were starting to tell on her otherwise excellent learning), was a tiny drop of sorrow in the ocean of bliss the two of us shared.

For myself alone, meanwhile, there was another, much greater burden brewing—one I was to carry unshared.

Yoska.

My first and greatest love was getting sulkier by the day.

Every night I returned to the marquee after walking Lyuba home to her unsuspecting parents. I found him in the stable, sitting on the hay, forearms limp between the bent knees, eyes staring down apathetically.

I would stroke his shoulder, kiss him on the side of the neck, and ask something insignificant, trying to sound lighthearted. At that, his entire frame would shudder, as if my hand were electrically charged.

He wouldn't hear me.

He'd jump up on his feet and then on Flame's back—and tear off into the night.

He left me nothing to do but hastily mount Businka, or Ezme, or Prince, and gallop after him along the pitch-black streets of the town.

I'd gain on him quickly enough.

Like two ghost knights, we would fly through the dark in complete silence, shattered only by the clatter of the hooves.

Thus we would continue till we were completely exhausted. Then, without saying a word, we'd turn back.

Leaving the horses in the stable to whine nervously (no amount of best oats, purest water, and affectionate back pats could convince the sensitive animals that everything was going on as should, when in fact it wasn't), we undressed and got under the wide goose-down blanket together.

He accepted my caresses; he returned them. But he refused to talk.

He was right, of course.

Words are not needed to tell a truth—they better serve to conceal one. In silence, on the other hand, truths grow most ruthlessly deafening. Pronouncing them is redundant. They fill the air; they leave an acrid taste on your tongue.

Yoska felt it; I felt it too.

This was my punishment, and he showed no mercy in administering it.

*

'Will you, swine, ever learn to stand properly when a superior is addressing you?'

That's Petko-the-prominent, tearing Vano off a strip, for want of Boiko.

Petko, this little gendarme, is going to miss his favorite scapegoat. Vano is no replacement for Boiko—Vano's too cunning, too thick-skinned. Too dodgy.

Still sitting on the bunk, I look up at Petko, and he trails off. The pockmark face is one of those who rarely need stimulation from Lavuta. A glance is enough, to be sure.

'What is it?' I ask.

Promptly leaving Vano alone, Petko explains there is a new arrival due at the second ramp, and immediate help is required at the selection, for particularly interesting twin samples are expected to be delivered.

More curiosities for Angel's freak theater.

I tell Petko it will be me who is going to do the job, and no one else.

Terrified of me as he normally is, the pockmark face performs an odd semi-squatting routine and lopsidedly nods, inviting me to follow.

Across the squelchy-soiled plain, along the sparse grove, which, for all its feebleness, starts showing salad-color signs of *majowa* awakening, we walk past a series of prickly fences.

Petko is using the time of the walk to pour out his heart to me. He is complaining of the stupidity of the Sonders who won't see sense and agree to swap tooth crown gold, the extraction of which from the mouths of the incinerated corpses they oversee, for extra helpings of the first-rate Cuban tobacco he, Petko, can offer.

'What good is gold to the miserable fools? They won't last more than another month or two, and they know it, the greedy bastards!'

I voice an assumption that the Sonders are probably in no shortage of quality tobacco without Petko's invaluable services and, at this, order him to cut out his whining.

There is something or someone in connection with the new arrival requiring special attention, and it calls for a tune-in.

Greeting us at the rail, first thing, is the sight of Obersturmführer Rhöde and Obersturmführer König having a lively conversation—the latter tugging at his sprouting mustache, the former distractedly fingering his right gorget patch.

'So, imagine,' Rhöde conspiratorially lowers his voice. 'This inventive American devil attaches live explosive to six dormant bats, then sets off the bat alarm clock. Then guess what—off go the awoken bats to seek shelter—and fly straight for the base. Then—boom. Up goes the airbase in Carlsbad!'

Rhöde hiccups with laughter. König stretches the left corner of his mouth up and sideways to express sarcasm and accentuate his mustache.

'Shame about the bats. Those Americans have no feelings for animals.'

'Right, but picture the effect!'

'A new Tesla, eh?'

Both Obersturmführers are scared, confused, and loudly drunk. Brazening through the selection, while neither of them is remotely a Mengele. Of all the doctors, only Angel can see a selection through sober and in style. And of all the doctors, Angel is one not present today. Detained by urgent business in the lab, he cannot make it. This is why help has been called. And this is why I'm here to extend it.

I scan the disoriented crowd.

High-cheekboned, concerned faces of handsome Jewesses in their laced-up ankle boots and unbuttoned overcoats. Dazed children with scarves wrapped around their heads.

The old folks—scowling and apprehensively clinging to their leather sac voyages.

Then finally I locate my task.

Two equally braided, equally green-eyed freckled palenesses. Two thin twigs in equal, burgundy-brown checkered cloaks. Serene. Well-behaved. Holding hands.

I put my arms around the girls' backs and move them aside.

'Maya and Yana. Correct?'

'Correct, sir,' Maya confirms in a musical voice as her sister politely bows her head.

'So. Tell me, exactly how much trouble does your mom have telling you two apart?'

'No trouble at all, sir,' Maya continues in her enchanting silver-bell manner. 'In fact, our mom says we do not even look so much alike at all. It always surprises her that other people sometimes mix us up. You can ask her yourself, sir; she will come to collect us any minute.'

'She is probably picking up our suitcases,' Yana, the quieter one, adds in a calm whisper.

This is true. In the crowd, just a dozen meters away from us, I spot the mother. Twig-slender, auburn-haired, and freckled like her girls, she has already noticed their absence and is frantically looking around for them.

Therefore, we must hurry.

*

'How was your journey?' I ask Maya and Yana. 'Did you girls like traveling on the train?'

'We quite liked it, sir,' Maya admits. 'Although... Mom got a little tired, I think, and my sister did too.'

'Is this so? Did you get tired, Yana?'

The quieter twin nods.

'And you, Maya? Did you not get tired at all?'

'I did not, sir,' Maya reports enthusiastically. 'In fact, I slept a lot. It is the way the train moves, it makes you sleep a lot. And I had most wonderful dreams. I'd never had such back home.'

'What did you dream of?'

'Oh, most unusual things, sir. I dreamt that our train turned into a swirl and was sucked into the sky, and we along with it... Actually, I drew it. Here...'

Absent-mindedly, she slips her pellucid hand into a sac which she and her sister share, searches through their messed-up belongings, fishes out a folded-in-four, crumpled sheet of paper, clumsily unfolds it, and hands it to me.

There is a bizarre, pencil-executed image of a locomotive going up, turning into a stream of smoke at the head, and spiraling into coal-black skies.

'Wow. Extraordinary. Is that your dream?'

'Yes, though… This picture is not very good, sir.'

'Is it not? I'd say it's splendid.'

'No, sir.' The girl shakes her head in a resolute denial. 'It misses something important. Something I saw in my dream. I tried to pull it out of the dream and draw it on paper, but it didn't come out. It slipped away. I wish I could bring it back…'

'You can still bring it back,' I assure her.

'Can I? But how?'

'You need to relax and concentrate. I have my violin with me here, see?'

I take Lavuta out before her and Yana's bewildered eyes.

'I will play you a melody, and you listen. It will help you recall what you saw in your dream. You listen too, Yana. It will give you some rest—you look very road weary.'

Maya makes a tiny movement and parts her lips as if to say something, but, much as I wish to, I cannot afford to grant her that last word. Her mother has spotted hers and her sister's checkered cloaks and is now striving hard to move towards us. Her struggling through the crowd will give us a maximum of two minutes.

So I go straight into playing.

The first bars suffice to get Maya's eyes to close and her weightless body to go limp.

And then, the life that was meant to last forty-seven years condenses itself to take a minute and twenty-one seconds to flicker under her pearly eyelids.

The first sketches.

The art school in Vienna.

The stormy student romance.

More sketches. Young boys shattered into million crystal shards.

Myriads of beautiful, gross, bizarre dreams. Color obsessions. Paintings. Worms crawling out of meaty pears. Mincemeat turned into bloody sunsets. More gruesome dreams. Skies the color of meat, meat tasting of skies.

The first exhibits, the first acclaims. Old men dissolved into benches they are sitting on; young oligophrenics laughing heartily in the kitchen, mixing their saliva with the sausage they are munching on. First recognition. First bad press. First ecstatic press.

Maya Pashkovski, the first European artist to truly reconcile expressionism and surrealism.

Large canvases. War cripples with their arm stumps entangled in the sleeves of their shirts. Street fighters with their fists frozen into blurry oblivion in the melees they got embroiled in. Gala art functions in Paris, London, and New York City. Fashionable salons. A posh condo-studio in Manhattan. Bohemian parties. Opium dens.

An explosive love affair with an art critic.

A betrayal. Sleeping pills.

The last dream—a long forgotten dream of early childhood: a train smoking away into dirty skies. Finally complete—acrid, corrosive, tasting of rusty metal, burning the eyes—the way this train should have always been. At last.

And then lightness.

Then there is little Yana.

Her life is softer, warmer, mellower—in washed-out watercolors.

Always by her sister. A friend, a comfort, a ray of sunshine, a medicine for Mayechka. A cup of hot cocoa, a warm plaid, a guard, and a protector. A shrewd manager. An indefatigable worker. A courageous fighter. A selfless defender.

Yet, unlike Maya's, Yana's life rewards her with a loving husband, two gifted children, a big country house, and a clever German shepherd dog as a much-loved house pet. Then, not long after Maya's parting, a rapid, ruthless breast cancer. But I spare her this—Yana reaches lightness synchronously with her twin, as though sharing the sleeping pills with Maya. This little bonus is Lavuta's and mine to give, so we give it.

This is also, for better or worse, as far as our powers extend. Not within them to undo AU, or Angel, or the Führer—for these are to undo themselves. But it is our duty and privilege to make Maya's and Yana's lives happen—even if a little over a minute is as much as these lives have to perform the task.

Therefore, happen we make them.

*

The dismayed Petko is breathing heavily, force-feeding his sauerkraut fumes to my nostrils. He is staring down in disbelief, taking in the dead bodies of two primary-school-aged twins—Maya's, whose face is frozen in the expression of a forty-seven-year-old suicidal artiste, and Yana's—whose delicate features are those of an aging nanny asleep in her rocking chair, her lullaby sung.

'The Pashkovski twins?'

'That's the ones,' I testify, much to Petko's chagrin.

'I have orders; Angel is expecting them! We must deliver them to—'

'I'm afraid there is not much left to deliver,' I interrupt his whimpering.

'What happened to them?'

'They are dead, or so it looks to me.'

'Why?' The poor prominent has a hard time keeping his hysterics in check.

'Well, I suppose you might report a simultaneous heart failure due to prolonged stress, extreme exhaustion, severe dehydration, and acute malnutrition. The bodies will still be good for the dissecting room.'

At this, I leave Petko to deal with his conundrum alone.

I have to withdraw myself quickly, because the girls' mother has at last made her way through other wearied, worried, bustling bodies and reached on us. Her grievous shock, her shrieking agony at the sight of her daughters lying breathless on the ground, is not something I can at this moment alleviate. The notion that they have been spared Mengele's freak theater where their veins were going to be sewn together and their eyes burnt out of the sockets would seem too nightmarish for her to believe; the far more important fact that they have been given back their lives and just lived them—and that those lives have been fuller and more colorful than many of us can dream of—too fanciful to comprehend. Not now, not compared to the screaming reality of their deaths in front of her.

Luckily for Anna Pashkovski, her own biological shell will be merciful and grant the relief I am helpless to provide. The poor woman is going to lose her mind and become desensitized by the deafening power of the grief. This shall render her insensible to the raunchy "escaping through the chimney" jokes she is going to hear aplenty on her way to lightness. Anna will welcome her end, and she will receive it in peace, like little Yana just did.

The new arrivals are now being rigorously divided into two columns—some to the right, others to the left. The able-bodied are going to taste some AU dank air; the infirm—some Zyklon B in the oven.

As I pick my way through, I catch a glimpse of David squeezed in between Schlomo "the Bagel" and Chaim, the blue-eyed bookkeeper.

What are the boys doing here?

I approach from the rear and, placing my hands on David's shoulders, take him out of the tightly packed group.

'What do they want you out here for?'

He looks away and asks me for a smoke. Then he explains, 'They wanted the talkative ones to help the Sonders organize the new batch...'

'Fast-talk them through the procedure?'

'To that effect.'

It is normally the Sonders' work to receive their tribesmen off the train, greet them, and explain that they are going to be given a wash, then fed, then accommodated, and then allotted a cushy job. The purpose of this is minimizing any possible stress-fueled commotion and facilitating the transportation of the exhausted yet agitated Untermenschen into the oven.

'You will not do this,' I say.

'Can you break me out of this?'

'Ought to be the second reason I came here for, all the way having to bear Petko's presence.'

'Then you sure have to make it count,' he lights up.

I nod, and firmly take his hand in mine.

'Come.'

No necessity for Lavuta's help—no one shall notice his absence. Schlomo and Chaim will forget he was with them in the first place. And even if they didn't forget, they wouldn't tell. No one would know, should I even lead him out of AU right now, never to return.

But it is not the time for that yet.

For now, we just spend a while together before I accompany him back to the Jewish camp. As one of the Gypsy superintendents of the Jewish camp, I can at times move its inmates in and out without arousing unnecessary curiosity.

Among the Monetesque, tremblingly leafing birches, we inhale each other's breath. His lips smell of custard cream biscuits, as if it were the only food he ate all his life. He says mine smell of fluent waters—rivers and streams. This is one thing he has in common with Yoska—the hot-blooded rider used to say the same.

Having safely delivered him—soft, warm, and drunk on my rivers and streams—to the barrack—I, all of a sudden, find myself playing. I am inspired, filled to the brim. By the taste of David's mouth, by the memories of Yoska's.

I start a new story. A memoir in D minor. A hymn to my boys, to their exhilarating stubbornness, their intoxicating naughtiness. Lavuta knows exactly what I'm on about. She adds the ever-expanding, multiplying, tortuous chromaticisms. All these glorious E-and A-flats. Then the melody reaches wider intervals—from D and E flats to D/Fs, and further—to D and C sharps…

Let's see where it lands us.

V
1st Violin

As the capricious Euterpe seems to be jibing at me these days, I have made a decision. It is final, and I do not intend to go back on it.

I am, with a firm hand, putting music aside. I am wholly devoting myself to the realization of The Idea. For it is not artistic but scientific progress that, in these troubled times, my country and civilized humanity as a whole stands in dire need of.

It would be wrong to assume that I now cast aside my sacred belief in the power of beauty. I am still convinced there are few things more pernicious for the human race than science without art, civilization without an aesthetic sensibility. In view of all historical facts known to us, one would have to be of a petty mind and small faith to relinquish this notion. While among the Hellenes a free man could not, of his own accord, dedicate himself to trade, then our pragmatic century condemns every artist to slavery from birth. Artistic expression is for us an indulgence, a whim. Not being a prerequisite for the State's wellbeing, it does not dictate for our social existence the maxim that the sense for aesthetics should be all-permeating. Already in Rome, it began to be perceived rather as a caprice, a folly, a luxury. There, it was the whimsical aspiration of an individual Maecenas, the patron of poets, who stood alone in calling beauty into life. And ever since, the loftiest summits attained by the most elevated minds have turned largely on a pontiff's ardor for construction, on the vanity of a sovereign happening to be a scholar of the classics, or on the flashy taste of a pretentious commercial guild.

No.

I still remain a humble servant of beauty.

It is just that, at different times, beauty calls for different building materials. There are epochs when it is poetry, painting, or music; yet there are others when it is scientific thought that is the most nourishing food for all things aesthetic. This is the explanation why Euterpe is not answering my call. All because the wise, strategy-minding Athena lays her claim, demanding investment in her departments.

Ignoring the fog in the head after another sleepless, fruitless night, I purposefully made my way into the family camp, first thing in the morning—well, first thing on my waking up, anyway.

My previous visit had been interrupted by the onset of unnatural somnolence—as though some daemonic forces conspired to withstand my goal and interfered, taking away my physical energy and draining me of mental strength.

This time I was determined to fight whatever fiend—real or imaginary—might stand in my way and make the visit count.

Damira wouldn't stop talking. In her habitual hyper mood, she bombarded me with news.

'Our Boiko—do you remember Boiko, Onkel Heidert? He is working with Obersturmführer Karp now! They are making experiments together! He may even get to work with Doctor Angel if the experiments go well. We are all so happy for him!'

So incredibly capable, Damira. Getting so good at German lately.

Giving her a hug, I could not help complimenting her linguistic talents and expressing support for her friend Boiko, whoever he was.

She mentioned Guido though, which puzzled me.

What business can the boor have in the Gypsy camp? He's always avoided it like plague, believing, an obscurantist he is, that noma and other "Gypsy diseases" are contagious. What could make the fool tangle with "the filthy tramps" now? What is he up to?

I did not have time to dwell on the matter anyhow. I had a purpose, and I was not to be distracted.

*

As Damira beamed at me, displaying the entire range of her endearing smiles, I examined the tiny ulcer on her left cheek.

I did not, at this time, observe any discharge of pus, even while she actively mimicked and stretched her froggish lips, especially wide.

I asked her if she had any difficulty opening her mouth. She shook her head insouciantly.

'No, Onkel Heidert, I don't!'

Self-oblivious as this child is, she is not noticing any discomfort yet. I even predict it might not bother her for another week or two. But later the swelling will start to show, and from then on it should progress rapidly.

This is when I intend to isolate her, as this is when the process will start manifesting itself in all clarity.

She, obviously, even now has intermittent fever, of which she too, seems quite unmindful. Another good thing is, she had a history of chronic cough since childhood; on the other hand, there is no previous record of trauma.

It all agrees; it all screams—The Idea holds true.

Force vitale it is!

The mechanism of self-distruction is activated early on, and then, even unaided by external factors, it evolves to eventually blossom in its ultimate form—tissue necrosis.

Damira smiled at me, as though, unknowingly, approving of my hypothesis, endorsing my effort. On her lap, hectically restless, there lay a little bundle—her baby brother. Dando is the boy's name.

There is not the slightest doubt the little creature will start showing signs of noma in the coming weeks too, and I have to suppress the urge of including him in my research as another incontrovertible specimen. Close relatives as Damira and him are, he may pollute the experiment. I must be as self-challenging here as I can. No possibility of inaccuracy can be admitted. Noma is not to be seen as a defect that runs in a family. It must—and it will be regarded exclusively as a means for an inferior race to cleanse the world of its contagious presence.

While I was examining Damira and listening to her prattle, baby Dando started emitting his characteristic grunts. It was not long before the grunts grew louder, and, soon enough, crescendoed in an ear-splitting squall.

'I'm sorry, Onkel Heidert!' Damira rapidly went into the routine of rocking the noisy creature. 'He is so nervous all the time. He won't listen to me or mom anymore. Only Jass can put him to sleep.'

Jass. I'd heard the name before. The fiddler. The daemon Indigo would have liked. The one who lullabied the baby into death-like stillness yesterday. The one who somehow bewitched me too, turning my brain into a somnolent mush and ruining my evening.

'So where is Jass now?' I asked. 'Shall we call him so he calms your brother down once again?'

'He is out now. Went to do some business, I think. Nowhere to be found.'

'Indeed? He can go out any time, as he pleases, then?'

'Oh yes, he goes out, Jass, when he needs to. Went to meet the new train with Petko this time, I think.'

'Went away and took his violin?'

'That's right! He always takes his violin where he goes.'

'A good violin player, Jass, then? Do you think he plays well, Damira?'

'Oh, yes, yes, Onkel Heidert, he does.' The girl nodded vigorously. 'Jass, he can play anything in the world. He can play your thoughts to you. He can play your soul to you.'

*

Engrossed as I was in The Idea, I'd almost forgotten all about the business of the new arrival. Damira successfully reminded me.

Thankfully, there were others, like Schlöhm, Guido, or even Anton, who would be there to gladly go through the ordeal for me. One advantage of running paperwork is not having to rake through some of the most revolting aspects of the actual work. Being, in some sense, exempt from the moral and physical carnage. My job is to meticulously collect and register the results of the others' toil. Which I do, to the best of my abilities—perhaps not always as impeccably as I should.

In this case, however, though I knew I would be too blatantly late to be given any credit for putting in an appearance on the ramp, I decided to go. Angel could not attend this selection, while word had been sent that some valuable specimens were arriving. There was also the Pharma-Ko order still hanging over me like a raincloud—oppressive, pregnant, waiting to be delivered. I was still in charge of the goddamn thing. No one—not even the anxious Guido—had yet officially taken it off my hands, so I had to at least pretend I was doing something to get them their coveted batch... Why not try and use some new arrivals?

On my way to the ramp I entertained the motivating thought that I might even be able to get my hands on more material for The Idea. I was far from holding out much hope, though. It is self-evident the Jews can never be as forthcoming in terms of providing observable data as the Gypsies. Not of noma, anyway. The Jews are too knowing, too pragmatic, too selfish to internally, each one of them as an individual, recognize their pestilent nature as a whole, and allow the salubrious *Force vitale* to cleanse the world of their rancid existence. No wonder it was Spinoza the Jew who egotistically proclaimed an individual's freedom priority. The Jews are too individualistic. In terms of biological honesty—the ability to recognize on the cellular level that you are a pest and must go away—they can't hold a candle to the ingenuous, children-like Gypsies.

Barely had I set my foot in the vicinity of the messily unloading cattle train when Guido accosted me, popping up out of the crowd like a jack-in-the-box.

'There you are, old shirker!'

Grabbing my elbow in a vice-like grip, he unsolicitedly and vehemently proceeded to put me in the picture of what had been going on in my absence.

'The two specimens of value Angel wanted dropped dead as they stepped off the train. Exhaustion and stress, they say, but the circumstances are being clarified... The rest are mainly oven-fed not worth mentioning.'

'No relatively healthy children among them? Aged 9–12?'

'Not that I know of, brother... Look. All this is crap compared with what I have to report to you.'

He breathed triumphantly into my ear. I distanced myself a bit to look him in the eye.

'All right then. Spit it out.'

'While you and Lauer chase inspiration looking at photographs of pretty ladies and rehearsing your music, the devoted admirer of your talents gets some dirty work done for you.'

He winked and took a dramatic pause. I smiled.

'Go on.'

'The bothersome Bayer-Raisko business has been successfully taken care of.'

'What, you got them off our backs?'

'Struck a deal actually.'

Guido's cheeks were glossy with self-congratulation. I encouraged him, 'Tell me more.'

'Höss is putting together a letter on the sale of one hundred and fifty female inmates as we speak.'

I gave him a punch on the shoulder—once again, not insincerely.

'Well done, my friend.'

At least this ordeal was now out of the way, and I was grateful to Guido. For all his infuriating habits, he can be useful sometimes; one has to give that to him.

'I knew you'd be glad to hear the news, old boy. Now, put in a word for me with Angel about Farma-Ko, will you?'

I chuckled. As is his wont, Guido immediately started pressing his advantage.

'Cause you know I'll happily rid you of that bitch too.'

'I know, buddy. You told me many times.'

'And when better than at The Evening? You and Lauer haven't forgotten about The Evening in the heat of your rehearsing, have you?'

I assured him we hadn't.

Ironically enough, the conversation on the ramp strengthened my resolve to devote myself completely and solely to The Idea. Guido's having been able to resolve the Bayer business overnight convinced me I might as well try and fob off Farma-Ko on him, given that he was so eager to snatch it.

It all now hinged upon Angel's agreement to free me of the irksome bureaucratic duties in the name of medical science. So I thought I would actually use The Evening to talk Angel round, just as Guido wanted me to.

*

'Two hundred RM per woman? Is that exactly for how much you people have contrived to milk Bayer? No way!'

Ziegmund Rudolf Schöneich, the ex-chairman of the Farma-Ko division board of directors, was so tickled he couldn't stop cackling like a hen over hatchlings. The eighteenth-century styled-bottled Moët & Chandon, no doubt, augmented his frolicsome mood.

Repulsive a snail as Rudimundi is, I had to keep in mind his word still carried most weight with the Farma-Ko nibelungs. It was with him Guido-related negotiations were going to be held, it seemed. For Angel, presiding over the four hundred-centimeter-gala party table in his impeccable snow-white shirt and a burgundy necktie, smiling brilliantly, cracking jokes, and sparkling in his witticism, looked like he would be talked into anything as long as it pleased everyone present.

It had been three days since Guido and I talked on the ramp, and, for me, they had been seventy two hours passed in some semblance of sweaty fog. Realizing that it was my last chance to put together The Draft before The Evening, where I meant to present it, I shook off my meddlesome hesitation and did it.

I spent most of these three days writing away, and my determination bore fruit. On the table, under my left arm, in between the silver cutlery and the crystal champagne glass, there now lay a brown leather folder containing the speech on the evolution-determined magic of *Force Vitale*, which I was going to give today.

Apart from laboring at my writing, I rehearsed with Anton and Birgitte for three evenings in a row. Having been absorbed, as I was, in The Draft, those hours are largely hazy in my memory, except for one or two emotional moments that stand out. I remember Birgitte running up to me in the beginning of each rehearsal and chirruping excitedly about Grisha (this is how she decided to name the puppy, after a smart Gypsy boy she works with). I remember her leaving Anton and me dumbstruck with her exquisite delivery of "The Nightingale" in Italian (she must've rehearsed a lot on her own, in secret). I remember Anton ended up having to finalize the repertoire list for me, as I confessed that my work on The Draft meant for me complete disability and out-and-out fiasco on all other fronts. Thankfully Anton, a true friend as ever, was understanding and agreed to give me a hand without a single word of reproach.

It certainly looked like Anton did a sensational job, for The Evening set out and went on fabulously, in no small measure, it appeared, due to the perfectly-paced entertainment we provided.

We hailed Farma-Ko with a minimalistic yet jubilant version of *Entry of the Gods* to which Anton had created brilliant last-minute arrangements.

It proved a genius move.

The nibelungs were flattered. Boy did they imagine themselves to be the majestic procession entering Valhalla—the greedy, grabby runts that they are!

May the große meister forgive me for wasting his divine music on so philistine an audience, but it sure did pay off. The glasses melodically clinked; the silver click-clocked on the porcelain; the voices clamored each to be the first to toast scientific progress, the fruitful collaboration, Angel, whose vision, courage, and intrepid mind made the collaboration possible;

the motherland, the führer, and the impending victory.

Rudimundi could not stop relishing the Bayer news.

'So did they actually pay you two hundred per item?' he was grilling me as he struggled to pick some stringy parts of an oyster out of his teeth with his long little fingernail. 'Tell me they did! Come on, make my day!'

'They did, believe it or not. And they certainly got their money worth.'

'Did they?' Rudimundi smacked, visibly thrusting his tongue into the cavity in his back tooth.

'No two ways about it. The transport arrived in perfect condition. All one hundred and fifty are now actively worked with and still in good health.'

'Won't they all die before any conclusive results can be obtained, as they are generally known to?'

The ugly slug was bending over backward to provoke me, but I was having none of it.

'Absolutely excluded. Specimens that Doctor Karp selects have the highest viability coefficient.'

On hearing his name, Guido, who sat next to me, moved the plate filled with foie gras pâté aside, stopped ogling the buxom wife of a Farma-Ko supervisory board rep, and began to take notice.

'Do they indeed?'

Much as Rudimundi was trying to mock, his voice, beyond his control, turned a tone more serious and an undertone more interested.

I grabbed the bull by the horns, 'I assure you. Oh, and allow me to take the opportunity to introduce my brave, resourceful, outside-the-box innovator colleague Dr. Karp, who is, incidentally, going to take the helm in our common effort from today on. And believe me, Herr Schöneich, you and the whole of Farma-Ko shall not regret it.'

'Oh, nice to meet you then, Doctor Karp,' said Rudimundi, sounding almost genuinely friendly for the first time. 'Me and my colleagues pin our highest hopes on you and your innovative resourcefulness.'

He stretched out his arm over the table across my chest to shake Guido's hand. Readily and beamingly, the latter proffered his spade-like paw and grabbed Rudimundi's sharp-nailed extremity.

*

Trimly attired in a midnight blue tuxedo, lively and nimble like a swift, Anton stepped forth to the piano. In his Hollywood box-office star voice, he announced our next number, Mozart's Fifth Concerto arranged for violin and piano.

I left the table, allowing Guido and Schöneich time to exchange pleasantries.

Cosima was clearly on my side today. Embracing, like I was, the frivolous baroque intricacies, she wove dandelion-fluff light sonic cloth from Mozart's ornate threads. The three of us—Anton, the piano, Cosima, and I—were celebrating my first success this evening, and Mozart lavishly spread our mood onto the audience.

Everyone in the hall felt elegant, elated, and erotic, and I sympathized with my listeners—even with the complacent Farma-Ko bosses.

At the table, König was loudly chatting up Amelia Feuermacher, the seductive Farma-Ko legal office secretary. Münch was planting the umpteenth kiss on the lace-gloved hand of Linde Klobber, the rakish consort of Klaus Tuhm, the head of Farma-Ko Financial Department, who had been taken sick after emptying two bottles of Château Lafite in record time, and withdrew into the water closet for the rest of the evening. Angel and his wife Irene did not seem to sit down a minute and, dividing the hall into two, tirelessly entertained he one half, she the other.

They weren't exactly perfect appreciators of the music, but it didn't bother me. They were happy, relaxed, supportive, and on the right wavelength—this was all that mattered.

The Evening was approaching its crescendo—my speech. I didn't want them stone-faced and buttoned-up serious while listening to it. I wanted them comfortable and open-hearted. I wanted their perception flexible and fluent enough to be able to reach beyond its habitual setting.

And I felt now this optimal state of their collective mind had been reached.

Two days before The Evening, when The Draft was well underway, and I knew with almost one hundred percent probability I would get the speech ready in due time, I notified Angel of a sensational phenomenon I had discovered and asked for his permission to deliver a brief talk on it during the upcoming Farma-Ko event. Angel nodded and promised to give me the floor.

Now, upon my request, he raised his hand and announced, 'Dear guests, colleagues, and members of medical and scientific societies! A minute of your attention, please. You are probably aware that here at AU we conduct advanced research fostering excellence in various spheres of healthcare and medical science. In the course of his work, our colleague Doctor Christian Heidert has made some interesting observations he would like to share with us today.'

He then nodded at me, bestowing upon me one of his most encouraging smiles.

'We are all attention, Christian.'

The hall quietened.

I opened the brown folder, cleared my throat, and took a breath.

'In the process of our work with Sinti and Kalderash hominid primates, we have come to a number of important conclusions,' I started confidently and paused for a moment to prepare my listeners for receiving the message.

All the eyes were on me. I then resumed—coming, as it must've seemed to them, from afar.

'Have you ever questioned yourselves, dear colleagues, how water and dissolved nutrients are conducted upward along the stem of a plant?'

There was a somewhat embarrassed silence. The little exam in botany caught them unawares, which was just what I counted on!

'Well, by way of the xylem, of course!' I helped them out, smiling magnanimously, the way Professor Schwarz would've smiled when he humored his beloved students while they were not being so quick on the-uptake.

My witticism was met with amused chuckles. Good sign!

'And what, I ask you, is the force that moves the vital juices up along the xylem?

Intrigued silence again. I took another pause and then charged forth.

'Let me disclose to you now that there is a special force—a vital force—that provides this life-supporting motion. Otherwise, how would the fluid reach as high up the stem as it does?'

The clarity of The Idea availed me. I almost did not have to consult the text.

'Allow me also to reveal to you the following: the same exact force is instrumental in developing the phenomenon known as "noma," or, in other words, tissue necrosis in the aforementioned Sinti and Kalderash hominid primates as a nature-envisioned means of purging the world of their own inferior kind...'

An explosive ovation and crystal jingling followed.

There were delighted smiles and enraptured outcries. The audience was loving me.

It was a triumph.

I had fought, and I had prevailed.

*

Angel came up and shook my hand.

'Good speech, Christian.'

Anton winked at me showing me two upturned thumbs, one of his favorite American-imported gestures of approval.

Guido slapped me hard on the back and, breathing booze in my face, loudly whispered, 'It's in the bag, brother.'

I was not sure if he meant his secured deal with Farma-Ko or the guaranteed triumph of my project, but it didn't trouble me much. If only for an evening, if only for an hour, I was celebrating, and right there and then nothing could cast a pall over my joy.

Birgitte blew me a kiss from across the hall. Her duet with Anton on Alabieff was coming next, and by bringing her fingertips to her lips, she made clear I was the one to whom her performance would be dedicated.

Dear Birgitte, my amber-haired Freia! She looked at her most autumnal, standing by the piano at full height—slim, royally straight-backed in her mauve, floor-length lace gown.

Her L'usignolo also came out autumnal, in contrast to both the season when this bird is supposed to sing and our current time of the year. But it was perhaps the most moving rendition of the romance I had ever heard. Her light voice, poignantly plaintive yet warm, flowed like a stream carrying golden leaves—making its agile way around trees and tussocks, slowing in grooves, speeding down hillocks, weeping and trilling.

This time she sounded even more magnificent than at our last rehearsal—a rich, textured coloratura, almost the bel canto standard. Eventually, it seemed, it was Anton's polished performance that proved the fine setting to the jewel of her vocals, rather than vice versa.

This was exactly what Anton admitted when I joined them by the piano.

'Looks like I was the one helping out on the instrument, don't you agree, Maestro? Our Undine is the indisputable prima today, not counting your inventive self, of course!'

Touched to the heart, grateful, I hugged him. Then, with all the tenderness and appreciation I was capable of, I pressed Birgitte's hand to my lips.

'Our true and only star.'

The gentle creature was so overcome with emotion she almost cried.

'Don't forget my reward, dear Meister,' she whispered with a catch in her voice. 'You promised to play Tongues of Flame tonight. I shall demand it.'

'Will be granted, my Freia,' I said, kissing her other hand.

Then it was my turn to perform—solo on a regular of mine, *Beethoven's Romance No. 2*, after which Anton and I duetted again—on Träume, as Anton had suggested. Both were a success, like everything else appeared to be that evening.

Predictably, success was what Guido proposed to drink to when I returned to the table. I drank a well-deserved glass of champagne. And another one.

Guido then proposed to drink to long-standing ties with Farma-Ko. I drank to that too. For once, neither the unrefined nature of Guido's cheerfulness nor the familiarity of his manner annoyed me. He was understandably happy, and I was happy for him much like I was happy for myself.

Guido insisted we drink to the members of the fair sex who inspired us. I drank to Birgitte's beauty and talent. I explained to Guido that, though I had proved unable to compose a proper romance for her, I could probably redeem my fault by playing Tongues of Flame tonight, a little piece of the poor oeuvre of mine which she favored.

'A true Freia she is, Birgitte,' I said to Guido. 'Don't you agree?'

He emphatically agreed and then, all of a sudden, raised an index finger.

'Wait, brother. Wait. Listen. You just listen to what these people are saying.'

Across the table from us, Farma-Ko's Reich and public relation, Achim Helle, was loudly arguing with Weber's new assistant (I believe his name is Jandel).

'No, no, no, man, I'm telling you, you are out of line disparaging the Poles! You just arrived here—well, I worked with the Poles for five years. The nation deserves respect! They are not less proud or ingenious than us. Nor are they to be underestimated. Keen as mustard they are, the Poles! The Brits would still be shaking in their shoes before our Enigma if it hadn't been for the Poles who sold them some domestic cryptology expertise…'

There was no telling what got into Guido, but he interfered.

'Pig shit!' he vehemently contended across a row of bottles in varied degrees of emptiness and a large, semi-ravaged hors-d'œuvre platter. 'You must be misinformed, buddy. That weasel Rejewski was no Pole. He was a goddamn Jew.'

Helle raised his eyebrows and, forgetting all about Jandel, turned enface to give Guido a disdainful look.

'I'm afraid the misinformed one here is you, dear friend. You must be confusing Rejewski with Noskwith, Turing's helper. That one is a Jew. Rejewski, to let you know, is as Polish as tripe stew.'

'Excuse me!' Guido boomed, banging his fist on the table. 'Sounds like we got our wires crossed somewhere, man. Let me tell you now that…'

He went on with some arguments, and I realized I'd completely lost the thread of their conversation, while the topic was of no interest to me anyway.

I knew it was now time for me to announce and play Tongues of Flame. I went to look around the hall for Birgitte and Anton.

There were many guests now asleep in their chairs. Schöneich was sitting with his double chin splattered over his chest. He was somnambulantly staring at his navel. Rhöde was folding a napkin into origami. Angel was standing by the door, discussing something quietly with Irene.

There was no sign of either Birgitte or Anton.

I understood I was late. I had failed her. Even her small, romantic request of a song I could not grant in good time. I offended her. She had left. She had left with Anton, who was always elegant, courteous, and obliging, while I manifested myself as inconsiderate and gauche once again.

My happiness was gone. I was sad, angry at myself. I wanted to cry.

I returned to Guido, who was now sitting quietly, hugging a bottle of Polish vodka. Helle and Jandel were gone.

'I failed her.' I sobbed, plonking myself down on the chair. 'I failed my Freia. I am a shitty composer. And I could not even play her a song she wanted to hear.'

Guido tapped me on the shoulder and poured me a glass.

'Don't despair, brother. Drink.'

*

The heavy smell was filling the nostrils. The smell that will haunt me to the end of my days. The cloying licorice of Bernie's cologne mixed with the odor of dust, male sweat and liquor, and something else, sickly and unnameable.

The hefty oak armoire was blocking the view. Behind it, in the cigarette smoke-filled semi-darkness of the room, there was activity going on: whispers, rubbings, muffled giggles, cloth rustle, and heavy breathing.

I was agonizingly fighting the urge to peek behind the armoire's polished side. I did not want to see. Yet some diabolical impulse was pushing me forward.

The whispers were getting louder, the breathing unsteadier, the smell stickier. It was clogging my throat; I was suffocating.

Unable to bear any longer, I pressed myself to the armoire's side, stretched my neck as much as I could, and peeked.

What I saw felt like a leaden punch in the stomach. A mighty billow of nausea heaved to my chest and gullet. Convulsively slapping my hand over my mouth, I recoiled from the armoire and cumbersomely struggled to the door, terrified that I might be sick while still in the room.

Too late!

A fountain of vomit tore out of me, noisily spluttering on the floor.

Dizzy, feeling another heave coming, I fell down on all fours. Before my eyes there pulsated, blinking in reds and yellows, the floral pattern of the carpet, which I'd messed up. A shudder raked through my entire frame, and I threw up once again, more violently.

I stopped fighting. I collapsed on the floor, my cheek pressing against the carpet, wet and foul with the sick. I was shattered and still nauseous.

I was past caring. *Let me die here, on this floor, at this door*, I thought. Let them find my broken body in the puddle of puke. Let it be my final statement.

Then I passed out.

What I found myself blankly staring at when I regained my senses was not the floral carpet in Wörishofen, but my own crumpled pillow in AU. The pillowcase was soaked, slippery, and unbearably stank of vomit. It was pitch dark in the room. I was fully clothed—still in my performance suit and shoes. My body felt numb; at the same time, every single part was aching.

The reality was slowly restoring itself in my consciousness—the Pharma-Ko event; my speech; Birgitte's request for Tongues of Flame; her and Anton's disappearance; Guido.

It was Guido, my newly found chum and confidant, who'd literally carried me to my quarters on his shoulder when I got myself drunk to the state of a floor rag. I hazily remembered having told him volumes of most personal things, but, oddly enough, I felt neither embarrassed nor apprehensive. In fact, I did not one bit care what Guido knew or thought about me now—or even how he might use the information I'd imparted.

A bizarre indifference to the present came over me. The world of here and now appeared distant and smoke-screened. What came to the fore instead, what stuck out like a sore thumb, insulting the eyes, ravaging the mind, poisoning the body (I did feel a new bout of nausea approaching) was the episode of seven years ago. A wound which, I believed, had long since healed became just another fragment of an elaborate network of scars.

I had not actually peeked from behind the side of the armoire that night. I had not had the courage. I had not, because I knew that should the foul sight accost my eyes, I would not be able to hold back the beast within. Breaking itself free from the confines of my frame, he would condemn and immediately execute the two bastards savagely, tearing them limb from limb. It would feast on their flesh, like they had feasted on the flesh of my strange, awkward, passionate, and naive child. My inkblot-eyed fluffy little imp, who found mundanity and mediocrity so abrasive she was ready to fling herself head first into any perversion, any trap, any fraud, or nastiness just as long as it did not smack of behaving as became a decent young woman.

My beast's teeth were especially itching for Bernie's throat. The creep who had so lowly exploited her misguided feelings, now offering a taste of her to his depraved friends, leeching on her romanticism.

It did not come as a surprise, however, when later Indigo herself, in frolicsome tones, related to me the circumstances of their "little adventure" with Ernst. That was as much as I'd expected from her. She took particular pleasure in making it sound like "the three of them were just whiling away a rainy evening and decided to have some fun together."

'Bernie was painting Ernst naked... and then Ernst suggested he paint the two of us naked... and then we just went on.'

'So do you... like this, Ernst?' I asked, trying hard to keep my voice from trembling. 'I mean, are you attracted to him? As much as you are to Bernie?'

'Well, he is attractive—you've seen him. A Rimbaud, and he is funny, with a great sense of humor. But you know me; you know the type I fall for. Ernst is not within my range. But Bernie is so fond of him, he says at the moment Ernst is the flesh and blood of his art. And they get along so perfectly. I'd like Bernie to have a pleasant companion here when you and I leave—and an inspiring model. I don't want him to feel lonely. And I want him to go on painting.'

Indigo told the truth; Ernst was not her type. He was Bernie's type. And, like many other young men Bernie fancied, Ernst did not particularly fancy him back but was quite fascinated by Indigo. Ernst would've not jumped in Bernie's bed in a hurry—however, given that there was a winsome female party willing "to share the fun," he, and many others like him, readily agreed to a *ménage à trois*. This is how then, and later, Bernie got to enjoy a little piece of his favorite male models—by feeding them a little piece of Indigo.

I wondered if Indigo would ever ask me if I was jealous.

She never did.

This did not surprise me either. Jealousy was not relevant in our relationship (whatever our relationship was). Jealousy was too provincial, too gauche a manifestation to cross my Indigo's sophisticated mind.

*

The consequences of my drunken night demanded a lot of cleaning to be done immediately. Having contemplated it for about an hour, I concluded I absolutely could not face the dirty work. So I bundled up my ruined sheets and stuck them in a garbage sac, to be disposed of in the morning. I decided I'd think up some plausible explanation for Pittypat Two later. My clothes—my best, cherished tail suit, which I used for important concerts—

also was in a deplorable state. I took it off and, overcoming the severe hangover, brushed it down with soap and water.

Then I prepared myself a bath and took it. It made me feel better—physically, at least. The sick memory of my delirious vision—the orgy in Wörishofen—lingered, however.

With revulsion I discovered I was, beyond my will, wondering if I could have, hypothetically, been included in their group as a fourth. Partake of their "fun" and have Indigo's body close, all to myself—possess it at least momentarily—even if I had to bear the presence of the other two. With even greater revulsion, I realized that the question had indeed been bothering me long since—actually since the very accursed night in the sanatorium.

An unnatural mixture of disgust and arousal overcame me. I could not stop seeing Indigo as clearly as if she were standing in front of me. I imagined touching her, caressing her, kissing her long, silky, calling lips. I could feel her warm skin under my fingers, I could smell its intoxicating fragrance—innocently milky and sweet, like a child's, and, at the same time, sinfully sensuous.

Unable to banish the importunate thoughts, I took Cosima out of her case (I should thank Guido for making sure in my senseless condition I hadn't left my instrument behind). The wicked jumble of feelings that held me in its grip incongruently had something of an inspiration to it. Perhaps it was just the suitable state for creating a thing as tormenting, torn, and controversial as Indigo Mind?

Siegfried touched the strings—and the two-decade-old feeling returned at once, enveloping and tantalizing. The feeling of what it should be like, what it should sound like. The rhythm permeating the entire piece, like a line, passed from instrument to instrument. The violin tonality, enabling the leading instrument to resonate with all its overtones.

And alas, once again, was I perfidiously betrayed, maliciously deceived, and bitterly let down! Once again did I set the sail for the siren's call, only to be smashed against the merciless rocks of my talentlessness, sunk in the depths of my shallowness, drowned in my eternal self-disappointment. The guileful chimera successfully lured and entrapped me once more.

Serves me right, for never must one allow oneself to be tempted by a treacherous mishmash of incompatible emotions. Whenever a man—

especially a creative man—bites onto that poisonous bait naively hoping something constructive may come out of the turbid cesspool like Venus out of the sea, he is bound to be led astray. Love cannot coexist with hate; attraction cannot peacefully alternate with aversion; good can never grow from one stem with evil.

It is the Jews with their gene—and history-molded duplicitousness, who have made it their task to teach the world that everything—time, space, speed, human feeling—is relative; that there is no absolute, and figures of any magnitude largely depend on what you measure them against. It has always been in their interests to confuse matters as much as possible. Talk of the proverbial fishing in troubled waters! Unfathomable indeed that such a dogmatic, such uncreative race should also be so inventive in everything aimed at muddling and befuddling. The Arian man who is by his nature creative and free but at the same time honest and straightforward in all he perceives and conceives of, must never follow in those paths—he will inevitably find himself stranded.

It was, of course, the fault of alcoholic intoxication, the momentary weaknesses I succumbed to, euphoric and stupefied by the success of my speech. Never would I have otherwise allowed the daemons to ensnare me so easily.

Surely enough, Cosima—ever the strictest judge—disapproved of my foolishness and showed me no support in my futile effort. I realize this. I firmly say "no" to the accursed bottle and all semblance of drink-released "inspiration" from now on.

Never again, I swear. Never again.

*

The punishment I received was all the more just because, apart from getting drunk and making a fool of myself the night before, I also broke my promise. Hadn't I sworn off all composing, at least for the time that my scientific project was being brought to a completion? Hadn't I already been given to understand that all engaging in art is irrelevant and to no avail at this moment?

Apologizing to Cosima, I humbly returned her into her mahogany abode. I gave a promise to never disturb her noble rest in vain. I hope another bout of weakness will not induce me to break my word, not again.

I set down to writing on *Force Vitale*. The first stage had been successfully—even gloriously—completed. I had passed the judgment of the medical society, and I had passed that examination with flying colors. Now it was time for the actual work to start.

After my speech and before Birgitte and Anton's duet, I had been briefly approached by Pharma-Ko's supervisor, Führsten, who posed me a question of, as it seemed to me then, little importance. However, thinking back to it, I now feel I should get this contradiction out of the way. For it is not a contradiction at all, but yet more evidence in support of my theory.

'I should say, Doctor Heidert, your hypothesis is groundbreaking,' he admitted to me. 'But, maintaining that *cancrum oris* is racially and "in-utero" predetermined, how would you account for poor oral hygiene as a factor observed in direct proportion to the incidence of the disease?'

I've made up my mind to be as exhaustive as possible. No sloppiness, no self-indulgent approximation can be excused in a work of the scale I am undertaking.

"As it is well-known and rightfully pointed out by a large body of my highly respected colleagues, the disease progression is contributed to by deficient oral hygiene, poor environmental sanitation, and exposure to animal and human fecal material," I wrote.

"This evident circumstance is not to be called into question and stands in no contradiction to the theory expounded in the present paper. Moreover, it can be easily corroborated hereby. We have pointed out above that the mechanism of *Force Vitale* is activated in Hominina subtribe as a genetically pre-programmed, self-effacing mechanism of liberating the world of one's presence, should the latter prove burdensome, ineffectual, and detrimental. We further contend that, just like *cancrum oris,* more colloquially known as noma, is the closing stage of the said process, so poor hygiene and self-exposure to contagious substances is its opening phase. The Sinti and Kalderash hominid primates' behavior is racially and genetically engineered to ignore the elementary hygiene norms, to self-pollute and self-abuse to the point where further, more effective means of self-destruction are ready to be launched. The poor hygiene is in many ways a prerequisite and a feeding agent of noma, so we maintain that it is not a chance occurrence but a purposeful practice initiated and preserved by *Force Vitale* in order to lead an individual specimen to self-demolition by means of *cancrum oris* when the time is right."

Then I expanded on it:

"The action of *Force Vitale* in the early stages is so subtle and wisely conceived that the objects do not notice it at all, let alone suffer from it. It largely acts on their subconscious level, molding their behavior so it leads them to incur deficiency of health, which eventually finalizes the process. More specifically, it inhibits in them the natural instinct to keep their bodies tidy, replacing in their mind the idea of how to maintain normal hygiene with contrived, fictitious concepts of "avoiding uncleanliness" or "staying clean" and with a number of superstitious taboos and rituals believed to ensure those states. Thus, they will not use everyday items which came in contact with women's clothes (the female body, especially its lower parts, are considered *mahrime* —"unclean"), but pick up and eat food from the floor; burn the straw where a woman has given birth, yet suppose it is normal that their babies are delivered on the ground; forbid a man to pass under a clothesline with women's underwear on it, while freely allowing their children to play in the dirt."

I went on to adduce concrete examples of violations of hygiene norms in the family camp.

Then I reread the passage and was pleased with it.

The main body of the paper had gotten off the ground. I was back on the right path; I atoned for my momentary weakness; I was working on what was timely and necessary. The powers of wisdom were on my side. I felt their steadfast support. Once again, the balance between my inner and outer world was restored—and I meant to keep it.

*

It was with some trepidation that I entered Angel's office in the afternoon.

While taking a few liberties with the Pharma-Ko task and handing it over to Guido seemed to have gone off smoothly to the contentment of all concerned, there remained a worrisome fact; Angel, our senior leadership figure, was still not aware of the new arrangement.

I frankly don't know why I dragged it until the last moment and never asked for his ratification. I suppose I was failing to find the right words. On the one hand, everyone could clearly see I was neither happy with the job nor particularly good at it, while Guido wanted it and would most likely do his best should he get it. Yet a direct request to be freed from an entrusted duty in favor of someone else smacked of defection, which was always a thing I despised, regardless of its form and circumstances.

Or it could have been that the three nights before The Evening—those nights filled with writing the speech and the rehearsals—were so overwhelming they simply left me with no force, while discussing the sensitive matter with Angel would have required a great deal of concentration.

For better or worse, I took my risks, entertaining a vague hope that the position in charge of the project entitled me to delegate part of the work to trustworthy colleagues, even without consulting higher authority.

Now, with not so low a probability, I was going to face the consequences of my arbitrary actions.

Contrary to my fears, however, no thunder struck. Angel was in one of his shiniest moods.

Shaking my hand once again like yesterday, he praised me for a perfectly organized entertainment program and asked to pass his gratitude to Anton and Birgitte in case he should forget to thank them both personally. His overall sentiment was that The Evening could not have been a greater success, on all accounts.

I reckoned, as things stood, raising the topic of our little deal with Guido was now redundant. It was certain Angel, with his perspicacity, had figured it out, and, judging by the fact he did not mention it and was in high spirits, we must have received his tacit authorization.

Instead, I plucked up my courage and asked him if my speech had indeed been good and what he thought of The Idea.

'Do you suppose my approach is perspective, not only as applied to noma, but on a larger medical science scale? Do you think it has a future?'

'Your speech was truly entertaining, Christian,' he assured me. 'As was everything else you contributed to. If I may put forward a suggestion, have you considered including a syphilis study in your research? Perhaps, even, relating noma directly to hereditary syphilis? You would have quite a solid ground to stand on there, since the prevalence of noma, as you rightly observe, is highest among the Gypsy children of the said age group, and syphilis is, conveniently, rife in the family camp.'

I said I found his suggestion brilliant, explaining that I had already cited deplorable hygiene as a concrete base for noma laid by *Force Vitale* and would now most definitely add syphilis to it.

'Very well.' Angel smiled. 'May the seeds of your endeavors fall on fertile soil, dear colleague.'

Immediately thereafter, with his characteristic abruptness in changing the topic, Angel invited me to accompany him to the dissecting room, as we had to attend a test dissection. One of the new arrivals, a Jewish forensic doctor, was being given an examination with a view to future work. We were to act as a jury.

Collecting Epstein and Bendel on our way to the barracks, we pulled up at the shed known as "the new dissecting room, up for refurbishment." Angel's plans to renovate the miserable little room had long since become a standing joke. However, now that this Hungarian Jewish forensic has come along, it looks like some actual steps may finally be taken toward realization of the improbable plan.

The two corpses were a suicide by hanging, and an electrocution (most likely self-inflicted too, by jumping at the wires).

As we watched the new prisoner doctor, a focused, intense fellow in his early forties, open the skull, the thorax, and the abdominal cavity and extract the organs, I, inexplicably, recalled my drunken vision of the room in Wörishofen once again. It must have been the raw smell of exposed death—so different from and yet so similar to the smell of exposed salaciousness—that once again brought about the sick memory.

And, in its tow—unsolicitedly, irrelevantly—the tormenting ghost of Indigo Mind followed, ringing in my ears, clouding my vision, tugging at my heart.

My greatest desire was to break out of the shed, rush home, grab Cosima, and make her play what I wanted. Force her, violate her, or rape her. Explode her complacent, conceited calm. Tear her arrogance to shreds. Bend her to my artistic will. She was, after all, only an instrument. I was the meister.

Though I knew compunction would eat me alive afterward, at the insane moment, no amount of self-reproach helped. The daemonic thoughts were attacking, like a swarm of bees attacks a bear; they were getting the better of me.

My head swam. I felt fevered. I was falling sick.

VI
2nd Violin

Doctor Heidert swang by today, not looking his best at all. Scared poor Damira senseless with his pale brow and the dark patches under his eyes. The compassionate girl flung herself into Onkel Heidert's arms, pleading with him to say he was all right. Christian gave her a hasty pat on the head, cast a quick look at the lesion on her cheek, and assured her he was well; just had been a bit indisposed for the last couple of days. He didn't sound too convincing, but Damira took his word for it and lightened up.

'Please do not disappear again, Onkel Heidert. I miss you when you don't come for three days.'

'I won't, child, I won't. I'll be coming to see you more often now. Promise.'

It is not Damira, however, the Onkel came for this time. We have a new twin pair, and another Onkel—Mengele—sent him to collect them. This is Christian's first task after several days of illness.

Two four-year-old Manouches bearing musical Greek names Leander and Nikander arrived with the last transport from Brussels accompanied by their aunt, who rather resembled a great grandmother. Somehow the boys got overlooked at the ramp, but no sooner did the little family join our AU extended *kumpania* than Baba Tanya took them under her wing and tipped off Lyalya, the aunt, about the incredible opportunities granted to twins by the camp's all-powerful medical wizard, Doctor Angel. Since Boiko's effective dispatchment into the labs, the *gicisvara* has been establishing herself as Mengele's personal propaganda minister. Surely the special offer extended by Doctor Angel was not to be missed out on, she emphasized to the shy, credulous Lyalya. Surely the boys were not to be robbed of that one-in-a-lifetime chance.

Lyalya heeded the elder's councel. Via Petko, Mengele was made aware of the twins.

Leander and Nikander did not seem to appreciate the outstanding opportunity granted to them. Holding firmly on to each other, they stood their ground—hand in hand, identical heads stubbornly lowered, two pairs of brown eyes scowling.

No amount of sweet talk from *Beebee* Lyalya or Baba Tanya mollified them. The twins menacingly hissed and growled. Four clenched little fists sent out a clear message that if anyone dared approach, he would be doing so at his own risk.

Christian, who had never been particularly good around children (unless they were girls with a soft spot for grownup, intellectual males with depressive tendencies), looked miserable. Leander and Nikander were neither Damira nor Rosa—his charms cut no ice with them. As for convincing arguments like "toys and sweetmeats showered on kids lucky enough to make it into Doctor Angel's lab," Lyalya and Baba Tanya had already used up the limited supply of those. Now Christian was at a loss for what to say or do. The poor man was inwardly cursing his beloved Angel boss and the new humiliating task the latter had thrown at him.

Then Damira came to Christian's rescue.

'Onkel Heidert, let's ask Jass to help!' She stepped forth. 'Jass can help! He can play them to go to Onkel Mengele. He even plays Dando to sleep, remember?'

Christian looked at me. His face reflected a funny mixture of hope and xenophobia.

'Can you… do this?' he addressed me hesitantly. 'Can you play them something to calm them down? Cheer them up, perhaps? Make them less afraid of me?'

I nodded and stood up. I gave the twins a big, clown's wink. Leander smiled. Nikander eased his grip on his brother's hand.

Then I started playing the first thing that popped up in my head—the silly English nursery rhyme about the girl Mary who had a little lamb. I even sang along in English.

After the song was sung, Leander and Nikander, now both laughing, took Christian's hand each.

'*Gehen wir!*' Nikander whispered, pulling at the grownup's fingers.

Damira clapped her hands.

'I told you, Onkel Heidert! I told you Jass will help!'

As Christian led the obedient pair away, Baba Tanya and Lyalya smiled equally broad, complacent old women's smiles. Their deal was accomplished. Against all odds, they secured two little boys—the most enviable lot one could imagine.

*

It was a good start of the day.

To begin with, Christian got over his anxiety at last and verbally acknowledged my existence. Thanks to Damira for this. Baba Tanya and Lyalya may see themselves as perfect matchmakers, but I'm the one to know they have nothing on this little girl.

Then, I should say, I rarely enjoy performing a request as much as I did this morning. There was indeed no better way to arrange the future of Leander and Nikander than sending them to Mengele's lab.

The fate of these two sturdy fighters is both a lucky and a sad one. It is their destiny to be overlooked. Always and everywhere. Just as they passed unnoticed at the ramp, so will Angel forget to make use of them in his death workshop. There will forever be something coming in between him and the boys—a more relevant job, a new pair of twins, paperwork to be completed. Never getting round to actual experiments with Leander and Nikander, he will keep postponing them for later.

Thus staying on the sidelines as a pair of lab extras, the boys will enjoy better food and greater comfort until their time will come to be transported to another camp, BB, along with those few ones who will still remain alive in AU. There they will be picked up by the British soldiers. They will be almost overlooked there too, but Leander will help himself and his brother out by raising his voice and greeting the victorious Allies in loud, articulate German, the intricacies of which, a capable boy he is, he will by then learn down pat.

Their jeering fate will accompany both twins till the end of their days (which will, ironically, be so long as to last into the next century). Passed over at work. Neglected by many a pretty lady.

But every single time life will try to shortchange them, Leander and Nikander will vociferously assert their rights and refuse to give up until their wish be granted and justice restored.

Two lives worth living.

Lyalya, their old *beebee,* has every reason to celebrate. In the celebratory mood, she will remain for the last month which is left to her in this world, and will depart joyously, knowing she has done what's best for her nephews.

Damira is happy too. She jumps around like a frisky kitten, sings "Mary Had a Little Lamb," improvising her own words, picks up Dando and dances around holding him, kisses her mother, and hugs Mihai. Then she cuddles up to me.

'*Ducaba tu*, Jass! You are my *chaphoro,* my magician, my prince!'

She curls up on my lap and closes her eyes.

'Will you tell me the story? How you ran away from Russia? With the girl you loved?'

Cuddly, sly Damira always knows how and when to ask.

So I resume my tale.

*

Shandor's circus did eventually have to cut short its Russian tour, and it was not Yoska's fault. It was mine. Thankfully, by the time it happened, Shandor had already accumulated more than a sufficient budget to cover whatever debts were weighing on his conscience.

It was not only my fault, but my will. The war was drawing closer. There were two months to go before Germany hit the Soviet borders without a declaration. I had to move Lyuba out of the country.

But there was a snag; my darling would not hear of leaving her parents. She especially took issue with the idea of leaving them in secret. She actually believed it was time to do just the opposite: introduce me to them. Became increasingly insistent by the day. Fantasied about how they would fall in love with me at first sight (for she argued ardently, how was it possible not to?) and welcome me into the family.

Much as I hated to disappoint the naive creature raised on Turgenev's novels, I did not share her rose-tinted vision. It was clear as day her parents would neither approve nor understand. Ever.

I tried to carry this notion across to Lyuba as tactfully as I could. All I got in response was:

'But, darling, even if you are right and you do not conform to my parents' idea of a proper husband for me, and even if after they see how much we love each other they still refuse to accept you—even in that unimaginable case—don't you have your violin? Can't you influence people's feelings? Can't you play something that will convince them you are right for me, simply because I will never love anybody else, because I will die if I cannot be with you? Can't you get them to trust you—to like you!—with the sound of your instrument?'

The enchanted soul, she so readily believed in magic. As the Russian saying goes, it would've all been funny if only it hadn't been so sad.

'Just look what a little hypocrite you are,' I teased her. 'You claim to respect your parents, and yet you so readily propose to deceive them—hypnotize them into feeling something which otherwise they wouldn't feel.'

She laughed and confessed to being "a scheming manipulator," but that semi-jocose observation of mine was, of course, no cogent argument.

I tried to explain to her, in the simplest possible terms, that the powers of Lavuta could not be turned on at as much as my whim; they only got activated to help along something that was *meant* to happen. At this I helplessly shut up, because next I would've had to tell her that neither was I meant to meet her parents nor were the two of us—to ever get married, which automatically took Lavuta's help out of the equation.

These last words remaining unsaid, Lyuba kept hoping. Kept insisting.

The best solution I eventually managed to think of was to shatter my poor darling's illusions by actually granting her wish and meeting her parents. Or one parent, to be precise—her father. Only that meeting would have to be an unprepared one.

Hitherto, Lyuba's dad had remained in the dark regarding my dating his daughter only because I'd been keeping the situation under mental control. All he needed to find us out was for me to lessen the control.

So I dropped my guard.

On a rain-soaked, mid-April evening, I was walking Lyuba home, as usual.

In the afternoon of the same day, her father had looked through her school diary. He was not satisfied with the result. Simultaneously, he recalled his daughter's repeated absences at a late hour going on for the last several weeks or months. It hit him that Lyuba and her best friend Zhenya had been frequenting a gypsy circus recently and exchanged many extolling remarks thereupon.

He remembered how feverishly Lyuba's eyes had been glistening of late, how her cheeks had that suspicious, hectic flush.

He suddenly made a connection.

Why had he been napping all this time? Why had he and Lyuba's mother ignored the alarming signs for so long?

He refrained, however, from worrying his wife before he himself found out what exactly was going on.

In the evening, he quietly left home a minute after Lyuba closed the door. In short runs, hiding under wet trees, prickled by the train, he followed his daughter on her way to the circus's marquee.

And then he followed Lyuba and me back, through the park. This was where he pounced on us—the moment she entwined her hands around my neck and pressed her lips against mine.

Indignantly, Lyuba's father yanked his daughter's hand. He tore her out of my arms. Grabbing her by the shoulders, he turned her roughly to face him. He slapped her hard on the cheek. Then on the other.

'Go home! Immediately!' he ordered her through clenched teeth.

Then he turned on me.

'As for you, young man, I strongly advise you to leave my daughter alone unless you want to find yourself in serious trouble.'

I felt painfully sorry for my fragile girl as she ran—tearful, hurt, terrified, and face buried in hands—toward their apartment block, pushed in the back by her infuriated parent.

Alas, this shock I brought upon her was the only way to break her out.

Now, the price paid, she was free from her ties. Her family were no longer an obstacle. Lyuba was ready to leave.

All I had to do was return to the marquee and wait.

*

The *kumpania* too was prepared to take off.

I warned them some days in advance, explaining that we had to make it out of Russia well before the war gained on us there. Shandor trusted my judgment unquestioningly in such matters.

They also knew we would be abducting a citizen. Only the citizen herself remained in the dark until the last day. My idea was that Lyuba should arrive at this only possible decision without being prompted.

She did.

In the depths of the night—actually bang at two o'clock in the morning—I heard her light step on the gravel outside the marquee.

I came out and received her in my arms—trembling, weeping, and spent.

For some minutes nothing was said—I just stroked her hair and back silently; she pressed herself against my chest, crying and shaking.

Then, through the sobs, she attempted to speak at last.

'I have written to them... left a note. Here...' She took a folded sheet of paper out of her coat's pocket. 'I've brought you a copy.'

I unfolded the sheet, lit a match, and read:

Dearest Mom and Dad!

Please forgive me if I'm causing you pain.

I deeply care for you and appreciate you, but I have fallen in love, and you have not understood.

Please do not try to find me. My place is with the one I love. Thank you for everything you have done for me.

Your daughter Lyuba.

I put my hand around her shoulders and led her inside. She looked up at me.

'We must vanish now, you and I. Just disappear,' she whispered. 'They will come looking for me in the morning, as soon as they find the note.'

'When would you like to take off?' I asked.

'Anytime. Tonight. Now.'

'Now it is, then.'

'How about the company? Shall they follow? Shall we join them later?'

'They are following. When you and I split, no one can stay behind. With your old folks coming in the morning searching for you, the others here would be the first to be questioned. This is why, if you and I vanish, so shall they.'

Her eyes widened.

'Will they be willing to go?'

'They will. They are. They are only waiting for my signal.'

The horses had been fed, groomed, saddled, and bridled; the props packed; the vardos cleaned. Dismantling the marquee was the only job left to be done.

With the many-decade experience Shandor's *kumpania* had, it was accomplished within an hour, well before daybreak.

We took off in our two vardos, making no noise, and leaving no trace. By the time the grayish Soviet sun diluted the ink of the night, we had been safely out of N.

Since then, for many a morn, as we were making our way toward the Polish border—nighting in fields, daying on washed-out roads—I woke up from my one love's kiss and went out of the tent inevitably to see my other love prancing on Flame's back, somewhere on the edge of my field of vision, often under pouring rain. Thus, Yoska was wishing me a good morning and saying goodbye. He was determined to pass soon, and there was no way I could stop him.

Each day he and I talked, walked, and rode beside each other, laughed together. Made love too. But that rain-veiled vision—him and Flame performing their sultry dance where the black field met the gray sky—is, and will, till the end of my days remain my last vivid memory of Yoska.

*

'It often rains in Russia, doesn't it?' Mihai interrupts me phlegmatically.

I was sure I'd been keeping my voice low enough for Damira alone to be able to hear. It turned out, however, that the more emotional the story got, the louder I spoke, because Mihai, while sitting on his bunk, had apparently been partaking of all the details without even straining his ears too much.

'Why? Russia is big, Babbo,' I reply. 'It depends in which part of the country you are. Where I was—yes, it does. Probably more so than in Poland.'

'This is why they are always so klutzy, those Russians,' Mihai observes thoughtfully, snuffing on a generous pinch. 'The rain sets mold in their brains.'

'Careful, Babbo. You are disrespecting the soon-to-be victorious nation.'

'Never, boy. Never. Too moldy-brained they are.'

The reason why the old man is bitter about Russians is clear to me—the consequence of his past traffickings with Pavel, the only Russian he ever dealt with. That Pavel was, apparently, the paragon of ineffectuality and used to cause our short-tempered Mihai much vexation.

The old man might be biased, but it strikes me that he, unknowingly, formulates a curious truth. The mentality of a nation must in fact be, not for a small part, determined by the climate of the area where the nation dwells.

It is well reflected in the lore.

Take the noire humor of the Latinos, or the Balkanians, for that matter. Death, feral as it is, is often wrapped in comedy and sentimentality—skeletons in floral dresses, skulls in wreaths, angels fluttering over the Grim Reaper, and twining roses round his scythe. Someone dies (is more often than not killed in a gruesome manner), and this forms the backdrop for a heartfelt family reunion, a fiery love affair, and a flamboyant creative endeavor. What can such an attitude be induced by, if not the reflection of bright sunny patches contrasting with deep black shadows—the characteristic weather pattern of those terrains?

Or take, indeed, the north-eastern Slavic lands with their quagmires, habitually gray skies, dankness, and slushy roads. Hence the resigned depression, the dreary acquiescence of many of their songs and tales—endless meditation instead of action, tearful regrets of the past, uncertainty of the present, submissive acceptance of a bleak future.

A triumphant cry: 'I'm going! Who's with me, *Phrali*?' derails my train of thought.

This is Vano, raspingly asserting his readiness for action.

With Boiko gone, Vano has been getting restless. Robbed of his best comrade in mischief, he plainly doesn't know what to do with his time. Learning German, telling scary stories, and playing Gile with Mihai is not much of an entertainment—not anymore. Vano is painfully bored. He spends most of his days lolling about the playground and reshuffling his card pack.

But, whenever Vano jumps to his feet in a sudden fit of pubertal excitement, one can be certain he is up to no good. And this is exactly what's happening now.

Petko-the-prominent has come to sound alarm. There is a brawl at the works in the Jewish camp, and Gypsy help is called on to break up the fight and mete out punishment.

Sure enough, Vano is the first to offer his services. What better opportunity to dissolve boredom, shake a fist, and show those Jewish *musselmänner* who's the boss. Well, the puny twelve-year-old has no shortage of valiance; one has to give him that.

On this account, I stand up, make my way to the doorway where Vano is jumping with impatience, place my hand firmly on his shoulder, and send him back to the bunk with the task of describing what the barrack dwellers are doing in ten German sentences. I instruct him to have the assignment done by the time I return from the Jewish camp. Ignoring Vano's twangy protests, I nod at Petko, indicating to him that I'm coming along.

*

By the time we arrive at the works, there's not a trace of a brawl anymore. There are just several scared, scruffy faces awaiting reprisal.

The faces are, namely, Schlomo "the Bagel," Marek the architect, and the Greek brothers Yossi and Yonas. Yonas's nose is bleeding; Marek's cheekbone shows a puffed, glistening promise of a black eye; the other two look ruffled but unscarred.

Across the dirt track from the four culprits stand their adversaries— also four of them, all *Bibelforscher*—the purple triangle bearers. As it is typical for adherents of their denomination, the four share an identical facial expression—benign and somewhat vacant. These seem to be completely unaffected by the clash. Leaning on some ground-digging tools, they peacefully stare across at us, the Jews, and the gathered Kapos.

I am puzzled. Jehovah's Witnesses are seldom known to pick up a verbal quarrel, let alone a physical fight. Yet I am told by the onlookers that they, and not the Jews, were the instigators.

A minor investigation yields a substantial degree of clarity. The witnesses, who, all four of them, work as the commandant's personal gardeners, were sent to the Jewish camp to get additional rakes and shovels. The moment they were at the works, Bushalo Karl (Sour One is here, of course, strutting about, tapping his boots with his whip) pushed Marek on the ground for some minor gaffe and, egged on by the other Kapos, dealt him several heavy blows to the midriff. After a minute of writhing in pain, Marek regained enough strength to stand up with the help of Schlomo, Yossi and Yonas. He then spat under his feet and whispered, 'What happened to this world, brothers? It's got to be turned inside out if I, an innocent intellectual, should take blows and insults from uneducated criminal scum.'

Luckily for Marek, Bushalo did not hear this, for he by then had gone off to train his whip on a new victim.

Who heard it were the witnesses. Those were standing in immediate proximity, waiting to be given the tools. One of them, for a vague reason, decided to poke his nose.

'This is fair that you, Jews, should suffer now,' he said in his clear, benevolent voice. 'If nothing else, then *this* is right with the world. Your kind should suffer and die, since your forefathers have betrayed Jehovah.'

Now one ought to keep in mind that Yossi and Yonas, two Greek-born, hot-blooded Jewish partisans, are always spoiling for it, even when unprovoked. Quite predictably, the candid pronouncement by the justice-loving witness set them off like a match ignites tinder, so the brothers laid into the purple triangle quartet with all their fist might. Schlomo and Marek—whatever vigor was left in him after Bushalo's assault—joined in.

The Jews were stronger and angrier. The fight would've certainly ended in their favor, should Bushalo and the Kapos not have immediately jumped on the opportunity to spill some gratis Jewish blood.

Little blood was spilled in the end, however.

The witnesses, not being avid fighters, they withdrew at the first sign of more violence from the Kapos. The brawl broke up by itself.

But the blood thirst of Bushalo and his brothers-in-arms was far from quenched. The punishment that the scrappy Jews faced could be a lot worse than any damage they might have sustained in the fight.

Holding the troublemakers under guard, all the Kapos were now waiting for, was the go-ahead.

I don't waste time on either the Kapos or the witnesses. For the former, a few bars of Lavuta's song suffice to have them forget what they are doing here and dreamily disperse. For the latter, I tell them to take their tools, hurry back to the commandant's quarters, and next time preferably mind their own business, if the tenets of their rigorous faith allow such a frivolity.

Then there is Bushalo, the main sower of discord. The instant he spots me, Sour One is gripped with a strong desire to sink through the dirt. He actually tries to do something to that effect, but in vain. I gain on him in two steps. I place my hand on the nape of his meaty neck and advise him, 'Should anyone, at any time, inquire about this little incident, you be a good boy, and tell them it was you, and you alone who provoked it. Understood? You take the whole blame and answer for it—alone. So, as you can probably deduce, it is in your best interests that no one ever recall about it. Nod if I'm making myself clear.'

I squeeze his neck, and Karl nods gloomily. Then, giving him a little slap on the back of the head, I send Sour One away.

'Don't you think he may squeal? Or lash back at the guys when you are not looking?'

This is my sweet-natured David expressing his concern.

He and his crew have just made their way to the scene and used my brief tête-à-tête with Bushalo to shake the four rebels' hands.

Everybody knows that while I am at the site, they are free to take rest and have a chat.

'Excluded, darling. Our boy is well aware that even when I'm not around, I can do to him things Himmler and Goebbels wouldn't think of if they knocked their imaginative heads together. He is sick with fear. No, he will not squeal.'

'Why can't you just destroy him?' my vengeful sweetheart demands as he presses his body against mine. 'Just make him die? Him, and others like him?'

'Because, dear, it is not time yet. The worst death I could give him now is a plain, boring stroke, or an infarction, or something similarly banal. While he deserves to shit his guts out and drown in his own excrement. This is the death I envisage for him. And there will come a time when I shall be able to finish him in this exact manner. Won't it be fun?'

'It sure will. But how many people will suffer at his hands before you realize your colorful scenario? Have you thought of this?'

'I will do my best to minimize that number,' I promise him.

*

While I'm saying this, a realization comes upon me: how smug the statement sounds, and indeed, how little bearing my chill self-assurance has on the grim reality. How many can I actually protect from the blows, should the current of life itself not conveniently carry me to the post of a protector?

And to what extent? And at what cost?

How much, on a daily basis, can I even protect David—from the humiliating labor, the pain, the deprivation—while I am waiting for the right moment to completely deliver him from it all? How much will he still have to take till that slowpoke of a moment arrives? And how unforgivably minuscule is this protection compared to the one I should like to have extended?

How much was I able to do for Yoska when my own feelings clashed in irreconcilable combat and the resolution demanded a sacrifice, and he offered himself up as one? Actually forced himself up as one?

It was on a bright day of July, in the green meadows over the Danube river in northern Bulgaria, that the sun-bathed, grass-caressed, and love-overflowing Lyuba ticklishly whispered in my ear I was going to become a father.

It was the night of the same day that Yoska came down with a bout of fever and severe cough. A malaise that started trivially, showing all the symptoms of a simple cold, abruptly took a turn for the worse and progressed with a satanic rapidity. Within hours, my rider was prostrated—his wiry frame reduced to a shivering bundle of ailing flesh.

Shandor suspected pneumonia induced by Yoska's matutinal outings in the rain. Insisted that if the reckless creature didn't get better by the morning, then we would have to fetch medical help from the nearby town of Nikopol or transport Yoska to a municipal hospital at our peril (it had been three months after Bulgaria terminated its neutrality policy and signed the Tripartite Pact, thus joining the Axis bloc).

I still wonder if Shandor, with all his intuition, really had no clue that the pneumonia was a self-inflicted one, and his nephew did not mean to outlive the night. Or did he know all the while and push the notion away in a grieved parent's denial?

With me, Shandor, Lyuba, Tomka, and Laila gathered around, and Yoska was burning out like a candle before our very eyes. Delirious, thrashing about on his velvet bedspread, he groaned and gasped through parched lips. I held his head; Lyuba dabbed his sweaty brow with a chamomile-soaked cloth, while Tomka, our self-trained herbalist and healer, was administering him a decoction from a silver ladle—the one we all drank when unwell, our surefire remedy for many an illness. Only this time the medication did not seem to work: the body, bent on self-destruction, rejected cure. As he swallowed a few drops of the infusion, Yoska's cough would subside momentarily; the wild shivering would cease. Minutes later, however, a new spasm would rake his body, still more viciously. Then Tomka inserted a new spoonful of the decoction in between his chattering teeth, and the cycle repeated.

This continued for hours.

At some point, finally, he appeared to have stabilized. There was a long break in the cough; his skin felt cooler; the pulse beat steadier. He looked exhausted and asleep.

This was when I knew the time had come.

I asked everybody, including Shandor, to go and take rest. I said I'd be with him alone till morning. Silently, grievously, they complied. Shandor's face was gray as he was leaving his nephew's bedside. If he might have resisted before, then by that moment the certainty broke him.

One on one with Yoska, I sat down on the edge of the bed. I took his hand and looked at the pale face—its exquisite features rendered ever more eerily refined by the malady.

He was not asleep. His eyes were semi-open, and, through his matted eyelashes, he was following my every movement.

I squeezed his hand in mine. He responded with a soft groan. His lips parted.

'A new life has been conceived for you,' he said, and smiled faintly.

'A new life has been conceived,' I responded. 'But not for me. *Your* life has been for me. And you want to take it away now.'

He nodded in affirmation.

'The price is too high,' I reproached him, clamping my will in a steel grip, fighting back the liquid in the eyes and throat.

Tears were not in order.

'Forgive me.' He squeezed my hand in return.

The effort of uttering the words and making the tiny movement triggered a new coughing attack. I took him by the shoulders to lift him up; pressed the pillow to his shoulder blades with my one hand while holding the back of his head in the palm of my other.

I looked at him.

As my dearest friend, the most precious creature in the universe was dying in my arms, I, to my horror and shame, could not banish the sinister, twisted lust aroused by the mere eroticism of his sickness—the fevered blood battling, the white cloth of his shirt clinging to the sweat-silked, luminous skin. Never had I loved him or desired him more piercingly than in those seconds.

He knew, of course.

This was his farewell present to me and his ultimate revenge. The delight of having him and the torture of losing him. The price was indeed too high, but he exacted it, and I had to pay. No bargaining was in question.

'I want to see Flame,' he said, when his cough-lacerated chest stopped heaving and he regained breath. 'Help me.'

I pulled him up by both hands, but that was almost redundant. Yoska slid off the bed quite nimbly and stood on his feet, his shiny eyes staring firmly before him. When he tried to walk, though, he staggered a little and had to lean on my shoulder.

Despite Yoska's feebleness, we left the tent noiselessly, without waking a soul.

Flame, the intuitive creature, was waiting in the dark a little way behind the tents—ears stiff, nostrils flared, pawing at the ground. At the sight of us, he neighed softly and, when Yoska came up, placed his long head on the rider's chest. Stroking the stallion's neck, kissing him, Yoska whispered something into Flame's tipped-forward ear—might have been words of love or a secret he trusted Flame alone to keep.

Then, at last, he addressed both the stallion and me, 'Let's take a walk.'

We walked slowly, the three of us—Yoska in between Flame and me, holding onto the horse's neck and my shoulder—along the narrow path up the dewy grass-blanketed cliff on the right bank of the Danube.

Yoska's temperature was rising. Several times we had to stop and stand through a fit of cough that left him out of breath. Then, as soon as he was able to breathe again, we would continue walking.

When we reached the flat summit where the edge of the cliff jutted out over the river, Yoska stopped. Turning to me sharply, he pressed his dry lips to mine.

'Don't name your son after me,' he then said with a broad smile. 'You don't want him crazy.'

With those words, he tore away from me, mounted Flame, and in the same fulminant movement did a handstand on the stallion's back—one of his coup de résistance at the shows.

Flame, the consummate performer, stood motionless on the edge of the cliff, his flank parallel to the river.

For the traditional ten seconds, Yoska froze motionless too. Straight like an arrow on his two hands, with his back to the precipice, he let the audience (which I alone was sentenced to be) admire his craft. Then, as his strength dwindled, he neatly flipped off Flame's torso into the dark sky, on which the first ray had already left a bleeding cut over the distant horizon.

*

David squeezes my hand.

'Check this out.'

A Steyr 125 pulls up, and the command 'Attention!' blasts from behind the brick mound. Alighting from the speedy vehicle are the very cream of the AU research body—Doctor Guido "Cabbagehead" Karp in the elegant company of Doctor Birgitte Junn, the pale Miss Academic Dowdiness.

These fine specimens head directly toward the works where the two Jewish crews are taking a smoke break under my shielding. Clutching onto Frau Junn is a grubby boy of about 10–12, over whom she every now and again leans with an unfeigned motherly attitude.

And—after blinking several times to make sure my eyes deceive me not—I ascertain it is actually Vano, our bored-out-of-his-mind, action-hungry ghost-storyteller who is entertaining Doctor Birgitte with his prattle while she is leading him by the hand to the work site where he is, to all appearances, impatient to get.

As I watch the unimaginable trio—Birgitte, Guido, and Vano in between, walking leisurely across the rubble-strewn field with insouciant smiles on their faces—it occurs to me that the three of them represent quite an idyllic metaphor of a young, healthy, and happy family thriving against the backdrop of an Armageddon.

When I shake my head to get rid of the clownish thought, my mind just goes blank. The picture is too surreal to try and make any sense of.

What brings me back to earth is Petko-the-prominent, who arises as if from the ground right before my face and starts rattling on about an urgent need for interpreting services. Doctor Junn, he says, is taking a special interest in Vano, but, Vano's German being a disaster, my assistance is necessary.

As the Jewish crews stare in amusement and David buries his soft giggle in my shoulder, I try to figure out what the hell is going on. It soon becomes clear, though, that simple concentration won't suffice. So I have to resort to tuning in.

I find out that since I left Vano in the barrack with an exercise in German, the bored kid has been getting busy, but not with the task I gave him. Desperate for attention, he went across the playground and behind the shed where Doctor Junn was having her usual session with the *glata*. While Frau Anthropologist engaged in animated talk with the kids, practicing her

Romani and meticulously recording the slips and logical inaccuracies in the little ninnies' babble, Vano went out of his way to get himself noticed. He tried cracking a joke. He tried singing a song. He attempted telling Doctor Junn's fortunes.

All to no avail. As at this stage of her research the doctor mostly targets younger children (from 3–8 years old) with their typical speech and skull imperfections, she was patiently but firmly waving over-aged Vano's efforts aside.

Then Obersturmführer Cabbagehead chanced to show up on the scene. Seeking more recruits for his commercial endeavor, he decided to see if he could utilize some of Birgitte's little charges. And, Guido being Guido, he also could not pass up the opportunity to exchange pleasantries with copper-haired Dr. Junn.

Absorbed in conversation, the Obersturmführer distractedly put his briefcase on the ground and got oblivious of it while examining the children.

It was then that Vano sensed his stellar moment. Disregarding the possibility of lethal consequences, pinning his hopes on *baxt* alone, he grabbed Obersturmführer Karp's briefcase. He laid it at the feet of fair Dr. Junn, winked at her frolicsomely, pointed at the nonplussed Guido, called on what German I'd managed to teach him, and delivered, '*Obersturmführer Karp, er gut ist. Er Zigeuner bestrafen. Ich Zigeuner bin. Mich nicht bestrafen—ich stehlen. Mich bestrafen—ich nicht stehlen. Obersturmführer Karp, er kennen.*'

In order to sound more convincing he snatched the briefcase away from Birgitte's boots and demonstratively placed it at Guido's.

To say that the trick worked would've been an understatement. It went down a storm. Dr. Junn started kissing Vano on the forehead, tweaking his cheeks, ruffling his hair, and squeezing him in hugs as if he were her pet puppy. Vano's speech was deemed an "invaluably capacious verbal realization of the characteristic mentality of Gypsy children educated in a manner inappropriate for their species."

So tickled Frau Anthropologist was that she temporarily put her work with the younger Gypsy subjects to one side and dedicated the rest of her day to cosseting Vano.

Was there anything the little clever darling needed? She inquired. Was there anything he wanted?

Without hesitation, Vano went about reaping the fruit of his success. He explained his greatest desire was to be useful. He said he wanted to go to the place where the Jews worked to help sort the brawlers out.

And without delay, Dr. Junn applied herself to granting the wish of her new protégé. She actually took advantage of Obersturmführer Karp's chauffeur for that purpose. Guido was not against giving Birgitte and her newly adopted Gypsy pet a lift, as he intended to take the latter directly to the lab as soon as the red-haired anthropologist got bored of him.

'Not punish me—I steal. Punish me—I steal not!' Dr. Junn recites her new favorite pun with a delighted laughter.

Every time she repeats it, she lovingly chucks Vano under the chin, while Vano, pink with complacency, casts victorious glances my way.

Guido stands nearby, clutching at his briefcase, leering at the sentimental anthropologist as she coddles the little Gypsy—waiting for his turn to use the object when the pretty female researcher is done indulging herself.

'Can you get him out?' David asks me quietly. 'Karp will have him rot away in his typhusorium.'

'No need,' I put my philanthropist's mind at rest. 'The scamp will admirably take care of himself.'

*

No need, to be sure.

Few in AU will do for themselves better than Vano will.

Not only will Cabbagehead never get a chance to put his hands on the little rascal—the Obersturmführer will actually be made by Dr. Junn to assist her in getting the kid out of the camp altogether. For Frau Anthropologist is going to be so captivated by Vano's savvy and witticism that she will end up actually adopting him—first as a house pet, later, when the Reich's goose is cooked—officially, as a son.

The move will prove a wise one, as it will clear Birgitte's name of her honorable membership in the Race Hygiene Research Centre, and of the foreword to her thesis stating that the author hoped to provide scientific cement for blocking the influx of "unworthy primitive elements" into the German population. It will render charges of proposed sterilization for Gypsies thrown against Dr. Junn by malicious tongues "ill-grounded and likely libelous." This is why the investigation into Frau Anthropologist's wartime actions will eventually be closed, as the magistrates will find insufficient evidence against and copious extenuating circumstances in favor of the good woman.

Especially hard will one find to believe that Frau Junn, the foster mother of Johann Junn (the revolutionary-minded JJ, a one-day-to-be-world-famous, extensively quoted star of anthropological science), once vehemently opposed initiatives to educate Gypsy adolescents. Not after she will have put her adopted Romani son through her own alma mater, the University of Berlin, help him write a brilliant doctoral dissertation and see him off to the United States, where he will find full professorship and a stellar scholarly career at the University of San Diego.

And emotionally too, much as Vano will profit by winning himself a German mother, it is arguable if *Mutti Bi* will not derive even greater benefit from obtaining a Gypsy son. Birgitte, after all, would have been going to die a spinster, broken in body and spirit, in an asylum in Frankfurt, were it not to be for Vano's rejuvenating presence in her life. Vano, our future Prof. JJ, shall, apart from his sensational academic success, prove the most caring child a lonely female soul like Birgitte's can hope to have.

Even in her late eighties, giving in to Alzheimer's, Birgitte's clouded mind will momentarily light up every time the elegantly silver-templed Prof. Vano will lean over her wheelchair, take her in his arms, and carry her out upon the verandah—for *Mutti Bi* to enjoy some fragrant Californian air in the rays of the setting sun.

*

'It's funny, you know; she reminds me so much of Batya...' David observes, as we watch Birgitte lead the disappointed Vano (the itchy-fisted kid cannot reconcile with the fact that he did not make it for the Jews—Jehovah's Witnesses sparring) away from the works and back toward the Steyr, with Guido tagging along.

'Who, Junn?'

'Yeah. Same nerdy grace. Same freckles.'

'Not the same motherly nature though, I bet.'

'Not indeed!' He cracks up.

Batya was David's geeky elder cousin from Warsaw. A zoologist, one of the not so many female honor graduates from the Major School of Rural Economy.

Of all the people he'd known, David tells me, Batya was the driest handful of dust. Even though not a completely hopeless case in the looks department, she managed to forfeit any chance she might have had of ever getting married by her utter disdain for mankind.

'Used to screw up her face whenever she heard a guy was seeing a girl. Me and Ad, we'd call her "dried roach"—when we were out of earshot, of course—or she would've pickled us alive in a tube and displayed us on the shelf.'

Adam was David's other cousin and a comrade in antics. The two pretty varmints would get slapped by the science-obsessed Batya every time they, taking advantage of a family gathering in her parents' spacious flat, dared approach her study.

Zoology was not only Batya's professional training. It was a passion. All the love she begrudged human beings, she seemed to invest in frogs and snakes. And frogs she had in abundance—magnificent sapphire blue poison dart frogs; harlequin mantellas; dainty, elven red-eyed tree frogs.

Batya's study at home was a kind of infirmary where she took those of her treasured creatures who were unwell—in most cases due to being deprived of their sweltering natural habitats—and needed more thorough care. There she treated them, and, when they got better, returned them to the state-of-the-art laboratory of the museum and Institute of Zoology, where she was steadfastly working toward full professorship and where the better part of her huge amphibian family was quartered.

In autumn 1940, Batya's Polish supervisor, accompanied by a member of Judenrat and a young SS officer, came into the laboratory and demanded that, by order of the Warsaw District Governor, she, as a Jewess, must vacate the premises and have her animals put down, as in the present conditions the institute did not have the means to keep them.

The scientist point blank refused. She purported that only over her dead body would the animals in her charge be removed from her lab or hurt. The supervisor tried applying some verbal pressure, which gave zero result. Unfazed, the obstinate woman sat at her desk, with her back to the numerous aquariums, her austere freckled profile to the visitors, writing a paper.

The supervisor, who over several years of Batya's work under him had formed a kind of attachment to the uncompromising female explorer, tried to talk the German officer out of using physical force.

He explained that Pani Strezhinska was a well-respected scientist and, in fact, a reasonable woman; he tried to persuade the representatives of authority to allow her time, promising he would bring his subordinate to her senses.

But the SS man was young and hot-blooded. He started brandishing a pistol and, in doing so, broke an aquarium containing a large yet inconspicuous gray toad.

This seemed to stir the unmovable Doctor Strezhinska. She lifted her head from her writing and looked at the three men over the top of her glasses. She stared at them a moment as if in perplexity, then put her pen down and, in a calm voice, asked not to disturb the animals. She said she would do everything that she must do herself.

With those words, she stood up, approached the broken aquarium, took the startled toad in her hands, and lovingly stroked its lumpy back. Then she slowly turned the key on an impressive-sized rectangular box right next to the remnants of the broken one—and the one closest to the SS officer. She sharply pulled the glass door open.

The container was a terrarium containing a two-meter-long western taipan—a generally placid, chocolate-brown creature who preferred to lie down, blending with the same color flooring and basking under the lamp, but, when provoked by abrupt movement, could strike swiftly and lethally. Batya's superior knew about the venomous inhabitant and took a panicked leap toward the exit. But the young Nazi, who was none the wiser, kept pointing his gun and barking his schnellers.

'It was so like *Siostrzyczka* Batya to feed a man to a snake for disrespecting a toad!' David laughs, gossipily emphasizing the "so."

When the officer felt a stab of pain, as if several fishhooks plunged into the flesh of his left palm, he did not immediately figure out what was causing it. Realization took him long enough for the taipan to crawl out of the open container onto the floor and into the perceived safety in between Batya's legs.

Eventually, though, the bitten military got over the shock. Following his first reflex, which was part retaliation, part self-defense, he shot the malevolent Jewess, her snake, and her toad, and then, clutching his bleeding left hand, frantically hollered for help.

Unfortunately for the officer, he was the only human being alive left in the room. Batya's supervisor and the Judenrat man had fled into the hallway. Moreover, for fear that the snake might escape, the supervisor had locked the door from the outside.

Upon hearing the shots and the officer's cries, the two men hastily returned and tried to reenter the lab. But the young Nazi's karma proved a bad one. It interfered.

Batya's supervisor was terrified; his hand was shaking. The key got stuck in the lock.

An inland taipan's bite, if untreated, can be fatal in less than an hour.

The youth's panic and ignorance of self-help first aid, combined with the language barrier between him and the two who were futilely ramming at the door to come to his rescue, exacerbated the situation.

By the time the door was breached, the ill-starred officer lay flat on the floor alongside Batya's and the snake's dead bodies. He was stricken with a cardiac attack and covered in vomit. A massive nervous system failure ensued, which eventually led to his death despite belatedly taken measures.

'So your militant cuz started the uprising even before the ghetto was built?' I joke.

'Kind of dealt the first blow… See her major difference from Dr. Junn? This one here prefers love to war.'

'Oh yes, and is sweet to kids! Batya detested children. Thought their presence endangered animals.'

'She sure would've not been impressed by Vano.'

'Bet not. This Vano doesn't strike one as a potential lover of frogs.'

'He will become a lover of dogs, though.'

'Will he?'

'Yes, this much is guaranteed. Birgitte's already got him a puppy to grow up with.'

VII
1st Violin

It is hard to resume normal functioning after an illness.

I've always felt that apart from being a blessing, generally good health is a challenge of a kind. Sometimes an out-and-out disadvantage, even. The lack of habit of working, writing, and reflecting while your body is falling to pieces. The pathetic succumbing to the unpleasantness of an inconsequential ache. The miserable inaction. While, at the same time, to think of how many geniuses, how many divinely prolific creators whose physical frames were entirely broken and apparently meant to be a curse to their owners, are known to history! The ones whose disability did not bar them from doing what they came into the world to do.

Makes one ashamed of oneself.

The only positive outcome of these several ruined days is that I did not need to invent an excuse to skip the Solahütte outing. Would've been a complete waste of time. Anton tells me it was indeed all about Höss and his pottering about. Should I have gone and tried to run *Force vitale* by the bunch of them again, it would've been drowned in the Commandant's moaning and done nothing but smudged the impression of my previous triumph. No. The Farma-Ko event proved an ideal occasion for the presentation, and none more is needed. Now it is time for real work.

And the real work is being done, even though not as efficiently as I would wish. I might have lost pace for a few days, but now I am regaining it. Slowly but surely getting back on track.

I am going to require at least three more objects apart from Damira. I think I'll ask Birgitte to help me out.

I have been watching her reference group closely the last couple of weeks. The children are the right age, and I have definitely spotted one or two with vivid signs of *cancrum oris* taking root around their lower jaw area. These subhuman youngsters are incurring noma, as they have been meant to, since birth. And those of them who are not afflicted yet, will sure be in the near future. There is no getting away from *Force vitale*. Sooner or later, it will catch up with every single one of them.

Birgitte has of course always been extremely scrupulous in all matters concerning her work. She is also highly protective of her objects. She might not be immediately willing to share them with me, especially knowing that after I isolate the selected children for my research, her own work with them will hardly continue according to the usual schedule. It may take some effort to persuade her.

I believe, however, that after my speech at The Evening I should be able to talk her round. The scientist in her will see things from the right angle. The intelligent, deep, and progressive human being Birgitte is, she will realize that while her own research is definitely useful, mine is groundbreaking. She will be able to put things in perspective, even if it means sacrificing several of her own refs in my favor. I doubt neither her generosity nor her wisdom.

There is another tremendous new decision I have arrived at.

It may be a folly. It may be outright insanity. It may even be a crime, as it runs counter to the oath I've recently sworn—it practically forces me to break it.

All things considered, however, I feel I have to follow my deeper instinct.

Regardless of how hard I try to chuck music out of my thoughts, Indigo Mind—this curse, this daemon, this bane of my life—keeps knocking on the door. Now more audibly than ever.

It haunts me at work. It raped my mind, marking the onset of an illness, just like it had done to me years ago. It was deafening me with its bewitching sound all through my feverish nights. It demands to be let out—and signals that now it is the time.

Simultaneously, there is a circumstance, a coincidence so twisted and bizarre I do not even dare name it. A thing I feel can help me. Something that has already given me a series of hints it can and will do so.

I may be wrong, but I take all the above as a sign. A message. An order, even.

Who knows if Indigo Mind, when finally born in sonic flesh, could not do for the motherland and the civilized humanity at large something as vital as The Idea. Who knows in what colossal motion this music might set minds; what new, unthinkable creations and inventions it might inspire.

All I, for one, know is that I am physically, mentally, spiritually, and sentiently urged to try, no matter how quirky it may seem even to myself—let alone others.

*

Birgitte threw herself at me in her typically compassionate way, asking about my health. We had not seen each other since The Evening, where I first triumphed with my speech, and then disgraced myself for getting drunk and forgetting to perform her request.

She never asked about Tongues of Flame, never even mentioned The Evening. All she wanted to know was how I was feeling.

I reassured her, saying I was now well and, in return for her tactfulness, refrained from any teasing about her having disappeared with Anton that night.

I decided to be straightforward.

I said I was completely and passionately engrossed in the work on the *Force Vitale* project. Said it was not leaving me time for anything else—even music—secretly hoping she would forgive my not having made much progress with the composition I'd promised to dedicate to her. I simply could not bring myself to play to her the shoddiness that had come out of the romantic vision of Freia's Reverie. Said I was badly wanting objects for empirical research. Asked if she could spare me two or three.

Birgitte, the perfect angel that she is, listened attentively to all I had to say. Then she responded by complimenting my speech exuberantly once again, saying I was a genius and the hope of contemporary German science. After that, without a slightest hesitation, she offered me three of her children, for, as she phrased it, "no one would make better use of these priceless resources."

I described the objects—those which I had in mind. She immediately put names to the descriptions. Mara, Patrin, and Grisha. And yes, she too had been noticing those tiny ulcers on the children's faces for some time now.

'You will love working with Grisha,' she sung the praises of her special ten-year-old. 'He is so smart.'

'Grisha, won't you miss him?' I asked. 'He's the one you've named our foundling after, isn't he?'

'He's the one!'

The little four-pawed Grisha, meanwhile, was whining delightedly in the kitchen, engaged in a playful skirmish with Vano, Birgitte's new favorite, and housekeeper.

I personally wouldn't trust this Vano much. He is almost grownup, has darting eyes, and a thievishly sycophantic grin. But Birgitte dotes on him. Who knows if he is not the reason why she sacrificed her Grisha boy and two others to me so easily. Or, perhaps, there are other, ulterior motives to her generosity. Something I am yet unaware of...

Whatever. I don't want to think about it. I prefer to see Birgitte as a good, understanding, and responsive friend. My golden-haired, amber-teared Freia.

*

Much as Birgitte's company was pleasing to me, I had to depart soon enough. There was an interesting twin study case Epstein and Bendel were on, and Angel insisted that I be present at the closure.

The case per se was a rather standard one.

Two Jewish seven-year-old female twins had both been given a series of injections of T14. As a result, one developed a malignant growth in her right kidney, which was predicted to kill her within a month. The other one, on the contrary, showed a curious resistance to the agent.

Angel wanted to have the two sets of kidneys, and he wanted them soon, before the cancer-afflicted twin died her natural death. Prior to nephrectomy, however, it was important to collect a number of urine samples from both twins.

Now while things with the sick twin were going more or less according to plan toward the closing stage, the healthy one started manifesting a behavioral-physiological idiosyncrasy. Namely, she stopped urinating. She also refused to drink.

No amount of verbal or physical stimulation helped, while it was established that neither force-hydration nor urinary catheterization was permissible in the case, for all interference would be contaminant to the experiment.

Eventually it was decided to close anyway; the tumor-afflicted twin was getting worse and could die sooner than expected. Angel appointed the day (today) for closure. And, before the twins received the lethal injection, it was our last chance to obtain an uncontaminated urinary sample from the healthy one.

So Epstein, Bendel, and I were, all the three of us, standing over the naked, shivering seven-year-old, awkwardly improvising means of inducing her to pee into a flask. Bendel, who spoke Miri's native Romanian, tried some sweet-talking in that language.

The girl was having none of it. Doggedly, she continued drilling the floor with her non-childlike eyes. Then at some point she raised those eyes to give us a second of intense, infinitely tired look.

'Where is my sister?' she asked quietly in German. 'Is she sick? Is she dead?'

Angel eventually ordered catheterization—there was no time to wait anymore. While we were performing it, I thought of the Gypsy with the violin. My daemon. How convenient it would've been to have him in the operating room. He would've surely known how to unblock Miri's urethra.

I might've even suggested calling the Gypsy in, if I hadn't allotted him a much more significant mission.

The daemon's business shall not be with the twin study.

It shall be with me.

*

Just as I was rushing to the car, impatient to be driven to my office in order to set about fulfilling my insane and beautiful plan, I had to be stopped, grabbed, and laughed uproariously into my face by the tipsy Guido.

'I have two pieces of news, one good and one bad, brother,' he bawled. 'Care to know which one's my favorite?'

Ever since Guido got the Farma-Ko job, he has been happiness-drunk, both metaphorically and physically. He just won't stop celebrating, which roughly amounts to him now perpetually being thrice his loud self.

It is not my place to complain, however, as it is this very Guido who not only once saved me from consequences of my own celebratory drinking but, most importantly, freed me from the aforementioned Farma-Ko job, allowing me time for indulging in follies like science and art. The mission I was on my way to launch had in no small measure been made possible thanks to Guido's help.

So as sacred codes of camaraderie prescribed, I returned his hug, laughed along with his guffaw, and in the most amused possible manner asked what the news was.

'Well, the good new-oos'—Guido hiccupped—'is that our brave Gestapo fighter Barbie has finally caught this Freemason frog Moulin in some unpronounceable shithole near Lyon. Latest update says the frog is having his warty hide torn off him alive and his flat head soaked in ammonia as we speak.'

I nodded and giggled, trying to make it sound convincing.

'The bad news,' he continued, 'is that those Yankees have gone so mad they are now training some of their negro apes to pilot! And—guess what?'

He paused for effect.

I squinted and shrugged, doing my best to look mystified.

'No, you'll never figure that one out! A troop of such flying apes crippled a couple of our Focke-Wulf 190 boys and sent them whining back to the base somewhere over Sicily the other day! And... this... piece of new-oos is my favorite, brother.'

It took him a lot of effort to have the sentence out distinctly, as a new outburst of laughter was choking him. At the last word, he exploded. He cackled so loud I did not have to try hard to show noisy appreciation. It was enough to open my mouth and tilt my head back—Guido would've outroared me anyway.

Then, quite abruptly, Guido stopped laughing, pulled a solemn face, and changed the topic.

'Have you seen Birgitte recently?' he asked.

'Why yes, I have. This morning.'

I was taken aback by his uncharacteristic mood swing.

'And? What did she say? Did she speak of me at all?'

'No... as a matter of fact, she didn't. Not that I remember.'

'Devil's puppet she is, this Birgitte!' he exclaimed with surliness. 'First she gives a man advances, sends him on a wild goose chase trying to smuggle a gypsling into her flat to be her private slave with a peacock feather fan, and, when a man gets that done, disappears without a word of gratitude!'

Now it was my turn to laugh.

'"The slave with a peacock feather fan" I have seen all right! No worries. Even if she didn't properly express her gratitude, she certainly appreciates your effort. This Vano boy—Vano is his name, isn't it? Seems to be the apple of her eye now.'

Guido puffed dismissively.

'She doesn't know where her bread is buttered, this girl. You won't believe it; I clearly gave her to understand I'm onto some money…' he took a dramatic pause again. 'No, I mean it, man. I have big plans on Farma-Ko. Real big plans, buddy…'

As I was walking slowly but steadily away, toward the car, he was expanding on some financial schemes he had in mind in connection with the recent Farma-Ko deal. But, having gotten rid of them, Farma-Ko were the last thing I wanted to hear about. So, although I nodded and grunted approvingly all along, I wasn't really paying attention.

*

Back in my office at last and finally left alone, I sank into the chair and turned Indigo's photograph so that her swampy black eyes looked straight into mine. I mentally asked for advice. Taking into account the delicacy of the matter, it was my intuition alone I could rely on, and my estranged muse's telepathic council was the only one I could seek.

How could I furnish it—an unheard-of arrangement that could have hardly entered my mind before the height of my despair coincided with the most surreal circumstances I'd ever become witness to? Somehow the décor and the presentation of the deal seemed important.

Upon reflection, I telephoned Klaus Ruffert, our resourceful steward, and asked for a platter of ham and cheese sandwiches and a pot of hot coffee to be delivered to my office. I explained I was having a strategic private meeting. Klaus, the good soul, promised to throw in a bottle of scotch on the house.

Then I summoned Petko, a shifty Gypsy *blokältester*. Swearing him to secrecy, I ordered to bring in the young tall inmate referred to as Jass.

*

He appeared taller than I'd expected. Definitely taller than he'd looked in the barrack. Taller and somehow bigger, although he was remarkably slim. He seemed to occupy the entire office space with his twilight presence.

He showed no surprise at having been summoned, nor did I feel any need to give immediate explanations. He nodded a hello; I nodded back. He silently asked for permission to sit at the desk and partake of the coffee and sandwiches. I, just as silently, gave one.

He ate and drank slowly, without greed and with laidback, sated grace. Inexplicably, while watching him at it, I myself had a fit of hunger, although I'd eaten a substantial lunch right before. So I too sat down, took a sandwich, and poured myself a cup of coffee.

The silence took a while, but it was not by any means strained. It was relaxed, and had a warm feel to it, like the silence of two friends between whom everything had been for years explained and understood. I knew, however, I'd have to start talking at some point.

And I did.

'Jass... Is this your real name?'

He moved his chin in the affirmative.

'I reckon it must be a short for something? A nickname?'

'Jassengro is the full version.'

His voice was low and had a soothing quality, like that of an old, wise, and amused storyteller.

'Jassengro,' I repeated. 'That's quite unusual. Does it mean something?'

'It does. "A runaway man."'

'A runaway man...' I marveled. 'Was it your parents' idea to name you thus? I mean, it doesn't seem to associate with much good luck, does it? I thought all Romani names were supposed to carry a spell of luck... no?'

'It was invented by my stepfather who considered the skill of disappearing at the right moment and without fuss a major talent.'

'So you did not know your real father, I assume?'

'Never seen him.'

He took another sandwich and topped up his coffee.

'Oh, I'm sorry I didn't ask before—do you take cream and sugar?' I offered.

'No, thank you; not at this time of day.' He chuckled softly. 'My biological father you've just mentioned was Italian, or so I've been told. Italians are known to only take their coffee with milk or cream in the morning and have it black for the rest of the day. I guess I've inherited the habit.'

I felt strangely at ease around him, although I could not shake off the impression that he was the host and I was a guest in the room.

'Who would be responsible for your excellent German then?' I inquired.

'My stepdad once again. A Sinti from Düsseldorf.'

'I've also heard that you speak other languages. Where did you learn those?'

'I was born in a circus composed of a motley crowd from various parts of the world. My mother was a Romanichal, she spoke mostly English. She and my stepfather, whose language was German, made up an illusionist act. Presumably, I was conceived from an Italian spectator during the circus's tour of Tuscany. The ones who raised me were my mother, stepfather, and an adoptive grandmother—an elder of the circus, a Ruska Roma. One might say, such an environment was conducive to a child's linguistic well-roundedness.'

'One might indeed… and the violin? Did you have a teacher?'

'None but my violin itself. She has been teaching me from day one.'

'I see what you mean. My own has been teaching me too… Oh yes, I forgot to explain that I am a violinist, like yourself… In fact, this is directly connected with what I would like to talk to you about.'

He lowered his eyes showing that he understood.

I was quiet for a while, at a loss where to begin. He prompted me.

'You are a composer, aren't you?'

'Yes, right. Correct. I am. I have been playing the violin since childhood, you see. It wouldn't be an exaggeration to say that, apart from medicine, music is the most significant thing in my life. For many years, I thought that it *alone* was my life…'

'I see.'

'And, as you have rightly guessed, I compose…'

I trailed off, wondering how to go on. Then once again I found my bearings.

'Say, do you compose too?'

'I do, when the mood takes me.'

'Yes, obviously. When you get inspired.'

'Correct.'

'So do I. I have written some pieces I am more or less proud of. But I cannot say this about all of them. Sometimes realization falls short of the idea. You probably know how it happens.'

'I certainly do. Please continue,' he encouraged.

My mouth felt dry. I took a large gulp of coffee—a deep breath—and lunged forth to the crescendo.

'So it happened once in my early youth that I was tremendously inspired and had an idea of a piece, but as much as I tried over the following years to embody it, I have always failed…'

I explained that The Idea was based on another musical work, an opera, which I had heard as a child. I almost began retelling the plot, determined to be brief and focus mainly on the line of Brünnhilde and Siegfried, when he gently interrupted, 'I know the contents of The Ring.'

I stopped, and, incredibly, felt myself blushing.

'Oh yes, of course you do. I'm sorry.'

I felt embarrassed. I might've known.

'Don't be,' he reassured me.

He said he admired Wagner's signature story—the tale of a fair and proud maid who was so devoted to her beloved one that she refused to relinquish the token of his love even on her formidable father, the god Wotan's demand, and later, believing herself betrayed by the hero Siegfried, led him to his death and threw herself on the flames.

'Initially it was supposed to be a celebration of her,' I described. 'Of Brünnhilde—her strength, faith, and beauty overpowered by the fire. Later, though, another female image entered my world. I made an acquaintance of someone. A girl who deeply impressed me. And then the idea of the composition transformed in my mind, yet somehow retaining its core and atmosphere. But it was of no help because my mind was where it remained locked up.'

*

I was narrating to him the convoluted history of Indigo Mind—leaping back and forward, losing the thread, dwelling on inconsequential details, and forgetting salient facts. And, the more I said, the more I realized the effort was redundant. All the while I felt I might as well have cut myself short and allowed him to finish for me.

He knew everything—not only what I was saying, but, more importantly, what I was, through sheer lack of adequate linguistic means, leaving unsaid.

I did eventually halt.

The topic of Indigo Mind drained me, so I changed the subject. Instead of expounding something I hadn't accomplished, I chose to show him what I had. That, after all, was why I had taken Cosima to the office with me.

I played to him—Tongues of Flame, La Imperfetta, and the prelude to Irminsul.

He listened most appreciatively, not so much with admiration as with an understanding which I felt every second I was playing. And I could without a shadow of a doubt state that it was absolutely the best performance of the said compositions I had ever given.

Somehow this fact did not even come as a surprise to me. The pieces simply could not have sounded any less than they did in his presence.

I complimented him on being the perfect audience. Redundant or not, this felt like the right thing to say.

'I heard you play in the barracks a few times,' I said to him. 'When you unmistakably found a way to tune your music to people's feelings, even changed their state of mind with it. Among your tribesmen, you are known to be able to "play people's souls to them." I thought that perhaps... perhaps I could ask you to assist me in finishing the composition I conceived of as an adolescent, but, because of some strange mental block, have never been able to properly bring it to life. Perhaps you could help me remove the block. Same way you get children to sleep, or not be afraid? And I should probably mention that I would like the piece to sound in the style of the compositions you've just heard. Same vibe, but on a different level... How should I put it? I'm not being too confusing, I hope...'

'You aren't.'

He stood up, or, rather, appeared in front of me in vertical position, having risen to his feet with such uncanny swiftness his movements had been imperceptible. In his hands he had his violin and baton, although I had not noticed him bringing them in the office when he entered (in fact I was planning to lend Cosima to him, should our very first conversation lead to him needing to play).

And, before I could say another word, the baton hit the strings.

*

Even a split second before he started playing—just by the expression his face suddenly assumed, by the way he held the instrument—I knew a change was being made to my world—one after which it would never be the same. A blast. A revolution. A new beginning and an infinite end.

I knew I had to stop him immediately, but I could not bring myself to.

At the first passages of the music, my heart sprung into my throat and swelled there, threatening to choke me. The explosive delight at feeling something that had for so many feverish years been lurking in the dark alleys of my subconsciousness actually vibrated my eardrums fused with the panic at the realization that my precious baby was about to be brought into the world by someone else.

Summoning all my willpower, I tore myself out of the enchanted stupor. I threw myself at the Gypsy; I clutched at him; I almost hung my entire bodyweight on his bent arms.

I begged him to stop.

'Wait. Please. Listen. This music means too much to me. There is nothing more mine, more belonging to me than it. I will have to learn to create it myself. I wanted to ask you to guide me. Be my tutor. Teach me to retrieve it. Do you think it can be possible?'

The Gypsy was willing to sell his skill in any format, it seemed. He assured me it was possible; just would take longer this way. I promised him in return that, even if it took twice the term I'd already waited, I would be the most patient of pupils, for I simply wanted to have it embodied before my lifetime ran out.

He lowered his eyelids with nonchalant comprehension.

It was agreed we would meet again in the near future. Perhaps tomorrow. Perhaps next week. I said I'd send Petko for him when I was ready. He said he'd be waiting.

At that, I asked him to leave. My feelings swirled in a tornado, and his very presence was too intense for me to bear any longer.

I needed to be alone, calm down, and collect my thoughts. I had to learn to live with this new reality I invited upon myself. I had to learn to make the most of it.

*

When the door behind him closed, it took me another immense exertion of will to tame the storm that was raging within. I could not allow emotions to get the better of me. Not now, not when the delivery of the dearest baby I'd ever conceived was in the hands of another—an obstetrician? A psychic? A sorcerer? Or just a scruffy inmate of the Gypsy family camp?

More imperatively than ever, I had to keep a level head. Make sense of things; assess them coolly. Give myself a straight account of what was going on.

What is he really, this helper of mine, the one that I have freely and willingly chosen in order to accomplish the greatest musical exploit of my life? Whence does his psychic ability derive? And more importantly, do I have any right to use those supernatural powers he possesses? Or would it be a theft, a fake, even a betrayal of myself as an artist?

But the more I contemplated it, the more I became assured that giving this creature access to my innermost world did not equal having his strength compensate for my weakness or allowing him to operate on my deficient creativity and extract the jewel that I was unable to deliver unaided.

It was, rather, an offer of collaboration on my part. Moreover, such a collaboration was justified in racial terms. For, when one recalled what the Romanies—especially Romani musicians generally were—it appeared that Jass's "paranormal" ability was most likely not paranormal at all. It was the natural Romani instinct for music which manifested itself, especially pronouncedly in his case.

Hasn't it been reiterated a number of times, after all, that some Romani peoples today are authoritatively regarded as an early cut-off branch of the Indian Arians? Aren't comparisons justly drawn between these peoples' whimsical sonic gifts and authentic Indian music? Aren't both cultures privy to the florid mysteries of a scale which comprises quarter notes and sometimes even minuter distinctions?

It is by those means that they obtain harmonic orders and progressions unbeknownst to Teutonic musical art.

Besides, the ardent—typically "Gypsy"!—passion of the melody and the lush, inexhaustible accompaniment which challenges our scale of notation is precisely consistent with what has been written or related to us in Indian music.

Haven't I myself had a chance to enjoy listening to a genuine Hungarian Gypsy Orchestra? When Franz, Oliver, and myself—"the Friedrich Wilhelm Maestros," as we were known—whiled away entire evenings in Der Weg Cafè? Didn't I, already back then, argue that there and there alone one could observe unpolluted musical genius in action? For this music, although based upon lightweight popular melodies, is always extemporized—inevitably called for by the moment.

True music is not, like a painting or a statue, created once for all—true music is directly projected emotion—breathing, vibrating, and alive. It is an intuitive understanding of what is felt by another and expressing it. Something that cannot be taught. Something that Jass does with such ease. Something the Hungarian Gypsy Orchestra would do, even without knowing what a note, an interval, or a key is—devoid of any theoretical background whatsoever.

It is self-evident that, born at the time of playing to express a unique feeling or a fleeting emotional state, such music must make quite a different impact on the listener's soul than one which has been carefully thought-out and laid down on paper.

Such a sonic product, however, comprises no elements out of which monumental artworks can be molded. The musical sphere in which Jass and his similarly gifted tribesmen dwell is not really art—not in any of its accomplished forms, anyway. It is rather the element from which art initially arises—not the sea-born Aphrodite, but the sea itself.

The nature of my collaboration with Jass-the-Gypsy is thus explained. He will provide the sea. I will carry my Aphrodite out of its waters.

*

Speaking of the racial side of the question, by the way, I am in the clear even from the official Gestapo point of view... or am I, really?

It is common knowledge that the Reichsführer himself spares no effort for the two main Gypsy stocks to be preserved, as he firmly believes those descend directly from the elemental Indo-Germanic race and keep their traditions relatively uncontaminated. Even Höss, our painstaking commandant, is well aware of this.

Anton related to me in most comical details what a poor figure Höss cut when, striving to demonstrate his awareness of the Reichsführer's purposes, he had given a whole speech on the subject in Solahütte, but, in his cups, forgot the names of the two particular Gypsy breeds which the great man singled out.

'Domari... eh... Lomari... no, different ending... Domarven?' Anton aped the hapless drunk's scattering (and he knows how to take off the drunken Commandant brilliantly, Anton does!).

"Maybe the Reichsführer just meant that pure Gypsies and *Zigeunermischlinge* were to be distinguished?' Angel ventured quizzically.

But Höss, as Anton tells me, paid no heed to the remark and stubbornly continued searching through exotic tribes' names, inventing new, ever more grotesque ones, as he mumbled on, 'Dimari? Larven?'

He has been manifesting himself as a most pathetic mess lately, Höss. Is visibly losing his grip... He is, however, well familiar with the Reichsführer's program, which stipulates that the pure-blooded members of the two main Gypsy tribes be collected and settled in the Oldenburg district on the Neusiedler See, while the rest are to be restricted to the AU family camp.

Given the fact that my Jassengro is in the family camp, and taking into account what he told me about his mixed origins, he more likely belongs to the latter, non-valuable breed. To the *Zigeunermischlinge*, that is. But, if I keep on the discreet side and refrain from blabbing to anyone, including Anton, who is ever going to find out about my collaboration with the "runaway man?"

Indeed, all these paltry contradictions and petty doubts pale in comparison with the sense of purpose. Yes. I have formulated it accurately and precisely. The sense of purpose. This is what my seemingly insane act—seeking the Gypsy out to offer him work on a joint effort—is redeemed by.

The sense of purpose was what permeated our entire meeting, our very conversation with Jassengro. He exudes it. Every word I hear him say reinforces my aspiration and fills me with greater will for victory.

This is also what makes me believe that, racially, Jass might be not so wide off the mark, after all. Even if his ancestors were not all pure Indian or Iranian natives, I can feel a distinctive Arian trace in him.

For it were the purest of the pure Arians—the pre-Islamic Persia's adherents of Zoroastrianism who have bestowed the sense of purpose (including creative purpose) upon the world. Along with Moses, Zarathustra was the first to perceive time as a linear magnitude. Abandoning the sweet poison of cyclism—the long-term indulgence of their Hindu and Buddhist counterparts—Zoroastrians found inner strength to admit that existence is finite and set themselves a goal.

In the case of Moses' successors, however, the idea of linear time led to the hideous phenomenon of a chronological religion. The Jews thought nothing of grabbing the mythology of the Greeks, stuffing it full with the historical superstition typical of their own people, and out of the whole spinning an abstract dogmatical web, materializing into empirical forms everything that was transcendental and allegorical.

The Arians, on the other hand, used the category of finiteness merely to imbue their existence with the feeling of aim. Proud and upright did they stand in front of the rising sun—not praying or worshiping, but rather leading an open dialogue with their benevolent God Ahura Mazda—seeking his council on what an individual could do in order to help good prevail over evil. It was this bravery, this noble attitude of feeling on par with God, that lit a fire in the hearts of the Persians, for a historical instant, turning them into the most strong-spirited nation in the world. And this indomitable spirit and a sense of purpose is what all Arians inherited. It is what Jass and I share. Or, more precisely, what I carry deep within and what he will help bring out.

I got so carried away by euphoria I failed to notice the moment that I began expressing my ebullient thoughts out loud. I might've happily continued holding forth if it hadn't been for Petko's knock on the door. He heard me calling out the name "Jass" and was puzzled, as he had already accompanied the one who went by this name back to the family camp—in fact, he returned to report it to me.

'You will say no word of this Jass's visit to my office. Anywhere. To anyone,' I warned the nosy *blokältester*.

The rapscallion gave a series of obsequious nods.

Then, on the crest of the sense of purpose wave, I spontaneously made up my mind to complete a momentous stage of the other great work of my life. *Force Vitale*. I decided to isolate Damira and Birgitte's children today without procrastinating any longer. The time for lab observation has come.

So I immediately sent Petko back to the family camp with a new urgent task.

VIII
2nd Violin

This Christian is not such a sissy after all.

I thought less of him. Wouldn't be an overstatement to say I'm impressed.

Offering him his magnum opus readymade on a silver platter was the acid test. I'd envisaged him standing there, jaw-dropped, drooling, with shaking knees, begging for more.

Like hell!

The boy passed. With flying colors.

Pounced like a panther. Pinched my wrists in a vice grip. Almost knocked me off my feet. Almost tore Lavuta out of my hands. In short, proved himself up to the challenge.

I'd expected to be disappointed. I wasn't. The material is not all waste. Can be worked with.

The main problem with Christian is though, he is envious. Full of pent-up envy, overflowing with it. He is envious of Anton Lauer, of Debussy, of Stravinsky. Envious, even, of his exalted Meister, Wagner. Of me.

He thinks it is his love for the doleful-eyed girl whose photograph he keeps on his desk that nourishes his creativity. This is, unfortunately, a lie. Christian's creativity is nourished—and poisoned—by envy, and envy alone.

The most comical of all is his envy of Orff. Christian simply won't get off the new court minstrel's case. Drowns himself in vitriol, discussing "the phenomenal ability of marginally talented individuals to worm their way into the affections of the dignitaries." Chokes on acrimony, talking of the unfinished Zarathustra. Calls Gisei "a miscarriage." Fumes at the ridiculousness of Carl's candidature being considered for writing a new version of *A Midsummer Night's Dream* after the ban on Mendelssohn's music—says it's nothing short of "a Jew being replaced by a converted Mischling."

Turns green at the very mention of the celebrated cantata. Ah, the haunting, impudent, and coveted sound—so welcomed by the gullible masses, so unattainable! How Christian wishes that a similarly "faux-cataclysmic, gaudily orchestrated piece devoid of harmonic texture, polyphony or development" could garnish him same degree of public acclaim as Carmina Burana has done its creator. How much he would, in fact, like to cater to those "lowly tastes on the lookout for tawdry sensation, those not knowing noble art from ignoble counterfeit."

And in what fierce denial he is regarding all these innermost desires that are tearing his soul apart.

Christian's greatest grievance against the world is the world's indifference to him. The global unawareness of his existence. If Christian cannot be loved, then he would settle for being hated. Just not for being unaware of.

In his wildest dreams, of course, it is not just loved or hated that he sees himself. Nothing as simplistic as this. His greatest appetency is for being envied. Christian would most ravenously have the world do onto him what he does onto the world.

He longs to be a mystery—infinitely fascinating, endlessly wondered about, incessantly explored. To be controversial, scandalous. An unsolvable enigma, even to himself.

Well, this last bit of Christian's multiple wishes can be granted, I reckon. At least for a while. As I have already pointed out, the material is not all basket case.

*

Shaking off Petko-the-chapherone on the traditional crossing under a birch and two pines, I took a turn to the Jewish camp to treat myself to David's lips.

And once again I was given a chance to admire my green-eyed love's keenly intuitive altruism against the backdrop of my own sensuous egotism.

The boy was restless, visibly uncomfortable. While I, in most entertaining tones (or so they seemed to me), recounted to him my meeting with Young Werther, he was not really listening. He kept interrupting with off-topic questions about how things were going in the family camp. He was, unimaginably, rushing to get rid even of my caressing hand.

He wouldn't stop sending me back to the Gypsy Ground. So I eventually obeyed and took myself off, quite mystified.

The explanation lay in wait for me, right on the threshold.

Petko loitered by the door, squinting, taking drags on a scruffy hand-roll. I thought he'd give me a wink or offer a smoke. I was sure the prominent's self-congratulatory airs were the result of being in my meeting with Dr. Heidert. He probably imagined he was now privy to some secret mission Young Werther and I were setting out on.

Instead, Petko threw the cigarette out and averted his eyes.

And then it hit me. There was another task he had been sent on by Christian, while I was in the Jewish quarters.

Damira.

Pushing the prominent out of the way, I tore the door open. In one leap, I was between Mihai's and Marusya's bunks.

In vain. She was gone.

Now I belatedly realize I have been so consumed by Christian business that I became detached from all other things around. I should've foreseen that the day of my meeting with Christian would become the last time I saw Damira. The billow of inspiration I'd invoke in him would be far too powerful to satisfy itself with music alone. It would demand science, roar for immediate sacrifice—and what better sacrificial lamb than Damira—the A list experimental object. I should've known Dr. Heidert was going to act upon his urge.

I chose to look away.

Starting on a guilt trip is the last thing I am inclined to do, however. For, regardless of what I knew or didn't know, there is null I could do to prevent what was coming. Damira's fate was sealed. The inevitability of it must've blunted my intuition.

Hell, I just wanted a chance to embrace the child before she was gone. Or maybe I didn't—and for this precise reason was not given one.

Occupying Damira's place at Marusya's feet was a character I'd almost forgotten all about, so long he'd been away at the Revier. In fact, he was never supposed to make his way out of that infirmary. To me, he had long since felt dead.

Sashko-the-clubfoot.

Outwardly, Sashko did not look much changed. Same watery eyes, puffy eyelids, sagging jowls, and glistening bowtie of a mouth. Same jovial chumminess.

One significant detail was missing, at a closer look—the one that had garnered Sashko his moniker. The clubfoot was gone, along with the entire right leg.

In one of his most voluble moods, Sashko was patting his bandaged stump while he entertained the audience with the story of his adventures.

The ravenous listeners were Mihai, Baba Tanya, Rosa, and Marusya with baby Dando on her lap.

'Three times a day they'd come to the ward, just to look at me. Three! All for me. They'd call me "a most curious case of thrombophlebitis!"'

Sashko slapped himself on the knee of the still intact left leg and laughed proudly. The others chuckled along.

"Hanke the nurse would ogle my leg like it was a pretty maid. 'You should never smoke again, drink, or eat greasy foods,' he'd tell me. 'Otherwise you'll work up a gangrene, and we'll have to cut it off! We'll cut your whole leg off!' he'd say to me. And then, at night, he'd pass me cigs, beer, and sausage through Bzhdynsy-the-Pole. Bzhdynsky, the greedy pig, he took half of the grub, but there was still mouthful left for me. They served me there like a king!"

Sashko smacked his glistening lips at the memory. The audience groaned in admiration.

'They cut the ugly baby off then. Clean up to the knee. Hanke said he'd write his dissertation, all about my leg! And imagine, *phrali*, how much I will score in the streets now. A real cripple, a one-legged. No cheat. No impostor. They will carry me in their arms, those *gadje*!'

This time Sashko refrained from laughing. The statement was too serious, the moment too solemn. He just closed his eyes, visualizing the future. The listeners gave a sigh of undivided approval.

"Doctor Heidert took my Damira to the lab today,' Marusya ventured cautiously, dying to share the story of her daughter's success.

Sashko opened his eyes.

'He did?'

'Yes! I thought maybe he'd take the little one too.' She looked at the cooing Dando. 'But the doctor said he did not work with babies so young. Now that my girl is in good hands, my greatest hope is for the little one to find his fortune. I pray that he grows up knowing where his luck is, like you do.'

'No doubt he will!' Sashko acknowledged her successful attempt at flattery. 'I will look out for Dando, like he is my own brother. I will advise him. I'm always ready to give wise advice to a *phral*, you know me.'

'Of course he will advise him!' Baba Tanya boomed her endorsement. 'Our Sashko is on the right path, and he will take Dando along. And, mind you, girl!'

She lowered her voice conspiratorially, leaning toward Marusya's ear.

'You listen to what your Baba Tanya says. Now that Damira is with young Doctor Heidert, who knows if Doctor Angel himself will not take interest in Dando? You hear what I say. It is not Doctor Heidert we need for Dando. It is Doctor Angel, the *bakalo*, we want for the boy.'

Mihai took a lungful of air to express agreement with the *gicisvara*, but baby Dando suddenly stopped cooing and blasted the air with an ear-shredding cry.

If Damira'd been there, she would've asked me for help, but her mother mistrusts me.

As the four of them tried a number of ineffectual means of calming the baby, I quietly sat down and looked at the spot by my bunk, which Damira used to occupy while she listened to my stories.

The barrack feels empty without her.

As I contemplate the splintery floorboards, I remember another emptiness pierced by another baby's cry that once filled me with a similar hollow aching in other rustic walls, little ways down south from these parts.

*

My son was born when nine months elapsed since the day I had lost Yoska, the fiery rider. He was delivered easily, without causing his mother much pain despite her fragility and narrow hips. He let out his first cry on the Romania-Hungary border, overlooking a Mureş-flooded gorge.

It was some weeks before his birth when Lyuba, who had never previously uttered a whine about the constraints of nomadic life, started asking for a stopover. Even though the perils a shelter would imply far outweighed the comforts, I found it difficult to argue. The coming baby would, admittedly, need minimal stationary conditions. Shandor, after his nephew's demise, saw Lyuba, me, and our future child as his only consolation, so, concerned for the baby's wellbeing, he pitched in on

Lyuba's side. The others too were exhausted and demanded rest.

In the face of their unanimity, I caved in and, despite a foreboding, agreed to seek harbor.

Just as we bypassed the town of Arad in a hurry to move out of the menacing Romania and enter the somewhat more benign Hungary, Lyuba's first pains began. The baby was, eventually, delivered in a vardo, under the neutral skies, before we were able to find a suitable roof for his coming into the world. As an ultimate expression of cosmopolitanism, this circumstance gladdened me, but now, with the screaming little bundle at Lyuba's breast, the search for that roof was becoming even more of an exigency. So I firmly shut out the inner indistinct yet importunate whisper and focused on the task.

The first living soul that we chanced upon on a Hungarian road proved the luckiest find one could hope for.

A full-breasted, wide-bloused, and wide-skirted fairy godmother must have noticed our caravan from afar. She did not hesitate to briskly greet us as she tightened her grip on the reins to hold a bulky, seal-brown Murakoz who was pulling her cart.

'*Üdvözlünk! Ki vagy és hová megy?*' she asked, like they do in fairytales.

Shandor perked up at the sound of his native speech and answered confidently, '*Üdvözlet, tisztelt hölgy. Utazó művészek vagyunk. Olyan helyet keresünk, ahol éjszakát tölthetünk.*'

But it was not Shandor's distinct Hungarian and engaging manner that ultimately won the local patroness over. It was our newborn's timely cry.

'*Van babád?*' she asked. 'You have a baby?'

'Indeed,' confirmed Shandor. 'We do. My grandson. Was born last night.'

As he said so, Lyuba came out of the vardo with the wailing bundle in her arms and bashfully approached the cart to say hello to the lady.

At once a smile of endearment lit up the woman's large face. She beckoned to Lyuba to come up closer. With a caressing gesture, she asked for permission to hold the baby, and, having been handed the tiny body, started rocking it tenderly, babbling and mumbling Hungarian nursery rhymes.

Comfortably sunk in the warm softness of this ample new bosom, it took seconds before the little creature quietened down and went back to sleep. It should be noted that Lyuba's maternal instinct had remained singularly dormant while she was pregnant, and did not seem to awake when our child was born. She wouldn't learn to properly hold, nurse, or bathe him. All the womanly love the girl was capable of must have been spent on me. Lyuba never has, nor will really become a mother, although it is owing to just this peculiarity of hers that she and our son will grow into true soulmates in a distant future, many years ahead from now.

With Shandor in between them as an interpreter, the lady started asking Lyuba all manner of compassionate questions. Where did the pretty darling come from? Was she a gypsy, like her companions? If she just had a baby, why then was she so painfully thin? Did she have enough milk to feed the little angel? And where was the little angel's father?

I showed my face and had a chance to enjoy the mixture of motherly and prurient attention that has invariably sparked in the eyes of matrons across Europe at the sight of me.

'So you left your parents and followed him all the way from Russia, for the sake of love...' she intoned. 'Well, now that I look at him, I guess I can see why.'

All the while the Murakoz, the gentle boy, was standing still, moving his ears and filling the March air with his steamy breath, stoically ignoring Businka's ingratiating neighs and raised tail (our nervous girl had been feeling depressed since Flame-the-Mad had chosen to follow Yoska down the precipice over the Danube).

And then, without taking a minute to think it over, our first Hungarian acquaintance pronounced her decision.

'You people are coming with me. On the road is no place for either the little angel or his mother, the poor emaciated dove. Both need proper care and nutrition, so they will be staying in my house as my daughter and grandchild. As for the rest of you, it looks like there is no safe place now on this continent, but my own village I can vouch for. While I am chief, you shall be out of harm's way.'

We followed Zsófia to her settlement called Változás—about an hour ride from the crossroads where she picked us up.

Outwardly, the quaint little place looked unremarkable. Distanced from the rivers, located in a narrow clearing reluctantly yielded by a gloomy, Russian-like fir and birch forest, it lacked the typical Magyar scenic allure. But it was inconspicuousness, not flashiness, we sought for the time being, so we were hardly disappointed. The good thing was that in times of war, Változás managed to prosper.

Zsófia was a widow, and it had been her late husband, the cheftain, from whom she inherited the position. As nature did not see fit to reward her with motherhood, she compensated for it by treating the village's dwellers as her own children. Under Zsófia's administration, the place had begun to thrive. She was the lawspeaker, the provider, the healer, and the negotiator. She oversaw the farming, distributed the rations, treated the cattle, settled the arguments, and maintained complex diplomacy with the district authorities. She was loved and respected. Her word was law.

Zsófia was also widely engaged in humanitarianism. We were not the first nomads she put up. Numerous Romani and Jewish groups in search of safety from the still banned under Horthy's leadership, yet stealthily fierce Arrow Cross, had found protection in Változás. Indeed, we would've been just some of many such wanderers if Zsófia had not taken a shine to the baby Roman (that's how Lyuba decided to name our son) and extended us a particularly hearty welcome.

Lyuba, Roman, and I got a spacious room in the lady cheftain's timber and stone house. Shandor and the rest wanted to remain in the vardos, but the villagers, fascinated by our horses, insisted we do a show. After a first short performance, the entire *kumpania* got lodgings under various local roofs.

The locals loved us; our hostess treated us with parental care. Things were looking up.

And so it went on, until Zsófia's inexhaustible hospitality allowed new characters to invade our temporary seclusion...

*

There's a stir in the barrack.

I prick up my ears.

It turns out, Petko, on the wave of his recent success with me, Damira, and Dr. Heidert, has tripled his diligence. Now it is Obersturmführer Karp's call yet again, and the prominent is swaggering along the rows, leaning over the bunks, shaking his pockmarked countenance in everybody's face, and quacking out Cabbagehead's will.

'Obersturmführer Karp wants volunteers for the lab! Heard me, stinkies? Clean yourselves up! Obersturmführer Karp is on his way to collect more volunteers.'

There is no shortage of volunteers. Vadim jumps up readily, and Shutka and Manfri. Marusya wants to offer up baby Dando once again, but Baba Tanya and Sashko-the-amputee stop her.

'It is not karp-shmarp we want for Dando. It is Doctor Angel alone we settle for, remember, girl?'

Marusya nods and sits down obediently. Dando is done shrieking and is now smiling and stretching out his dimply arm to grab the tip of his mother's nose.

Guido arrives in a boisterous mood. A bit tipsy too. He punches the able-bodied males in the chest, smacks his lips skeptically at the women, and makes monkey faces at the children. He and Petko form a perfect duo. The latter trots along behind, imitating the Obersturmführer's every gesture and gibe.

Guido is anticipating a jackpot, so who can blame him? A man had better celebrate in advance, for who knows if there will be what to celebrate in the end?

Along with the volunteers, Guido takes Sashko-the-amputee.

Sashko is perplexed. Frustrated, even. He's had his brilliant one-legged future all planned out. Guido's decision comes as a bit of a detour.

Sashko tries to object by saying he has just been released from the infirmary. In fact, he has only recently been operated on. Maybe Obersturmführer Karp is confusing him with someone else he had in mind? Maybe he will reconsider his candidacy?

'*Du kommst! Schnell!*' Guido barks in response.

Apparently the Obersturmführer already knows Sashko's medical history. Apparently Sashko is just what he needs for his research.

'Go, boy, go with Doctor Karp,' Baba Tanya prods him. 'You don't wait for them *gadje* dupes in the streets; you look out for your good fortune here and now. You listen to Baba Tanya. Baba Tanya will not give you bad advice.'

Looking utterly disconcerted, Sashko takes his infirmary-provided crutches and hobbles along with Guido and the three healthy volunteers.

This is the last we see of Sashko-the-amputee.

This is also the last time this barrack shall see a happy, carefree Guido. The events to follow are going to rub the cheerfulness off Guido's well-fed face. The man will find himself embroiled in a hell of a tangle of laborious paperwork, messy menial jobs, lame diplomacy, and other unpleasant tasks in desperate efforts to cover up his roguery. Not to mention the financial loss, of course. But, against the backdrop of all the nastiness to come, the foiled profit plans will strike Obersturmführer Karp as the proverbial drop in the bucket.

*

I follow Guido to the Jewish camp, where he proceeds straight after accommodating his new objects in block 32. Now that the sham research he has launched for the toothie shark of a pharmaceutical is in full swing, Cabbagehead will keep scouring about for whatever extra guinea pigs he can lay his hands on. Gypsy lab meat is more easily obtained than Jewish, but, when push comes to shove, one has to be prepared to take greater risks. One has to pull out all the stops.

Although David is out of danger, I know I must keep a close eye on Guido now. He is too hyper to be harmless. Apart from this, I need a precise record of how many victims he will eventually drag into the lab, and whom exactly. I need their identification numbers, names, and faces.

David greets me with a reproachful look.

'Damira's gone,' I mutter morosely.

He turns away, grabs the cement wheelbarrow, which he dropped when I approached, and trudges off with it.

He disappears for quite a while.

Why do they always have to be so punishing, these sulky loves of my life?

When David returns, he takes as long as possible to refill the wheelbarrow, with his back to me. Then, finally, he faces me and talks.

'You meant the world for that little girl. You were the only real, alive human being she had in her life. You were like an adored and respected big brother. She trusted you. She believed you would protect her. Why didn't you? Was it too much of a task for you, with all the things you can do? Was it so hard to get this precious Heidert of yours to forget all about her, just throw her out of his head, especially in the midst of all the riveting musical fantasmagoria his mind is now occupied with, with your help? Why do you sometimes look after complete strangers but let down those who love and really need you?'

He is even more judgmental than Lyuba ever was, this green-eyed boy. But, thanks to Lyuba, the practice of giving self-justifications as confronted is not new to me.

I give them once again. I start with the inevitable "this is not the way it works." I explain that my "help," however it might be defined, is not attachment-regulated, or relationship-sensitive. I reiterate that it can only take part in those who have been dealt certain cards to begin with. I clarify that it is not even with living beings as such—rather situations—the "help" concerns itself. I add that Damira's situation was not to be meddled in; that interference would have definitely not made things better for her but might have entailed disastrous change for other, associated situations.

As I say all this, I realize how lame I sound. Certain phenomena and verbal expression make lousy bedfellows. David is by no means satisfied. Yet he gives a deep sigh and finally raises his eyes to meet mine. A good sign. Even unconvinced, my idealistic judge seems to have relented.

Meanwhile, Guido appears on the scene in the jolly company of Bushalo Karl. For the lack of a more imaginative means, the two decide on the least resistant way to select lab material. Guido points out a more or less strong and healthy-looking man among the workers. Then Bushalo leisurely walks up to the selected man, and, while the Jew bends over to pick up a tool or refill a wheelbarrow, strikes him with all his might across the back. The Jew who manages to hold his ground stays at the site—there's too much labor potential in him yet to commit him to block 32. The Jew who crashes under the blow is ordered to come along with Obersturmführer Karp; although not yet a *musselman*, he will probably soon become one. The weakling will end up in the oven anyway, so it is just the right time to use him for medical experiments now, while he is still in passable shape.

I keep close tabs on Bushalo's movements. I miss no face, no name, and no number.

Isaac, Boris, Dmitry, Saul… *Kleine Nummer*, all of them. Recent arrivals.

All of them, alas, "situations" that my "help" has no business tempering with.

*

Sullenly, David looks on.

'Later I will have to double check and record the numbers, digit by digit,' I tell him, trying to sound matter-of-fact. 'I may need your assistance.'

The tactic works. As soon as asked to give a hand, he turns and reestablishes eye contact. The tension that almost started to build up again, dissipates. David talks to me once more—still reproachfully, but no longer accusingly. It is curious rather than bitter that he sounds now.

'Say,' he begins. 'Is there any chance of disposing of Karp completely, perhaps? You said once you could not terminate Bushalo just yet because you meant to arrange a more intricate death for him later. Heidert is your pet. Damira's situation could not be reversed. I thought, how about Karp? You want to take his money, right? Is this why you don't want to, say, push him in the oven instead of some condemned inmate, and rescue all these men Bushalo has selected for him?'

I shake my head.

'Absolutely not.'

'Why? Is this really because of the money? Do we have to wait until…'

'No. No, dear. The money will be ours anyway, with Karp dead or alive.'

'Why then?'

'Because…' I sense a good moment, so I move in and get my arm around his waist. 'Because Karp is to swing. Death by hanging is a highly gravitational lot. Cannot thwart that one. Understand?'

Once more, I'm not sure he understands, but this time he surrenders. His hand slips into mine timidly. His shoulder blades grind against my chest. I brush my lips across the slightly protruding bones of his shaved head, find his ear.

While Guido and Bushalo are lost in their game, the others will not be looking our way either.

We have around twenty minutes. Not longer today, regrettably.

It is my second visit here during the evening, and this is the first little reward I get. An unbearably short one, but after a day of Christian's all-embracing envy, Damira's lethal exile, Guido's final selection, and David's resentment, I am grateful, even for this much of what I would like to never end.

*

Indeed, this much—and not more—has the best nutrition value for music. Just enough to mix the right chemical cocktail in the nervous system; not enough to get sated with it.

This is what I plunge straight into doing after Guido leads his newly selected batch away, and David has to go back to work.

The piece I've decided to name Le Storie. The dedication to David, Yoska, Lyuba, and the likes of them. Those dead or alive who have moved me and will do so in the future. Those few ones out there imbued with the inimitable *je ne sais quoi* that makes their opinion count for me.

The format is not yet clear, but, quite spontaneously, Lavuta and I have chanced upon the comet element: a glissando on one string, top down. Easy on the ear, quite novel too. A swoosh at the crescendo—and then a clean cut—flown right past…

*

'This is some strange music you're playing, son.'

Mihai. Sneaks up on me at the moment of the most fervent fiddling; jolts me out of tune.

My own fault. I've been somewhat unfocused since Damira left the barrack.

I lower the baton.

'Not yet playing, Babbo. It's not ready. I'm creating it.'

'Did I stop you when I shouldn't have?'

'You did. But this is for the best. You startled me and gave me an idea of a link I was missing. You've helped.'

He gives an understanding grin.

'How's that gingerhead of yours doing? Mad at you, is he?'

'He was. A little. Not anymore.'

'Your strange music sounds like he still is.'

I shrug resignedly.

'Lavuta knows better.'

He waves his parchment hand.

'You don't worry. He'll get over it. But you keep it in the music. Your strange, angry music sounds right to me.'

*

Then he calls me out.

'Speaking of your "victorious nation," boy. How are they holding up there, in their swamps? Any success? You follow their every step, don't you? Their hugest supporter, aren't you now?'

In the same breath. Mihai will be Mihai.

And how can I let the old man down? I pick up the gauntlet.

'Is it the British you mean, Babbo? Or the Americans? Or the Russians?'

'You know damn well who I mean. The swamp dwellers.'

'This will be the Russians.'

'Yes, your favorite swampy wimps. How are they coming along there, in the east?'

'To the best of my knowledge, they are successfully engaging field marshal von Manstein near the city of Kursk. The Führer has enough on his plate, as it happens—in the Mediterranean. His forces are being diverted to Sicily, and this is going to cost him in the east. Losses, Babbo, grave losses, of men and tanks. The swamp folks are going to grab the strategic initiative and never let go of it ever after…'

'No wonder,' Mihai is as surly as he can be. 'Do you know what they say about the weather in that land?'

'They say, whoever complains about it ought to remember that the climate in Russia is first and foremost aimed at destruction of the enemy.'

He grunts.

'You know everything.'

'Why, of course, I experienced this firsthand, Babbo. I've been there. This used to be a standing joke with us while we were in N.'

'And do you know that their nasty weather is not only the enemy of the Russians' enemy? That it is also the enemy of the Russians themselves, because it sets rot in their heads?'

'You have expounded this theory to me, Babbo. It is a plausible one. I mostly agree with you.'

'Mostly…' He smirks. 'Well, boy, here is something you may not know; I've been to Russia too. I just didn't tell you yet.'

*

I do, in fact, have some knowledge of Mihai's brief sojourn in the maritime city of Odessa, a short while before the war broke out.

'You actually told me about it, Babbo. It was when you and that Pavel fellow ran a barbershop together, correct?'

Mihai doesn't answer. Instead he throws a quizzical look my way, takes snuff, and lowers his eyelids. There is a silence, during which he seems lost in thought—remembering the past? Considering if I deserve an answer?—It's hard to tell, probably both.

After a long pause he decides in the positive regarding the latter and starts telling me the story, somewhere from the middle.

'It was me who scored all the smuggled French brilliantine, and dyes, and shampoo, and shaving cream, and whatnot. Straight from the port, just as those Turkish ships came in. It was thanks to me, that his *sharashka* had the best clientele. I brought in the punters, he pocketed the dough. He would sometimes get whiny about his life—work, relatives, women, and the *sharashka*. Then he'd get drunk at night and sleep it off until two o'clock, and I had to cover for him with the barbers and the clients. Never a thank you I got. Instead, he shortchanged me whenever he could. Jibed at me. Called me *proydokha-tzigan*—"lovingly," as he'd say.

And then once the militia came and busted the *sharashka*. And this Pavel klutz up and took the fall. Said it was himself who ran things with the port smugglers, turned himself in for all the under-the-counter trade we'd pulled. I was standing behind the big client lounge chair when they handcuffed him and led him away. He never mentioned my name. I'd despised him all the while, and he got me off the hook.'

Mihai takes snuff, stares into emptiness, then grins broadly.

'You never know with those Russians. Now they are bastards; now they are heroes. They are like… like the long word you say about something that is one thing, but, also, the other thing around. All in one. What's that word, boy?'

'Paradox?' I venture.

'There. That one. Para-ducks.'

His contentious mood appeased, the old man chuckles.

'Boy, do I miss Vano *schav*! He used to figure out all those clever words for me! You say he's doing well, right, son? And now he speaks

177

German just like you?'

'Right, Babbo. Almost like me. But soon he will speak German and some other languages much better than me.'

'Right, right.' Mihai nods. 'I always said the boy has a future with that bright head on his shoulders.'

Now completely satisfied with the global state of things, the old man dozes off on the bunk while Lavuta and I pick up the unfinished Le Storie just where we left off.

IX
1st Violin

Today was easier than I'd expected. Almost no crumblings. Ah, the blissed feeling of fluid lightness that it brings!

Whenever a crumbling occurs—that is, whenever we have to change something that I've been hearing in my mind all along—be it completely dispose of, reverse, or even slightly modify it—I am afflicted with self-doubt. And a strange kind of self-doubt it is.

The fact remains; all Jass's ideas prove the best thing that could have ever happened to my music. His precise knowledge of what I want as a result and his hunter's instinct in how to get it technically accomplished renders all my hypothetical objections irrelevant by default. And he certainly has a way of convincing me that what he suggests is exactly what I myself conceived of to begin with—I just haven't learned to hear myself properly yet. And then the music sounds so overwhelmingly my own true creation that I am, for the umpteenth time, left speechless, ecstatic, and humble. And then I readily swallow his theory.

But the trace of a muted discord lingers. As if something has been chipped, and never subsequently repaired. A crumbling.

Today was free from those. Every bit of his movements—every expression, touch, and gesture seemed too in accord with mine.

The fluctuating second theme, which had been, I remember, one of my most basic initial findings, was a bit of an effort to retrieve. It took me stopping altogether, and him holding Cosima, pressing it to his chest for a while. Not playing, just holding. Then he gave the instrument back to me, and there it was—unstoppable, unhindered, and stunning—performed by Cosima and me, as if freshly delivered out of my adolescent fever.

The work does indeed take diverse and whimsical forms; occasionally it involves me closing my eyes and him placing his hands on my head one on top of the other, as if he were hypnotizing me; or him holding Cosima and me touching the strings with Siegfried's tip; or him standing behind my back, embracing me and directing my arms while I try to play. At other times, it takes his mere presence for me to proceed for myself.

Only now that I, step by step, sound by sound, have come to weaving my dream into playable cloth with my own hands do I begin to feel the true power of my creation. Only now I see that when Jass first attempted playing it to me, it still had a lightweight, ephemeral quality. Now, at my own, its real meister's touch it is coming alive in all its excruciating tangibility, fully revealing its abysmal emotional depth.

I am now tying up the endless fractionations of the sixteenths with one long melody. Have transferred the sixteenths into the accompaniment, while the melody in the orchestra will be quarters in the subdominal. There remain a couple of episodes to complete; then the time will come to work on the form.

*

Only a little while ago, a period of depressing futility drove me to a state in which I came to believe art and science made poor cohabitants in my nervous system. I even almost forswore music altogether.

Well, from the height where I soar today, that gray patch of miserable stagnation looks like a bad dream. Never have I known artistic expression nourish scientific thought so richly, and to such a fruitful effect as it is happening for me now. The panacea has turned out to be not quitting art but giving it the fullest vent possible, turning it into the powerful tool it has always been meant to be. Now that it is done, Indigo Mind and The Idea finally become facets of one gem. The sparkle of one obscures not—but complements and augments the shining of the other.

The lab work is at full tilt. The progressing of the disease in all the four objects manifests itself precisely according to the scenario dictated by the power of *Force Vitale*. In fact, the degree of accuracy exceeds my wildest expectations.

The children, all admitted at an approximately equal initial stage of the condition, have so far been also showing a strong tendency for following a similar course in its progression.

Damira had a visible swelling on her cheek in the early days; Grisha was marked with just an ulcer at the corner of his mouth the look of which, nevertheless, left little doubt that it was the onset of *cancrum oris*; Mara's sore above her upper lip showed minor pus discharge; Patrin, the youngest of the four, complained of an itchy scar running from the corner of his mouth, almost as low down as to his chin—he wouldn't stop scratching it bloody.

By now, all the four have developed unmistakable peripheral evidence of necrosis around their respective lesion areas. There is apparent purplish discoloration, which followed severe crusting of the lips accompanied with foul odor—again, in all the four cases under study.

But infinitely more revealing than the physiological indications are the moral signs. These gypsy children are, as is their wont, not just resignedly prepared, but willing to accept the physical suffering which is meant to help correct the mistake of their having arrived in this world in the present form. Indeed, they are grateful for this trial. Oh, with what utmost appreciation does little Patrin now trace his elongated lesion with his index finger, with what unchildlike reverence does he compare it with Grisha's roundish erosion! Grisha, who is every bit as clever and mature as Birgitte described him, graciously allows the younger boy to examine his mouth over and over again, touch it—press and pinch at it—although it obviously causes him unbearable pain. Damira does her best to hearten the meek, crybaby Mara, completely ignoring—even, it seems, welcoming—the reek that the girl's putrid upper lip emits (of the four, Mara seems to be working up the greatest amount of pus). Undaunted, Damira hugs the other girl, strokes her head and assures her.

'You are lucky Vano is not here with us, with his scary ghost stories. Vano, ewww, that's who is nasty! We are all lucky he is not here with his ugly faces and mean jokes! If he was, then we would all have something to cry over. Without him, we are the luckiest four in AU!'

Blessed be *Force Vitale*, for its undeniable might and the wonders it works.

*

Blessed be also love. My love for Indigo. The only true feeling in my life. For, from whatever angle I look at it, one fact firmly restates itself; it is by this feeling that my real music is nourished. Same goes for my scientific ideas—for those that are going to leave a trace in the world, anyway. It is to her these achievements are dedicated, no matter if they bear her name or not, or if she was or not the first association that set in motion the breakthrough train of thought. She was always there—an invisible galvanizing presence—an electric spark in my nerves, a conductive current in my bloodstream.

I only hope the magic I am living now should somehow extend onto my love herself.

Will the glorious results I am going to achieve win her over? Will she finally see sense? Appreciate me? See me for what I am? See the two of us for what we have always been meant to be—two souls created for nurturing, augmenting, and completing each other? Bringing each other's potential out to the full; filling each other's depth to the brim?

Will she realize this?

Or should I talk to Jass? I still cannot bring myself to. What if he turns out to already know all about this too, even without my telling him—about Indigo, my feelings for her, her infatuation with the accursed Bernie?

I cannot. This is even more intimate than the music, damn it!

So many things I only wish I could forget. So many.

My graduation concert.

Franz, Oliver, and myself—our glorious trio—the three honored students, the pride of the university, the hope of the academia, the three young doctors, "the Friedrich Wilhelm Maestros"—there we were, lauded, applauded, and loved. Our studies completed, our Bach and Schumann done, we were standing on the stage in the Great Hall, receiving flowers, handshakes, and congratulations. And what was everybody in the hall waiting for? They were all looking forward to that grand encore, to young Meister Christian Heidert's performing his Friedrich Wilhelm Rapsodie (or Mes Études), a piece I'd composed specially for the graduation.

As always, I had been unwilling to play my own music. As always, I had been talked into it. The professors, the alumni, fellow graduates, their parents, and my brothers-in-arms Franz and Oliver, they had all persuaded me.

And why did I agree after all? Who was it for I was really playing? Whose inkblot eyes was I seeking in the audience and never found?

Indigo did eventually show up in her miniature black dress and multiple pearl strings by her adored French designer Chanel. Breezed into the hall at the closure of Mes Études—all flustered, her pale olive, hollow cheeks atypically flushed. Following her close behind, forcing their way past the seated, perplexed spectators were Bernie in a torn black silk shirt and another youth in whom I recognized one of Bernie's latest passions, another disheveled Ernst-Rimbaud type—Tommy? Nicky? I wouldn't be able to recall.

As it was explained later, the young men had been asked to come by Indigo without my knowledge and turned up at the site before she did. As they tried to muscle in into The Great Hall on the grounds that they had been "invited by one of the honors graduates," they were stopped by some Jugend kids who were outraged by their behavior (Bernie and his friend were loudly drunk, publicly holding hands and locking their mouths).

Brought to the police station, they insisted they were a relative of one of the university's late professor, and both were close friends of an honors graduate. Indigo was subsequently located at the entrance into The Great Hall, brought to the station, and spent another hour clearing her cousin's and his friend's names.

The three were eventually released, and allowed into The Great Hall by the end of my encore performance.

Indigo was to never hear Friedrich Wilhelm Rapsodie.

I only wish I could forget.

And forgive.

*

All along the past week, I've been planning a gratitude visit to Birgitte. To tell her how *Force Vitale* work is progressing, thank her for the three invaluable objects she sacrificed to benefit my research; say of what tremendous help her Mara, Patrin, and Grisha are being. Every day I have been setting time, and then deciding to postpone. I could not help feeling stabs of guilt whenever Birgitte came to mind. Those oddly washed with an achy undercurrent of pity, tenderness, and longing, as though for something precious, touchingly vulnerable, and irrevocably lost.

Today, at last, the exceptionally smooth Indigo Mind session in pair with all the evidence of steady success with *Force Vitale* heartened me. Once again, I overcame my misplaced qualms. I felt I could look Birgitte in the eye again. I stopped procrastinating on the visit and confidently crossed Rynek Główny Square.

I found her busy penning down the results of her own study. Her golden hair was offhandedly done up in a loose ponytail; her feet bare. Grisha the dog (who is now grown at least thrice the size I'd picked him up, complete with a low, bossy bark) was thoughtfully chewing on one slipper; the other, already chewed out of shape, was gaping, open-mouthed, from under Birgitte's desk.

Vano (I assume he is the creepy character whom Damira believes she and the other three children in the lab are lucky to be rid of) offered to make me a cup of coffee.

Birgitte, for once utterly unembarrassed by the deep cleavage in her bathrobe, didn't allow me to get a word in edgewise. Unquenchably on about her own work, she lavished love on Vano, explaining to me that without this sweet child's help, tact, discipline, and phenomenal memory, nothing of what she had got done would ever come near to accomplishment.

Remembering Damira's account of Vano, I had half a mind to joke about differences in taste, but decided to contain my witticism. I was there to thank Birgitte for what she had done for me, and I would be atrociously out of order mocking her own achievement, whoever she believed was her helper and guardian angel. So I congratulated her on her success and briefly shared news about mine.

Overjoyed, my gentle Freia jumped up from her desk, squeezed my shoulders, and kissed me on both cheeks.

'I'm so happy we both finally got our main work off the ground, Chris, dear!' she whispered in my ear hotly.

Though the gesture was luscious in appearance—the bathrobe cleavage came so wide open I was allowed almost a full perspective of her pearly-skinned, palely freckled breasts—it was completely devoid of sensuousness. Merely an unconfined expression of friendship, mutual appreciation, and common triumph.

So like Birgitte. So like my sweet-natured autumnal nymph.

I hugged her—warmly, friendly—in return.

My conscience is almost at peace now. Everything has been explained between us. Everything is simple, clear, and sincere.

*

While I was crossing the square on the way back home, an important thought occurred to me. I might even have called it a new bout of inspiration, but it was rather more like an idea. A clear-cut and brilliant one.

Thinking of Birgitte, of her lightness and warmth, I realized that Freia's Reverie, though keep it simple I had tried, was, perhaps, still too overloaded, too pompous a piece to truthfully reflect her straight forward and loving nature.

I decided to reshape the romance. In fact, I decided to compose a new one altogether.

I remembered Birgitte touchingly asking me to say hello to Grisha and the other kids in the lab for her. I replayed in my mind the heart-melting scenes of her caressing Grisha the dog. I could not help admiring her tenderness toward the helper-boy Vano (although he looked thoroughly knavish to me and I didn't trust his snaky smile).

The motherly nature of hers. This was what truly defined Birgitte. Her motherly nature.

I recalled that Freia, as the myths of old relate to us, had two daughters, Hnoss and Gersemi. Freia was a mother. I imagined her leaning over their rustic wooden cradles in an expression of infinite tenderness and care.

It was that warm, mellow, and simple yet divinely feminine element I was now going to try to put across in the music. It was not to be Freia's Reverie. It was to become Freia's Motherhood.

Free from compunction, I closed my eyes and, under the cover of my eyelids, re-pictured the milky hemispheres of Birgitte's breasts. The image was not a lewd one. It was poetic; therefore, I did not begrudge myself a seemingly licentious fantasy. I did not desire Birgitte. I was merely enthralled by her womanliness, motherliness, and lovingness. The vision of Birgitte transformed into Freia nursing Hnoss and Gersemi, her golden curls streaming down, almost covering her naked flesh and her baby daughters' faces. Then Freia metamorphosed into Leonardo's Madonna Litta, and that lofty image, further still—into the one of the Sistine Madonna. Not a breast-feeding theme, but Raphael was perhaps the only one by whom the right degree of sublime concern and care in the eyes had been nailed. He, the Divine Pagan, was the sole artist to have also successfully blended the spirits of Madonna and Freia in one transfixing canvas.

Without opening my eyes, I reached out for Cosima.

Tenderness and simplicity. Love and simplicity. Care and simplicity.

A single movement. Not E minor, F minor after all. A sonata. A light, lacy melody leading up to a clashing theme, yet of a related character. Like two sides of a coin. Then a more restive, uneasy theme—the ultimate concern swelling up to a stentorian climax. Then serenity—a return to initial themes, mildly flowing into an F major denouement.

I played it. I played it again. And again.

As I tried and tried, I became acutely aware of missing Jass's presence. Should he have been there, it would've all come aligned. Without him, I felt stumped. I couldn't tell if it was any good. I needed his guidance.

Maybe I should bury my reservations and talk to him about leading me through this long-suffering composition of mine as well. Perhaps I shall do so.

*

In fact, the reservations which I am, by reflex, still talking about in my head, are nothing but pure inertia.

Indeed, I am done self-doubting.

For by now it is clear as day I have every right to the Gypsy's help with any musical composition I work on, as the civilized world's history screams at us; it is only through a Teuton that an Indian or a pure Romani can transform his florid sonic ramblings into art. Therefore, a Teuton has every right to turn to a pure Romani for a little helping of the ramblings to be able to finalize the art.

Schiller has formulated the law for the future generations to abide by: "Music must become form." The Teutons were the first people to show the world the magnificent fruit of living by this law.

Because, as I it has been established by many an observer, critic, and scholar, the prominence of the musical talent is an intellectual property of the Teutons. Undoubtedly, the Indians also cannot be denied exceptional aptitude for the sonic arts, but, in their rendering, everything blended and drowned in something enormous, overly complex, and, thus, amorphous. The nine hundred and sixty different keys distinguished by Indians excluded any possibility of completion or technical growth.

The Hellenes, in their striving for perfection, took a fling into the opposite extreme. Armed with a mathematically integral but rigidly restrictive musical science, they built up their music so tightly cemented into one block with their verse—music being, as it were, the flesh and blood of the poetry—that it never achieved any freedom, and, for this reason, never evolved in any loftier shape. The melody of speech, not the melody as such, always formed the pivot of Hellenic music. Despite their unquestionable artistic gifts and their certainly being theorists extraordinaire, the Greeks were never able to rid their music of its linguistic fetters; cultivate it apart from poetry.

The Indians, on the other hand, whose sonic art is characterized by such exuberant instrumental embodiment, prefer the format of song as a kind of frame around which to develop their music. Your average gypsy of today unerringly chooses to play nothing except what is based on a definite song; should you tell him that you dislike the tune, that it is incongruous with the spirit of the moment, he will think up a new one or modify an already popular one into something virtually novel. But if asked freely to extemporize, he will be all at sea, and understandably so. For music not borne by a certain poetical movement of the soul is but meaningless juggling with vibrations.

Well, it was neither the Indian (or the Gypsy) nor the Hellene that was the first to truly—harmoniously and intimately—bind up music with poetry.

It was the Teuton.

Enough to remember our Troubadours, who were as much musicians as poets. Enough to call to mind the glorious name of Guido of Arezzo, with whom, the eleventh century onward, our music began its victorious progress toward technical impeccability and tremendous lushness of expressivity. The thorough training of the ear, the step-by-step evolvement of harmonic variations, the marvelous artistic texture of counterpoint, by which music builds itself a temple where it can rule as goddess. We, the Teutons, have attained it all by saddling and bridling the genre of song; by masterfully riding it.

This is what those Gypsies of today freely borrow and use to their advantage. This is why I, a Teuton, am fully entitled to borrow a bit of my own gypsy's witchery, to bring a piece of my music to perfection.

Aren't I?

The Reichsführer-SS maintains that everyone has his special Jew.

In my case, I suppose, I have my special gypsy...

The Reichsführer is indisputably a genius, perhaps only second to Angel in his brilliance. Take, for one, his idea of a living museum for pure

Romani, one which would feature each of the main tribes.

Reminds me of my own idea of a modern type zoo. I have always been against keeping animals in captivity. I believe depriving a noble living being of its freedom is utmost cruelty. If we, on the other hand, consider the rate of the recent technological progress, it is easy to imagine what it can do to our neighbors on the planet in the course of the century; what havoc it is likely to wreak on their natural habitats. In such conditions, one would perforce change one's views and conclude that, as the major predator on the planet, it is the responsibility of man to also be the major rescuer. Be a Noah. Take two of each kind to be saved on his arc; create reservations in which our four-legged fellow creatures will be granted shelter and protection. Perhaps the "zoo" will indeed be their only chance to avoid extinction, but it will be a new type of zoo, where instead being kept in cages they will but roam freely, breed, and hunt.

This is, roughly, along the lines of the Reichsführer's suggestion for the thoroughbred Roma. A project in realization of which I would gladly participate.

I wonder what Jass will say about it. I shall ask him. This might become one more epic decision he will help me make.

*

Another great helper in decision-making is Anton Lauer.

My dear Anton. How boring life would be without his lighthearted company!

Feeling I needed a gulp of fresh air after tinkering around with Freia's Motherhood, I went out to take a stroll down to St. Mary's Church, and, incredibly, Anton was the one I ran into by its red brick walls.

'Is it the dormant Catholic in both of us, simultaneously awakened, Maestro? Or is it my infallible hunch telling me that you miss me and providing me with the precise geographical location where you'd be walking off your sorrow?'

Anton, at his best.

I was happy to see him.

'Your intuition, dear friend, is as keen as ever. And indeed I am here, alone, lost, drowning in questions, thirsty for answers, and subconsciously drawn to this place in search of your wise counsel.'

'In this case, lieber Meister, I suggest we proceed somewhere we could take the load off our feet and talk whatever genius undertakings you're up to over a single malt, as becomes two self-respecting philosophers. I don't know about you, but yours truly is dying for a drink.'

At Anton's insistence, we relocated to U Barbary, just off Leśna. Not a place I would frequent alone, but with Anton, even this sleazy dive can somehow get away with its vulgarity.

I didn't mind. Besides, they do, surprisingly, serve decent whiskey.

As we occupied a table in a dingy corner, away from the drunken Belgians loudly hitting on some tomato-rouged, rustically blond local meat, I started interviewing Anton from afar.

I wanted his opinion, his support—but I meant to disclose no details.

'Do you think the Jews are, in general terms, a nation not devoid of common sense?'

'Is this practical interest?' he hooted. 'Do you mean there is a Shylock you owe a pound of flesh to? Are you concerned he might not agree to refinance?'

Then, quite swiftly, he turned serious.

'Why, I suppose they are. They have proved it many times over. No two ways about it...'

'Do you think they are a wise nation?'

'Well... One can look at the example of the Sephardim for evidence. The genuine purity of the race, plus the expression of true wisdom on the scale of a nation. Besides, even the now frowned upon Ashkenazim have, beyond doubt, shown the world how the wisely applied gift of turning money into more money can be the instrumental force that ultimately pulls the world by the ears out of a pool of excrement.'

'And the Romani? Are they wise people?'

Anton took an unhurried, relishing connoisseurs sip of the whiskey. Raised his eyebrow.

'Most definitely, Maestro. They are. They descend from the Brahmans, don't they? And it were the Brahmans who pronounced the most elevated piece of wisdom onto the civilizations to come. Weren't they? The concept of Brahmanism as silence? That bottomlessly deep idea of language and thought turning away from the great joy of knowledge, as they are unable to reach it?'

The truly wise one here is Anton, who merely feeds me bits of the lecture I myself delivered to him once, in the course of our late-night discussions. This is the trick he pulls every time he doesn't know what to say but wants to come across as historically savvy.

And I welcome this little trick of his, because, unlike myself, Anton makes it all sound convincing.

'So if an Arian... a Teuton, like you or me, were to make use of some Jewish or Romani wisdom in order to make the most of his own contribution to the world... I'm not sure I'm making myself clear, but do you believe it is permissible? Justifiable? Not altogether base or self-degrading?'

'I believe if it is an effective means to an end...' He struck up and lit a Lucky. 'There can be nothing self-degrading about it.'

Then he stirred in his chair, and I almost visibly perceived him pinning his ears back.

'What, are you planning to ask your young noma team for instructions on how to best benefit from their *exitium sui* mechanism? I hear you are working wonders in that lab...'

Anton will be Anton. There are no flies on him. Irony inexhaustible; instinct for success unerring. The inroads I'm making with *Force Vitale* have stolen his rest, I bet. He wants a piece of action, my Peter Kreuder. Angles for co-authorship.

It was now my turn to take a pause and a sophisticated sip of the drink.

'This is, actually, about music,' I said. 'Thought I might use some Gypsy violin for a piece of gratitude I'm composing.'

I surprised myself with how pleasing it was to suddenly deliver the unplanned truth.

The joke, this time, was on Anton. Music appeared to be the last thing on his mind in regard with our conversation. It was, therefore, perfectly safe to tell him that much of what was really going on.

'Wow, really?'

He could barely contain his disappointment. 'Great to hear you're composing again... A piece of gratitude, you say? Am I allowed to ask who the gratitude is to? Or is it a secret?'

'It is not a secret. I am grateful to Birgitte, and the piece will be dedicated to her. I will never be able to thank her enough for the help in my noma work.'

Leaving Anton Lauer puzzled and wondering is no small feat.

I had that achievement to congratulate myself on. I also had his—an impeccable Arian's, a brilliant doctor's, a gifted musician's, and a good friend's—support and approval of what I had been doing hitherto and would do henceforth.

Disconcerted as he momentarily felt, Anton could not now take it back.

*

We were about to take our leave and move on to the cafeteria when Guido Karp emerged in the doorway of U Barbary.

It would be no exaggeration to say Guido was looking his best. The flawless *feldgrau* shirt, jauntily open at the neck. The ruddy complexion pleasantly paled a tone; the straw-color hair, for once, styled and dashing (Guido has recently started growing out a cowlick). He even appeared to have slimmed down somewhat—at least his face looked leaner.

His loud joie de vivre was still there, however.

'So how do you like those wops, brothers?' He boomed straight from the door, ecstatic to find me and Anton at the place of booze and debauchery.

'I mean, this shitface Mussolini never fooled me—an out-and-out weakling with a big voice and no balls he has always been, and a shameful buffoon.'

Guido took out a handkerchief and blew his nose loudly, in a scornful gesture.

'But that the crony Badoglio should think he can go blowing hot and cold on us—this truly beats it, brothers! Well, our boys are now giving them what for, those *Makkaronifressers*! Leading them a merry Bella Ciao. Let's see if their newly found friends, the Saxons—or is it really the Yankees?—can save them now!'

Anton Lauer did not deliver me from the society of Guido Karp.

Instead, Anton masterfully, mysteriously disappeared—practically dissolved into thin air—while Guido was raging and fuming about the Italians and their disloyalties. Well, Anton is no admirer of Guido's inelegant loudness.

Next thing I knew, I was seated at the same corner, with Anton gone, and Guido in Anton's chair across the table from me, with a quarter pint of whiskey.

'What we need is more objects, brother, more recent arrivals… We are doing great; we are doing swell. And not that we are short, but we would totally roll if we had a dozen more, you know, just in case.'

All I could glean from his drink-slurred outpourings was that he felt immensely proud of himself, that he wanted something from me, and that both were in regard with Farma-Ko business.

'Do you think you couldn't try and get me some of those? Some *Kleine Nummer*, I mean? Angel still likes you more than anyone else; you have his ear. He'd do it for you.'

He shouted for a top-up, slapped the buxom waitress on the backside, and belched loudly.

'If only you could get me those, and perhaps also some control…' He yawned; took a sip. 'We could double the profit. We would be in clover, amigo.'

*

I remember effortlessly shaking my head and explaining to him that I wanted to hear nothing of Farma-Ko anymore. That there were truly marvelous things occupying my mind these days, and I had no desire whatsoever to spoil my present disposition with all the worthlessness I'd consciously and wholeheartedly washed my hands of.

I reminded Guido he had been the one who insistently asked me to arrange for the project to be given over to him, and, his wish granted, assured me he would be taking it from there—completely so—for which, I stressed, I was to this day grateful to him.

I felt no remorse telling Guido so. Nor did Guido seem to feel any resentment.

Having allowed me to speak my mind, he raised a hand in a defensive gesture.

'All right, all right, all right, sorry for bringing this up, brother. I know you want nothing to do with this. You've told me so many times. Apologies. We shall go there no more. Promise.'

He did not even attempt to entice me further with those "profits" he had been obsessively on about the last weeks. The subject was honestly and completely dropped—a tactfulness I would've never expected from Guido Karp.

Instead, he started telling me about his elderly mother; his young sister Claudia, who had recently gotten married. A girl he used to know in Karlsruhe. Several girls, in fact. One, he said, a gingerhead, looked exactly like "the manipulative vixen Birgitte."

Birgitte's name rang like an alarm clock.

I knew I had to be off. I wanted to reach home while I was somewhat intoxicated, but before I got drunk. I meant to use that state of the nervous system to try and work a little more on Freia's Motherhood.

I firmly stood up and made my excuses, leaving Guido to hit upon the plump waitress.

Guido did not mind at all. He nodded lightheartedly, almost in Anton Lauer's fashion, and wished me a wonderful evening.

I must admit I find quite agreeable what Guido's attitude has been of late.

*

The moment I brought Siegfried to Cosima's strings, I thought I was holding the sonata in my hands. Those light ripples, those lacy vibrations on the tips of my fingers.

As I approached the first clashing theme, however, I knew it was all… not wrong. Just deficient. Incomplete.

Generally, I was on the right track. But something was missing. Yet again.

The realness. The sensuousness. The effortlessness. The texture, the truth.

Jass was missing.

And I patiently, with parental care, put Cosima back in her case. I placed Siegfried by her side to stand vigil over her.

Let them rest. I shall not force them. Not until Jass is around to ease our interaction. To add the missing agglutinant that makes us one.

I reasoned, since I had Anton's (a highly respected independent party's) approval, I should not anymore question my inalienable right to get the Gypsy's help—in as many creative endeavors of my own as I wish. Indigo Mind. Freia's Motherhood.

It was all justified. All worth it.

The thought of Anton prompted me to cast a glance at the present he had given me on my birthday. The one I had been keeping on the shelf, jealously. The record of his operatic idol, Rosa Ponselle.

My general disapproval of Anton's leanings toward all things American many a time urged me to argue with him bitterly, asserting doubtless superiority of Flagstad, or Lehmann—the glorious Wagnerian sopranos—over the obscure, Connecticut-raised, Italian immigrant. Having, however, once heard Ponselle's rendition of Einsam in Trüben Tagen, I had to admit that with all Flagstad's epic grandeur, Bori's feline tenderness, or Gigli's caramel mellifluousness, Rosa Ponselle stood somehow apart.

Not only did she encompass all the best qualities of her rivals. Her voice—sumptuous, mysterious, and infinitely complex in layering— also had one unique property. It did not just engage your ears. It flowed, in a luxuriant sonic stream, straight through your nervous system. A musical ablution Anton called it, and I could not help but share his feelings. Even the majestic Caniglia failed, it seemed, to reach that degree of sensuousness, inconceivably combined with purity.

The record slipped out of the charcoal-grey sleeve into my hand, and I cautiously put it onto the gramophone. Lowered the needle.

"Casta Diva, che inargenti
queste sacre antiche piante,
a noi volgi il bel sembiante
senza nube e senza vel..."

The scintillating voice heaved—a wave of ominous power; an enchanting threat.

"Tempra, o Diva,
tempra tu de' cori ardenti tempra ancora lo zelo audace,
spargi in terra quella pace
che regnar tu fai nel ciel..."

Bellini's heathen, passionate Norma, the druid priestess, always struck that innermost chord with me. Touched on the ever-aching string.

The Brünnhilde string.

So many similarities.

The brave creature throwing herself on the pyre, driven by the unresolved love that burns hotter than the flames.

The wild, dark-minded, and noble pagan.

"Quando il Nume irato e fosco,

Chiegga il sangue dei Romani,
Dal Druidico delubro
La mia voce tuonerà.
Cadrà; punirlo io posso.
(Ma, punirlo, il cor non sa..."

The proud, white-tunic-shrouded figure, the pale brow, the striking eyes, and the cloud of unruly dark hair on the sleeve that I still held in my hand inevitably ignited another agonizing association.

Indigo, of course.

The love of my life.

My Brünnhilde. My Norma. My deity, and my priestess. My tormentor, and my healer.

"Ah! bello a me ritorna
Del fido amor primiero;
E contro il mondo intiero...
Difesa a te sarò.
Ah! bello a me ritorna
Del raggio tuo sereno;
E vita nel tuo seno,
E patria e cielo avrò...)"

No matter how my day, my dream, and my work or my rest should begin, it is always Indigo who is its opening and closure.

Why would the erratic creature be so privileged?

Why would I be so mad?

Is this a curse?

Is this a blessing?

X
2nd Violin

It is not the monetary reward nor the hilarious consequences that makes it all worthwhile in the long run. The former is too material, the latter too surreal to deliver undiluted creative joy.

It is the object's face that ultimately does it.

Guido's face was priceless. I only wished David could be there to share the spectacle with me. My green-eyed partisan certainly deserved the prize, after all the work he'd put in.

All the information he'd collected for me through his ubiquitous Polish-Jewish grapevine. About the brave German boys breaking out in a red rash in Naples. Clutching at their tummies in Sicily. Hawking—dry and phlegmless—in Kharkiv. Vomiting their guts out in Smolensk.

The frontmost destinations Farma-Ko has been delivering their new development to, with Dr. Karp's full, laboratory-tested endorsement and educated rubber stamp.

All the freshly, in-the-field obtained data he dutifully compiled for me about our own AU sacrificial lambs thrashing about and dying in block 32, with the same symptoms as their German co-sufferers. Purposely infected, Farma-Ko drug-treated under Dr. Karp's supervision. Isaac, Boris, Dmitry, Saul, Boiko, Sashko, Manfri, Shutka, and Vadim. All the names and numbers were neatly recorded.

Never to be deleted.

Never to be forgotten.

Well, I admit having allowed myself some artistic license with the names of the German officers. If they were not as precisely taken down as those of the AU victims, then at least they were devised carefully enough to sound true to life.

Every time David provided me with new numbers, names, symptoms, and whereabouts, Lavuta and I got my favorite object, Chris Heidert, itchy for another session. And, when Chris called us around, we safely drove him into the state of complete submission. The one in which he fiddled on believing he was playing by himself, and forgot all about us.

Meanwhile, I got hold of Angel-stamped and signed blank sheets on his desk. Along with his Remington and Olympia Elite. Then I spent a fruitful hour drawing up evidence. As I typed away, Christian, mesmerized, accompanied me on Cosima, frantically playing out the ideas I was transmitting to her strings.

Today the day has finally come.

After two hours treating Christian with violin therapy, I safely sent him home—drunk on his own genius creation coming, note by note, into life under my unobtrusive instructions.

While Dr. Heidert went off to enjoy well-deserved rest, I stayed behind in his office. It did not take Lavuta much effort to get both him and Petko amnesiac regarding my biological existence for a couple of hours and leave me in the block, all by myself.

Guido showed up some twenty minutes after Chris left, just as expected. Drunk—as expected, too. High-spirited—all his immediate needs having been indulged and satisfied in U Barbary, where he was coming from.

Dr. Karp's office is, these days, next door to Dr. Heider's. For Dr. Karp is, these days, an important man.

And, that door left ajar by the office's merry resident, I had the pleasure to observe his reaction to the pack of papers I had previously planted on his desk—on top of many other papers, files, and folders.

I had the utmost joy to contemplate his jaw dropping gradually—millimeter by millimeter—as the ripe fruit of David's and my labor sank in. The fat package of evidence was accompanied with a brief note asking Dr. Cabbagehead to kindly put all the RM received from Farma-Ko (namely nine hundred at this point—good to buy a modest Volkswagen) in an envelope and leave the envelope at his favorite *knajpa* U Barbary, tomorrow, sharp <u>at eight o'clock</u> in the evening, on the table in the corner—the one which he was a patron of.

In case of non-compliance, the typed note went on to say, the attached bulk of documentation confirming numerous German and AU inmate deaths from the faulty drug shall be forwarded straight to the Reichsführer's desk.

We are watching your every step, Dr. Karp, warned the anonymous typist. *We strongly advise you to cooperate, lest you see your career finish before a firing squad, for High Treason.*

*

'Chloya, the barmaid, is one of us, Babbo. She is collecting the dough. Then, through Vatslav—the technician in the Jewish camp—she will pass the envelope to David.'

'Hold-hold-hold there, boy!' Mihai interrupts, leaning forward in anticipation of his favorite part of the story. 'Tell me the barmaid bit once again! What does she look like? Tell me!'

As Mihai, the obedient disciple of Baba Tanya, is no respecter of Obersturmführer Cabbagehead (the *gicisvara* famously holds Guido in disdain, prophesying that "karp-shmarp will never get anywhere"), he is delighted with my meting out a bit of justice at Guido's expense. Although he doesn't understand nor really cares to know the particularities of the scheme, he finds it the most epic act of *Bujo* he has ever heard of. But the most delicious detail for Mihai is the envoy of ours—Chloya, the barmaid at U Barbary. Ever since I first described our voluptuous ally, he has been demanding more elaborate descriptions.

Through Chloya's fiancé Vatslav, I contrived to obtain a full-size photo portrait of her, especially for Mihai.

The moment Mihai laid hands on the precious sepia became, it seemed, not just the climax of his months in AU but of his entire lifetime.

He now keeps the photograph in his trousers. He takes it out when he thinks nobody's watching and contemplates it for hours, with a dreamy smile. He quietly talks to it at night, by the moonlight.

The feelings for the succulent Pole appear to have even surpassed Baba Tanya's formidable influence on Mihai's world. Our political activist is going through a massive outburst of concupiscence, which I, for one, find an optimal application for his abundant free time.

Although Mihai now has an actual photograph of the belle, he, as a true sensualist, still indulges in listening to verbal descriptions of her, and I dutifully provide new ones for him to relish.

'So, this Chloya maid, she has got long curls, the color of ripe wheat, right, boy?'

'That's right, Babbo. And a tiny dimple in her left cheek.'

Mihai casts a stealthy glance at the photograph for confirmation.

'Correct, correct. You've told me so. A dimple.'

'So she's picking up the *lové* for us, this toothsome wench.'

Mihai fidgets and giggles and rubs his hands. He even pats me on the back, lovingly.

'And she will continue doing so,' I go on. 'For as long as Cabbagehead continues to receive it from the fraudulent pharmaceutical I told you about.'

'And how long will it be, son? I mean, how much *lové* will you and David kid shake out of him?'

'Quite a lot, Babbo,' I say. 'Enough to keep us afloat for the first months that we're out.'

While Mihai is thrilled with the idea of Guido's mammon of unrighteousness going to steadily flow into my pocket over the coming months, I must admit I exaggerate a little for Mihai's benefit. The curtain for Farma-Ko will fall earlier than the term needed to ensure David's and my complete financial comfort. The good pharmaceutical's board of directors will get too carried away all too soon, its foul practices will leak, and the rivaling Farben will be only too happy to abordage them in an act of a most annihilating merger, under threat of turning the culprits over to the Gestapo. Thereby, Farma-Ko will disappear from the market, and its name as an independent entity will be wiped off the map. In other words, Farben will treat Farma-Ko pretty much the same manner David and I are treating Guido.

As for the latter, just like I said before, his personal hell hiding his sloppy tracks is only beginning.

The funds that Farma-Ko will transfer to David and me within the relatively short time left before its debacle are going to be partly spent here in AU. There are arrangements to be made, mouths to be shut, and tears to be dried. There is an All American Five receiver to be obtained for the Jewish camp (Marek-the-architect's special request). There are some pretty dresses to be bought for Rosa to facilitate her first steps outside (for all her cool, the epileptic will feel lonely and lost the first months after she gets out, even though some incredible and unexpected patronage will come her way), and I owe it to Boiko to render her some—if only minimal—support. There is a number of baby things to leave behind for little Dando—the only future AU survivor in his family. There's snuff to be got for Mihai while he is still around.

And then, there is the time I spend with Christian that imposes its own requirements. Our communication is getting increasingly intense. We discuss philosophy, literature, art, politics, and science. I feel I may need some books to swot up on a couple of subjects.

I do enjoy our clashes—those brief moments in between creating Indigo Mind. The numerous disagreements, the heated discussions—and, in the end—the inevitably shared conclusions.

It is in these conversations with him, my Young Werther, that I come to fully appreciate the touching, friendly quality of the German language, despite all the seemingly unwieldy words. How well-organized and logical, how gently forthcoming and self-explaining the language of Goethe is, as compared to, say, snobbish, metaphor-obsessed English, or the self-indulgent, "tongue-twisting" French!

You only realize you are in love with the German language when you discuss the world's deepest wisdom in it.

As Young Werther swims and drowns, dies, and rises back to life in his ostinato sea, I navigate my own psycho-sonic universe.

I experiment, practice, and exercise.

Chris wonders how it is possible for Lavuta and me to operate on his mind and on Cosima's strings by, so to speak, retrieving ideas from his cerebellum and uploading them to his cerebrum.

I set myself a different challenge.

I'm interested in how to get Chris and Cosima to play out my own ideas. Or, rather, what level of precision can be achieved in this process?

Every now and again I throw in an allegro giocoso of my own into a movement of Indigo Mind; or work a number of themes into a rondo; or variate Christian's favored D minor with E minor.

Cosima follows Lavuta's lead with endearing German pedantry; Chris implants my interventions into his vision as readily as a sweet-natured child would accept his parent's version of a fairytale. Enraptured, enthralled by the abilities of his own mind—its potential for innovation he could hardly have conceived of hitherto.

I find it touching to see Chris so moved, but what truly fascinates me is not him playing Indigo Mind, even with generous helpings of my creativity, which he adopts to be his own.

The greatest psycho-sonic indulgence for me is having Chris and Cosima create Le Storie under Lavuta's and my guidance, with zero awareness on their part. That's done in the brief intervals between our work on Indigo Mind—and that I deem the only fitting reward for my troubles.

*

Le Storie, the one thing I don't talk about with David. The piece is dedicated to him, so not until it is completed I cannot. Has got to be a surprise.

Yet I don't intend to finish Le Storie before Chris is done with Indigo Mind. The pieces have to be created in parallel, by my mind and Chris's hands—it makes the entire experiment twice as captivating.

It's a shame I have to be keeping it secret from David. The green-eyed Mr. Curious would've had a million questions; the musician and explorer in him would've been enthralled.

Well, he will ask those questions one day, and I will answer. As a bonus gift to Le Storie, which I hope he will like...

For now, David and I have other, more pressing matters to discuss. Our first harvest of Farma-Ko's funds, for example.

Today we are busy taking orders. I know exactly what's needed for the Gypsy camp; the Jewish camp has a number of needs too. Apart from Marek's radio, we get a request for a blanket from Shlomo. Max would like toothpowder to last for some time. Abi wants pens and pencils. Most want food and cigarettes.

Normally, within AU, such commodities might be "organized"— obtained by means of slavish work and draconian arrangements made with Kanada servicemen.

David and I can circumvent the ordeal, and free the others from the necessity to "organize." We can buy. Purchase—from the outside, not off the bodies of those sent to suffocate in the ovens.

Vatslav-the-guard and his buxom fiancé Chloya-the-barmaid are going to be our faithful procurers from now on—Farma-Ko's investments will ensure their loyalty.

Money talks.

But it is not only money that motivates people. Many around us here in AU—including Chloya and Vatslav, who are and will be going the extra mile for us—would be doing just the same without any material coaxing.

Incredible, but a fact.

What truly stimulates them is being entertained. The Guido story has gotten around. The local folks are well acquainted with Obersturmführer Cabbagehead and harbor different degrees of negative feelings toward him, ranging from downright hatred to plain squeamishness. They are clamoring for continuation of the show—and it has been promised.

Panem et circenses—even highly moral human beings in the direst circumstances will overtly or covertly crave them.

So too it was in Változás, the village of our Hungarian benefactress Zsófia. It was for the entertainment that the people of the settlement embraced us.

'They would've probably gone on embracing us,' I tell David. 'If it hadn't been for another remarkable trait of human nature. Two remarkable traits, to be more exact. Gullibility and innate passion for witch-hunting.'

Since I lost Damira as my most grateful listener, it is David's ear I've been bending with my past. The green-eyed darling, bless his heart, is patient with me.

I mean the story of how I was separated from Lyuba, my son, and Shandor as an object lesson in what people are capable of doing, but David doesn't seem to be taking it as a lesson at all. After an hour of meticulously penciling down everybody's orders, he is happy to place his shaved, finely-shaped head on my lap (much like Damira used to do) and listen to whatever tales I tell—just relax and be entertained. For nothing human is, thankfully, foreign to David.

*

The moment I saw that heart-shaped face and brick-red braids, I knew our sojourn in the hospitable Hungarian settlement was coming to an end. I also knew that, for me personally, a whole stage of my life was about to be over, vigorously ousted by a new one. What new one—I at the time had yet no way of knowing. I just felt there would be trains and faces. A light-limbed silhouette against white snow; sparkly, speckled eyes. Nothing more.

*

I spotted them from afar.

Zsófia's house was immediately in front of the main Változás's gate, and the gate was open. I was standing on the timber-frame porch, which I'll never forget, leaning on a beam, enjoying a cup of morning coffee (real coffee—Zsófia and the villagers had the luxury in the times that even potatoes were scarce) made by Lyuba.

I saw them in their festive pinks, reds, and yellows, with similarly colorful sacs across their shoulders, with their boisterous kids in tow. They were coming out of the fir and birch tree forest. They were noisily walking toward us.

'*A vendégek!*'

A vendégek. The guests. That word was repeated many times.

Zsófia went out to greet them with a broad smile; so did, it seemed, the entire village.

Immediately they flooded the tiny square in front of the gate, filled the mellow early autumn air with their merriment. There were around fifteen of them, together with the children, but their presence felt like a crowd of at least fifty. They played a lot of music—accordions, guitars, and harmonicas. They sang and danced; clutched their feathered fedora hats; hugged the villagers; and slapped the children. Zsófia glided busily amidst them, hugging, kissing, and pinching cheeks, like a happy mother hen.

At some moment I became aware of a pair of eyes zeroed in on me. Greenish-yellowish eyes, the color of unripe acorn. High cheekbones. Full hips.

Separating herself from the crowd, she moved toward Zsófia's house, straight at me. She was biting on a green apple. I heard the crunching between her glistening teeth, saw sweet and sour juice trickling down her dirt-stained chin along the side of her scruffy-fingered hand and her sun-browned forearm all the way to her pointy elbow.

She halted in front of the porch, never taking her two unripe acorns off me. Her moist lips parted.

This was when Lyuba came out onto the porch, with baby Rom in her arms. She approached me and placed her head on my shoulder.

'Would you like more coffee?' she asked languidly, rocking the baby against my left side.

Their eyes met.

The stranger threw the apple stub into the dust under her feet and took her thumb between her lips. Sucking on it noisily, she slowly turned and went back in the direction of her tribesmen.

*

They were part of an extensive Romungre *kumpania*; they spoke some Carpathian Romani, but mostly Hungarian. Barnat, the leader, had some long-standing ties to Zsófia based on an old friendship with her late husband. It was said they'd shared decades of mutual assistance. Exactly what kind of assistance I never quite figured out, but the exuberant reception the villagers gave him and his people made one think they were all not only permanently indebted but also sincerely grateful to him.

And, looking at the *vendégek,* it was hard not to share the locals' feelings for the convivial group. Except for their overly noisy ways, they were the most pleasant people imaginable—warm-hearted yet straightforward. They took a shine to us from the start—wanted to know all about us, see the show, even partake in it. Shandor and the bubbly Barnat got on like a house on fire: it had been a long time since I saw Shandor so talkative in his native Magyar—even Zsófia had never been able to draw him out that successfully (a common childhood language combined with a common ethnicity must've worked as some super-powerful conductor).

They arrived in the morning; on the night of that day, on Zsófia's instruction, five long wooden tables were placed in a long line across the square in front of the main gate, and a feast was thrown in the honor of the *vendégek*. There was the Hungarian bold Egri Bikavér by the jug, lángos bread, a variety of cheeses, Változás-grown vegetables, and fruit. There was, of course, music galore—Danior and I joined the newcomers' guitars and harmonicas for a hearty jam; at some point a tightrope was stretched in between two mighty old oak trees (the village's pride and subject of local legends), and Yanoro performed some of his pièces de résistance; Laila and Tomka danced with the *vendégek*'s frolicsome kids and chirruped away with their mothers—festive, flirty in their frilly skirts—for the first time in a long while enjoying the spirit of a true holiday. Even Lyuba, though burdened by her early motherhood, did not look exhausted that evening. Her morning spirit of languid sensuousness lingered on—she seemed uninterested in socializing with the others but gave all her attention to me instead, leaning on my shoulder, stroking my chest casually, or playfully biting me on an earlobe. Now I'm thinking back, I realize Lyuba was instinctively marking her territory. And she had every reason to be doing so, for across the table from us the acorn-eyed apple devourer sat, never taking her clouded stare off my face.

As dusk fell, fairy lights were lit above the tables, and Zsófia's gramophone was played. The women took the children by the hands and led them in a circle dance around the tables. The men joined in.

In the middle of the castanet-clicking Rio Rita, baby Rom suddenly started crying on the porch, awaken by the vivacious pasodoble. Lyuba hurried to the house to attend to him.

The moment she was gone, my wrist was grabbed by a hot female hand. A steamy whisper moistened my ear.

'Come with me.'

Every time I know a portion of existence lies beyond my powers of fiddling with it, I know it by one sure parameter: I feel an irresistible desire to play along, however absurd, dangerous, or even ugly it may appear. That desire is final—I never, even remotely, have the sufficient amount or the right quality of power to withstand it. This is how I know.

This is how I knew then.

She pulled me by the hand past the scampering children, the dancing adults, the endless tables, through music and twinkling lights, into the darkness. Around the little square, behind Zsófia's house, into the barn. In fact, she halted right in front of the entrance first and asked me for a smoke. Her voice was coarse, yet had incongruously capricious, girlish undertones.

I gave her a cigarette and matches. She lit up.

'So,' she began slowly, after taking a deep drag and blowing the smoke in my face. 'You live with that *gaji*? And her *chavo*—yours too?'

In the darkness, her face blurred into a puffy inkblot. There was something of an inkblot to her entire frame—sloppy, brazen, wrong, and indelible. She threw the half-smoked cigarette, unextinguished, under her feet—brusquely—like she'd thrown the apple stub earlier that day. She snatched my hand again, pushed the barn door, and pulled me along.

Her breath was steamy, like that of the horses. Her nails sank into the skin of my forearms.

'Pull my hair,' she said. 'Pull it hard.'

I did so.

Getting hold of her two rope-like braids, I wrapped them around my arm. I pushed her down on her knees, pressed her face into my groin, and smeared it all over my crotch.

She tore at my trousers, gnawing on the belt, and biting off the buttons.

She sucked my flesh in like a hungry, greedy vampire.

Before I climaxed, she demanded I enter her.

I lifted her to her feet and propped her against the stable. She hoisted her skirt.

As I penetrated her, I covered her lips with mine. She tasted of soil and blood.

Pressing on my head, clutching my buttocks, she forced me deeper into her mouth and into her vagina. She smashed her tongue against mine. She thrusted and writhed, growled, wheezed, and hissed.

Before we finished, I had to place my hand over her mouth, for fear her howling might drown out both the horses' neighing, and the music outside.

When finally it was over, she slid down to my feet, curled her arms around my legs, and covered my groin with noisy kisses, frantically murmuring in intervals between them, "You're mine, you're mine."

I stroked her hair absently. For some time—maybe minutes, maybe seconds—my mind went blank.

What abruptly brought me to my senses was a panicked cat's scream, immediately followed by a jerky movement around my knees and a throaty yell.

'*Teh kurel tut jooklo!* Dirty animal!'

She sprang to her feet and made a sharp leg movement, aiming to hit something.

There was another plaintive cat's cry. I saw two horrified feline eyes flash eerily and caught a glimpse of the little animal retreating through the crack under the door.

'Filthy beasts they are. Lick their own assholes,' she said, whipping her skirt with her hands frenziedly, trying to brush off the fur that might've accidentally stuck.

'Don't you hate them?" she asked in a softer voice, looking up at me. "They are creepy, no?'

I pulled up my pants. Holding them at the fly with one hand, I firmly moved her aside with the other and went out of the barn.

*

Zsófia was still outside with the guests; Lyuba was in the house with the cooing Rom in her arms. Upon seeing me, she put him swiftly into the large basket we used in place of a crib and came up to me. I was still holding my trousers up with one hand, but she ignored that. Instead, she looked me in the eye—not accusingly or reproachfully—just attentively.

'She is going to cause you to leave me, isn't she?'

As was her way, Lyuba was not really asking—she was affirming.

I looked away.

We both knew the answer, much like we always did. I was just unprepared to discuss it right then. But Lyuba was not going to spare me the discussion.

'Have you obliged her?' she demanded.

I nodded silently.

'But you will not be able to anymore.' she stated.

I shook my head. 'I won't.'

She sighed—deeply and painfully.

'I'd rather you went on obliging her than she caused me to lose you.'

'Don't worry. Causing something like that is way over her head.'

Lyuba said nothing. Instead, she went to the doorway and picked up Mitsa, Zsófia's cat, who was sitting on the threshold grooming herself, getting over the knock she'd recently taken in the barn. Scratching the animal under the chin, Lyuba took her to the corner where the cat's bowl stood, poured fresh milk into it, and placed the cat down in front of the bowl.

While Mitsa was lapping up the milk, Lyuba did not for a moment stop stroking her silky calico fur. Mitsa purred audibly.

*

I did not completely lie to Lyuba. Litka was not to be the cause of our separation. The true cause lay in the time that got ripe. Litka was just a tool.

As autumn moved on, swathing the skies in a pearly veil, splashing ochre and burgundy over the trees, mellowing the sun, and edging the air, Shandor got increasingly more confidential with Barnat. These two spent hours in the fir and birch tree forest walking the horses, or riding them in the field that lay beyond; or tinkering around with the vardos, or some villager's fence, or cart, or roof; or simply lounging on the yellowed grass, smoking and chatting. Sometimes they came over to Zsófia's and spent an evening entertaining her and Lyuba with jokes, playing a game of chess with me, or nannying little Rom like two tenderest grandpas.

There was another circumstance adding to the idyllic picture.

Our vivacious chatterbox Laila fell for one of Barnat's lads, Gabor, and the attraction was mutual. As a decent *chivala*, in order not to commit a *bino*, Gabor ceremonially requested an audience with Shandor and begged for his permission to woo the flirty creature.

That having been granted, Gabor and Laila took to whiling away whole afternoons leaning on the fences, which Shandor and Barnat mended, eyeing each other longingly, holding hands, and exchanging sweet nothings.

To say that during those months Litka fiercely persecuted me would be an overstatement. All she ever did was emerge from around the corner when I was alone outdoors, approach with a semblance of a sassy smile, and ask for a smoke. Upon receiving what she asked for, she'd smirk for another second or two, but, as soon as I started walking on past her, she would pull an angry face and scowl in my back.

That was all. Not once did she attempt following me, grabbing my hand again, or offering herself openly.

Then one day I was in the yard with baby Rom, introducing him to Businka. Holding the swaddled little body in my stretched-out hands, I brought him up close to the horse's head so that he could look straight into her chocolaty eye. Rom was giggling along with the horse's soft neighing. Gabor and Laila stood nearby, admiring our father-son pastime.

'Thick as thieves they are, eh?' Litka's husky voice came out of the blue.

This time she'd approached from behind. Her red hair was loose, her face made up. I noted that with cosmetics on, it looked scruffier than ever.

'Thick as thieves,' she repeated, pointing her finger at Gabor and Laila. 'They are. Only you and I are not. Pity.'

Casting a murderous glance at Businka and Rom who immediately started whimpering in my hands, she turned away and walked off.

*

Once I was returning from an outing in the woods—it was my turn to run Businka and Ezme.

Walking across the little clearance toward the main gate, I saw a kid perched atop the fence—one of Barnat's bunch. I remembered he was called Balint, and he was as pretty a child as the sound of his Hungarian name—flaxen curls and blue eyes. That Balint boy had usually seemed quite sweet-natured—smiley and cuddly, much like everyone in Barnat's company. This time, however, he was sticking his tongue out and making faces at me.

Businka jibbed and gave and offended whinny, as if the slight was directed at her personally. Ezme echoed.

Then I knew something was amiss.

I wasn't surprised—I'd been expecting it any day. I was only wondering what method Litka had eventually chosen to get back at me.

The answer came soon enough.

Zsófia met me at the gate with a nervous smile and, coming in between the two horses, started stroking their manes and speaking—in a muted, fast voice. Most of her monologue was lost on me (my Hungarian was still in the germinal stage). The only words I made out clearly were "Lyuba *a lányom*", "Rom *az unokám.*" "Lyuba—my daughter." "Rom—my grandson." Several times, as she pronounced Lyuba's name, she covered her ears with her hands, then placed one hand over her mouth, and made several short, low, mooing sounds. I understood. "Lyuba is deaf and dumb."

Then she walked with me and the horses to the house, continuing to talk—now in her normal voice and a business-like manner.

There was quite a crowd on and around the porch: several villagers, two Barnat's men, some children, and Litka, who smacked her lips at me. There were all of ours—Danior, Yanoro, Tomka, Laila, looking bewildered.

I led the horses into the stable and followed Zsófia into the house as leisurely as possible.

Sitting in the autumnal, copper sunlight-filled room at the large, rectangular table were two mustached men and almost an equally mustached woman in swamp green uniforms. On the opposite side of the table, facing them, sat Shandor. Rom's basket was empty. Lyuba was out of sight.

'There,' Shandor indicated me to the uniform-clad trio. '*Fő társam*, Jassengro.'

'My main companion.'

I was instructed to sit down and answer the trio's questions, with

Shandor and Zsófia providing interpreters' help.

They wanted to know my full name, age, and citizenship. They wanted to know the circumstances of my joining Shandor. They also inquired about our other companions and demanded details of how we'd met Zsófia and what exactly we were doing in Hungary in general and in Változás in particular.

'This is only a registration, a standard procedure, innocent enough,' Shandor managed to whisper to me in a momentary interval between the questions. 'No need to be alarmed. One of Barnat's girls seems to have blabbed about foreigners staying in the village, so they've come to make sure we are normal and cause no trouble.'

For as long as I'd known Shandor, every time he sensed his nearest and dearest could be hurt, he inevitably slipped into denial regarding the danger he himself might be in.

This seemed to be one of such times.

It was tragic, because the instant I saw the mustached trio, it became clear to me that their presence meant serious complications for all and certain death—for one. Shandor.

Shandor needed to run.

I was desperately looking for a way to open his eyes to it and couldn't find any.

He was calming himself. His instinct of self-preservation, which had never been particularly keen, went from bad to worse after Yoska's death—all but completely deteriorated.

One by one, those who waited for their turn outside were called in and questioned at the table. Ours mainly gave their names and personal data; Barnat's and the villagers were more meticulously interrogated—the quagmire-colored trio wanted to know everything about our conduct toward them: were we always well-behaved? Decent? Did we ever try to dupe them? Steal from them? What exact truck and dealings, if any, did they have with us? Are they sure we always acted in good faith?

Litka, as the reporter, was questioned the longest time and gave the loudest speech. Barnat's answers were opposite to Litka's—succinct and quiet.

Our Laila, who seemed the most distressed by the interrogation, asked with Shandor's help.

'I am a foreigner, but what if a Hungarian were to marry me?

Officially, before law and God? Would I be allowed to stay in Hungary then?'

'Who is the Hungarian that proposed to marry you?' inquired the mustached woman.

Gabor's name was given, and there was an order to call Gabor in for questioning, but Gabor was nowhere to be found. No one knew where he had gone; no one had talked to him or seen him that day.

The distraught Laila buried her face in her hands and started sobbing. Shandor wanted to hug and comfort her but was curtly told to stay clear.

While the questioning went on, we were required to keep distance from each other.

Zsófia managed to smuggle me into the back room, where Lyuba was shivering and crying over Rom's basket. The baby was asleep.

I took her in my arms and held her long and tight.

'Zsófia passes me off as her deaf and dumb daughter,' she whispered into my chest. 'But I don't want to do it. I'll turn myself in. I'll follow you where they take you, or, if they don't let me, I'll kill myself. My life has no meaning without you.'

I lifted her chin gently so that her eyes meet mine. Every time I did so, she knew I was going to announce a new stage of her life.

'Listen,' I said. 'You have to let me go. It is time. Your own way lies before you. You cannot turn your back on it. Besides…' I paused. 'You have our child. My child, part of me. Yours and his paths mingle into one at this point.'

She closed her eyes and shook her head slowly, new tears streaming down her pallid cheeks.

'I am no mother.'

'I know. Do not force yourself to be one. Just be yourself, be an egotist, and do what you want. Rom will find his feet, and he will find his way into your heart. You will not have to take care of him. He will take care of you.'

*

'Them—Roma? Them—our people? You cannot be serious! Wake up! They break every law in the book. They mess with *gajos*. Their women are sluts. All their men, we hear, are sodomites. They entered this country illegally. *Nyilaskeresztes* are coming for them anyway. We don't call the authorities on them first, we'll be nabbed along with them—they'll drag us down.'

These were the words of Barnat, retold to me by Shandor in a hollow, unbelieving voice.

The interrogation was adjourned for the night. The village was cordoned off. The square and the streets were empty—Barnat's people and the villagers were hiding in the houses; ours were all under guard on Zsófia's porch.

'He says he couldn't do anything; his folks leaned on him. Even Zsófia couldn't interfere on our behalf—this is a *vitsa* matter. A matter of *Kris*.'

Apparently, there had not only been a "council of elders," but also a kind of condemning petition against us, started by Litka and signed by every single person in Barnat's group.

Having related all this to me, Shandor fell silent. He looked crushed. The notion of an "innocent registration procedure" he had been clinging to hitherto now wore off.

'Run,' I said to him. 'Please. I can get you out—you alone. I'll take care of the rest. Just go.'

This was a lie. I could not get him out. We both knew it. But maybe—just maybe—if he'd agreed to try and cheat the preordained, I would've gone for it, even if it were to tangle the paths that lay before us into a deadly knot which would slowly and painfully choke us and all around us.

He didn't agree, of course.

In the morning, some more questions were asked and some more forms filled out.

Then we were handcuffed.

Three tarpaulin-draped cattle cars pulled up at the gate.

Yanoro, Danior, and I were ordered into one. Tomka and Laila into another. Shandor was to go into the third.

It was at this point that Shandor raised his voice.

'*Kérem, engedje meg, hogy elmenjek a lányokkal!*' he pleaded. 'Allow me to go with the girls. Look at them; they are shaking and terrified. They have never been on their own; they are defenseless; they will die. Please, let me come with them—I'll go to any place and will do any work.'

The mustached men in swamp-colored uniforms tried to load him into the truck by force, but he kept baulking and pleading. Then the mustached woman took out her gun and shot him in the head.

I did not see him die.

Uncuffed for a moment, I'd been sent into the house to fetch some heavy boxes prepared by Zsófia that the trio wanted to take along.

I only heard.

The bark of the shot was followed by a high-pitched shriek—Rom went into wailing in the back room.

I think I also heard Tomka's and Laila's horrified cries; Lyuba's and Zsófia's stifled sobs. But these were muffled, dulled, as if coming from underwater.

What burned through my eardrums and punched through my brain was my son's voice—the only true dirge for Shandor.

All I could see was the wooden floor; all I could feel—squeezing pain, akin to the one I was to feel for a little girl, Damira, years ahead, in my new life.

Another living being I would love but would not be able to save.

The feeling of helplessness enraged me. I needed a vent—there and then. I needed revenge, and it had to be bloody and dirty.

So I willed Litka to show up on Zsófia's threshold.

There she was—disheveled, large mouth semi-open, in smudged lipstick and rouge. The craving to see me led away in handcuffs exceeded the fear of being punished.

She should've known better.

Pushing her out of my way so that she fell and hit her head against a wooden beam, I gave her a brief overview of the events to come.

'There will be a town called Komárom. You will be marched there. Once arrived, you will be shaved bald, dragged through the dirt, beaten, spat on, and peed on. No one will bother to rape you because you will be too filthy and stinky to use. Besides, you will be contagious—you will have typhus. Eventually, you will be thrown into a pit covered with quicklime and left there to rot.'

While I was saying this, I spotted Mitsa, Zsófia's cat, on the front door canopy—body flattened, eyes rounded, and darkened. Preparing to strike.

Cats are vengeful creatures; they neither take kindly to being kicked, nor forget their grudges.

So I concluded:

'Alas, the ugliness that awaits you will not look any less ugly for being seen with just one eye.'

Noiselessly, Mitsa swooped down on Litka's screwed-up face. With a sound similar to that of a tearing thread, she masterly scratched her right eye out of socket and shot through the open door back into the house, past me.

Litka's rumbling roar of pain and her face bathed in blood did not get even close to alleviating my anguish inflicted by Shandor's death.

I just hoped Litka's swollen, one-eyed countenance could be my parting gift to Lyuba, delivered by Mitsa's paws.

I only wish I could have offered the woman who loved me a better present before I took off into my new life of which she was not to be part.

XI
1st Violin

Guido has mystified me today.

I was sitting at my desk making a fair copy of the first movement of Indigo Mind.

Jass had just left—I'd asked him to leave a little earlier. I needed time alone.

Today was a special moment—one that I'd once almost despaired of ever coming. The day on which a third part of Indigo Mind was completed. *The* actual Indigo Mind, née Brünnhilde's moods—the one borne out of the very blaze of my childhood fever, purified and verified by its heat—not some tortured simulacrum or a pitiful compromise.

So I got out the beautiful rosy-cream note paper that I'd once bought in my favorite music shop in Hohenzollerndamm and been saving for this fair copy. What a leap of faith that had been! All these years hoping against hope that a day would come when I'd be able to rightfully use it...

Well, as it turns out, my hope was not in vain.

As a schoolboy, I was often commended by my teachers for neat handwriting, in which I never took any particular pride. Today, however, these delicate, slanting whorls and intricate calligraphic loops I am gifted with penning have at last come to serve a verily suitable purpose.

In the middle of the top line, in silvery black ink, I traced out **INDIGO-GEIST**. Then, on the line below, closer to the right-hand side, and in smaller letters—***In Liebevoller Erinnerung An Meinen Vater, Ludwig Heinrich Heidert***.

The flame may have been kindled by the rebellious mythical maiden and made brighter by Indigo, but it was my father who took me to see the meister's greatest work—the core and nourishment of my inspiration. So it is he, the profoundly wise man, the adoring husband and intuitive father, to whom the concerto shall be dedicated.

I paused, cast a meticulous glance at what I had written, and was pleased with the result. I knew the coping would occupy most of my evening, and it was the sweetest anticipation I'd ever experienced.

Enchanted by the process, I drew a treble clef when I became aware of indistinct grumbling and importunate paper rustling noise coming from the corridor.

This seemed unusual—I did not doubt that, save for myself, not a living soul remained in the block after Petko had led Jass away.

I went to check.

As I found out, it was not the corridor the noise came from, but Guido's office. Incredibly, at nine o'clock in the evening, Guido was still at work. Moreover, he was so engrossed in sorting out something on his desk he didn't hear or see me enter, even after I audibly knocked and cleared my throat.

Albeit puzzled by his late-night work zeal, I was in such an exultant state of mind that Guido's presence gladdened me—I suddenly felt I wanted company, and I wanted a celebration.

'Heil!' I saluted him. 'One would've expected to find you at U Barbary at this hour rather than here.'

He flinched and dropped the folder he was holding.

His cowlick was sweat-darkened and messily stuck to his perspiring brow. His hands were shaking.

'Don't you want to be teleported there?' I went on, employing his own jovial manner as I usually do when I want to poke mild fun at him. 'There is a good cause. Our boys kicked some Tommy and *Makkaronifresser* butts in Leros—really gave them what for, those disorganized suckers. Let's show this town we are proud of our victories!'

Guido attempted a smile but failed. Instead, he made a jerky movement as if undecided whether he should salute me back or pick up the folder first. Then he tried to say something, but what came out was just a scary, squelchy grunt. His face was pale, with cranberry-red splotches.

Then, at last, he pulled himself together enough to mumble a string of words which, if I heard correctly, amounted to, 'Sorry, brother, I happen to be in the middle of something urgent here. You go, all right? I'll catch you later.'

Having forced that out, he took a hasty dive under the desk, apparently for the dropped folder.

I may be mistaken, but I'm pretty sure I saw tears welling up in his widened eyes.

What on earth can be happening to the good fellow?

*

Though he did nonplus me, I asked no further questions. There was something plaintively defenseless about his posture, his voice, and his wild stare—something of a hunted animal.

I sensed that any persistence or curiosity on my part would at that moment only add to his anguish. I wished to do no such thing. I nodded with a casual smile as if I hadn't noticed anything out of the ordinary and said I'd be next door, also raking through some accumulated paperwork.

'Just give me a yell whenever you're done—we might still go for a drink,' I added.

He muttered something in response, but I don't suppose my words had even reached him, so faraway he looked.

Truly speaking, I was overjoyed to return to my desk and resume the work. Besides, the more I thought about Guido's odd behavior, the more convinced I became as to possible reasons.

The girl from Karlsruhe must have carried out her threat.

In our moments of sincerity Guido often tells me about a liaison he had with a feisty redhead—Magda? Martha?—whom he met in Baden-Württemberg where, after a number of times quitting and resuming medical training, he enlisted in a *Freikorps*. This perky young nurse was in his training team and, according to Guido, knew how to stand up for herself better than any man around. "A she-devil in a white apron—saucy and stubborn—but the more they are like that, the more you want to pull off their knickers and slap their butt" is how Guido usually summarizes the emotions she evoked.

While he becomes uncharacteristically coy every time the conversation is brought around to the subject of their last meeting, I've heard enough to conclude the consequences of that final fling are an object of nagging concern to him. The girl, it has been implied, is not averse to correspondence with her ex-lovers' superiors. A letter describing "lewd and lascivious conduct unworthy of a German officer" composed by the disgruntled Magda (or Martha) already once landed before a chief of Guido's back in Karlsruhe. Guido and the girl reconciled afterward, but she repeatedly threatened to lodge a similar complaint with whatever figure of authority Guido would be answerable to in the future, should he upset her again. Such a figure currently being Angel, Guido obviously shakes in his boots at the thought that it will be to him the *gnädige Fräulein* might address her next grievance. As is commonly known, Angel, in his moral flawlessness, does not connive in dissipation.

The other day in block 32, I caught a glimpse of Angel flicking through a ledger, grumbling irritably. I think I heard him pronounce Guido's name. I didn't give it much thought then, but now, putting two and two together, I believe I understand why Guido looks so distraught.

The girl has written to Angel, and Guido has been hauled over the coals.

*

Should Guido now, God forbid, seriously fall out of favor with Angel; should Angel decree he be stripped of heading the Farma-Ko-Farben project (for this, no doubt, is the prospect that scares Guido out of his wits), I would personally bend over backward to whitewash him in Angel's eyes, even if he did indeed commit a number of indecorous acts against fair Magda-Martha. I would make every effort to help Guido restore his good name and ensure that he stays on the job.

For, any way you slice it, were Guido to lose Farma-Ko, I would be seen as the one and only plausible replacement. Because, who else? Anton? He will easily talk his way out of it, the glib tongue he is. Anton never wanted anything to do with Farma-Ko—he always felt it was a shaky ground. I, who have never been as perspicacious, stupidly allowed myself to be entangled. I got in on the ground floor, I know the business like the back of my hand—or so everyone believes. Surely I will be required to take over if Guido falls flat on his face.

While now is the time that not for any ostensible profits—not even at Angel's behest shall I agree to be lumbered with that dead weight again.

Not when I am approaching my personal summit, both in science and art.

The further I advance, the more I feel the inextricable connection between the two. Music is recast in thought; thought—sublimated in music. The flight of sonic fancy crystallizes into the strict splendor of scientific innovation. The more resplendent the sound, the more rampant the mind. The former nourishes the latter; the latter renders wing to the former—and the two soar to exalted heights, hitherto unattainable.

Jass is right when he says, "The more you raise the bar, the more it reveals to you the infinite elasticity of your abilities. Those impossible tasks we set ourselves are not only possible, but they have a way of bringing forth the accomplishment of whatever other impossible tasks we can potentially throw at ourselves in the future."

*

Another thing Jass is right about—I need a listener. I feel it; I sense it with my entire being.

Jass tells me stories—lots of them. One is from his time back in London.

'There was this elderly lady,' he recounts. 'One Miss Limms, a cheesecloth-cheeked little spinster—one of those quintessential wilting English roses. She would come every Saturday, leave generous tips, and listen ravenously. She seemed tireless. For hours she would stand in the middle of the circle, closest to me, leaning on her cane. She smiled, laughed, and applauded, clapping her wrinkly hands more than anyone else in the audience. I ended up providing a chair for her and insisting that she take the load off her feet while I played.

It was a rule with me to do orders for my regular listeners. Miss Limms, as the most honored patroness, was invariably the first one I asked what she would like to hear. And, from the wide choice I offered, it was never Tchaikovsky, Schubert, Von Vecsey, or The King's Way she ordered. Nor was it a melody of my own composition. No. It did have to be something of my own, but something not composed yet. She wished for me to play whatever came to mind, creating a song in the process. Improvisation appeared to be the only music she deemed worthy of the name.

So I gave it a free reign.

She participated a lot—closed her eyes and moved her chin up and down slightly, tapped out the rhythm with her cane; even stood up from her chair occasionally and attempted dance moves. She was wonderful.

As for myself, I was sometimes truly happy with my playing; at other times less so. And, every time I thought I was doing well, Miss Limms (or

Alicia, as she demanded that I address her) would observe, 'I am being quite fancily eloquent today, aren't I, Jassengro?'

But whenever I felt I'd given a lackluster performance, she'd apologize, 'I'm sorry, son, I didn't seem to have much to say today. Must be the weather. It really starts affecting you as you get older. Hope I should be more articulate next time.'

*

The listener as a co-author.

How ingenious. And yet, how transcendentally true.

As the only non-metaphorical form of artistic creation, music is the most direct one—one that endues the artist with the power of an absolute maker. Its impact, therefore, is immediately vectored at the listener, endowing him with a capacity for co-making.

Imbibing new musical forms elevates everyone to the level of a genius. Hence, as I have many times noted throughout my years of actively engaging in the art of composing and performing, the technical side of things dissolves entirely in the process of transmitting music to the listener—indeed, it may almost be asserted that at the moment of execution technicalities cease to exist. Isn't it ironic that I, who has always been an uncompromising perfectionist in terms of skill and form, have also repeatedly arrived at the paradoxical conclusion: in music (at least in true music—the one able to fuse the performer and the listener into the whole of a Creator), technique possesses minor significance.

Having said this, I must repeat it is music alone that's capable at times of defying the restrictions of the technical, and soaring all the higher for that. No other art, be it verbal or visual, can ever afford to neglect the dictates of form, for no other art is free from the fetters of allegory.

Least of all, it is painting that can get away with poor execution. This I always felt, and of this I became completely convinced after I'd been, against my better judgment, made to try to promote substandard specimens of the craft. The wretched Bernie's, no other's. To please my beloved Indigo, who else?

*

That breezy late May—early June stands out in my memory for more than one contrasting reason. Those emotionally dipole moments, which have been tearing my mind apart ever since.

My triumphant graduation—and the execrable stunt Bernie and his companion in depravity pulled on me. My confident first steps in academia—and utter disillusionment with my colleagues. My bright idea for a future doctoral thesis—and instant frustration due to the egregious lack of support on the part of my new supervisors.

Finally—the evening with Indigo in Treptower Park—the very following day after my commencement ceremony.

She looked so charmingly repentant, so sincerely conscious-stricken after the night before. She would not stop taking my hand, pressing it to her cheek and apologizing for the embarrassment Bernie and his disreputable acquaintance inflicted on me. She pleaded with me to forgive her having missed the concert.

'Please, darling, do not hold the sorry accident against the one who, as you well know, roots for you with all her heart and is the most spellbound admirer of your music!' she whispered, her lips rustling like the clusters of blossoming lilac around us, her breath scented with lilac too.

Then, at some point, while holding one of my hands up to her cheek and the other—to her chest—in the same fragrant breath she addressed me.

'Chris, darling. Listen. I need your help.'

Completely beguiled with her vulnerable softness, all my senses enswathed in her plaintive tenderness, I let my guard down.

Stroking her cheek, I asked what it was.

She livened up a little.

'Have you heard of the art exhibitions in Munich? Those opening in July?'

'The one in the new Haus der Kunst? The Great German Art Exhibition? I have, of course. Hasn't everybody?'

'Yes,' she said. 'The Great German Art. And the other. There will be a second exhibition. Have you heard of the second one?'

I paused to think for a moment.

'Um... Not that I remember... What about them? You would like to attend the inauguration, perhaps?'

She fingered the gauzy cowl neckline of her lilac silk dress slightly with an almost imperceptible touch of nervousness.

'This is not for me personally, Chris. The openings in mid-July coincide with Bernie's birthday. I have thought of a truly mind-blowing present for him. One that might initiate a new era of his life. Bring him the recognition he deserves.'

Indigo stopped and squeezed my hand delicately, making me stop too. She looked me in the eyes, took a quick shuddery breath, and lowered her voice, as if about to divulge a secret.

'I want Bernie's works to be exhibited in Munich,' she said.

*

To say my heart broke would have been an exaggeration. I suppose by then I had developed a kind of immunity to blows of that kind. If anything, I was amused by the preposterous nature of her wish. As she enlarged on the details of her plan, she amused me all the more.

The plan was clear and not devoid of logic: to use an old acquaintance of my family's to propel Bernie's canvas smearing into the most influential art show in the country.

'That Alois Jänzen of yours? Your father's good friend? You told me he was one of Ziegler's leading mentors in the Academy of Fine Arts.'

'Not quite so,' I corrected her. 'Alois Jänzen closely knew Ziegler's master of technique, Max Doerner. And yes, he knew Ziegler too; tutored him a little. But he never was one of his leading…'

'Never mind,' she interrupted impatiently. 'They are still in touch, and on good terms, aren't they? Jänzen and Ziegler. You told me they were.'

This was, unfortunately, true. I had on several occasions mentioned to Indigo and Bernie that an old friend of my father's, a painter, was a long-standing academic connection of the President of the Reich Chamber for the Visual Arts.

Exactly what purpose I had in sharing this information was a mystery even to myself. Boasting? Hoping against hope to impress Indigo by trying to look more steeped in the world of fine arts than Bernie "the painter?" Most likely so.

For Bernie, my efforts to beat him at sophistication were like water off a duck's back—I doubt he even heard me. Indigo, however, heard and remembered.

I could have kicked myself for my indiscretion and foolish bragging.

The joke, once again, was on me.

In a lame attempt to cool Indigo's ardor, I voiced an assumption.

'From what I've heard, the exhibition may not even occur this year at all. They may cancel it.'

She snapped.

'Who did you hear it from?'

'From that same Alois Jänzen. The Führer is said to have looked in on the preparations in the Haus der Kunst and found the quality of the suggested pieces so outrageously inedequate that he disbanded the Jury of Selectors and called the entire thing off. Alois tells me, in his wrath, the Führer ripped paintings off the walls with his own hands; he even…'

'Stomped his feet, waved his fists, hissed, and spluttered like the Rabid Roach he is,' Indigo interposed coolly. 'This is all hearsay. The exhibition will not be cancelled.'

'Well…' I started on a new attempt, still less confidently. 'Indie, you should understand… You should realize that the style of Bernie's art is looked askance at by the state. Both Ziegler and Jänzen take exception to avant-garde. And this is to put it mildly. Paintings of the kind Bernie produces would be indignantly rejected, and proposing something like that would cost me Jänzen's friendship. He would never talk to me again, even out of respect for my father.'

'You may be slightly off the mark regarding the state, dear.' Indigo smirked. 'The Rabid Roach's preferences are thoroughly philistine; this is true. But the Mad Rat has been hailed by *Kunst* and *Deutsche Allgemeine Zeitung* as the proponent of all things expressionist, futurist, and new objectivity. Guaranteed absolute freedom for the arts some years ago—actually around the same period that he was burning the books—but these are perverted times we are living in, aren't they, so, I guess, this fact doesn't strike anyone as the most heinous example of hypocrisy. And, last time I checked, the Rabid Roach gave the Mad Rat carte blanche in culture-related matters.'

"The Rabid Roach" and "the Mad Rat" were the monikers Indigo had invented for the Führer and the Minister of Propaganda, respectively. Every time she started throwing these expressions around with a certain hysterical fervor, it was a sure sign she was bent on some outlandish idea and would brush aside any reasonable arguments one might offer.

I tried another mild objection, nevertheless.

'Your information is outdated, Indie. This is all in the past. Since the Führer explicitly proclaimed his will to overcome the degeneration of our culture by cleansing it, the Minister has firmly adopted the *völkisch* stance.'

She turned sharply, got hold of my forearms, and squeezed them—a little harder than earlier she had my hand—more insistently, urging me to "cut the nonsense" and pay attention.

'Chris, look! Do you seriously believe I want these loutish impostors to approve of Bernie's art? Do you honestly suppose I wish to see his works in the *soi-disante* "Great German Art" show, alongside all the kitsch? God, that would be a murder! What I really want is for them to hate his paintings, curse them, and be scandalized by them to the extent of wanting to exile them into another exhibition—the one that is going to be held some streets away, the one that they are going to call "Degenerate Art," and where they will be shoving the most outstanding works by true geniuses—the real art, which is a thorn in their side! This idea may seem insane today. It may sound entirely unreasonable to you and even to Bernie. But it is a step into the future. The impostors will go; their shoddiness will be washed away by the tide of history. Real art will remain—and the more it is demonized now, the more iconic it will be in epochs to follow. Don't worry about your relationship with Jänzen—it is not going to be hurt. You will not have to be associated with Bernie or his art at all. All I want you to do is tell Jänzen that you know of a painter who is a bit crazy but quite prolific and eager to be exhibited in any quality. Tell him you have no idea in what style the artist works. Just arrange a meeting between him and Bernie. The rest I take upon myself. Chris, they are desperately short of material for both exhibitions—they are raiding museums and taking pieces by force to fill up the "Degenerate Art." They will be grateful for any willing contribution, trust me.'

Was I ever able to deny her whatever she asked for? I allowed myself to be persuaded all over again.

*

The sound of a slamming door returned me into the present.

Guido's departing footsteps boomed in the corridor. Another door banged downstairs. Looking out the window, I saw him trudging toward the Steyr, shoulders hunched.

He'd never looked in, even to say goodnight. For Guido to manifest such sociophobia, he must be entirely downcast.

The sight of him filled me with momentary unease again, but I drove the dim thoughts away. It hit me that, instead of notating the first movement, I'd been sitting idly, staring at Indigo's photograph, and nursing my bittersweet recollections already for some time. One thing about Indigo seems to be undeniable—she has a way of turning even the most exasperating memories associated with her into some sort of sentimental reminiscing. She also has a way of trickling into my thoughts at moments when I am at the acme of my creative and intellectual efficiency. My main inspiration she does remain—the driving force of both my music and my science. Not for nothing it is that I have renamed the greatest work of my life after her!

As I returned to notating, the astonishing idea of music reliving itself in science struck me again.

It becomes an obvious thing when contemplated in the process of simultaneously generating new material in both spheres. The living, breathing correlation between Indigo Mind and *Force Vitale* is a phenomenon only deaf, blind, and intellectually torpid would fail to notice. I can trace the interlacing in every note of the concerto and every symptom of *cancrum oris*; they reflect in one another so dazzlingly that even I, the creator of one and discoverer of the other, am left awestruck.

Take Baroque—the style in which I envisaged my musical magnum opus.

The very essence of it is polyphony, where a variety of seemingly disparate melody threads are spun simultaneously to form a homogeneous canvas. Then take the pathogens of a noma lesion. The microbiota of *cancrum oris* are so diversified that indeed it would be a challenging task to locate the main culprit. The counterpoint of Borrelia vincentii versus Fusobacterium; the contrasting actions of fusiform bacilli and non-hemolytic streptococci and staphylococci—all at play to shape a formidable unison.

Even the name "baroque" itself derives from *barocco,* which means "deformed pearl." And doesn't noma spell "deformed face"?

In the mood, which since the very first seconds of the music's fevered genesis proclaimed itself as *furioso* or *feroce*, one can easily hear the onslaught of a force that furiously devours soft tissues, ferociously destroys the bone, and is relentlessly fatal. The name of the force, originating from the Greek *nomein*—"devour"—speaks for itself.

Then there is the key—D minor, which is by right regarded as the most somber of all keys—the sonic incarnation of necrosis. Then the pitch—flat, or *bemolle*—"softened" in Italian. Once again, the sure indicator of soft tissues, primarily affected by the disease.

And the chromatic elements so favored by Jass—those breathtaking tangents the music flies off at? What are they, if not the incongruously elevated moods my objects manifest as the disease claims increasingly greater parts of them? Those surges of curiosity Patrin shows; Grisha's smiley stoicism; Damira's briskness; Mara's cuddliness—all against the backdrop of pain and putrescence.

And then, finally, *Force Vitale* itself. The idea of my life. The immaculate, implacable power that moves fluids up xylem and brews noma in the flesh of subhumans.

The obstinate force. The one that also guides my composing head and my performing hand; the one that persistently glorifies itself in the *ostinato* patterns.

More parallels need hardly be drawn.

*

'And where else would the meister be, if not at his desk, working away, when everybody else has long since gone home?'

Birgitte's voice came to complete both my reflections and my notation, like a chrystal-bell coda.

'You are the best end of the day a lonely worker might wish for,' I said, blinking at her dazedly. 'What celestial winds bring you here, angel?'

'Was taking Vano to visit the kids in the family camp. Chris, you should've seen them! All the hugs and tears. It got so emotional I was almost weeping myself before I knew it. Luckily, Guido was stopping by. I insolently exploited his car once again and sent Vano back home with his driver. But myself, I felt too sentimental to go home yet. Thought I'd benefit from a walk and see how my friend the meister is doing. Guido told me you'd be here... He doesn't look himself, by the way, Guido. All rattled, face like a rain cloud, barely talked to me. Do you have any idea what's going on with him?'

She jingled away, and I bathed in the sound of her voice. The delightful surprise of her presence, paired with the knowledge of a substantial part of my musical and scientific work having been realized, suddenly filled me with warm, lazy, and cream-caramel joy.

'Chris! It's not fair—you are not listening!'

She giggled, shaking me by the shoulder. I caught her hand and brought it to my lips.

Her eyes fell upon the notepaper, and my writing.

'Hey, what is it, Maestro? Music? Something incredibly beautiful? Your raison d'être piece?'

I was covering the title with my elbow—she could not have possibly seen it. Still, she cottoned on. I must have exuded an air of triumph, and Birgitte is a highly empathetic being with a perceptive mind.

I saw no reason for prevarication.

'Yes, it is. But it is not ready yet. I have only finished work on the first movement today.'

She threw her arms around my neck ecstatically.

'Don't forget I called Dibs on the premiere.'

'I shan't.'

She kissed me on the lips, yet in a friendly manner. I returned the kiss.

Birgitte did not say so, but somehow it hung in the air that she was not just calling in on me. It was clear she was picking me up—making me stop whatever I was doing, leading me outside, and taking me home.

I did not keep her waiting.

I carefully collected my papers, put on my coat, gave her my hand, and followed her out.

Never had I been so happy to be abducted, and I told her so.

*

It was music and medical science, anthropology, and mysteries of human nature that we discussed on the way to the Rynek Główny. This long autumnal walk across the clammy emptiness of AU unstabelivably felt warm, light, and fragrant. I could almost compare it to my Treptower evenings with Indigo. It had the same sensuality entwined with friendship and appreciation.

While complimenting my progress in music, Birgitte showed an even livelier interest in my noma work. She wouldn't stop asking about the children: was Grisha being a leader? Was he as comically protective of grownups as ever and as patronizing—was he trying to teach me how to do research? Was Mara the same withdrawn, lonesome thumbelina, or was she now changed? Did Patrin demonstrate his secret mischievous side, or did he keep playing at a little saint?

I gave her the fullest possible account—of the children's behavior and their interaction, of how *Force Vitale* penetrated their flesh and mind—even of the mystical interlacing between the inexorable justice of nature and the creation of music I had established.

'All right, Maestro Heidert, that's it. It is inhumane to intrigue someone to such an extent and leave them in the dark. You've got to play me that first movement of yours. I can't wait till you have the entire piece ready, I'll die of curiosity.'

We were standing by the entrance to my block, across the square from Birgitte's. Her hand was in mine.

We flew up the stairs—me leading, she behind.

In the musty dusk of the storey, I took out the key, habitually slipped it in the keyhole, turned twice, pushed the door open, and stepped inside.

'I shall not leave you in the dark, my Freia,' I whispered, pulling her in.

As I kissed and undressed her; as she gave herself to me—sweetly, obediently, and tenderly like I had known she one day would, it was Freia's Motherhood that played in the back of my mind—for the first time unclouded and undiluted; for the first time crystal clear and true.

XII
2nd Violin

Guido never ceases to amuse me.

I don't bother to tune in much on his account, so there truly is no telling what he will get up to next.

His latest idea is to frame Chris Heidert.

No sooner had I shown my face in the Jewish camp today, and immediately the hard-working squad transformed itself into a flock of giggly schoolboys.

Yossi let go of the welding machine, nearly causing Yonas a burn. Both abandoned the piece of pipe on which they were working and simultaneously plonked their scrawny backsides on the ground strewn with clamps, wrenches, and pliers. Then, as if on cue, both guffawed (twins will be twins—if Angel has not got his lab hooks into them yet, it is probably for the sole reason the two make too good a workforce).

This alone got me suspicious something was going on, but when Marek doubled over with hilarity and Shlomo started clucking and shaking so that the pliers in his hand clanked, whatever remaining doubts dissipated. A wildly entertaining scenario was being played out, with me as an unconscious Charlie Chaplin.

Soon enough, David appeared with a heavy-duty cartwheel and explained everything.

'Do you know what these impossible men here took to calling you and me?' he said, barely containing his own velvety mirth. '"Job creators!" Get a load of that.'

Then he explained the rest.

'Karp came today with a very special task for Yulek and Leo.'

Now Yulek used to work in a registry office, and his finely honed calligraphy skills have earned him campwide renown. Leo, before he was interned, had been a stamp maker.

'He wants Yulek to forge Heidert's signature and Leo—Farma-Ko's stamps.'

*

Guido's plan is, once again, the paragon of simplicity. Guido wants to shift his ex-cathedra approvals of Farma-Ko's pills onto the unsuspecting Young Werther. Technically, retype all the paperwork and sign every medical certificate with Chris's name instead of his own.

What pushes Guido toward this desperate move is the fear the anonymous extortionists might actually carry out their threats, even if he should regularly effect enveloped payments via U Barbary.

Not that Guido has such a low opinion of the nameless gentlemen he is dealing with. Not that he supposes them capable of a deed as vile as blowing the whistle on someone who honestly holds up his end.

No. Deep down, Obersturmführer Karp is a believer in the goodness of people.

The thought keeping Guido up at night is one of an accidental information leakage that may occur.

What if the nameless gentlemen should not be discreet enough? What if they, themselves, should be put pressure on? What if someone—even a complete outsider—should, quite by chance, overhear a bit of a conversation or catch a glimpse of a document?

In order to safeguard himself against these ominous possibilities, Guido would like to stock up on counterevidence. Should he be confronted with allegations, he will shove Heidert-signed forms in the alleger's face. Heidert was, after all, the one who actually came in on the ground floor. He was in charge of the whole thing to begin with. The signing over to Guido was never anything official—if Angel ever noticed it, he must've forgotten by now. Heidert simply tried to dump some tasks he was too disorganized to do himself on his colleague Obersturmführer Karp, but surely Heidert's sloppiness did not make him any less in charge or any less responsible!

Guido's plan B is, in itself, innocuous. It would lead nowhere and change nothing, either for him, or for Christian. The only two men who would suffer from it are Yulek and Leo. After they got Guido's special order fulfilled, they would become expendable. Guido would never find rest while the two Jews who have done such a delicate job for him drew breath and could be made to talk. Yulek and Leo would be in for the gas.

The only way to get the two forgers out of the oven is to have them escape from AU. This should be done relatively soon, before they finish the work for Guido.'

'So how do we go about it?' David demands, hungry for action.

'Yes, how does one escape from AU these days?' Shlomo-the-Bagel chimes in quizzically.

'Well, let me think.'

I tilt my head, chewing my lower lip and stroking my chin. I am enjoying the moment, and so, I know, are my listeners.

'One of the most effectual breakouts in the history of this place had been accomplished some months before you and I got here. None of us present now was lucky enough to witness that deed. Four hotshots drove through the gate in the commandant's personal tricked-out car, sporting SS uniforms, yelling at the guards, and carrying a detailed report which the main AU underground knight had drawn up to pass to the leaders of the resistance army.'

'In the commandant's personal car? Seriously?' Marek makes little attempt to hide his incredulity.

'Indeed so. They heisted it.'

'Some men have a pair,' Yossi breaks his habitual silence.

'Some do. And we can hardly ever hope to match the unprecedented gallantry of those four. A car we are going to need though, just like they did. Not the commandant's, of course, nothing so grand. Guido's. As well as himself as a driver. The employer is going to have to take care of his employees who will be doing an exclusive job for him. It is only normal, isn't it?'

*

Gnädiger Dr. Karp!

We find it expedient to inform you that your art project, which involves falsifying the signature of Dr. Christian Heidert and one of Farma-Ko's executives, Ziegmund Rudolf Schöneich, as well as counterfeiting the stamps of the said pharmaceutical company, is known to us and carefully monitored by us. We would like to reassure you that the trinkets in question will be duly manufactured to your order, and you will be allowed to have them in your possession. However, as you might expect, the granting of this little whim of yours is contingent on your obedience and full cooperation.

Here is your new mission: on the date and time which we shall specify in further instructions, you will provide the inmates Y. and L. with civilian clothes, drive them out of the camp in your car, and bring them to the place we shall indicate.

Noncompliance shall entail immediate punishment, the extent of which you can approximately calculate, given that the crime you have committed against your country is now aggravated with the fabrication of evidence with the purpose of slandering innocent and loyal citizens of the Reich.

'We need a grand finale!' Shlomo demands ferociously. 'Write him if he as much as thinks of disobeying, or if someone harms one hair on Yulek's or Leo's head, he will burn alive in that car of his before Himmler and Gestapo can get to him!'

'Nah, this is anticlimactic,' David objects. 'He fears his precious Reichsführer's ire more than burning alive. Might even take it as relief…'

'Then add that what he's done will be made known to the Reichsführer, the Führer, Angel, the Minister of Propaganda, and the rest of the Reich immediately after he's burned!' Shlomo insists.

'You are, each of you, both right and wrong,' I end the argument. 'Cabbagehead does in fact care for his hide more than for being in the Reichführer's good books, though he may not realize it. Nothing human is alien to him. We shall, however, not add any crummy endings—first and foremost because it is bad taste. Besides, one does not lie in such letters; otherwise, they lose their power of persuasion. Telling Karp he will burn would be a lie, because, as I might've already informed you all, Karp is to hang.'

The bilious "Bagel" is not quite satisfied, but the draft is finalized, regardless.

*

'Where will you land them?' Mihai inquires when I tell him the latest news. 'Those two kids. Where will Karp take them?'

'Chloya will decide where. Some quiet, isolated place out of town where the men of resistance will pick them up.'

It will mostly be Vatslav who is really going to take care of the matter. Chloya, our money administrator, will be on the sidelines this time. But Mihai does not know Vatslav is Chloya's fiancé—the fact that the delectable barmaid is betrothed would upset him greatly. All the remarkable goings-on in Mihai's mind are linked with Chloya and Chloya alone, and in my long conversations with him, I carefully maintain her image of a golden-curled fairy with a magic wand.

Mihai fishes the photo out of his trousers, casts a contented glance at it, and tucks it back in.

'And where will they go? What will they do outside?'

'Will each follow his own path. Yulek will successfully go into hiding, reconnect with his girlfriend after the war is over, retrain as a historian, and teach at college. All search for him will be in vain, so his parents and elder sister will be interned in reprisal for his escape. They will die here.'

'Nothing you can do about this?'

'Nothing, unfortunately.'

'Bad, this,' Mihai sighs. 'But then we don't know if they wouldn't die outside, just as well, because they're old, sick, and hungry. Here at least they feed you; they treat you. The *Deutsches* have respect for old age, and they know about order. They are not all like Cabbagehead. Right, boy?'

I choose to leave that without a comment.

'Leo will join the Polish Home Army, become a soldier there, and fight bravely. Later, though, the communists will hold him prisoner for two years and eventually shoot him on charges of espionage.'

This sends Mihai into a rage. He bangs his fist on the edge of the bunk.

'I always said those Poles are chickenshits! Especially their commies! Like Russians, even worse! Tito, the hero whom you badmouth—that's a true communist for you! But they are not like him. I say, if not a communist like Tito, then better a national socialist like the *Deutsches*! Those Poles and Russians, they think nothing of murdering their own. Turds, not people.'

'Poles and Russians are quite different from each other,' I attempt an objection, but there's no stopping Mihai now—he's mounted his hobby horse.

'Different, eh? Do you believe yourself, boy? Different how, tell me! Only in those ones sell themselves openly, and the others kid around they don't?'

I keep quiet, and Mihai spits angrily.

'Tell you something, boy. If what you say is true and the Russians win the war, then the word "win" will not mean the same anymore. Winners!'

He screwed up his face. 'The heroes that rat on each other and fear their own children! And it is not for nothing they fear, I tell you. Their children will treat them like garbage. Will take the rathole flats that the Commie state gives their parents, turn them into *love,* and run away from the shitty country. And the parents will rot in stinky Commie homes for old people. Serves them right, the fodder generation they are.'

It is not so often that Mihai prophesies, but when it happens, his prognostications have a funny effect on Baba Tanya—for some reason the *gicisvara* gets as irritated as hell. This time, according to the usual pattern, she turns her head heavily, bringing her corpulent frame into a wavy stir.

'You're giving me a headache, old man. Do you ever shut your trap? When will you swallow your tongue already?'

Mihai's moment of demographic vaticination is over.

Humbly apologizing to the irascible *gicisvara* for shooting the breeze, he takes a snuff and falls silent for a while.

*

Upbraiding Mihai makes Baba Tanya feel visibly better. Her big face relaxes—as if a storm cloud suddenly transformed into a porridge bowl. She turns back to her new pet, the boy Vasil.

Vasil is a meek, bleating-voiced human being with drooping eyelids and a perpetually blocked nose. He is one of the few in the family camp hailing from Bulgaria. While the tenacious efforts of Bulgarian secular and clerical intellectuals keep deportation cases of the country's Jews as well as Roma scarce, Vasil, the luckless creature, managed to get himself caught and deported on the border with Macedonia. After the sudden demise of King Boris, who had been massively and mistakenly lauded as "the protector," Vasil's kumpania panicked, believing that the protection provided for them in Bulgaria would now cease, and took a hasty, ill-thought-out move toward the border with the intention to clear out. This was exactly what they should never have done. The group eventually dispersed and most managed to escape, but the not-so-adroit Vasil lagged behind and got apprehended.

The moment Baba Tanya set her eyes on Vasil's plaintive countenance, her maternal instinct went off the charts. For a while she abandoned her other numerous charges, including Mihai and Marusya, and focused entirely on Vasil. She diagnosed him with a number of ailments, which she proceeded to aggressively treat. She endlessly complained to him about her own health. She edified him with countless anecdotes, fables, and parables, but mostly with stories from her own life. The latter would set her off reminiscing into the late hours, and every time the bleary-eyed Vasil listened with his mouth opened in awe. Baba Tanya gossiped with Vasil about the inmates, warning him to have no truck with those she saw as a bad influence. She instructed him which of the camp doctors were to be sought the friendship of and which—not worth wasting time on. Finally, she graced Vasil with showing him her treasure box.

Everybody who is remotely acquainted with Baba Tanya knows that as a sign of the *gicisvara*'s most favorable disposition.

Baba Tanya's treasure box is actually a round biscuit tin full of bric-a-brac: buttons, coffee spoons, metal figurines, brooches with broken fasteners, and earrings without a pair. She claims the box is charged with mighty healing powers and magic spells, which I assume to be true because otherwise it is not entirely clear how Baba Tanya managed to smuggle her treasures into the camp intact (it is especially remarkable considering that the box contains a few sharp objects—pins and clasps). A still more amazing fact is that, apart from preserving, Baba Tanya somehow contrives to augment her property within the confines of AU. The tiny statuettes and glittery bibelots in the box seem to steadily multiply.

When Baba Tanya is not busy treating, counseling, or scolding someone in the family camp, she likes to spend time in her corner with the open treasure box on her lap, taking out one little piece after another, inspecting and admiring, then putting it lovingly back into the tin. While she does so, she usually hums or mumbles something under her breath, and every now and again her cracked lips stretch into a dreamy smile.

Mihai, who is torn between jealousy and reverence regarding the *gicisvara*'s biscuit tin (he never made it into the select few who have been honored with a closer look), at some point dubbed Baba Tanya's treasures *biryul'ky*—a word with a vague meaning he'd apparently learned during his time in Odessa. Although no one understood exactly what that strange combination of letters stood for, the name stuck.

Everybody in the barrack knows well; whenever Baba Tanya is sorting out her *biryul'ky,* it is not advisable to bother her with trifling matters, for the *gicisvara* enters a very special emotional state.

The boy Vasil's secure position as Baba Tanya's favorite is not for a small part explained by the fact that, despite his crybaby voice and patsy look, he has a knack of saying the right words to the right person. Moreover, he never gets tired of repeating those words.

Ever since Baba Tanya found this out, Vasil has become a permanent partner in the *biryul'ky* sessions. The treasure-owning patroness sits him in front of herself, opens her biscuit tin, and slowly pulls out a shiny specimen. Then she dangles it before Vasil's nose and singsongs.

'See this *brelok*, boy? See how it shines and sparkles? Tell me, do you like this *brelok*, boy?'

'Yes, Baba Tanya, I do,' Vasil singsongs in return, stretching out a hand to touch the object ever so slightly. 'It shines like a real diamond! It is beautiful; I like it very much.'

'Well,' Baba Tanya booms, stretching every word with relish. 'You should know; this *brelok* is one of a kind. Your Baba Tanya has been everywhere in the world, and nowhere has she seen another one like it. It is a gift. It was given to your Baba Tanya by a Russian princess in exile, in gratitude, because your Baba Tanya cured her daughter from an incurable disease.'

Vasil gives a solemn nod.

Then Baba Tanya dips into the tin again and fishes out another glittery object.

'And this *brelok*, boy, is also unique and also a present. Was given to your Baba Tanya by a Polish merchant, *o baro rai*—a rich and powerful man—because your Baba Tanya prepared medicine that made his back pain go away.'

Vasil gasps in admiration.

Then the *gicisvara* takes a *brelok in* each hand and dangles them both in Vasil's face.

'Say, son, which of the two do you think is prettier?'

Vasil takes time to consider, tilting his head left and right. Then he pronounces.

'I really do not know, Baba Tanya; it is hard to say. They are both so pretty.'

'Because I thought, maybe we should give one away? To Marusya, maybe. Or to Rosa. They are pretty girls; they deserve to have pretty things, yes? Which one do you think you and I should keep? And which give away?'

Vasil sucks his lips in, shakes his head.

'Hard to say, Baba Tanya. I like them both so much.'

'This one?'

'Hard to say.'

'Or this one?'

'Hard choice.'

'To Marusya?'

'Mmm…'

'Or to Rosa?'

'Ehhh…'

'Or shall we keep them both, son? You tell me! Shall we keep both *breloks*, or give one away?'

'I don't know, Baba Tanya… If you ask me, and because they are both beautiful and the only ones in the world, I say, let us keep them both.'

Baba Tanya's face melts into a buttered pancake; she smacks Vasil on the forehead.

'That's my smart boy!'

Vasil beams at Baba Tanya.

The *breloks* return into the biscuit tin.

*

'Our *gicisvara* is too wise to part with any of her *biryul'ky*,' Mihai observes. 'One doesn't just give away a piece of one's magic powers.'

'Give away not,' I express an agreement. 'Share them one can though, maybe.'

'Much like you share yours with Doctor Heidert. Right, boy?'

Mihai likes to throw in an effortless line every now and again, showing that no matter what is or is not discussed with him, he always keeps on top of things. He does it with a special panache.

'You nanny Doctor Heidert even more than Baba Tanya does Vasil here,' he goes on without bothering to lower his voice, as Baba Tanya and Vasil are too absorbed in the treasure box to hear him.

I disagree this time.

'It is not quite nannying, Babbo. You might call it a mutually enriching experience. An exchange, if you like.'

237

Mihai coughs skeptically, and I purse my lips, assuming an obstinately self-assured stance for his benefit, as in "me, my arrogance, and my long clever words."

Mihai finds it easy to believe. He is satisfied enough to leave the delicate subject of my relationship with Christian alone, at least for the time being.

*

The old man is right, however. Partly at least.

I do mollycoddle Chris sometimes.

The Young Werther that he is, Chris gets overexcited, maudlin, and self-conscious. He gets carried away. He becomes sulky and bitter.

Since I made him seriously addicted to chromaticism, he has been flying off at a tangent every now and again, and I have been indulging it, even where it felt like going a bit overboard.

Chris prefers to think of all tonal indeterminacy as "The Großen Meister's blessed influence," which I choose not to refute. Sometimes though he feels compelled to pay additional tribute to the meister and then goes forcefully Wagnerian. "To the point of introducing leitmotifs," as I like to joke.

It is at such moments that I gently intervene and return my musical ward back on track—without him noticing, naturally.

Or, at other times, he puts the instrument to one side and switches to channeling Wagner ideologically.

'Only the meister, with his almost supernatural insight, could perceive the tragic paradox of the German! Only he could formulate it as an insurmountable cleft between what the German public wants and the aspiration of the lofty mind of the German artist!'

Now "the tragic paradox of the German" for Chris is as much of a pet peeve as "the miserable lameness of the Russian" for Mihai. When either starts holding forth on his own, it is easier to let them burn out the fuel then try to shut off the engine.

So Chris continues, and soon already follows his venerated meister in reconciling himself with the tragic paradox and looking on the bright side instead.

'The genius couldn't be more prophetic when he said that we Germans would never be great politicians, but perhaps we could be something much greater if we judged our capabilities rightly…'

Here Chris usually takes a triumphant breath before soaring upward to the exalted conclusion.

'…something through which we may be destined to become, not indeed the rulers, but the ennoblers of the world!'

*

Riding his Wagnerian tide, Chris orates some more on the meister's philosophy. He relates to me in intricate detail exactly why the Great One was so moved by Feuerbach and Schopenhauer, not particularly touched by Kant, or repulsed by Hegel.

'Only that which is purposeful and spontaneous springs from a real need, and need alone is the source of life!' Chris exclaims, his eyes shining feverishly.

Exclamations of this kind tend to complete the mental transformation which my musical ward undergoes, reincarnating his favorite composer in his own body and mind. Then, having securely convinced himself that he is the Schopenhauer-inspired Richard Wagner, Chris starts pontificating about art and creativity.

'Only when the artist's choice falls on what is necessary does it become art,' he muses out loud. 'As long as the artist is devising and selecting means his work is not yet art. Not until the choice has fallen, and has fallen of necessity…'

This quote has become a slogan.

Chris loves reiterating it during our sessions, thereby, I suppose, again and again striving to justify his choice of me as the mentioned means.

*

Eventually his motley Wagnerian ramblings dovetail into the most morbid theme of all—the one of fair sex and love.

'The große meister,' Chris says, 'could never become completely and purely a philosopher. He was too much of a poet, and he was too much of a man. He could not—nor ever tried—to fight his natural admiration and sublime tenderness toward women. While for Schopenhauer women were nothing but "foolish attendants on the sick," Wagner's elevated attitude was reflected in his Elisabeth, Senta, Brünnhilde, and Isolda. While the philosopher disdained love between man and woman, the poet placed it on a pedestal of a transcendent scale. More often than not, perhaps, the philosopher was right, and the poet naive and foolish. But he was a poet. He felt exactly the way he was destined to feel.'

Then, as expected, from the meister's premises, my musical charge trampolines to his own empirically grounded conclusions.

'...Not to love her was impossible because her entire being was permeated with love. Love streamed from her deep, liquid, melancholy eyes—love even for those she hated, even for those she reviled, derided, or tried to hurt.'

This soliloquy is inspired by Indigo, the black-eyed affliction of Christian's life, and the pretty face in the frame on his desktop.

'A woman's existence is about love, emanating love, and without love there is no woman! Indigo was... is... about love. And while being that, she has always contradicted her own nature, denying the value of love! "A man's love for a woman is unnatural," she'd say. "There should be more compelling things in a man's life to be in love with—creating, working, learning, and winning... A woman should mostly be a means to satisfy his sexual drive, and, at that, he should have a lot of women, effortlessly drifting from one to another, without compunction, guilt, or pangs of missing the previous one. This is what separates a man from a needy wimp." Can you imagine such words on the tongue of a woman—a lovely, delicate, and love-emanating young girl!'

At this point, tears well up in Chris's eyes.

'Being a woman is about being a mother. If a woman is not a mother, then her entire womanhood is compromised,' he continues winding himself up. 'There was no telling her that. She wouldn't listen. She'd over and over again repeat appalling nonsense. "I'm annoyed by people who are too attached to their parents. Or children. Or motherlands. Something they haven't freely chosen. Parental instinct is nothing but atavism, while patriotism is a dusty, blood-drenched relic of the past." Sometimes I think she did it on purpose, knowing what deleterious effect her verbal poison had on my soul... Yet I know she did not hate me. Indeed, I know she loved me. This is the painful enigma I am not able to resolve.'

*

'She did not hate you,' I throw him a straw.

He clutches at it.

'She did not! I know she did not! All the things she said were merely a reflection of her infinitely loving nature, no matter how outrageous they sounded.'

And he goes on obsessively retelling those things, not unlike Baba Tanya won't stop playing with her *biryul'ky*.

'She'd confess she always sympathized and cooperated with a pale, miserable frotteur grinding against her in a crowded streetcar,' he whispers, his voice hoarse with terror.

'Let him act upon his desire—it won't exactly make a piece of my body fall out, will it? Let the poor sick soul have his pleasure while I use him for a little extra warmth in the freezing tram. It's not my business to shame him or try to cure him—if there is anything to cure. He is a fellow in misery of sorts—I am the same; l rub against the bodies of men I fancy, dream of doing that in my sleep… Only, I am lucky to have been born a rangy female brunette, so I get away with it, while he is cursed to be confined to his pasty, slobbery, and sweaty carcass, for which he is perpetually hated, scolded, and hounded. Why would I add to his anguish, if it costs me nothing to temporarily relieve it?'

His face twisted in a grimace of revulsion, tears of self-pity now streaming down his cheeks, my poor ward all but spits on the floor.

'Any foulness she'd pity, and perversity she'd sympathize with! Would give herself to sodomites! Yes, actually open her legs for one pederast in order to pleasure the other!'

The stage of maudlinness is replaced with the one of righteous fury.

Pederasts of all kinds are a particularly corrosive poison for Christian Heidert's soul. He has a score to settle with homosexuals: Indigo's affection for her limp-wristed cousin Bernie can never be forgiven. All buggery bastards in the world owe Christian a blood debt for that slap in the face.

'If he hates the buggery bastards so much, remind him of his adored meister's son.' Mihai, with whom I have been sharing stories of Chris's tribulations, interposes. 'Wagner junior. You told me once he fiddled with boys.'

'Siegfried Wagner was indeed attracted to men, Babbo, but, although a good composer, he never rose to his heterosexual father's standard, so holding him up as an example would hardly win homosexuality many points. Besides, why would I hurt Christian's feelings even more by taking his idol's name in vain? He has enough pent-up misery as it is.'

'I'm joking, son.' Mihai chuckles magnanimously. 'I would never want you or anyone else to offend our gentle Doctor Heidert!'

XIII
1st Violin

All my senses seem singularly sharpened these days: sound amplified, vision brightened, smell keened, and touch refined. Sometimes they get so painfully intense I even fear they may be deceiving me.

Today, while in the family camp for a quick check, I clearly heard the old Gypsy Mihai pronounce my name.

It was not because he saw me that he uttered it. It was evidently part of the conversation, which had been going on for some time before I showed my face.

Moreover. This conversation was between him and Jass, and apparently it had been held in strange tones.

Pitying? Mocking?

My hearing is too acute for my own good.

Upon seeing me, the old man did not lower his eyes or his voice—merely nodded with brazen familiarity and smiled a smile which, I could swear, was pitying too! As if he and Jass had been discussing a common pal who they both in a way cared for but saw as naive and puerile. A patsy. A soft touch. A ninny who everybody took advantage of, and the two of them were trying to protect—if only he would listen to their advice!

Jass seemed to have barely noticed me. It appeared he had the eyes for the old codger only. When Mihai gave me the impudent smile and actually, while nodding, had the effrontery to repeat my name again: "Doctor Heidert!" Jass was looking at his face intently. I believe I discerned a complex mixture of emotions in his eyes. A shadow of an effort, as if he wanted to stop Mihai from addressing me. Then, after the effort failed, his expression changed to that of deep sorrow. Pity too, perhaps. Only, this time his pity was not on my account. It was on Mihai's.

I did not simply feel it.

It screamed at me. It burned me. It was drilling holes through my eyes and ears.

I won't stand for this. This is not right. This must be stopped.

It is clear as day the filthy old rat is a foul influence on Jassengro. He dares pity me, and he convinces Jass I am to be pitied.

He poisons our work. He defiles it.

Jass must never look down on me.

I am the meister; he is the guiding force of my instrument. Without me, he is emptiness. He makes no sense without my creativity and Indigo Mind. The whole point of our work is my giving meaning to his existence, and he is helping me make the most of my creative powers.

Jass would of course never dare to condescend if it were not for this Mihai Vermin.

Now, clearer than before, I can see the importance of the Reichsführer's decision to, so to say, separate wheat from chaff. Insure that the purebred descendants of the original Indo-Germanic race be preserved, and that they should at all costs be prevented from interbreeding—or, for that matter, interacting—with mongrels and half-castes. For the latter may lead to egregious consequences.

Jassengro and this old cur Mihai are a glaring example.

One an Indo-Germanic (at least in essence), the other a contemptible mix through and through. A genetically noble mind contaminated by an ignoble one, put up to disrespecting his holy of holies—his meister who breathes sense, spirit, and order into his otherwise hollow life.

This must be nipped in the bud. This Mihai creature must be removed.

And removed he shall be. I shall make sure of this.

*

It is indeed astonishing that while having developed an unhealthy attachment to the old stinker Mihai, Jass rarely ever shows any feeling toward other inmates. Even those who have a clear affection for him leave him cold. Even the children.

Damira Girl is a case in point.

Not only does she love him dearly, as if he were her elder brother or even her father—he is also her undisputed hero. One should only hear the stories of "the fearless and powerful knight and wizard Jassengro's" exploits that she tells the other little, *Force Vitale*-driven redeemers.

'…and once Jass saw Vano—I told you about Vano and how nasty he is!—try to call the spirit of Count Dracula... Do you know what Count Dracula is? He is the most terrible vampire ever existed! And do you know what a vampire is? It is a monster who is already dead, but he comes alive at night to prey on people and suck their blood!'

The timid Mara's eyes widen and fill with tears of horror. She snivels.

Damira stretches out her arm and strokes the edge of the Mara mattress, like she would have stroked the younger girl's head, could she have reached it from the confines of her own bunk (none of the children can walk anymore).

'Don't cry, don't be afraid! This story has a happy ending, all thanks to Jass,' Damira's tale goes on. 'He saw Vano calling Dracula's spirit.'

'And how did he know Vano was calling the spirit?' Grisha the clever boy interrupts inquisitively.

'Vano was telling stories about Dracula after sunset, and when one does so, Dracula can hear them—he wakes up, turns into a bat, and flies to look for the one who is telling the story. Then he sucks out his blood and the blood of everyone around him.'

'So that means Vano was calling the vampire on himself?' Grisha presses on.

Damira rolls her eyes at his skepticism.

'I told you many times already—Vano is dumb... So Jass heard him tell the stories, and then he saw Dracula appear! Jass alone could see him; others could not, because Dracula is very sly and can make himself invisible—only people like Jass who have special eyes can see him coming. He flew into our camp, then into our hut, and then he flew straight at me! I was the first one whose blood he wanted to suck.'

'Did you see him too?' Mara whispers tremblingly.

'Only at the last second when he was about to grab me. I saw his huge black bat wings, his crooked nose, and his blood-red eyes. I was so scared I screamed! I was sure I was going to die. But Jass saved me! He took his violin and started playing. I told you Jass could make anything happen by playing his violin, right?'

'Right!' The children respond in unison.

'He fought Dracula with his music, and he made him disappear. The vampire turned to dust, I saw that happen! And he never came back for me again, even when Vano was telling his stupid stories.'

'Is it safe to tell stories about Dracula before sunset?' Patrin inquires, struggling to move his gangrene-devoured lips. The last several days, the disease has been progressing in him twice as rapidly as in the others.

'It is still better not to. Unless, of course, you have Jass around. Then you can fear nothing... Jass can make all evil things go away. But not only that. He can also make good things come. And his violin can talk to birds and animals. I once saw him play for a sparrow—and the sparrow sang along!'

Her Jassengro tales never end.

Whenever she sees me, it is "Onkel Heidert, please tell me how Jass is!" that I hear first thing. And when I leave, "Will you be seeing Jass, Onkel Heidert? Can you pass him a *hello* from me?"

This endearing attachment and tender admiration would, one might think, melt a stone colossus's heart.

Yet when I mention Damira's name to Jass, he looks vacantly past me as if my voice didn't reach him.

What would account for such an indifference to an affectionate child— and such disproportionate cordiality toward a despicable old mongrel?

*

We are now on the second movement, and this is a moment when I should more than ever be on my guard against all poisonous interference from the side. The intensity of the work is at its very peak. Now it is crucial that Jassengro be my all-feeling, all-knowing, and unconditionally obedient instrument; that no whiff of negativity or falsity should come between us. For it may ruin the sublime creation, half of which has already been born— which is already tremblingly alive and breathing.

The ignoble will always be lying in wait to befoul the noble. The noble, therefore, should stand vigil over the precious fruit it bears.

Note by note, passage by passage, we are proceeding toward the moment of ultimate glory.

The form is now completely clear; no need to be thrashing about in hesitation any longer. A simple eight-bar structure. The main theme with a development, a short recapitulation, a transition with an episode in the middle, and a coda. Then a great crescendo on the main theme; a tutti. And, in the end, a theme in D major.

A symmetrically concentric shape.

He is in fact tractable, Jassengro. A good and faithful means to my lofty end.

My fears of Mihai the cur poisoning him against me are, of course, a chimera.

Nothing to worry about there, truly.

It is I who mostly plays during our sessions. Jass almost never does. But at the rare instances that he lays his hands on the instrument, it feels to me as if my soul left the body and observed it from a distance. Or, more precisely, as if this soul of mine observed my *improved* body—looking exactly the way I always wanted it to look.

While he still harrowingly reminds me of the daemon character, more often than not the apparition is eclipsed by another image Indigo religiously adored—the one of Orpheus playing the violin. Needless to say, in our better days, Indigo used to compare me with that anachronistic fantasy by Cesare Gennari, an Italian painter.

It is those dramatic hands caressing the instrument, the svelte torso, the chiseled yet vulnerable chest, and the Baroque grandeur I see enveloped in the amber dusk of my office when he plays.

Jassegro.

Through contact with my music—through this alone—he assumes the appearances Indigo has associated me with. And why does such a mystical metamorphosis occur? To guide me to my better, ennobled, elevated, and accomplished self. For nothing else.

Nothing will be allowed to stay in the way of this.

No impediment shall be tolerated.

None.

*

Any tragedy is always a demonstration of the elusive power of individuality, which is eventually compelled to be cast into the nameless depths. Man does not exist in a vacuum. The Arians, in their wisdom, spoke of the concept of individuality as a deceit; and every masterpiece of a tragedy reaffirms the same principle in the straightforward, persuasive manner of art.

The epic musical work created by the große meister is an impeccable specimen of such a tragedy. Brünnhilde, Siegfried, and Wotan all represent types of individuality who, in different yet interlaced ways, meet each their own demise.

Brünnhilde, the daughter of a God. Not just some god—the reigning deity of Walhalla, the mighty Wotan. She relinquishes her immortality in compassion; forsakes her wisdom in love. She is the goddess become human; the power bestowed on her by right of birth is forfeit. What she is left with is a heart aching for the world, and the ability for superhuman anguish.

In stark contrast to Brünnhilde, there stands Siegfried, the "witless hero," the human becoming god. This perfect hero's soul is "free from envy, glad with love"; he knows neither fear nor covetousness. It is of him that the meister writes, "In him I saw man in the natural, joyful fullness of his sensible existence; no historical dress yet obscured his form nor were his movements obstructed by any force external to himself; his acts spring from his own joyful existence; the error and confusion arising from the wild play of passion rage around him and involve him in destruction, without once his inner impulse being stayed; nor even in the presence of death does he allow any control over his actions save the restless stream of life flowing within himself. He is the spirit of spontaneous impulse, the one eternally productive principle embodied in human shape, the doer of real deeds, the *man* in the highest and most direct plenitude of his powers, and above all things lovable. His acts did not spring from any desire for love gained through reflection; they lived and swelled every vein and every muscle of his body to rapturous fulfillment of their functions."

Then there is Wotan, the central figure of the epic, "the spear's strong lord," to whom "all things are eternally subject." His destruction is not the doing of an outer force, for there is no external foe powerful enough to be able to break the mighty ruler of Walhalla. Intellectually and morally, Wotan is above all living beings; and it is in the depths of his own soul, which is torn between the desire for power and the longing for love, that the cause of his downfall lies.

And what of me? What of Indigo Mind? Having been inspired by the große meister's creation, what can my humble work add? How can it further develop the meister's noble ideas? Here I am, a lonesome Siegfried, mourning for his estranged Brünnhilde, without whom he is incomplete. How can I, in my incompleteness and yearning, augment the wholeness of what the meister created in his integrity and wisdom?

Here is how.

I shall not strive nor even attempt to take a step further from what the meister established in his greatness. What I am making will be an entirely new world, unrelated to the one created by the genius of the meister. I shall certainly learn the lessons the meister taught, but in doing so I shall arrive at my own new conclusions. The meister sang a requiem for individuality; I shall sing its resurrection. In the sadness of the dirge, I shall try to sound the triumph of what should stand immortal—the undaunted spirit of Brünnhilde, her love for Siegfried, his survival through this love. He in his righteousness shall be her savior, and she—in her passion—his.

This is the scale of what I am doing; this is the mighty tower Jass the Gypsy is being utilized as a tool for mounting.

I should never stop reminding myself of these core principles. These irrefutable truths.

*

And then there is something else to remind myself about—Freia's Motherhood. My other child—by now quite legitimately so. Another dedication, another story. Not even quite another one—rather a different theme of the same saga. The saga of my life.

In my earthly story, Indigo came first. She was, in all senses, the beginning. Birgitte made her entrance later. In my saga, however—the creative reflection of my material existence—the two swap places. Birgitte, my Freia—the primal goddess of love, fertility, and motherhood and *seiðr*, Wotan's sister, the guardian of the golden apples and the possessor of a cloak of falcon feathers which avails other deities—is there to begin with. A stronghold of wisdom and balance, sensibility and composure, things eternal. The guarantor of peace of my mind.

Indigo—the Brünnhilde—conversely emerges subsequently against the Freia-woven backdrop of peacefulness and plentitude. The restless and tortured one, the one whose feelings tear her apart and set her aflame—she is the igniter of passion, disturber of the peace.

And then it is Freia's turn again to step in and restore the balance.

Should I at some point try and actually bring the two themes into one musical epic?

I shall perhaps. As soon as I have Indigo Mind completed.

As to Freia's Motherhood, after the night Birgitte and I shared love, this child of mine has been finally born. I am as happy with its present form as an adoring parent can be, and I decided to keep it to myself. I won't ask for Jassengro's help, not this time. I've said what was to be said in this sonata. I think I am ready to play it to the one it has been inspired by.

And it is with a trembling delight that I anticipate her reaction—how overwhelmed, how entirely enthralled my Freia shall be! God bless the tender, appreciative heart of the gentle creature, for I know her joy will know no limits when she hears F. M.!

*

When I think back to the magical moment we shared, the memory of how demurely yet ardently she surrendered to me, I myself can barely hold back the tears of endearment and gratitude.

Has Indigo, my one and only true love, ever given me an instant of such intense happiness?

A ludicrously rhetorical question.

Remembering the glaring disproportion of how I felt about either woman and how each repaid my feelings convinces me that indeed I owe Birgitte more than just a serenade.

Besides reciprocating my love, she has also played a crucial role in my academic triumph. *Force Vitale*. The work that will immortalize me as a medical scientist. If it had not been for Birgitte's emotional support and practical help, attaining the results which I have by now generated in the lab would have hardly been possible.

With this in mind, I now seriously contemplate the idea of dedicating my *Force Vitale* project to Birgitte, apart from the F. M. sonata. It will still only be a very modest "thank you" gesture, but it will make the unfair situation a little fairer. For I have not yet told Birgitte so directly, but she is discerning enough to suspect that my main musical piece, I. M., is dedicated to a rival of hers, a troubled soul whose place in my heart can never be occupied by another, even an infinitely worthier one.

*

The troubled soul who not only threw my love away—preferring to chase a phony—but also exploited my feelings to help her forward that phony's miserable excuse for art, and, by doing so, put me through yet another embarrassment—one of the most burning embarrassments I had ever been cursed to suffer!

Almost seven years have elapsed since the summer of 1937, when Indigo managed to drag me into a new disgrace.

I did what she had asked.

I introduced her and Bernie to Alois Jänzen as the daughter and nephew of my late university mentor. I was sure Bernie's daub would be cast a token glance at out of pure civility, then politely rejected on the pretext of "not quite fitting the format of the exhibitions," and this would be the end of it.

I was wrong.

The end of it was a lot less decent. Nothing prepared me—or, for that matter, Indigo—to the utter and complete mess Bernie would get us into.

*

Indigo worked out a scenario.

According to it, I, a brilliant university graduate and the darling of the academia, deeply moved by my commencement ceremony, was to "have an idea" to throw my own "tribute party."

To this party I would invite people who inspired me in my younger days or influenced me as a future creator and scientist: my leading university professors, school teachers, and closest friends; some friends of my father's whose achievements made an impression on me as a child. Alois Jänzen was to be included in the latter category; Bernie and Indigo would be present among "the closest friends."

'You will not even have to introduce us,' Indigo assured me. 'I will approach Herr Jänzen with a cocktail and strike up a conversation myself.'

Indigo really pushed the boat out for me to host that sham party.

She rented a villa at Wannsee, hired a chef, a bartender, and waitresses, and ordered luxurious wines and exotic flowers.

Just a little over a month remained before the opening of the exhibitions—time was tight. Invitations to about twenty people had to be delivered within one day by a team of couriers—a courier to each person. That day was Monday; the party was planned for Saturday.

The impression of a spontaneous and extravagant decision made by an over-emotional university leaver elated by his triumphant graduation was meticulously—and successfully—created. Everyone who was invited, without an exception, fell for it. No one seemed to mind a short notice; everyone expressed enthusiasm.

Everyone, without fail, showed up at Wannsee the following Saturday.

Indigo revealed enviable organizational abilities, single-handedly arranging it all in less than a week's time—such that I had never suspected in her. She also revealed her (or, rather, her late father's) financial might and the grotesque extent of her obsession with Bernie—which I had been well aware of even without so lurid a demonstration.

*

Even though the whole arrangement was a hoax, I, contrary to my expectations, found myself taking pleasure in it. For Indigo it might have been a travesty staged for Bernie's special benefit, but for me it incredibly turned into a real tribute party. I was happy to reconnect with my old mentors, see the good friends of my parents' who had known me as a little boy; once again make music with Franz and Oliver as the inseparable Friedrich Wilhelm trio.

Indigo's Wannsee Act bestowed on me another deeply emotional, singularly real, and exhilarating experience of reuniting with those who mattered. She was later to tell me that if no other good came out of it, then at least she was happy to have given me a beautiful party. It was, she said, the very least she could do to thank me for the years of being her "guardian angel," while she herself had mostly behaved "like a spoilt brat and an ingrate" toward me.

Her own words, quoted.

She understood...

Needless to say, she played her part impeccably from the beginning to the end. Though generally an introvert, events of that kind were her element—they provided a backdrop against which she could glow. If the preparation was a challenge she'd admirably coped with, then starring as a professor's socialite daughter with an arty cousin in tow was the pure reward she reveled in.

Indigo and Bernie arrived at the scene a little later than everyone else; their vehicle was a specially hired, chauffeur-driven *Großer Mercedes*. Her slimness was set off by an open-back *rose pâle* dress that nipped in at the waist before falling to a skirt layered with striking swathes of diaphanous black tulle. In her hands she carried a bunch of black and cream roses which she gave to me with greetings and kisses. Bernie was wearing a black velvet one-button peak lapel coat whose strict elegance contrasted with his artistically tousled locks over a hollow-cheeked, alabaster pale countenance. He was also wearing an absent expression and a slightly dreamy, slightly arrogant half-smile.

She made virtuosic use of her Junta-from-Das-Blau-Licht magnetism to bewitch poor old Jänzen. After offering him a drink and introducing her cousin, she fell practically silent. It was Alois who followed her every step and did the rest of the chatting. Indigo merely listened with her dainty breasts heaving; made swift movements with her slender hands; assumed feline poses on the sofas and armchairs. Every now and again she took her eyes off her interlocutor and momentarily stared into emptiness like a frightened doe.

As to Bernie, he loitered around distractedly, drank copious amounts of Absinthe, approached Indigo and Alois occasionally, and inserted some benign utterances. Eventually he got bored of them and sauntered into the back veranda to have a smoke in the company of a strapping, ruddy-complexioned youth—the nephew of my Gymnasium St headmaster.

I did not watch the three of them much.

I was occupied with a lot more rewarding activities: receiving congratulations on my success and wishes of an even more successful future; catching up on the news of the many dear friends I had not seen for ages; sharing further academic plans with the Humboldt folk; listening to the Gymnasium headmaster (my elderly *Herr Direktor*) and the guidance counselor reminisce on the scraps I had gotten into with the other scallawag schoolboys while having always been their indisputable creative leader; performing with Franz and Oliver.

Indigo, Alois Jänzen, and Bernie were accidentally in, and just as accidentally out of my field of vision as I spent time enjoying the party. Now I saw Indigo showing Bernie's portfolio album to Alois; now I overheard Bernie commenting on the style of some paintings on the walls of the villa; now I caught sight of Alois ceremoniously stooping over Indigo's hand to kiss it.

At some point Franz and Oliver started insisting that we play Mes

Études again—the miniature I had dedicated to my alma mater. I found myself looking around for Indigo, hoping that, as she had missed the piece at my graduation concert, perhaps she could hear it this time.

But, once again, Indigo was suddenly nowhere to be found.

Ironically, she re-emerged to the sound of the final chords—much like she had done at the ever-memorable concert. Face flushed, all of a dither, she fluttered up to me.

'Chris, have you seen Bernie?' she whispered agitatedly. 'I'm looking for him everywhere. Jänzen is ripe; all that's left is some final small talk and a handshake—and Bernie has to disappear just the moment he is most needed!'

I looked around.

Bernie was not in sight.

Alois was sitting in a wicker chair by a coffee table with Bernie's portfolio album across his lap, munching on a canapé and sipping scotch.

I told Indigo that last time I saw Bernie, he was following Dieter Meier, my ex-Principal's nephew, out of the door. I assumed they could still be on the veranda or in the garden.

She swiftly nodded and rushed out.

My guess proved right, for a minute later she stepped back in, dragging the disgruntled-looking Bernie along by the arm.

Next thing I saw, the two of them and Alois were standing by the coffee table engaged in a lively conversation.

I then got distracted and once again lost track of the trio.

Toward the end, when I was seeing some of my guests off (many stayed overnight), Indigo pulled me aside and breathed into my ear ecstatically.

'It's done! Jänzen disapproves of Bernie's style yet finds it "intriguing." He knows we don't mind being—and even want to be—at the alternative exhibition. It didn't surprise him much. He is arranging a meeting with Ziegler in Bernie's studio next week! This practically means Bernie gets exhibited. It is in the bag, Chris! We did it. You and I did it.'

*

Next time I heard Indigo's voice was three days later.

It was Wednesday.

I heard it on the telephone belonging to Eugen Fischer, the rector of

Friedrich Wilhelm University. During the party, I had mentioned I would visit the rector on that day regarding participation in the Rhineland Bastards project, which he invited me to join.

It was in the rector's office that Indigo managed to find me.

Fisher's secretary looked flabbergasted as she was passing me the handset.

'Doctor Heidert? It is for you. The young woman says she is Indigo Schwarz, the daughter of late Professor Schwarz. She sounds terribly upset and insists this is absolutely urgent.'

My heart sank into the pit of my stomach. Uncomfortably leaning across the rector's desk, I took the handset.

'Indie?'

'Chris...' She gulped back a sob. 'Do you know where Bernie is? Did you talk to him today? Or yesterday? Did you see him? Do you have any idea?'

She sounded distraught, but I felt an immediate relief. Nothing terrible had happened to her. It was once again something about Bernie.

'How should I know where Bernie is, Indie?' I started, lowering my voice as much as I could. 'I don't chaperon him—you do. I am the last person he reports to.'

She burst into unrestrained sobs.

'He disappeared! Just vanished! We had an appointment with Ziegler today. Ziegler and Jänzen waited for an hour outside the studio—the door was locked, and Bernie never showed up! I didn't know what to say to them...'

Now that my initial pang of worry was gone, I felt embarrassed by this absurd scene in the rector's office. Covering the mouthpiece with my free hand I implored Indigo to calm down, promised we would find Bernie and decide how to save the situation, said I was on my way, and returned the handset onto the hookswitch.

'Is Fräulein ...eh... Schwarz all right?' Fischer asked, clearing his throat sarcastically.

Both he and the secretary were staring at me in bewilderment.

'Whatever gave her the idea of telephoning *here* in search for *you*, Christian?'

I could have sunk through the floor.

Mumbling vague apologies I turned and left. Any other actions or reactions felt entirely inappropriate.

Indigo's hysterics on the rector's telephone thwarted my chances of ever taking part in the Rhineland Bastards project. In all fairness, however, I never regretted this particular outcome much.

I found Indigo at Frau Treder's—sitting on the bed, hair in a messy contrast with her smart black and beige tweed suit. The ashtray on her bedside table was overflowing. She was nervously fingering at a small tilt hat which had landed on her lap. Her makeup was smudged with tears.

She gave me a pitiful look when I entered.

I embraced her and petted her disheveled hair.

'Tell me what happened, darling.'

It was predictable; there had been an agreement with Jänzen that he would get Ziegler to visit Bernie's "studio" (a kind of art room which Indigo rented) and look at his paintings, after which Bernie's works of Ziegler's choice would be transported directly to Munich. The latter, according to Indigo, had already been decided; Ziegler had preliminarily approved on Jänzen's recommendations, so his visit to the studio was needed as a pure formality. Indigo was positioning herself as the artist's official representative and publicist.

Only, the day before the planned visit (Tuesday), Bernie said he was going to "meet up with a friend," went out, and never returned. As such spontaneity was by no means untypical for her cousin, Indigo refrained from worrying until the end, hoping he would arrive at the appointed time, directly at the studio.

He never arrived.

Ziegler waited for an hour and left in righteous indignation; Jänzen followed, shrugging his shoulders and marveling at the "irresponsibility" of Christian Heidert's young circle of acquaintances.

'Did Bernie name the friend he was going to see?' I asked. 'Or mention his approximate whereabouts?'

'Dieter…' She closed her eyes and shook her head wearily, trying to recall. 'Dieter something. He met him at your party, I believe.'

Dieter Meier. The Gymnasium headmaster's nephew.

Indigo had enough on her mind as it was, so I spared her my own apprehension. I doubted little, however, that, apart from Alois Jänzen's, my name was now also disgraced in dear old *Herr Direktor*'s eyes.

My fears were confirmed.

Bernie returned.

Emerged in the doorway an hour or so later—all ruffled up, in a torn, dirty shirt, with a bleeding cut across his shoulder and a black eye.

'What happened? Where have you been?' Indigo cried in exasperation, ignoring her cousin's miserable physical state.

'Keep your voice down, will you!' Bernie screeched at her. 'You will scare the hell out of mother, and I don't want her to know I've been out at all. Besides, I have a splitting headache. Don't make it worse, please.'

'What happened, Bernie? Where have you been?' I repeated Indigo's questions as peacefully as I could.

From Bernie's hungover ramblings, it could be gathered that, apart from "this ungrateful pig," Dieter Meier, he had spent the night with a bunch of Dieter's pals whom he wined and dined in several *Kneipes* of their preference out of his own (meaning, Indigo's) pocket. But, as soon as Bernie attempted to isolate himself with Dieter, the latter started calling him all kinds of bad names. Dieter's "boorish chums" chimed in. They said Bernie had better beat it if he didn't want himself reported to the authorities. Some of the chums saw fit to reinforce the verbal message with physical action—hence Bernie's injuries. "The Pig" Dieter, reportedly, added that he would let his uncle, a respectable Gymnasium headmaster, know with what kind of creepy perverts his former favorite pupil Christian Heidert hung out these days.

'Bernie!' Indigo screamed when he finished, as if she heard nothing of what had been said. 'Where the hell have you been? We had an appointment with Jänzen and Ziegler about the exhibition! They waited for you outside the studio for over an hour! Where, for devil's sake, have you been?'

Bernie raised a bloodshot eye at her and gave her a bored look.

'Ah… The exhibition… I forgot, sorry. Well, I never wanted to be exhibited, anyway. It was your idea, and I always thought it was a stupid one.'

With those words, he flopped on the bed where Indigo was sitting and passed out.

Thus I was dishonored in the eyes of some people whom I held dear, and Bernie proved too degenerate even for a degenerate art exhibition.

XIV
2nd Violin

"My views on mankind become more and more dismal; it generally seems to me that the race must perish entirely."

Wagner's reflections on humanity, which Chris loves to quote.

The zigzagging quality of my musical ward's discourse escalates by the day. His misanthropic musings now more often than ever before alternate with fits of charitableness; his fierce discontentment—with humanitarian gestures.

Damira's name is permanently on his lips. She has become another of Chris's pet obsessions. He habitually starts off with some wisdom of the große meister's, then flies off at a tangent and lands in AU's block 32, where he has been given a personal lab for working on his *Force Vitale* project.

The children whom he refers to as "the little, *Force Vitale*-driven redeemers" are now all in a bad way. All the four, including Damira, of course. The more of their flesh he feeds to the disease, the more Dr. Heidert craves to delve into the depths of his objects' souls. He is overwhelmed by his many discoveries: stricken by coincidences, rendered speechless by discrepancies, spellbound by differences, dazed by similarities.

'Never in my life have I seen four living beings so ennobled—so, in the deepest sense of the word, matured—by the act of, first unconscious, and then almost conscious surrender to what has to happen. For no other reason than it simply being the ultimate justice done. Their profound, unchildlike understanding of what is going on, the appreciation of the transcendent wisdom of the force that is acting on them, the unconditional acceptance of the rules that it dictates, the uncomplaining obedience—and more than other things—the mutual educating—reinforcing that mystical inner knowledge in each other…'

At this point, Christian usually stops to dab at his eyes and blow his nose. Thus the poetical line is often left unfinished.

*

He finds a particularly spicy pleasure in telling me how dear Damira holds me, how she misses me, and what incredible escapades of mine she tirelessly relates to the other children.

This is a good thing.

The sincerity of Christian's wallowing in schmaltz (David's favorite word) is unblemished. Unpolluted. This means Lavuta and I can use him as a messenger. Or, rather, a courier.

A rarity, an invaluable alignment—not to be missed.

I listen to him intently as he speaks—never interrupting, asking no questions, staring aside. I wait for the climax. The moment he reaches the peak of feeling, and before he takes out the handkerchief to blow his nose again, I press Lavuta to my chest and chin.

I start playing—anything that occurs to me. Being the musical tutor and technical support, it is tacitly agreed I can grab the instrument and play at any moment—whenever instinct takes me. If my fiddling interrupts Christian's reflections halfway through, all the better. This means we are on the same wavelength. Any such spontaneity of mine is understood to be for the good of my meister's musical cause.

So I play.

Christian may or may not stop to listen. In fact, in most cases, there is not much to listen to—just a lumbering of notes. «*Très avant-garde*», as Maurice-the-painter, a new arrival at the Jewish camp, might describe it.

But, regardless of him paying only minimal attention, or none at all, Lavuta's sounds get implanted in Dr. Heidert's memory. So that next time he goes to the lab to look at his objects, he should unthinkingly take his pedantic Cosima violin along and, once there, feel an inexplicable urge to entertain the children.

Chris barely remembers these occasions; the children remember Doctor Heidert's strange desultory performances even less. However, every time the doctor delivers Lavuta's and my little message, Damira's brain gets specific instructions to sink every bit of the pain she feels in jolly memories of her hero Jass and pass the anesthesia on to the other three.

The good girl does the job dutifully.

How can she disobey?

*

Mihai started a game with me a while ago.

When he perceives a bit of information as a particularly pleasant one, he pretends not to understand it. Plays the senility card; asks to explain over and over, repeat again and again. The new ruse is aimed at getting to numerously relish a tale that's only meant to be exciting once, or even told with altogether different purposes than tickling the listener.

He has continually tried the stratagem when our conversation turned to Chloya the barmaid or when I mentioned overhearing that Baba Tanya complimented his hygienic habits. Naturally, while raising these topics, I quite expect having to serve them to Mihai a dozen times anew under various verbal sauces, spiced up with different wisecracks and with helpings of new gossip every time. Indeed, I enjoy being a chef who knows how to concoct a delicacy and indulge my customer.

Lately, however, the customer's taste seems to have gone a tad too exotic. The old man has developed a palate for most unlikely subjects. One of recent favorite treats are the chronicles of my relationship with Doctor Heidert. Mihai wants to know everything in minute details. He insists I should explain to him what epic music piece it can be the doctor wants to compose that it makes him agree to bear long hours of my company on a regular basis (Mihai assures me that if he were in the doctor's place, he would've long since shot me, or himself). He has to know everything we talk about. He is respectfully curious about the doctor's political views and philosophical reflections, even if he understands little of the former and even less of the latter. But more than anything else, Mihai craves stories of Doctor Heidert's past—especially the trials and tribulations of his love life. Mihai's attitude toward Indigo, Christian's flame, is an ambivalent one. On the one hand, he gets mad at her for having been such a beastly bitch to the gentle and all-forgiving Doctor Heidert. On the other hand, this Indigo has obviously become Mihai's hero. He can't get enough of anecdotes about her.

*

'Listen, boy,' the old man starts, and by his tone, I already know he'll be asking for another treat. 'There's something I can't understand. For the life of me, I cannot. You have to explain it to old Mihai, or old Mihai dies a fool.'

'Yes, Babbo. What is it you want me to explain to you?'

'That Indigo lass. Our doctor's… you know.'

'I know.'

'Did she really hate the doctor because she could not love him? Did she do all the things she did to jeer at him? Teach him a lesson? Maybe she even wanted to shame him in front of others? Show him up on purpose?'

'I don't think she hated him, Babbo,' I start noncommittally. 'I believe maybe sometimes she felt guilty because she could not return his feelings and unconsciously sought to rile him so that he fall out of love with her.'

'Right, right,' He nods, taking a snuff. 'Like that birthday party of her girlfriend's she dragged him to. She wanted the doctor there to show him what sins she got up to. No? Come, tell me the story again, boy! Cause I want to understand.'

Sure enough. Another act of *Bujo* Mihai rates high. And if it is *choribe* tales that warm the cockles of Babbo's heart, then be it. I retell the story of Indigo's practicing her secret foible for the third time in the last twenty-four hours.

*

'So it was, Babbo, that Fräulein Indigo took Chris—Doctor Heidert, that is—to her ex-schoolmate's birthday party. Indigo's cousin, Bernie, the one our Christian is perpetually jealous of, came along too. That party was to take place in a big, splendid house in one of the poshest residential areas of the city of Berlin. And the area was so posh, and the house was so splendid because Indigo's ex-schoolmate was the daughter of rich parents who allowed her to buy chic things, go to expensive venues, throw luxurious parties, and do what she wanted. And this girl always had generous pocket money to entertain herself and her friends, and she liked to boast of it, so everybody in her circle, and beyond, knew she had *lové* on her.

Fräulein Indigo spruced herself up well for the party—chose a fancy outfit, styled her hair, and hired a swanky car. She insisted that her companions—Christian and Bernie—be dressed up to the nines, coiffured, and perfumed too. So Chris and Bernie did not doubt Indigo was one of the birthday girl's very special friends and a highly awaited guest, as they saw her prepare so carefully.

But, when the three of them arrived at the gate and rang the melodious doorbell, it turned out Indigo had hardly been expected—maybe had not even been invited at all. The birthday girl seemed clearly surprised to see her and the two strangers she brought along. Out of decorum, however, the *Geburtstagskind* put on a smile, pretended she was gladdened by the visit of an old schoolmate, accepted the flowers Indigo brought, and allowed her and her entourage to enter.

Seeing that they were not really welcome, our discreet Christian and even the usually impudent Bernie felt abashed and out of place. Indigo, on the other hand, looked perfectly in her element; ignoring the snide looks and pursed lips of the other guests, she lightheartedly chatted, danced, ate the birthday girl's oysters and caviar, and drank her champagne.

As all the guests were getting increasingly drunk, Indigo was becoming jollier and jollier. At some point, after a cheery Lindy Hop, which she shared alternately with Christian and Bernie, Indigo took the arms of her two companions and asked them to help her find the room where she could fix her makeup.

Past carpeted seat benches on which young men were lounging—some exhausted by the swing, others by too much champagne and cognac; past the kissing couples; past girls who gabbled away twenty to the dozen, the three of them glided across the spacious hall, dissolved in the cigarette smoke, and dived into a darkened corridor. On they marched along the endless corridor—Indigo pulling the two young men by the hands. Instead of stopping to enter the bathroom, she urged her friends to take a sharp turn at the end of the passage and then follow her up the steep stairs to the second floor.

'Where are you taking us?' Christian demanded.

'You'll see soon enough,' Indigo whispered excitedly.

Finally, they halted at a semi-open door.

'I've only been in this house once as a kid,' Indigo said. 'But, as I remember well, this is our precious Renata's very own bedroom.'

Renata was the birthday girl's name.

Without a moment's hesitation, Indigo walked into the dark room, monosyllabically ordering Chris and Bernie to follow her there too.

In the cool, drapey darkness, they could make out the outline of a wide canopy bed, a nightstand, and a dressing table.

Indigo went straight to the nightstand, pulled out the top drawer, and slid her hand in, felt for something.

'There it is!' she announced contentedly. 'The old girl remains a creature of habit.'

With those words, she took something out of the drawer—apparently a velvet envelope—and, ignoring her companions' (well, mostly Christian's) indignant protests, slid it into her own patent leather clutch bag.

'Listen to me, boys. We now go back downstairs, blend in, and exchange some more small talk with those bores of Renata's guest. You watch me all the while and wait for my sign. When I see that our sweet hostess is approaching the right degree of inebriation—which, I expect, will be occurring in the next half hour—I kiss her on both cheeks, wish her a happy birthday again, and thank her for a lovely evening. This will be the sign. Immediately after we say our goodbyes and leave—preferably along with some others. I know I owe you two an explanation, and I will give one as soon as we are out of this place. I promise.'

No matter how much Christian was exasperated by Indigo's behavior, he saw there was nothing else for it; he and Bernie would have to follow her instructions and play along, lest they, all the three of them, got in trouble. Bernie saw that too, and, unlike Christian, did not seem to mind. He looked, if anything, rather amused by the whole situation—but it was typical for Bernie to take pleasure in such shenanigans, and it was also the reason why Christian always detested Bernie, believing him a corrupting influence on Indigo.

In that case, however, it was clear the idea belonged exclusively to Indigo herself, and the criminal act went off without a hitch, from the first point to the very last one.

*

Mihai rubs his hands, chuckling.

'So this Indigo *chey* snatched some of the rich girl's *love*; nice and clean, she did!'

'Indeed she did, Babbo.'

'And when Doctor Heidert demanded his "explanations," what did she say? Tell me again what she said to him!'

'As soon as the three of them got off the hired car at Bernie's place where Indigo was staying, Indigo explained her act to her two companions, just as she'd promised.'

She said, 'All through the school years I was trying to figure out; what is wrong with me? Why are they doing this to me? How, or what must I be to get them to stop it?

'I was kind to everybody. I shared. I was polite.

'How did I deserve this?

'The rich, smug, snout-nosed, potato-faced Renata, who was considered "the prettiest girl in class," and the gang of her suck-ups, some of whom you've seen at the party, tortured me in every possible way: pinched me, pushed me, spat at me, called me names, and took my books and toys I brought along and tore them apart.

'The worst thing was that sometimes they unexpectedly became friendly—played with me, talked normally, and accepted me as an equal. Renata even invited me to her tenth birthday party—that's when I visited her house for the first time.

'But then, just as I relaxed and thought the nightmare was over, without any reason or explanation, they would in a matter of a second turn on me again—and taunt, hassle, and harass with a vengeance.

'I tried telling my father, but he was too gentle a man to believe "girls" could be evil. He thought his sensitive little wild flower was just overreacting a bit.

'I tried complaining to the teachers—and it worked—several times Renata and her stooges got detention and desisted for a while. But it only helped temporarily; some days passed, and they resumed.

'The teachers, meanwhile, got bored of my complaining. They started advising me to "ignore" Renata. They said the tormenting would stop if I paid no attention to it—the tormentors would lose interest then. I was wondering though: how long exactly will the period of ignoring have to last for it to stop? Just one ignored tormenting session never seemed to be enough… How much pain will I have to endure, pretending as if it didn't hurt and I didn't care, before they lose interest in inflicting it?

'Renata and her gang never used my name—they called me "rat," because I "ratted them out" to the teachers and because of my "ratty" appearance.

'Well, as years went by, I realized rats were some of the sweetest, smartest, and loveliest animals in the world—but they could be quite fierce too. I felt more and more like a proud rat—much like back in kindergarten I had felt like a proud crow, as that was how other, younger "girls" had labeled me back then. I decided I'd always be as much a rat toward the "girls" as possible. I will truly deserve the name. Not only will I rat them out at every opportunity, not only will I break their every code. I will do something else rats do. Steal. Take from them. Take their money and buy myself the loveliest things for it.

'Renata always liked to boast of her pocket cash—of how much her parents loved her and indulged her.'

'I knew I would come for that cash of hers one day.'

'I did today. You saw it happen. I'm going to buy myself a sapphire necklace I've wanted a long time.'

*

Mihai is in a celebratory mood. He won't stop grunting contentedly.

The show for my one-man audience is not yet over, though. Babbo wants an encore.

'But our Doctor Heidert was not happy with the explanation the girl gave? Was he, boy? He still gave her a spanking, right? Told her off, well and proper, no?'

'Verily, Babbo, our Christian was not satisfied with Indigo's excuse. And he continued to reproach her bitterly.'

'What did he say?'

'He said, "The things these girls did to you may have felt terrible; I can well imagine that. I hate them for having hurt you. But their beastly acts as children do not justify your vile behavior as an adult. They did so unwittingly; they were little, they didn't know any better. You, on the other hand, are an adult now, knowing what you do, able to think critically, and answerable for your actions. You are a grownup avenging children. You repay their age-bound folly of a long gone past with a truly immoral and unlawful deed in the present. Moreover, you make me and Bernie accomplices to your crime. Stealing is despicable, Indigo. No circumstances justify it."'

'And what did the girl say to that?'

'She asked Christian whether he thought torturing a sentient, intelligent being was justified in any circumstances.'

'And he?'

'He answered, "Taunting is a nasty thing, Indie, but it is characteristic of children. Almost every schoolchild at some point gets teased and bullied by his or her mates. I was a victim of other boys' cruelty many times as a schoolboy. So, I'm sure, was Bernie, or anyone you ask. But such infantile little conflicts always resolve themselves. Kids get older and cleverer; they grow out of stupidity. They recognize their former little mistakes and apologize to the mate they once picked on. And usually later they become his friends, and he may even end up becoming their leader and role model, as it was in my case.'

'And she then?'

'And then she interrupted him, "Did your tormentors apologize to you, Chris? Did they say "I'm sorry"? And did you forgive them?'

'To which he?'

'To which he exclaimed, "Of course they said they were sorry! And it came from the heart. And of course I forgave. Never would even a thought enter my mind to hurt my comrades for something we all did as children, especially employ such a dastardly means as thieving for the purpose! I do not doubt, Indigo, that Renata apologized to you too. I am sure she said she was sorry."'

'And then the girl interrupted him again, right, boy?'

'She most certainly interrupted again, Babbo.'

'And she said something our gentle Doctor Heidert still cannot get over, didn't she, boy?'

'Precisely so.'

Mihai fidgets in anticipation. He leans forward and licks his lips.

'Tell me what she said.'

*

'She did not just say, Babbo. She wrote. To make the account of her actions complete, she promised to write a letter to Christian and Bernie, a sort of explanatory essay.'

'And she did?'

'She did.'

Upon giving this last confirmation, I recite to Mihai a piece of belle-letters authored by Fräulein Schwarz, which Chris, in his emotional turmoil, has repeatedly read to me out loud.

This little soliloquy is what Mihai is truly looking forward to—a cherry to top his cake.

Dear Christian and Bernie!

I am writing this letter to explain why I took you along to see what to you may have looked like iniquity, but for me it was merely justice.

I am especially addressing the following words to you, Chris, who reproached me for not having had the magnanimousness to forgive a person who had tormented me for years when she apologized to me and said she was sorry for what she had done.

You see, I generally do not believe there is any intrinsic justice in the world. I do not believe good prevails, evil ends up punished, and everybody gets what they deserve. They don't. Unless you make them.

The place where the kind are rewarded, while the malevolent get their comeuppance is mostly fairytales.

There is no wise and beneficent god to stand guard of the righteous cause for you. There is no proverbial "boomerang." The man-made concept of law is, let's face it, a freedom-crippling, despicable, yet toothless farce.

YOU are your own god, law, and boomerang.

This is the only religious view I hold and adhere to.

Hope I have not bored you too much with this preamble. Now we come to the point.

I do not know about you, dear friends, but I personally have a problem with the phrase "I'm sorry."

Let's analyze it. They have done something nasty to you, and then they go and exempt themselves, proffering this lightweight, commonplace, and sure-fire tag. And once they have thrust this coat-check stub at you, you officially have no moral right to punish them or even blame them anymore because "Hey, I've already said I'm sorry, haven't I?"

This means you are now alone to deal with the pain they have inflicted, the consequences of their irresponsibility, and sort out the mess they have made without any compensation or help on their part. Because after they have admitted they are "sorry," it would be incredibly unkind of you to demand any, wouldn't it?

Well, this "I'm sorry" bit does absolutely nothing to me apart from aggravating me even more. It is of zero use. It cannot be converted into an exotic trip, an erotic massage, or even an ice cream. And, I believe, if they sincerely regret the damage they have done and actually feel as "sorry" as they claim to, it should be their natural urge to want to, at least in part, undo it. And this is where the fundamental social regulator, the universal lubricant of human relations, the all-purpose remedy, the genius invention comes in (or should come in)—money.

I am convinced that any moral or physical harm—be it a rude word or a partner's betrayal—must be financially compensated—in the amount approximately equal to the size of the loss, which is ultimately determined by the aggrieved party.

It is a perfect solution because it both punishes the offender and recompenses the offended.

You see, it would not make me feel any better to, say, slap them on the cheek or smash their nose in for having done dirt to me (well, in most cases it wouldn't—there are exceptions, but they are rare). Usually when I am hurt, my first care is to stop my own pain—not make them hurt too. I am not sadistic. When I am hurt, I want comforting things for myself—usually of the variety that money can buy.

And, if they are not willing to fork out... well, I consider it my moral right to take their money without their consent, in the amount calculated according to the formula designated above. At the earliest opportunity. About as soon as they look away from their wallet, purse, or bank account.

I hope, dear boys, I have now fully stated my position and explained why I dragged you along to Renata's party. I did it in order there should be witnesses to me exercising what is right in my book.

In case, even after reading this, either of you still resents me for doing what I have done, I do not say, "I'm sorry."

I rest my case.

*

Mihai applauds and thunders with glee, his head tilted back, a long, lazy tear maneuvering its way down his wrinkled face. At this point, the amount of brouhaha generated by him overfills the cup of Baba Tanya's patience. With a squelching clap, she vigorously lands the stumpy palm of her right hand on her fleshy right knee and booms.

'Is it the fables the young rascal here tells, or your own stupidity that makes you crow so loud, old man? I told you a thousand times I have a headache, and you always make it worse with your racket. You do it on purpose; you must. Clearly, you want me to die. Well, let me promise you, old fool, you are not getting your wish granted in a hurry! God who sees everything knows I still have things to do in this world. Do tie a rope round your beak, or I shall!'

Mihai obediently covers his mouth with his hand and continues laughing into it, quietly and shudderingly.

We lower our voices, but do not stop our dialogue.

Both Baba Tanya and Mihai have their clock ticking, they will both be gone soon. One has, therefore, to make them happy in the days that are left. With Baba Tanya, it is Vasil, the Bulgarian boy, who does the job; Mihai is my responsibility. So I must take care that Baba Tanya and Vasil coo over the *biryul'ky* undisturbed in their corner, while I continue telling the old man my "fables." It is his snuff, Chloya's photograph, and talking with me that sets Mihai's mind at rest these days. I make sure the latter should go on uninterrupted—yet without disturbing Baba Tanya's and Vasil's never-ceasing, giggling, and whispering rites.

'Do you think it is real love, boy? The one our doctor feels for this naughty Indigo *chey*? Forgiving her everything? Always wanting the best things to come to her? Letting her go with another and still caring for her?'

Somehow speaking more softly modulates Mihai's mood, switching him from the mirthful mode to the romantic wavelength again.

I take a moment to reflect on it, then answer, 'If by "real" we say "sincere," I suppose it is, Babbo. In as much as all things Christian feels or does are real. He doesn't have an insincere vein in his body. He always means it. And he always means well.'

'Yes, yes, yes!' My interlocutor nods frantically. 'So kind, so obliging, Doctor Heidert! So polite always! Still… there is something I cannot wrap my stupid old man's brains around, boy.'

It is now Mihai's turn to indulge in a thoughtful pause, and he makes the most of it—takes snuff, coughs into his fist, frowns, wrinkles, and unwrinkles his forehead, and stretches his lips into a meditative half-smile. Then, at last, he pronounces.

'To want a girl, and yet stand for her going out with another man. Not only stand for it, no. Help them be together. Help him alone even. What kind of saint would do that? What kind of sucker? Isn't it against a man's nature? Or are you, the young men of now, different from what we, the old ones, were back in the day?'

I resist the temptation to tell him the approach he describes is a classic and elegant stratagem inspired by the libertine poet Cyrano de Bergerac somewhere in the seventeenth century and popularized by his imaginative biographer Edmond Rostand two centuries later. Mihai wants to think of the saintly pattern as specific to Doctor Heidert's mentality. Or at least repeated after someone great who has been Doctor Heidert's major influence. So I briefly retell Mihai the word-tone drama story by Christian's creative and spiritual lighthouse, Meister Wagner. The one whose main character Chris wants to be associated with even more than with Siegfried of The Ring.

*

'Once, Babbo, in the merry German town of Nuremberg there lived a hard-working, wise, and kind man named Hans. Although a shoemaker by trade, Hans was also a talented poet and musician. So skillful he manifested himself in these arts that Nuremberg's guild of Master Singers recognized him as a great authority—as their best one, in fact. The recognition of that society was a great honor, for not only did the guild comprise many distinguished poets and singers, but also had a devilishly complicated set of rules which dictated how to write and perform songs correctly. This was so because the Master Singers of Nuremberg were, most of them, master craftsmen of various trades, and they believed music was also a kind of craft, so it was to be played craftily. Their traditions were intricate, the principles rigid, and the rules were to be followed to the letter. Any musician who broke a rule dropped out of the guild.

'One day an elder mastersinger and goldsmith announced to his fellows that he would give his daughter Eva's hand in marriage to the one who won the song contest, which the guild traditionally held on Midsummer's Day. Eva was sweet of character and lovely of face, and many men wanted her for a wife. Hans had long had tender feelings for the girl—and she also was kindly disposed toward the best mastersinger. And, as Hans was so great at singing and composing, no one doubted that, should he enter the contest, the fair maid's hand would be his.

'But it so happened that a short time before the contest Eva met a young knight by the name of Walther, and the two fell in love with each other at first sight. Hearing of Eva's father's will that his daughter should only marry the mastersinger who won on Midsummer's Day, Walther decided to join the guild and take part in the contest.

'It was, however, no easy task to be accepted as a mastersinger, let alone win the contest. The young knight almost had no time to learn the complicated rules of composing and performing established by the guild.

'It hardly came as a surprise that Walter's first attempt to become a member of the exacting association utterly failed. The song he presented to the jury broke every rule in the book, both in composition and delivery. The young man was harshly criticized; his candidature was rejected. The day of the contest, meanwhile, was approaching. Walther and Eva almost despaired.

'The two young lovers would have probably ended up separated and miserable if it had not been for the wise, noble, and golden-hearted Hans who intervened on their part. The song Walther had performed before the Master Singers' jury, though it may have been faulty by the guild's standards, touched Hans's soul, and he felt a deep sympathy for the youth. Besides, watching Eva's reactions, he could clearly see that the knight was her heart's choice. And, as he wanted the one he loved to be happy, Hans sacrificed his own desire for the girl and made up his mind to help Walter win her hand.

'Hans took the young knight under his wing: he explained to him the rules of mastersinging and trained him to perform in accordance with them. On the day of the contest, he spoke before the other mastersingers in Walther's defense, insisting that the guild's decision to reject the knight had been premature and he should be given another chance. After many arguments, Walther was granted a second trial, and, with his improved technique and Hans's authoritative support, he was not only accepted by the guild but also won the contest.'

'And took the girl?'

Mihai, who has been all this time listening with his eyes wide—ensorcelled like a little boy by his nanny's fairytale—now finally started getting impatient.

I nod.

'And took the girl.'

The old man shakes his head in a mixture of admiration and disapproval.

'And the young lovers were overwhelmed with gratitude to the kind, wise, and selfless man and the people of Nuremberg all sang the praises of Hans, their beloved mastersinger,' I add.

'This fable inspires our Doctor Heidert, right, boy?'

'This fable was put to music by his favorite composer. And the character of Hans is his moral benchmark. It definitely inspires him.'

'And he is just like this poor soul Hans himself!' Mihai exclaims with a catch in his voice. 'Too good for this world, too gentle. Even what he loves he gives away. Even whom he ought to dislike, he helps. Who'd be surprised all these ingrate girls and the rest of the world use him without shame?'

Not finding any plausible objections, I grunt in agreement, and Mihai gulps for air to continue his muffled lamentation of Doctor Heidert's softness and the world's taking advantage of it.

The old man, however, is too slow in formulating a new argument. Petko, the pockmarked harbinger, touches him on the shoulder just as Mihai is about to set off belaboring the point.

'On your feet, oldie. Follow me. Doctor Heidert's orders.'

It seems like Mihai and myself are the only two who did not hear Petko enter.

Marusya, Rosa, Maxim, and Emelian—all the rest are frozen before him, habitually cowed—staring up at the smug, mud-like face in anticipation and fear. Even Baba Tanya has hidden her treasure box and leaned on Vasil's bony knee to be steady while keeping the suddenly inflicted, heavy-breathing, and questioning silence.

Mihai scrambles into a vertical position. He is astonished and excited.

'Hear that, boy? Hear that? Speak of the doctor, eh, boy! See, it is not only you, Doctor Heidert needs! Sometimes it is old Mihai. Wonder now what it is that Doctor Heidert is calling me. What do you think it is, boy? Bet you'll never guess. Tell you when I'm back. You wait, boy. You wait.'

Prodded in the back by Petko, Mihai hobbles to the door.

The door creaks, sighs, and coughs.

The grayness outside swallows the two slouchy figures.

I shall not see the old man again.

XV
1st Violin

Though a minor thing, it is a relief. Akin to having got rid of an importunate insect—a fly banging against the windowpane or a mosquito whining at the ear.

Guido has proved unexpectedly helpful.

I asked him, quite on the off chance, if he would, perhaps, need a control object for Pharma-Ko.

What with the bewildering reticence and inordinate nervousness Guido has been demonstrating lately? I expected he would bolt from me like a horse from a fire. Pharma-Ko has recently been one of the most fraught subjects to raise in Guido's presence. His face begins to change color, rapidly going from the bluish red of a plum to the greenish pale of a death cap, after which he usually mutters something indecipherable, hides his eyes, and vanishes before one has time to repeat the pharmaceutical's name. And that is the consequence of a mere mention. Asking a direct question in regard with the project may provoke a still more violent reaction, like crying out or even tears, which Guido never manages to fight back, although he visibly tries.

Given this and a number of other recent instances in which Guido has manifested inexplicably out-of-character behavioral patterns, my chances of palming the Mihai creature off to him were nearing zero.

Something, nevertheless urged me to try.

I did, and, contrary to all logic, it worked.

Moreover, he seemed uncannily aware of everything I was going to say and ask.

'Mihai, the wrinkled-faced, coughing Gypsy, which stinks of snuff, is that the one? You are reading my thoughts, dear colleague! It is precisely him I wanted as a control; I was just about to tell you myself! So, when are we transferring the oldie to the block today?'

He sounded almost anxious.

I surprised myself at how reassured I actually felt to have the old, chummy, and enthusiastic Guido back—if only momentarily.

*

Guido is a good man.

An understanding colleague, a supportive comrade. Honest, upfront. Optimistic. Cheerful, faithful, simple.

Salt of the earth.

As for his recent crankiness—well, who is without sin?

Who has not been taking things close to heart? Who has not had his nerves worn thin?

It borders on treason to stay placid these days, if you ask me. Peace of mind becomes an untimely and unaffordable luxury.

There is betrayal and incitement everywhere. In AU, in Berlin, in Italy, in France, and in the East.

In Italy they have, I hear, executed a traitor, Benito-the-Clown's son-in-law. Anton jokes that whenever they happen to be family—a daughter's husband, a wife's cousin, even flesh of one's flesh—they all end up getting the axe—almost without an exception, the literal one.

'The hoary Georgian highlander Stalin refused to swap his son for our Paulus, mind you!'

Anton being his not-giving-a-damn, sarcastic self.

'And the Leningrad embarrassment—do you want to know the cause? As easy as two by two, my good fellow…'

'Spare me this!'

Not another betrayal story told in Anton's amused manner. Not now.

That would be more than I'm able to handle.

I need to be talking to Anton, though. To be talking to someone. I wish I could tell him so much, but I feel I should not.

Should keep it all to myself.

Try.

Do my best.

*

Jass is being cranky too.

Those silences of his. The sombreness. The self-assuredness.

He thinks he is always right. Infallible. Well, he is, most of the time—there is no denying it. His every outlandish assumption proves scientifically correct. Every little tweak he makes to the music explodes like a goddamn bomb.

He is, however, so screamingly aware of all this that sometimes it becomes intolerable.

He suggested I should start with a grand orchestral intro instead of going straight into the main theme.

'We need a buildup. A fertilizer…'

While he was saying it—merely uttering the words—that intro of his played in my head and immediately claimed the title of the best bit I had ever heard or composed.

The complacency of the gypsy trickster!

Come to think of it, there is something Jewish about his attitude and the role that he took to playing in my life. Something brilliant yet illusory. It is not Romani effortless, artless magic anymore. It is double-bottomed Jewish "science."

I found him playing the other day—just stepped into the office to an opulent stream of sound.

Jassengro was standing with his back to the door, and although he most certainly heard me open the door and enter, he did not stop or turn his head.

At first I had a strange auditory illusion: I thought he was playing Indigo Mind. That feeling, however, got immediately ousted by an acute realization of its absurdity.

It was a completed piece—something deeply, viscerally, and primally mine, yet something as torturously unreachable as Brünnhilde's Moods had been when, as a child, I woke up from my febrile dream; or as Indigo's beloved daemon; or as Gennari's Orpheus.

The form of the piece I could not quite define, but the association that sprang to mind was with a comet—I remember a glissando down one string. A vertiginous slide into a crescendo—and an abrupt cutoff.

It flickered past, blinding and deafening me for a brief moment.

When Jass finished, I asked him what it was.

'A piece dedicated to a friend,' he answered.

*

I know he has a friend in the Jewish camp—someone Anton once mentioned to me.

He did not specify who exactly he devoted the music to, but somehow I immediately made a mental connection with this spindly, darting-eyed inmate.

It is irrational, of course, for that "friend" of his could be anybody. But Jassengro's thoughts are mine—he cannot hide them from me. Or, rather, he doesn't want to. Sometimes I believe he even forces me. Rubs my nose in his world on purpose. Holds himself open to me as though he were a didactic book and compels me to read, like an exacting teacher might a slothful pupil.

The price I have to pay for using him as a tool.

A heavy constituent of the price is him having Jewish "friends." Getting inspired by a Jew to write music I could have written.

Somehow it feels as if my own creativity were now all leached through and befouled with Jewishness. I might have felt less repulsed, if only the very idea of inspiration invoked by a Jew did not seem, in its very essence, entirely perverse to me.

The reason for my attitude is that there is simply nothing inspirational about the Jews.

Naught.

For only what is—at least in some way, or to some extent—creative itself can ignite another creator.

The Jewishness, as is universally known and historically corroborated, presents a phenomenon which is the very antithesis of creativity.

The two pillars the Jews have at all times leaned on are faith and racial purity.

Never on living and breathing thought. Never on imagination. Never on freedom.

The Jewish faith is probably the sole reason why the Jews, albeit their limited intellectual resources as compared to the Hellenes and the Romans, triumphantly prevailed in the age of post-Christ chaos. "Faith wide, narrow the thought" has always been the phrase that best described them.

The Hebrew soil could never have breed a real philosopher, poet, painter, or composer because the very sound of the Hebrew language makes the interpretation of metaphysical thoughts completely unrealizable. It is the same reason why the Semitic people could never weave into their scanty culture a mythology in the same sense as the Indians and the Teutonic peoples.

It is, therefore, begriming for a Romani creator to be inspired by a Jew—not to mention a Teutonic creator.

I only wish I could somehow put this self-evident truth across to Jassengro and make him seek his muses somewhere outside the Jewish camp.

*

Jassengro can hear my mind just as well as I can his.

Keen as mustard, my Gypsy instrument.

While I carefully search for a proper way to word my wishes (there is no question of expressing them openly, as it might rip the delicate emotional cloth sustainedly woven between us), he blurts out a crude objection.

'Whatever our attitude to Christianity and Christians, the person of Jesus Christ as one of the most inspirational entities in human history can hardly be disputed. European culture owes the Jewish race quite a bit of building material—perhaps as much as it does the Greeks.'

He winks at me impudently.

Little does Jassengro care about preserving that emotional cloth between us intact. It is I who should worry lest I inadvertently disrupt the precarious balance. It is I whose need is greater. I suppose by now I had better reconcile myself with my dependent position.

Nevertheless, I advance a counterargument.

'In a personality whose spirit shines so brightly as Christ's did,' I say, 'the peculiarities of race pale into insignificance.'

He nods.

'They do beyond doubt.'

I know this manner of his to agree too easily. It is fraught with subsequent mocking and bodes ill for my preserving inner harmony during the rest of the evening.

I press on with examples.

'Take an Isaiah. Regardless of how much he may transcend his coevals, he remains an unadulterated Jew. Every word he ever uttered grew out of the historical and spiritual soil of Jewishness. Even when he vehemently denounces what is typically Jewish, he, by this, confirms himself all the more as the Jew. While in Christ, we do not perceive even a tiny drop of that Jewish liven. Or let us look at Homer! In order to be able to open the eyes of the Hellenes to their spiritual and cultural identity, he had to absorb and nurture in his own bosom the very essence of entire Hellenism. Christ, in contrast...'

'I agree,' interrupts Jass.

'Then,' I continue, 'I hope you will also agree that it is not in Judea where people have earned themselves the right to claim Christ as their own! Galilee in Christ's times had almost no political or intellectual ties with Judea—it was perceived as a foreign country. Even the name "Galilee" itself stood for...'

I trail off and search my memory for some seconds.

'*Gelil haggoyim*,' prompts Jass. '"District of the heathen."'

'Exactly. Even in the earliest times when Israel was still powerful and united, Galilee had served home for a number of non-Israelitic tribes. Then, most significantly, in the centuries before Christ's birth Phoenicians and Greeks had flocked there in their thousands! Indeed, enough purely Aryan blood had been transplanted thither to almost confidently claim Christ's belonging, for the most part, to the Aryan race!'

'I thought we proceeded on the premise that in a personality whose spirit shines so brightly as Christ's, the peculiarities of race pale into insignificance.'

He grins and gives me another cheeky wink.

*

He jeers.

My instrument.

Sneers at me.

When Jassengro does something, it has to be swallowed and digested as an inherent part of reality. I would not think of asking him to stop or change his ways, because I would not even know what exactly it is I would be asking for or how to formulate it in such a way as not to humiliate myself further.

And, because he still very much accommodates me as an instrument, I know I will have to put up with his sneering and jeering, like I put up with so much else.

Scoffing generally seems to plague me on a daily basis. The blight of my existence.

Everybody scoffs. Anton does. Weber. The great man of pure genius that he is, Angel, unfathomably, scoffs too.

Don't they understand scoffing is impermissible in momentous times like ours? That nothing heroic, nothing lofty has ever grown out of mockery? Mockery is incompatible with great deeds, like a crooked smirk is unimaginable on a truly noble face.

History has known scoffing as a rancid product of distemper, a cultural regurgitation provoked by periods of chaos of people.

There was, for instance, Lucian—the second century's most celebrated lampoonist. No matter how many distinguished philologists will froth at the mouth trying to prove to me that Lucian's remarks about religion and philosophy are profound and that he was a daring opponent of superstition, I shall never fall for it. No. Religion and philosophy were hopelessly over this Syrian mestizo's head. He sneers at the systems which had been created before him, but it is only the shallowest, the most primitive element of those systems that he comprehends, utterly incapable of looking further or deeper than the superficial wording; never grasping the idea itself. It is not in the manner of Voltaire or Aristophanes that Lucian sneers. Those two men may have been sarcastic too, but their satire hinged on positive, constructive thought, on fanatical love for the people of their homeland. Lucian sneers without a noble aim, deep conviction, or firm principles; without a notion of belonging to a home, a land, or a people. The only thing Lucian truly understood, and the satirical scourging of which he indeed excelled, was the world whose motives and approaches he knew well, as he himself was the quintessence of that world—the totally bastardized, depraved, and degenerate reality around him—the chaos of people which followed Christ's demise.

"Our very own" Heinrich Heine is another case in point. One more worthless, wit-cracking wreck on the sea, devoid of pride, people, or homeland, daring laugh at something the depth and complexity of which is plainly beyond him.

As a matter of fact, I must correct myself regarding Heine: unlike Lucian, he did belong to a certain people and was thereby marked with certain pronounced facial features; Lucian's physiognomy was a lot less clearly defined.

The truly laughable property of these otherwise not unintelligent men is their failure to see what a caricature their life is on the destiny of the really great. How otherwise could a Heine have put himself on the same pedestal as a Goethe?

*

It is nature's way to begin with making the nucleus; the shell appears as a later accretion; the flesh must be created before it can be clothed; the hero's heart must beat before he can set out on his exploits.

Mockery erodes the nucleus; jeering individuals like Lucian or Heine have neither a kernel nor a root or a stem.

Wagner, the große Meister, must've felt this deeper than anyone else. One of his finest creations was well-nigh renounced by him in the earliest stages of its birth, just because he discerned a faint odor of base derision in it.

His only real comedy was meant to ridicule the formal approaches of the public art, but creative intuition, high morals, and artistic tact revealed to the great composer that what he was embarking on could be interpreted as an attack on tradition. The thought was so repulsive to Wagner's nature he laid the sketch aside for over fifteen years and, instead of *Die Meistersinger*, wrote Lohengrin.

When he eventually returned to work on the former, it was with a series of cardinal additions that he agreed to complete the comedy.

The initial sketch contained no indication of Sachs's love for Eva. Wagner subsequently introduced this crucial detail, thus bringing inner conflict into the heart of his cobbler-poet. He also put the glorious and prophetic monologue into Hans's mouth in order to counterbalance his previous call on his comrades not to follow the mastersinger's protocol too formally and allow for a situation when some of its most rigorous clauses could be waived. A situation in which true love of two human beings as well as true love for the art is involved, for instance.

In his final address to his fellows, Sachs proclaims.

What is German and true none would know if it did not live in the honor of German masters. Therefore I say to you: honor your German masters, then you will conjure up good spirits! And if you favor their endeavors, even if the Holy Roman Empire should dissolve in mist, for us there would yet remain holy German art!

Meanwhile, real, good humor—"lofty mirth which heals our pains"—is by no means wanting in the opera. It must be, however, regarded rather as an ornament than the dramatic center of the piece—a setting to hold the gem. The center, the gem, the core is solemnly asserting tradition rather than making it a laughing stock; it is also deep personal pain rather than gaiety, the pain of relinquished love.

For Wagner, comedy was only acceptable if it served as a means of bringing more nobleness into the world. And true nobleness, as Schopenhauer brilliantly observed, is always marked with a certain trace of silent sadness—"a consciousness that has resulted from the knowledge of the vanity of all achievements and of the suffering of all life, not merely of one's own."

*

I spend hours trying to bring it home to Jassengro. Read my mind he does; my musical alter ego he is—true. But to further my creative will, it is necessary that he should embrace my morality on a conscious level and bow to it.

Ignoring his mockery, surmounting the barriers of ridicule he builds up, I struggle to get through to him.

Have been speaking to him of *Die Meistersinger* a lot—probably more often than even of Der Ring. It is crucial that he should see Hans Sachs in me—I've been telling him so directly.

'Wagner's most Schopenhauerian character,' I have been saying. 'One that is closer to my soul than the intrepid Siegfried or the longing-stricken Tristan.'

In his characteristic manner, Jassengro first nods full understanding but then suddenly shrugs.

'Far it be from me to underestimate the value of renouncing one's desires, but, knowing you and myself well enough by now, I'd venture to argue that Diderot's philosophy is far closer to both our hearts than Schopenhauer's. Remember his *l'esprit d'escalier* alone—doesn't it just about sum up your entire life? It sure does mine, at least some of its turning points. Would you care to hear one such story?'

And, smiling in my face, he starts recounting another gypsy-Jewish anecdote.

There is a daemonic irony in one circumstance; Anton too has recently used Diderot's name paired with French wordplay to tease me. It was when, after the umpteenth sardonic remark he made about the prospects of the war, I reproached him for being cynical. He said, 'You should perhaps read some Diderot, my idealistic friend. He coined a special word to name the attitude for which you upbraid me so often, and some of which, in my humble view, you should learn—*je-m'en-foutisme*.'

*

I may sound obsessive, I know. Yet deluded or delirious I am not.

All around me sneer. Including Birgitte. My Freia. Even though she is supposed to be the preserver of balance in my soul. For all her sweetness, she too pokes fun at me; I can sense it.

This notion is the reason why I still haven't played Freia's Motherhood to her. Not that I feel it is inferior or fear she may dislike it. I know it is a masterpiece, almost as sublime as Indigo Mind. I have no doubts she will like it. What makes me apprehensive is that, in a way, she may like it too much.

With her never-faltering collectedness and composure, I can well picture Birgitte finding F. M. overemotional. Inappropriately candid. Embarrassingly sensual. Disproportionate to the scale of our relationship, or the meaning of what happened between us.

I can hear her coy, slightly didactic voice saying, 'Oh my goodness, Chris, I'm overwhelmed! I can't believe it is to me all this splendor is dedicated.'

She will want to add, 'You really should've not...' but will contain herself.

Her eyes will probably fill up with tears, but lurking behind the glistening liquid there will be unease and irony.

This is what I am afraid of. That the grandeur of my music will make her feel both uneasy and ironic toward me.

How can I be sure the love we shared matters to Birgitte as much as it does to me? She most likely sees it as nothing but a little naughty episode—a childish prank she was never going to either repeat or dwell on. She will interpret F. M. as reprovable dwelling on it.

Ever dignified, ever moderate, Birgitte will inwardly giggle at my puerile romanticism.

Maybe I should have used Jass in my work on F. M. after all. He would've not made the sonata any better, but he could've made it immune to irony. Whatever this Jew-loving Gypsy touches somehow becomes impossible to ridicule. No thinkable needling, teasing, or taunting feels relevant anymore, as soon as he turns his hand to a piece.

I must learn this skill from the Gypsy. I must, and I shall. No property a tool has is unattainable for the tool's master.

Reflecting on the recent events of my life has made me wish more than once I could apply this Gypsy tool to more spheres than music. My scientific apogee, *Force Vitale*, must be securely protected from derision or underestimation, just like the music. Another piece of pure greatness I created, and another one I wanted to devote to Birgitte. I use the verb "want" in the past tense because I now have reasons to suspect that Birgitte's attitude to this work of mine is not derision-free either.

I was reporting to Angel on one of the usual Mondays, and she looked in to ask him some question. When she heard us discussing the results of my *Force Vitale* work, she tapped me on the shoulder playfully and whispered, 'Aren't you overworking, Christian, dear?' While she was saying it, I could swear she was looking past my face at Angel and that she gave him a wink. I believe I may even have seen him wink back at her.

This is when I saw through Birgitte's autumnal serenity and unearthly sweetness.

*

Oh well.

I don't find it much of a comfort, but I probably ought to remind myself of some events from five years ago. The proof that, if not happiness, then there is some kind of severe justice in the world, after all.

It is painful to be unfairly derided by a woman for something brilliant you have achieved. But I am convinced it is well-deserved to be despised for something at which you have shamefully failed.

The former has happened to me; the latter—never. I simply never failed at or betrayed either my science, my art, or anything I have undertaken.

The latter happened to Bernie.

Unsurprisingly, the talentless cynic he is and the unvengeful soft touch I am, Bernie's downfall in Indigo's eyes did not either sadden him or gladden me—one bit.

Indigo's disillusionment with her Pierrot-resembling cousin Bernie started on the day of his non-appearance for the meeting with Jänzen and Ziegler. Maybe the exhibition incident was the proverbial straw that broke the camel's back, and Indigo's patience, which Bernie had been trying for years, eventually wore thin. Or perhaps Indigo, who for all her blindness was always a keenly intuitive creature, could feel that Bernie's drunken vagary signaled a permanent change in him. A change which was bound to shatter all the mystique he held for her.

There were several personality features Indigo found irresistible: physical attractiveness (especially one with a morbid flavor), an independent mind like her own, and talent. She could madly and all-forgivingly adore an owner of those three even when far more essential qualities, like honesty, generosity, or moral integrity, were lacking. But when one of the three magnetic jewels, for some reason or other, lost its glow, Indigo's interest in the object had a way of vanishing abruptly, relentlessly, and irrevocably, no matter how complex the history of the previous relationship, how great the object's other merits, or the attachment to her had been.

The Berniemania, however, proved a clingy parasite. Her disenchantment with him did not happen all at once but developed gradually over the course of almost two years, in several bitter stages.

That unforgettable summer after the failed exhibition endeavor, she spent hours with me in Treptower, pacing the alleys, speaking of nothing but Bernie. Of how, since the notorious day, he had become reclusive and gloomy. Of how he was spending entire days sulking around and being rude to her and his mother; how he, who had always been such a dandy, suddenly stopped looking after himself; how—most heartbreakingly—he stopped painting.

'Last time he went to the studio was before Wannsee,' she lamented, at times with indignation, at times with tears.

Months passed, and at a certain point her stories somewhat changed, both in tone and content. She now sounded more amused than upset and told me how Bernie's glum mood sharply switched to a perpetual dreamy smile, bleary eyes, and occasional bursts of laughter without a reason.

'He lolls about the place with a volume of esotericism,' Indigo noted with a contemptuous shrug. 'This deranged Blavatsky woman. Quotes passages from her out loud. Auntie Mag is terrified; she thinks the tuberculosis has eventually gone to his brain!'

Soon after that, Bernie himself paid me a visit.

One morning he telephoned and said in a triumphant voice, 'Listen, pal, there is something tremendous I have to discuss with you. Mind if I drop by?'

I was not exactly missing his company, but curiosity got the better of me.

Bernie arrived within the following hour.

He looked unkempt. His hair was matted, face unshaven, and overcoat crumpled. His lips, however, were stretched in an inextinguishable smile Indigo had warned me about.

'I bring a vital message, pal,' he announced pompously. 'My life has turned upside down, and it is the best thing that has ever happened to me. I'm a new man now.'

He went on to tell me he decided to go to Tibet and be converted to Buddhism. Next thing he told me was he didn't paint anymore, because he had been given a "sign" to quit art.

'I have destroyed all my self-portraits. There is a dream I had—it told me what to do and what not to do from now on. Just listen; you will be astonished!'

He proceeded with retelling the dream he'd had, which took a good half hour, and from which I heard almost nothing. The thought pulsating in my head, drowning out Bernie's voice, was the one that Bernie was finished. Done for. There was no way Indigo could go on loving him when he looked like a bum from the Anhalter Bahnhof, spouted obscurantist drivel, and created no art.

As to the purpose of his visit to me, Bernie made it clear right after he finished retelling the dream. He wanted me to go to Tibet with him and also convert to Buddhism.

'You are the right person for this, trust me. I have recently done a lot of thinking about you. You and I are alike in more ways than you can imagine. Our life paths are entwined.'

'Trust me,' he repeated weightily. 'I've had a dream about you too.

About us together.'

If nothing remotely entertaining had been happening in my life for the past few months, then Bernie generously compensated me for the lack of a good laugh that afternoon.

XVI
2nd Violin

I was sure I had thought of everything.

The Christian-Guido scheme per se seemed obvious enough; its realization came easy.

What was essential to remember though, knowing the old man's fickleness, were the details, garnishing, and sentimental dues.

Gods existing and imaginary know Mihai's tastes are prone to changing, as are his views. But it is also common divine knowledge that when the old man takes to loving or hating something (or someone), he does so with utmost fervor, for as long as the passion holds him.

Mihai's emotional life falls into periods, and in different periods different people, memories, and ideas become a focal point. Today it may be Tito, tomorrow Ribbentrop. Now it may be Vano the chime-in whom Mihai makes his associate; then it is, all of a sudden, Emelian.

The two characters Mihai held dear in the last weeks were Chloya, the winsome barmaid, and Doctor Heidert for whom he developed a protective tenderness through conversations with me. These two were the ones I mostly focused on in terms of references, mentions, and physical contact.

And just as I congratulated myself on having done a neat job, a big reminder of an inexcusable omission made her voice heard.

'At last someone is taking this blabberer of an old man away! I already thought God was angry at me and sent him here to drill a hole in my head with his chatter!'

I looked up at the grumbling Baba Tanya who pulled out the treasure box from under her skirt just as Petko led Mihai out of the hut.

Then it hit me.

Baba Tanya, the *gicisvara*!

How could I forget about her?

True, she and Mihai have not been fighting the ideological war against me lately as unitedly as they used to. She has been too occupied with her adopted grandson Vasil; he—with listening to my tales of Doctor Heidert, the Jewish camp, the resistance, and Chloya. She has been mostly yelling at him to cut off his ramblings, he—apologizing for not cutting them.

Yet, the *gicisvara* continued to hold a special place in Mihai's heart. He still venerated her; her words were prophetic, her opinions irrefutable. Without *her* approval, his jigsaw puzzle would not be completed.

There was nothing else for it—the situation had to be blitzed by Lavuta.

We burst into an impertinent, loud *kolo*—a tune which used to be one of Mihai's favorites—right into Baba Tanya's ear.

The startled Vasil emitted a bleating cry; the *gicisvara* hiccuped.

'*Dyrlyno*!' she roared, raising a fist at me. 'Are you mad or possessed? If the old gabber is not here, then it is you who must murder me with your moronic music!'

Baba Tanya was as livid as only she could be, and her fist, chunky like a bulldog's head, was about to crash into my left eye, but it stopped an inch away from it, as the *gicisvara*'s gaze fell upon Mihai's snuff tin.

She froze momentarily. Her wrath-distorted face relaxed.

'The old fool forgot his box,' she muttered. 'What if they keep him long? He'll die without his snuff…'

Then I was privileged to observe one of the most sublime miracles Lavuta had ever worked.

The *gicisvara*, who had almost never left her queen bee corner before, now promptly brought her rippling mass of flesh into a vertical position. With an agility one could hardly assume compatible with her age and physique, with Mihai's snuff tin pressed to her ample bosom, she maneuvered her way in between the bunks, stretched-out legs, protruding knees, toward the door.

I quietly followed.

Like a cargo ship, Baba Tanya steered her formidable frame across the field. She gained on Mihai and Petko well before the two could reach the gate. She overtook them and blocked their way with her width.

'Here, old man. Don't you leave behind what's yours.' She thrusted the tin into Mihai's hand. 'And don't you be gone with Doctor Heidert too long. I'll miss your conversation.'

If both Petko and Baba Tanya hadn't been holding Mihai by one arm, he would've keeled over.

'Bless you, *Gicisvara*! Thank you! I will miss yours too,' was the only reaction his boggled mind was capable of delivering.

Reeling with joy like an eager schoolboy unexpectedly praised by a strict headmistress, Mihai followed Petko on the way to new delights.

*

The wonderful surprises awaiting Mihai had been, like I said, relatively easy to arrange.

First off, the time had come to write another letter to "gnädiger Dr. Karp."

The new message instructed Guido to chauffeur one more inmate out of AU—a certain M. from the family camp. The plan contained a specific condition: M. had to be pulled out via Guido's colleague, Christian Heidert. Namely, Guido was to approach Dr. Heidert with a request to help him get his hands on M. as an object for the Pharma-Ko research. In the likely case of Dr. Heidert himself approaching Guido with the corresponding offer, Dr. Karp's task was reduced to simply accepting it.

The latter scenario duly came to fruition, convincing Mihai that Petko arrived to escort him somewhere unknown on gentle Dr. Heidert's—not the nasty Cabbagehead's—orders.

Till his last second, our new Count of Monte Cristo would see the noble, soft-mannered Doctor Heidert as his own Abbé Faria.

This mattered, knowing that in his long life, childless Mihai only ever had two fully-fledged son figures, both of whom he conceived in AU—me and Christian. We had to fulfill our filial responsibilities therefore, just like Baba Tanya—her parental.

The only role Mihai will mentally attribute to Obersturmführer Karp will be of his personal driver, who is also obeying someone's orders—very probably Dr. Heidert's.

Such a state of things alone would be enough to make the old man's day, but the crowning glory of his adventure will be still before him.

*

Upon arrival at block 32, Mihai will be greeted by the obliging Doctor Heidert, who will shake his hand and express gratitude for Mihai's consent to serve the causes of science. Doctor Heidert will also give Mihai a quick medical exam for the protocol, in the middle of which Guido will join them.

Guido will assure Christian of his readiness to take it from there, and Christian will be off, contented that he is leaving the old man in reliable hands from which he will not escape back to his barrack in the family camp.

Then our Monte Cristo will be shown into a separate ward, served sandwiches and coffee. While wolfing those down, he will be politely asked by Guido to "wait here a little."

The waiting won't be so little—it will take several hours. The mystified Mihai will spend those blessing in the name of Baba Tanya, who's made sure he'd have his snuff about him.

When the marshy darkness falls and chokes the life out of the camp, Obersturmführer Cabbagehead will reappear in the ward and tell his guest to change into a long overcoat, dandyish trousers, and a fedora, which he will bring along.

At this point, Mihai, who's many times heard the story of Yulek and Leo's recent escape, will cotton on to what's happening.

As a child, Mihai was taught to sell old books, touting them as out-of-print rarities and collectibles. He was taught card tricks, thimble games, and a little bit of accordion play.

He was never taught to drive a carriage, nor had anyone in his surroundings who owned one. Yet, since childhood, it was one of Mihai's dreams to be driven around, like some of those imposing *gospodines* to whom he peddled the books.

The night ride through the camp, out of the gate, and into unknowingness in a Steyr 125 with an Obersturmführer at the wheel will far surpass the wildest fantasies little Mihai's mind was remotely capable of conjuring.

*

There will come a moment for Mihai to be left on his own.

In the far end corner of a murky side street where Guido will ask him to get off and wait for "a friend" who should pick him up, the old man will feel even more like a benighted little boy.

But the feeling will not scare Mihai, nor will the waiting be long this time.

For out of the piss-drenched fog, into the stale light of a single street lamp, there will soon come a fair creature of bluebell eyes and a dimpled cheek. With her lace-gloved hand, she will throw back her cowl and shake loose her wheat blonde hair, which will fall in long, luminous curls around her shoulders.

Her lips will part in a coy half smile, revealing the glistening teeth.

'*Dobry wieczór, mam na imię Chloya. Proszę, śledź mnie,*' she will say quietly and take him by the hand.

*

David, my green-eyed spy, proudly takes credit for all Mihai-related arrangements with Vatslav and Chloya. Not my, or Lavuta's doing—we only set the tune. The main body of practical work has been David's and his nimble "little chipmunks's" on the outside.

The arrangements are as follows: Vatslav shall leave for the night in order not to get in Mihai's hair. Chloya shall take the old man to her place, carefully leading him by the hand all the time.

At home, she will give him a towel, a bathrobe, a piece of perfumed soap, a shaving set, a phial of cologne, make a hot bath for him, and leave him in the bathroom to relax for an hour or so.

After Mihai's done bathing, Chloya will treat him to a glass of cognac, a fried chicken dinner, and a sponge cake she will bake herself in his presence.

While her guest will be enjoying his meal, she will tell him the recent *Armia Krajowa* news, most of which he will fail to understand, but this will hardly matter, for it will be the velvety voice of his beguiling hostess, not the words he'll be greedily drinking down along with the coffee.

Chloya will hand him a fat envelope with pages of typed text, stamped blanks, and attached photographs. She will ask him to pass it to the resistance people who are to come to get him tomorrow. She, as a resistance agent herself, will invite him to join up.

'*Będziesz dla nas nieocenioną pomocą,*' she will assure him.

This Mihai will understand.

In Romani and Serbian, in German, Russian, and Polish, he, to the best of his abilities, will swear to serve the cause of his lady to his last breath.

However, the chivalrous knight will soon feel wearied of his day full of adventures. The bath, the meal, the liquor, and the company of the otherworldly creature he had hitherto only met in his dreams will, little by little, start to lull him to enchanted drowsiness.

Upon noticing this, Chloya will lead him into the living room, lay him down on the sofa, cover him with a plaid blanket, and tuck him in. She will ask him to sleep tight, so he will be well rested, because tomorrow serious resistance work is going to start for him. At that she will kiss him on the cheek lightly and be gone from the room.

For he has sworn to obey the wishes of his fair dame, Mihai shall do as he is told and sink into sleep almost immediately.

Of this sleep—deep and velvety like Chloya's voice—he shall never awake, dying from a heart failure during the night.

The men of the Home Army will indeed come in the morning, as Chloya will have promised Mihai. They will pick up his dead body, transport it to Wolski Forest, and bury it there under an ash—the tree under whose crown Mihai always wished to one day find eternal shelter.

*

Young Werther is as happy as a clam.

Walks into the barrack whistling, flirts with Rosa, and bows to Baba Tanya. Even occasionally asks for Marusya's permission to hold baby Dando and rocks him in his arms, while Dando screeches with baby glee.

At our sessions, he stops in midplay, kisses Cosima's strings, whispers to her, paces up and down excitedly, and resumes playing with dewy eyes.

It is not so much for the nearing completion of Indigo Mind that Christian's spirits are so high. He has more or less come to take the accomplishability of his masterpiece for granted; besides, my participation gives him mixed feelings about it.

It is mostly on account of Mihai's absence from the family camp that Christian is stoked.

Getting rid of a thorn in one's side invigorates one more than placing a crown on one's head.

The old man was this very thorn in our Young Werther's side the last weeks. He poisoned Christian's existence.

Mihai loved Doctor Heidert for his intellectual's naïveté; he thought of him as a put-upon saint; Mihai sympathized with him. Unable to contain his feelings, the old man smiled pityingly every time the doctor showed up.

With his pity, the accursed old Gypsy murdered all the joy the visits to the family camp had been for Doctor Heidert. The more Mihai liked the doctor, the more the doctor cringed at the sight of Mihai's affectionate wrinkled mug.

All because one of the doctor's greatest fears is to be pitied, especially by an ignoble.

It is remarkable how instead of being drawn to those who love us and care for us, we are magnetically attracted to those who see us for what we would like to see ourselves, even if at that they should despise us. Conversely, our most ill-wishing enemies do not sicken us as much as the friends who fail to discern our coveted features in our souls, bodies, or faces, but instead detect something we are loathe to admit we have—even if the loathsome attribute should be the very one they love us for.

*

When I look at Christian in his moments of cringing and elation, I am reminded of a face from my past—that of Laila.

That girl, before she met her only true but treacherous love in Változás, had never been deeply interested in any particular man, although she was desired by many. Pretty as a picture she was, with cocoa brown, slanting eyes, caramel-color skin, and a sparkling smile—a Joséphine Baker look-alike. The semblance she bore to the "Black Pearl" profited the circus greatly; Laila's dance number in a banana skirt and a long multilayered necklace used to enthrall the audiences even more than Yoska's bold acrobatics.

Laila's attractiveness had a twist—she was a little bit on the plump side. Those rounded shoulders, generous hips, and dimpled thighs were a temptation to men but a source of covert discontentment to their owner. Laila dreamt of a lean, brittle body—the kind of translucent grace my Lyuba had (when they met, Lyuba simultaneously became our little own Joséphine Baker's soul sister and object of envy).

One of the most passionate admirers of Laila's charms was Danior, the circus's drummer. Though he tried hard to convince everybody around, and primarily himself of Laila being his "sister," and he—her "big brother," the poor lad could not fool nature. He desired the slanting-eyed dancer so much that, as Yoska used to wit crack, "when she was in Danior's field of vision, his hormones ignited the air and threatened to burn down the circus."

An orphan who'd had Shandor as a replacement for both his absent parents and never knew motherly love, Danior's taste in women was determined from the cradle (which, having been born in a vardo, he'd never really got to sleep in).

In Danior's opinion, a real woman was supposed to look like a potential nurturing mother. Full-breasted, ample-hipped, milk-and-honey-dripping was his ideal. Shandor called him "Rubens on the drums."

Oftentimes, unable to contain his emotions, Danior approached Laila with dithyrambs.

'*Luludi miri*! You are such a masterpiece! Just look at your lovely curves. How wonderful it is you have soft womanly flesh on your bones—not like some of these rake-thin, moth-pale, prissy ladies who come to the shows!'

Little did he know that every such compliment he paid her was a nail driven into the coffin of their potential romantic future in each other's arms. Even though swarthy-complexioned, Laila would blush, shiver, and recoil from the gallant, barely holding back tears.

Danior put such reactions on the account of the girl's bashful chastity, and this flared his passion even more.

In reality, however, Laila would run off, hide in the little corner she called her "room," draw a curtain around it, throw herself on the makeshift bed, face down, and cry silently, biting the pillow in frustration, because she felt she had been called a "fat cow—and rightly so, because she really was one."

Several times the disconsolate creature worked herself into such a state I had to invisibly call on Lavuta's help to make her calm down and smile again.

Notwithstanding her feminine softness, girly touchiness, and giggly charm, Laila was in fact a tough cookie. When she wanted something, she eventually had her way—at least in the cases when the outcome depended on her alone. A lot of tough men I used to know might've envied the little artiste's willpower.

At some point, driven by Danior's praises, gifts, and sweets he showered on her into utmost vexation, she firmly decided to lose her rounded forms and get the slim figure she craved.

She took to hiding in her corner behind a folding screen for hours, doing scissors, upper torso lifts, and waist-trimming twists. She swore off chocolate, which she generally adored. She ate no more bread. She would secretly feed her dinners to stray dogs.

Time passed, and a moment came when Laila's efforts began to bear fruit.

The result was not equally obvious to everyone. Laila herself noticed it in the mirror and rejoiced; I noticed it; Yoska and Shandor did. But Danior, set on seeing his preferred, habitual version of her beauty, seemed to observe no change, and, despite Laila's now flatter tummy and leaner legs, would still tenderly call her "our chocolate muffin."

Once we were performing in a Belgian town.

Laila was on the stage, in her tropical outfit, strutting her Charleston stuff, ogled by the rowdy, mostly male crowd.

Suddenly a tall, loosey-goosey punter in a pince-nez, which contrasted with his otherwise loutish countenance, rose, spat on the floor, and started pounding the table with his beer mug.

'*Maigrichonne! Misérable! Gitane osseuse!*' He bawled over George Olsen's Jollity.

Laila's eyes flashed, as if two stars were lit in their depth.

She slowed down her routine, fluttered to the edge of the stage, and leaned forward to hear the man's words better.

'Some Josephine Baker you are! Josephine Baker, she's got a body; she's got a butt and a pair of boobs! And you? Your ribs stick out like on a xylophone Josephine might've been playing.'

The crowd, which had been till then showing lusty enthusiasm for Laila, now instantly swayed to the bully's side.

'*Maigrichonne!*'

'*Gitane maigrichonne!*'

There came whistles, hoots, and boos.

A half-eaten apple described a bridge in the air and landed at Laila's feet, smashing into purée.

Danior and Yanoro had to rush to Laila's rescue; the show was ruined; Shandor was upset.

But the look on Laila's face reminded me of El Greco's Virgin Mary's at the Annunciation. The girl was in a state of bliss.

As the lads dragged her backstage into safety, Laila repeatedly turned her head in search of her offender—lips parted, eyes shining with gratitude and joy.

It is Laila "Josephine Baker's" rapture at being insulted, and her irritation at being praised. I now remember when I think of Christian's, my vulnerable Young Werther's suffering, which Mihai (may he rest in peace under his ash tree) was causing him, and of which he is now delivered.

*

David is mistrustful of me again. Looks askance. Interrogates strenuously.

'Are you sure he was actually going to die?'

'Yes, dear. He had a bad heart. His time had come. If I hadn't been sure, I would've not set this entire merry-go-round in motion, had you and others risked so...'

'This is not what I'm asking!' he interrupts fiercely. 'You know very well what I mean. I'm asking: Are you sure he would've died that night and that minute, even if we hadn't sent him out? Would he have passed in the family camp, on his bunk? All the same? Are you sure seeing Chloya did not rush him into his grave? With that weak heart he had?'

'Seeing Chloya made him happier than he'd ever been in his life—not precipitate his death,' I explain softly.

'Again, this doesn't answer my question.'

'Of course he would've died that night anyway, dear. In the barrack, or elsewhere. This much was unquestionable. But he was meant to die a happy man. That's why...'

'Are you sure *that's* why?' David won't desist. 'And not because you were indulging your beloved Chris-the-puddle-of-piss once more?'

'David!'

'I'm sorry...' The green-eyed snide brushes his graceful fingers along the back of my hand. He is now switched to his conciliatory mode.

'I'm sorry,' he repeats. 'It's just that sometimes you seem to care about this creep's psychological comfort more than anything, or anyone else.'

David is bitterly jealous of Christian—of the time we spend together, the conversations we have, the music we play. Explaining to him, for the thousandth time, the nature of my communication with Young Werther is useless. He knows all about it, but it does nothing, or almost nothing, to stop him being jealous.

An understandable thing, who would argue? Christian's outer and inner allure is too obvious to all who see him; having him as a hypothetical rival (even just imagining it as a never-to-be-realized potentiality) would turn anybody's eyes green.

I've long since reconciled myself with the impossibility of alleviating this bittersweet pain my elf chooses to inflict on himself and allow him to rant at Christian's expense as much as he pleases.

'So,' David usually starts like a petulant child. 'When is your genius boy Heidert's turn to swing? It is the gallows we have prepared for him, isn't it?'

'No, dear, it isn't,' I correct him with utmost patience. 'Karp is going to swing, not Heidert.'

'Karp is, and Heidert isn't?' David clicks his tongue. 'How so?'

'Swinging is not what's going to happen to Heidert. As simple as that.'

'Is the gallows not his lot? Or do you mean to interfere and save him from it?'

'I wouldn't be able, nor will I need to. His lot is different.'

'You and him will get married, live happily ever after, and die on the same day?'

'He will certainly not die on the same day with me. Or on the same day with Karp or anybody else here.'

'Oh, of course, I'm so sorry; I won't stop forgetting he is exceptional,' David taunts. 'He deserves a better end.'

'I don't know about better. A cleaner one, perhaps. More dignified…'

I keep quiet a moment, then I add spice to my love's bittersweet self-torture.

'Yes, he deserves one.'

*

David swallows the bait and explodes in the most adorable manner. He's still trying to camp it up—but now it is mostly meant to disguise the real storm that is raging within and shaking his lithe frame.

'Deserves, eh? And why does this perverse murderer deserve something clean or dignified? Illuminate this mystery for me, in my stupidity! Will you? The one who has children die in a torture chamber in the name of his false science, causing them infernal suffering? The one who sends people to death because they looked at him the wrong way? How is he better than all these Karps, Angels, and Eichmanns?'

David's jealousy may be intense, but more powerful still is his sense of justice, and it is this latter one that will be driving him from this point on. At least for the rest of this particular conversation.

I dare not tease him anymore. I have to speak in earnest, and it is one hell of a task.

'I am not saying he is better,' I play for time. 'I've never said so. The categories of better or worse are hardly applicable... He is just different.'

'Different in what? A prettier face?'

'He is creative. Not creative for the sake of "The Cause," although he tries to convince himself that, even in his art, he serves it. Creative for the sake of being. In other words, creative is the only way he can be. And he feels in a different manner.'

'What does it matter how he feels if what he does are atrocities? One is judged by one's deeds, not feelings—correct?'

'Not always so. Sometimes feelings matter. It is hard to fit into a rational framework because feelings per se do not change the material side of things (unless, of course, they are embodied in actions). But in certain circumstances, under certain conditions, feelings may be woven into that cloth, which forms the background for a different reality in the future. People who feel pass away, but the material of their feelings stays. It envelopes the world, and how the world will be in the times to come depends on the aggregate nature of the many feelings which form up the cloth.'

'He must be completely and quite hopelessly in love with you,' David observes. All rancor is gone from his voice, replaced by a touch of contemplative melancholy.

'He certainly has a strong passion for me.' I nod. 'But the constituents of this passion are, shall we say, more diversified and richer in texture than those included in what's traditionally perceived as love. Although, of course, if we assume there are as many kinds of love as living beings multiplied by the number of randomly formed, emotionally intense, and polisemantic states of mind these living beings may hypothetically enter, then yes, he is in love with me.'

'Bet you stir him even more than that muse girl of his.'

'Ironically, the reason I stir him now is precisely that she stirred him once in the past. And continues to stir him. Or at least he firmly believes she is still the guiding star of his existence.'

'She dumped him, didn't she?'

'Not exactly. He never lit her fire to begin with. He intrigued her; they were friends for years. But at some point, even the friendship grew burdensome. She dropped the burden; he still carries it.'

*

'Intelligent, good-looking, talented, perspective,' David counts, one by one unbending his elegant fingers. 'Obsessed with her. What else did the spoilt brat of a girl want?'

'As I gathered from Chris's accounts, she was the kind of girl who preferred to be obsessed herself rather than become the object of an obsession.'

'A convenient trait in a woman.'

'Perhaps. But not for Christian, since he didn't make it into the elite league of her chosen ones. As to the rest of the world, her demands were high. She didn't much care for being adored or worshipped—she wanted to be researched and understood. *Known*, as she defined it.'

'"If they cannot know me, let them at least love me." That tune?'

'That was one of Indigo's aphorisms which used to drive Christian insane, right? Did I tell you already?'

'You must've... So he didn't do such a good job *knowing* her, then?'

'Apparently not. Although he researched her, he did it long and methodically. Dedicated years of his life to it, and still goes on doing so.'

'But came to all the wrong conclusions.'

'Mostly.'

'And Doctor Junn here hasn't cured him of his Indigo ailment either,' David goes on speculating. 'Their short-lived affair is over, I understand? Despite your joint efforts composing a sonata for her?'

'Oh, the sonata is decent enough work; in fact, it might've forwarded matters between them. But he won't play it to her. He is wary of her now.'

'Not without a reason, maybe?'

'May very well be. A hunch of sorts. Generally, Chris's intuition is fair to middling, but who knows if he shouldn't have a lucid moment once in a blue moon.'

'Will she hurt him?'

'Not intentionally. But the fact of her existence will contribute to his demise even more than the fact of mine.'

'Incredible...'

David wants to say something else, but a metallic rumble cuts in, followed by someone's plaintive whine and Bushalo's barking.

We come out from behind the stack of rusty beams where we were having a smoke.

Going on around us there is a nonsensical pipe-laying work—in fact just a collective burying pieces of pipe in the ground after arranging them in a chain-like sequence. No one has a clue where the pipe begins, where it will end, or what it will serve for. As per normal, a job like this invites hours of carrying, pushing, shoving, swearing, shouting, hitting, kicking, and lashing, with Bushalo running the show.

What happened this time is Arkadiy, a delicately built, diffident young man dropping a piece of pipe on his foot and writhing in pain.

For Bushalo, someone's physical suffering is a trigger—he has to double it, and one lash is never enough.

Bushalo's hand is raised to strike; his whip hovers over Arkadiy's bent back like an airborne snake, but this is the instant Bushalo sees us. The hand freezes; the whip sags and helplessly falls—a cut rope.

'It looks like the Bushalo boy is constipated again,' David hisses loudly, enraged and emboldened by our discussion of Christian. 'Let's send him to the latrine till lights out, shall we?'

Bushalo knows he has been caught red-handed—it is useless to hide or plead. Lavuta is with me, but I don't play a sound. The very sight of her in my hands instantly detonates a bomb in his belly and squeezes his colon like a wet rag.

'Don't drop it all in your trousers; save some for the latrine!' David shouts for all to hear as Sour One beats a hasty retreat with his overalls in a mess.

'He will save something to make his eternal rest bed smell better,' Shlomo echoes from the opposite side of the ditch to everyone's hearty laugh.

XVII
1st Violin

In his letter to Goethe, Schiller once introduced the concept of an aesthetic man. It was, Schiller wrote, one "in whom the sensual and the moral are not diametrically opposed in aim." The poet believed such a man "needs no immortality to support and hold him."

This is the type of man that will save the civilized world and Germany as its undisputed leader. Aesthetic—*aisthesthai*. The Greek for "perceive."

A perceiver.

It is not a chance thing, therefore, that my sensory perception, which has, for as long as I remember myself, been quite acute, is now, at the aesthetic acme of my life, growing almost unbearable.

I must receive this lot as both a blessing, and a cross to proudly bear.

An aesthetic man, a perceiving man. A creator, an inventor. A server of The Cause, a scientist of the art, an artist of the science. The hope of civilization.

*

I hear, I see and I feel.

A lot.

More than a man can handle. An ordinary man.

For the extraordinary, however, hasn't it always been precisely this way? Has this cup ever been taken away from an aesthetic man?

He wouldn't have been worthy of the name if it had.

The more colossal aesthetic men history has known always stood at the junction of arts and sciences. Didn't Aristotle amalgamate physics and philosophy? Leonardo—engineering and anatomy? Goethe—natural history and poetry?

They all welded the scientific with the scholarly; the artistic with the technical. They wedded the fiercely natural with the loftily sublime.

Should I wonder that I am no exception? Should I not glorify my "predicament" rather than lament it?

*

What once began as bold hypothesizing based on outlandish parallels has molded into a firm conviction. Not just a conviction—a realization and acceptance of a sacred duty.

It has now revealed itself to me in all its dazzling clarity that my mission as an aesthetic man is joining music and medical science into an indissoluble unit.

The Gypsy does not comprehend. He thinks he does, but I know he does not. He is not able to.

I try to open his eyes to the spellbinding relation between the dolefulness of D minor and the perniciousness of the gangrene. He half closes his eyes, stretches his lips in a half smile, as if intrigued by a curious thought, and whispers.

'The mawkishness of art smashing flat against the crassness of reality.'

'Yes! Precisely!' I exclaim, prematurely rejoicing at being understood. 'Flat, as in *bemolle*—the *soft* tissues which get penetrated and eaten away…'

And then he throws a bucket of cold water on me, interrupting, 'This is not exactly what I meant.'

Should I be surprised?

Can his Jewry-loving, dubious-origin-Gypsy mind ever be attuned to the meaning of an aesthetic man?

Vain hope.

I spare no effort to illustrate for him the majestic drama of the illusive microorganisms which induce the disease under my research, translating into the exquisite deformities of Baroque.

He responds with the same all-knowing half-smile.

'Correct, it makes sense. I wonder what Bach, who lost many of his children to vague medical conditions, would've had to say to that. He might've agreed.'

Once again! *Tries* to speculate and *believes* that he grasps the depth of what is taught to him.

Alas!

Even the triteness of the examples he adds shows how shallow his perception is.

I seek to enlighten him in the dramatic interplay between the fierce physical affliction of noma and the ferocious mood of the music.

'Music imitating life? Or life imitating music?' he inquires quizzically.

More spurious reflection—and, essentially—mere word juggling in the typical Gypsy-Jewish fashion.

I tire not of describing the relentlessly obstinate mechanism at work in both vascular plants and subhumans whose existence turns against itself. I won't stop spelling out to him the inextricable connection between this vital force and the musical patterns of Indigo Mind.

In response, I get yet another smart comment.

'Obstinacy may be a reprehensible quality in a woman, but in some women it is the trait that cements their personality. In this case, it may also be their major incentive—truly a vital force. If such a woman's mind is inspiring enough to become the theme of a musical piece, then I definitely see the connection. As for the link between that and the disease you are studying, I have to take your word for it, as my medical knowledge is exiguous. Your colleague Anton Lauer should appreciate your idea, though.'

I can barely hold back the tears every time I mention the chromaticisms, so much I've come to associating them with the emotional throws of my objects—in particular with Damira's.

'I will remember her incredible liveliness on deathbed long after she is gone,' I confess my not entirely professional sentiment to Jassengro.

'She will remember yours too,' he delivers a nonsensical reply, by which I realize he is not listening to me at all but is lost in his own entangled Gypsy thoughts instead.

An exercise in futility!

*

He says I should not open the piece with the main theme but add a big escalation intro in order to "gain momentum."

I know exactly what he is talking about. The instant he uttered it—even a second before—I'd had this intro playing in my head. Thunderous, fiery, transcendental, and divine. The crowning glory.

I wish, however, that he had never advised it. That he had never thought of it.

I already feel too much of his importunate presence—in my music, my life, and my thoughts. In fact, I wonder if my thoughts are any longer mine, if he hasn't used his witchcraft to replace my mind with his own.

Besides, if he does not comprehend the supreme goal of fusing music with medical science, how can I be guided by his judgment any longer?

Even if the intro proves to be the final stroke that transforms I.M. from a simple work of genius into an over-worldly bestowment on the cultured humanity, I shall not add it. Not until I locate and register some deep touchpoint it has with The Idea. Should I fail to find one, I shall relentlessly banish the very thought of that intro, as if exorcising the mental intrusion the Gypsy Daemon has inflicted on me.

Every single musical movement of mine must from now on be congruent with the movements of *Force Vitale*.

*

It was with this load on my mind that I entered the ward in block 32.

I had to see the objects and find the touchpoint.

At first, I had attempted seeking the link in the underlying factors of the disease. The self-destructive behaviors of the subhumans; the poor sanitation; their propensity for picking up and consuming semi-edible objects; maintaining superstitious rituals at the expense of necessary hygienic measures; unhealthy alimentation. It had appeared to logically conform: the multiple accretion factors, the escalatory quality of the development—all jibed with the idea of an introductory passage.

Upon an hour or so of pondering, however, I realized such an analogy was too simplistically obvious, yet at the same time somehow far-fetched.

I then turned my attention toward the onset of the condition per se. The early symptoms like tenderness, mild swelling, slight fever, and minimal pus charge—those fuzzy first indicators largely ignored by the hominini (their "first aid" to the children who display the symptoms is typically splashing the sore spot with water, more often than not dirty)—could they be encoded in music in the form of an intro?

The answer did not take long to hit—nonsense. Not the intro that Jassengro and I envision for I. M. The sound we hear there is pierced through with a bare nerve; it is raw and opulently ominous—intimidating in its splendor. Something as unclear and habitually dismissed as the initial stage of noma could not be reflected in such conspicuous a part, even if one were to factor in the insidious nature of the early *cancrum oris*.

It then became clear as day that only my actual experimental material—the objects with which I work and whom I observe daily—could provide me with the correct answer.

So I rushed to block 32.

The reward came, and it came at once.

All four children in my care have by now developed distinctive features of orocutaneous fistula. Different in shape—a gaping abyss in Grisha's case; a grinning slash in Patrin's; a tongue-exposing cavity in Mara's, and a kind of deep, "drilled" hole in Damira's—they all communicate one unmistakable truth. A pathway. A tunnel. A corridor.

An entrance.

An entrance was what I needed to see, and the fact of this "entrance's" being, instead of an initial, rather a late stage of the disease, is the ultimate allegory I was looking for. The very entrance that contains the whole story with its inevitable ending. The "soil preparing," escalating, and ominous introduction.

Once again, *Force Vitale* has built me the bridge to the music I required.

I am satisfied. No more proof is needed.

I. M. shall open with an intro.

*

Once again, I ought to rejoice.

Another answer found, connection made, resolution achieved.

And once again doubts come to gnaw on my soul, corroding it, eating through it like worms through an apple.

But I correct myself.

Doubts they are not. I am not doubting anymore, nor have I been for a long time already.

It is derision that tarnishes the joy.

The rare flower of creativity, however vigorous it may be, is vulnerable to mockery, toxic skepticism, or disbelief. The precious fruit of inventiveness will easily parish, oxidized by the choking fumes the cynics disgorge.

Derision surrounds me. It gnashes its teeth at me, snarling at my work. The more I progress, the fiercer its attacks.

It is hard to withstand—an unremitting toil. A never-ceasing combat. An hourly fight.

As I was exiting the block—the harmony between me and the world restored—something had to immediately occur to disrupt the balance.

It was Rhöde and König I ran into. Our inseparable pair. The two gossipy, good-for-nothing boozers. The dead loss of AU.

The two were, as is their wont, loudly discussing something that was no concern of theirs. Japan, apparently.

'It was Hideki himself, they say, who came up with the idea of giving the chinks flea showers!' König blared.

'Hideki? The prime minister? Nah, not likely,' Rhöde argued. 'He is not so adventurous, the four-eyes. It was the cutthroat Kitano, it must've been. Or that other one... also a four-eyes... That wizard, what's his name? Ishii! No?'

'Or maybe the chinks have grown the plague in their own cells since birth?' König guffawed.

'Like by some magic biological force?'

'Exactly! Maybe it's in their chinky nature to break out bubonic and croak at some point, and the flea-showers are all a fantasy?'

At that, they both, as if on command, looked at me.

'Heil Chris, how is the work going?' König asked, and Rhöde grinned inanely.

I could swear that was not the first instant they noticed me. I had been standing by the door collecting my thoughts for some time; they could see me all the while.

They had led their poisonous conversation to the "greeting" moment on purpose.

They had made sure I could hear their every word.

Curse them.

Curse them.

*

This whole establishment is rife with malice and envy. The snide faces—malignant presences exuding vitriol like putrid sores ooze pus.

Alas, it is not only my existence they contaminate. It is the motherland they befoul.

Few understand this, and there is certainly no explaining such subtle laws of nature to mockingbirds like Anton. There are, nevertheless, consistent patterns whose existence is undeniable, even if I should be the only living being sensible enough to acknowledge them.

Just like art or science, patriotism is never to be joked about. Facetious remarks in regard to what's sacred are not only inappropriate or blasphemous. They are carcinomatous. They invade a lofty cause, attacking its sensitive tissue and eroding its very building blocks. Cynical attitude spreads through the air; it metastasizes. It belittles a genius creation, underplays a brilliant idea, and makes a heroic deed sound as if it were an unnecessary overreaction or simply a folly. By doubting or deriding what has been done, it undermines potential success in the future.

This is why I say mockers are traitors!

I hear their treachery echoing around the place all the time. And when I hear it, I clearly realize it is not something I build up in my mind or exaggerate out of proportion. It does not always concern me personally or my creations that they mock at, so it is not my hurt pride getting in the way of objective judgment. More often than not, it concerns The Cause. I am only a witness, and I know a treacherous act when I see one.

Just the other day I overheard those same Rhöde and König gossiping about the Roman terrorist attack.

'Surely Mälzer has no better idea than ordering to shoot some more Jews in retaliation, and his loyal Kappler, Priebke, Hass, and the rest are only too happy to oblige. Why Jews, I ask? Why not Italians?'

'I thought they shot Italians too. And the Jews are condemned anyway, so...'

'Spot on! Condemned anyway! I mean, don't we already condemn them enough? The Jews have a load to answer for, no denying that, but why make them answerable for Italian wrongdoings? I tell you why. Because the Roman units are all bloodthirsty, Jews-eating ogre—Mälzer and the company!'

And the two explode with laughter.

Or Anton, who won't stop gloating about the Red offensive west of the

Dnieper!

How can one sleep peacefully at night being aware of treason—even if the treason is only in words, and the word is uttered by a friend?

The latter circumstance only makes it that much harder to take.

Over and over I reflect on the irony of the fact that Guido Karp now seems to be the only one around who reacts to things as becomes a patriot and simply a decent man—Guido whom I had once regarded as one of the worst boors and gloaters!

Guido, "our one truly *Völkisch* element," as Anton says of him. Anton makes fun of Guido the way Anton makes fun of everything—the way I myself used to do.

However, I suppose there is some truth in this observation. Guido, if anything, is the archetypal *Völkisch* soul—honest and kind at heart, even if sometimes a little unpolished. These days I might have applauded such a definition of Guido, except I have my own personal reasons to dislike the word *Völkisch*. Instead of evoking the image of blood and soil, it unpleasantly reminds me of Bernie and his "Buddhist period." Personal associations are stubborn things, and memories can hardly be obliterated at will.

*

Though Bernie's gradual fall in Indigo's eyes failed to gladden me, it did, in a tragicomic way, amuse me.

His appearance at my place when he suggested that the two of us should go to Tibet together proved only the first one in a series of similar calls he paid me over a period of several months.

What earthly reason did I have to entertain him in my flat as a guest for so long? I still wonder. For Indigo's sake once again? Not likely. She never came to our meetings and spoke of them with undisguised ridicule. Now that I'm thinking about it, I believe it was some warped curiosity on my part. I observed Bernie like an entomologist might observe an unpleasant yet rare dying insect in its exotic death throes. Was I gloating, perhaps? I might have, and of that I am now ashamed. Did I pity Bernie? I most probably did. Moreover. There were moments at which I quite sincerely empathized with my old-time rival—contrary to all conventional logic of love triangle relationships.

Bernie would turn up on my threshold in all sorts of outlandish attires—loose robes of orange, brick red, or yellow, tattered rope bracelets, and layered bead necklaces. He would sit down on the floor barefoot and cross-legged, sit me down in front of him, lock his fingers together, close his eyes, and mumble at length something he said was a chant in Sanskrit. He would bring along sachets with strange herbal concoctions and treat me to improvised tea ceremonies. He talked incessantly about "taking refuge" and his newly discovered, zealously observed "practices." While talking, he never stopped smiling.

Not long before his transformation, Bernie had befriended a group of people whom he maniacally insisted I also should befriend. The group claimed they were Buddhists, but in actuality, as I could glean from Bernie's rather tangled accounts, were an eclectic sect of ragtag people with obscure goals led by a man known by the moniker of Dragon. Bernie and the rest of the group deferentially referred to him as "guru Dragon."

The philosophy guru Dragon preached boiled down to rejecting all commitment, responsibility, or human attachment and hymning the existence of complacent inactivity instead.

'If you don't want to get disenchanted, don't get enchanted in the first place!' Bernie quoted his mentor smilingly, trying to put across to me that any friendship, love, reliance upon, or feeling responsibility for another person were nothing but emotional slavery and deplorable weakness.

The attitudes Bernie's guru denounced were divided into two intriguingly named groups: "those who rubbed against the minus" and "those who rubbed against the plus." Roughly, the former meant persons who complained about their lives and wallowed in self-pity, whereas the latter defined individuals who prioritized achievement and took pride in their successes.

It was, as I came to realize, in order to avoid "rubbing against the minus" that Bernie smiled all the time, while the aim of his quitting art was to nip in the bud all "rubbing against the plus."

At first, I thought guru Dragon's teachings were the primary factor attracting Bernie to the group, as they chimed with his own outlook. Buddhism, or any similar philosophy, is for the likes of Indigo's cousin nothing more than an excuse to laze through their lives and betray indefinitely.

Eventually, however, Bernie let slip that the group contained a still more powerful "magnet."

*

There was a young man, of course. How could there not be one?

Even before Bernie mentioned this, during the period of his strange obsession with me and the preposterous idea of our ending up in Tibet together, I had suspected that the Tibetan idyl was not planned for just the two of us. Bernie had a third member of the brotherhood in mind, and I was to learn his name soon.

The name was Peter. The age was sixteen. Though several years Bernie's junior and still in the HJ, this adolescent became Bernie's ideological guide. As I found out, it was Peter who'd introduced Bernie to Dragon's sect and turned him on to Buddhism.

'You will fall in love with Peter!' Bernie cajoled me into meeting his new passion. 'You two have so much in common. You will find you are kindred spirits, believe me. The way he looks at things—so primally simple, so fiercely true, and yet so poetic! The very quintessence of *Völkisch*!'

Bernie would use this word a lot to describe his young friend.

He did eventually bring Peter along, as I could find no plausible excuse from being introduced.

Cornflower blue eyes, turned up nose, open smile. Strapping; healthy complexion.

Peter certainly had the exterior to become an addiction for Bernie. Also hailing from Bernau, he was entirely devoid of morbid jadedness with which we, big city dwellers, are tarnished from an early age.

In spite of my initial prejudice, I found Peter's candidness and youthful vigor quite disarming.

Young as he was, Peter turned out to be a mature server of The Cause. He intended to make it strait out of the HJ into the Waffen-SS. Apart from that, he aimed at membership in the Ahnenerbe.

'They unearth our living and breathing history—incredible facts,' he raved about the association's research. 'Next time they organize an expedition to Tibet, I mean to be on it!'

Peter rattled off passages from Günther, whose *Kleine Rassenkunde* he seemed to have perused inside out.

The desire to establish Buddha's Nordic descent was, I came to understand, what ultimately drew the ardent youth to Buddhism. As to the suspicious sect with whose help he and Bernie chose to pursue this goal, Peter explained that Dragon had direct connections with the Ahnenerbe, apparently had been on their latest mission in Lhasa, and guaranteed that his disciples would be taken along as soon as a following similar journey was arranged.

We'd had the discussion not long before Dragon, predictably enough, proved an out-and-out fraud. Once he simply failed to show up at a planned group meeting. Later it was established the impostor ran off with the money which he had been regularly collecting toward future expeditions and other promised undertakings.

But young Peter seemed to be endowed with an indomitable spirit and enviable social skills. Far from despairing, he took the loss of a guru in his stride. Moreover, he wasted no time in finding a number of other potential links to the Ahnenerbe and hypothetical ways to get to Tibet, even without direct Buddhist patronage.

As for Bernie, Bernie was like water—he always took the shape of the one he poured himself into.

When Peter's enthusiasm for Buddhism waned, so did Bernie's. While, at the same time, Peter's general loyalty to The Cause grew, Bernie bent over backward to mold his own outlook to match that of his younger friend's.

*

Bernie joined the Allgemeine SS not long before Indigo's 22nd birthday.

He had attempted following Peter to the Waffen but was declined due to health reasons. Despite this little failure, Bernie loudly celebrated his new status. He flaunted his Oberscharführer's insignia. He spent hours strutting up and down the corridor of his mother's flat, every now and again stopping in front of the big mirror and marking time.

Frau Treder's joy caused by her son's abandoning what she'd called "awful clown rags" (meaning the Buddhist habiliments) for the dashing uniform was immense. She would telephone her girlfriends and, after a token exchange of health news, cooingly deliver a speech on how she knew her life and motherhood had not been in vain, for she finally saw "every reason to be proud of Bernard."

'Oh yes, my dear!' She would repeat into the mouthpiece, relishing the sweet notion. 'You are talking to a proud, proud mother.'

On my occasional visits to them (ironically, it was now mostly Bernie who asked me over), I happened to witness Indigo's reaction to Aunt Magde's outpourings. Her eyes narrowed with utmost disdain, and a vaguely mischievous smile hovered on her lips. When Indigo assumed such a look, it was a sure sign she was plotting a vicious prank and she didn't mean to hide it. But I was by then the only human being around who knew Indigo well enough to understand her expressions and was interested in her enough to notice them at all.

Indigo got quiet and reclusive those days, rarely talking to Bernie, almost never to her aunt; only exchanging occasional glances with me when I came. She spent hours locking herself up in her room with her cat, her music records, her books, and her writings.

Bernie was clearly not her Pierrot anymore—he turned into a fun figure, and she silently laughed at him. Aunt Mag was just a miserable old ninny, an object of contempt.

But there was someone in the immediate surroundings who positively got Indigo's back up and made her sick to her stomach. Someone whose cornflower blue eyes she would've scratched out if she hadn't felt squeamish about touching him.

Peter, the charming *Völkisch* soul, was a frequent guest at Bernie's, warmly welcomed by his mother.

It was not that Indigo exclusively blamed Peter for the metamorphosis in Bernie, which murdered her love for him. The change in Bernie had commenced before Peter appeared on the scene and would probably have gone full cycle just as well without his participation.

What she did detest Peter for was completing Bernie's metamorphosis in a way that, of all possible outcomes, she regarded as the most repulsive.

I could see how she felt, and I assumed her revenge, whatever shape it took, would primarily have young Peter as its target. She understood I was able to guess her intentions, but she knew I would never denounce her, even if I utterly disapproved.

XVIII
2nd Violin

I never saw stealing as a particularly wicked act.

It does depend on the circumstances, of course—what one steals, from whom, and how, but in most cases the goal of a thief justifies the means. Even if his purpose is not serving a dire need but simply having a good laugh, it is usually worth it.

I probably take after my mother in this attitude, though in other aspects, as I've been told, I do not resemble her much.

There's never any telling how exactly your parents' genes will manifest themselves in you, or yours in your children. After years of lying low, they may kick in midlife, reflecting in your face, body, or character in quite a bizarre fashion.

Or, reversely, it leaves you dumbfounded at how much outward or inward semblance you suddenly happen to bear to a genetically unrelated human being. I have always seemed to have a somewhat narcissistic tendency to be attracted to those who looked and felt like me, even if I never noticed it much in the beginning of a new love. People would chronically take Yoska for my twin brother and Lyuba for my sister; even David, whose freckled creaminess and green eyes objectively contrast with my dusky appearance, is commonly found to have my "smirk and swagger."

Sometimes, apart from its purely fetichistic value, sharing bodily features with another might be of practical use. Which, I foresee, will be the case with me and Christian Heidert. While being rather striking, our outer similarity has not yet been really noticed by anyone—and this is the best thing about it. Our identical height, built, and facial bone structure is a factor of subconscious pleasure to Chris; to me it will be a gate-opener.

The plan is only vaguely outlined in my mind yet, but I still have time to think it through.

*

The further I. M. nears completion, the more nervous Christian becomes.

"Nervous—very, very dreadfully nervous"—just like Edgar Poe's woeful character.

It is astonishing how accurately Chris's emotional state is described in that story. Sometimes his painfully turgid speeches sound exactly like the narrator's—I wonder if he read "The Tell-Tale Heart" as an adolescent and is unconsciously quoting passages from it now.

My nervous protégé mostly uses our sessions to cry on my shoulder these days. He laments everything and complains of everyone. He tells me endless stories about his naughty Indigo's irreverence toward all what he ever held dear.

'She would show me loathsome caricatures of Wagner's audiences drawn by this other pervert whose so-called art she deified!'

'Oh, but Aubrey Beardsley did not mean that drawing as a caricature at all. His admiration for Wagner was no lesser than yours—he even wrote his own novel dedicated to Tannhäuser.'

'He did!' completely enraged, Christian bangs his fist on the table. 'And she quoted that foul scribbling to me as well! How dared the sickly, twisted queer Beardsley touch any subject concerning the meister? And why did Indigo insist on showing me the filth? To insult me? To spite me?'

'I don't suppose it was her intention,' I go on with my appeasement strategy. 'She wanted to share something she liked, and you just didn't happen to be an admirer of modern style.'

Poor Chris is, predictably, not appeased and goes on seething.

*

But more bitterly than of Indigo, he has now taken to complaining of his AU closest circle.

His best friend Anton Lauer teases him mercilessly. Everything Anton says is said to rile Christian.

Christian knows it. He feels it. He hears it. All of these and more, separated by grave full stops.

Anton glorifies the contemptible Yankees. Anton speaks of Haeckel as "a funny fellow with funny theories." Anton refers to George Patton's speech in Knutsford as "the most prothetic joke of the month." Anton has also recently turned out to be a raving admirer of Napoleon, whom Chris never calls anything but "the scourge of history."

Christian, who with his Young-Wertherish mindset is more than anyone prone to idolizing, never takes kindly to such proclivities in others.

'A million times I tried to hammer it home to Anton that a personality—no matter how remarkable—is only a product of its historical and demographic medium,' he fumes. 'The field allowed by history for arbitrary self-expression and impact of the outstanding personality is negligibly small—a nothing! Would there have been a Napoleon without a chain of Richelieus, Voltaires, Rousseaus, and French Revolutions to prepare the soil for him? Without the national character of the French to lay him, like a poisonous egg, on that soil? Without the weakness of Friedrich Wilhelm III, the fickleness of the Habsburgs, the turmoil in Spain, and the misery of Poland to allow him to further his criminal ends? The ends, none of which, by the way, found realization, while the one who conceived them was duly cast into ignominy, as soon as the society, once again, got enough of the preeminence of individual will…'

Here Christian trails off and slaps his forehead in exasperation.

'I waste my breath talking to Anton, and he, as though deaf, goes on about the virtues of the Code, "the first serious attempt to unite Europe," and other Jewish-Napoleonic machinations.'

The most amusing fact about the described polemic is that in reality it was not with Anton Lauer Christian held it. It was with me a little while ago.

It is now a usual thing with my nervous protégé to confuse me with Anton, or Indigo Schwarz with Birgitte Junn.

His thoughts have become awfully entangled of late and will, I expect, only get more embroiled in the coming days.

*

It is not only people Christian now habitually confuses one with another. He's begun to manifest a curious tendency of mixing his words with those of his interlocutors, voicing ideas of his opponents as his own, and, conversely, attributing his own to them.

His recent outburst in the family camp is a case in point.

Apart from Anton there is Birgitte—Christian's part-time muse and a single-time lover—who has become one of his greatest tormentors. Not that she has a clue about it.

So the other day Chris and Birgitte clashed at the site of Dr. Junn's research—across the playground from our barrack, behind the shed.

Chris happened to be passing by when Birgitte was outside with the *glata*, basking in the timid April sun and teaching the kids how to play twenty questions.

The rules of the game are quite simple: one player thinks of a noun, and the others ask him yes or no questions, trying to figure out what thing he's thought of. Supposedly, within the framework of twenty questions, one should be able to guess any object pertaining to any sphere.

The completely innocent and amusing game roughly aims at teaching the players how to ask the right questions; it is also good for language learning. This, I assume, was Birgitte's purpose when she gently demonstrated to the children that "officer," "horse," and "barrack" were too easy to guess—that they had to think of something less obvious.

This (namely, teaching the children some language and deductive reasoning—not slighting Christian) was, I bet, her wish when she decided to lead the game and chose the word "music."

'Is it big?' The little players started tentatively.

'Is it food?'

'Is it alive?'

'Can a man make it?'

'Can **you** make it?'

Then a brisk though squint-eyed girl whose name is Stasya spotted Christian standing a little way off. Stasya thought of nothing better than pointing a finger at him and loudly asking.

'Can Doctor Heidert make it?'

Birgitte glanced up the way the girl was pointing, saw Christian, smiled radiantly, and affirmed.

'Bullseye, Stasya! Doctor Heidert can most definitely make it, better than anyone else I know!'

After a bit of struggling with the abstract word, the children somehow approached the right answer.

'Music it is!' Dr. Junn exclaimed triumphantly.

Overfilled with her ever-growing parental love for Vano, exhilarated by her success with the *glata*, invigorated by the spring, she winked at

Christian, who, after hearing his name, remained at the scene to learn what it was he "could most definitely make."

'Children can't be fooled, can they, Chris? They know the right question to ask, don't they?'

In his peculiar emotional state, what was meant as innocuous flattery struck Christian as a subtle way to needle him.

'No Birgitte!' he blurted out. 'It is you who is fooling yourself. The cliché about children's keen intuition is a hypocritical lie. Children are the most corruptible beings in the world. Most children will applaud glittery tastelessness, take kindness for weakness, obey the whip, and betray a friend for a piece of candy.'

He then turned on his heel and marched away, leaving Birgitte entirely perplexed.

*

The remarkable feature of this episode is that Christian's tirade about children was a borrowed one. He plagiarized his other muse, Indigo Schwarz, who'd often expressed such feelings.

Indigo's cynical attitude toward children was one of her properties, which used to affront Christian most of all. The day before the incident with Birgitte, he had quoted her those very words to me, trying to illustrate the baffling nature of his love for a young woman who'd said and thought monstrous things.

Next thing my protégé does—he unconsciously parrots his first love to scandalize his second love's motherly nature.

How ironic is this?

The spinster's sentimentality of Dr. Junn, which Christian labeled "motherly nature," is the trait which ensured Vano's bright future and inspired Freia's Motherhood—the sonata Chris painfully strove to compose without my help. This fairly innovative piece lurked in the back of his head for weeks, really distracting him and obstructing our work on Indigo Mind. After we muddled through the first movement of I. M., I got enough of it, tuned into Dr. Junn's spinstry-motherly world, and with a brief solo on Lavuta, got her all cuddly and horny for Chris. They spent a night together, and, though only one, it was enough to break down the barrier in his head and release the obstinate tune. F. M. got completed; Chris soared on the wings of a new infatuation and creative realization. Thus the little obstacle was out of the way, and we calmly continued giving our full attention to Le Storie and Indigo Mind.

Those were the days.

Over now, for better or worse.

The "motherly nature," which Christian once adored, has turned into a source of suspicion and anxiety for him.

My nervous Young Werther will never play F. M. to his red-haired lady. He will not make love to her anymore; or ever trust her again.

From now on, his soul will only grow darker, day by day. Birgitte and Anton will innocently and dutifully continue pouring more black paint into the darkness.

These two Christian's good friends will become his executioners. Them and little Damira—she will deal one of the final blows by which Doctor Heidert will be felled.

*

Damira the martyr will like and respect her tormentor till her last second. She will be spared the knowledge of having been the weapon that killed him; she will never even know he's dead.

'She will outlive him, won't she?' David asks hopefully.

'She will, yes. Not long, just by one day, but she will. And this last day will be the happiest day of her life.'

Damira's passing will bring her the blissful message that everything is right with the world—the notion she strove for and painfully lacked during her short earthly existence. All the good tidings will find her; all the bad ones escape her. She will have lived to hear of me and David making our way out; of her baby brother's, the toothy Dando's escape under Baba Tanya's protective wing.

Damira's final moments will grant her clairvoyance. She will see, as if lit by the young sun of May, the lifelines of those dear to her. Belonging to the type of creatures who are happiest dissolving in the happiness of others, she will melt in me, David, and Dando.

This is what will make her complete.

As I pour this sentimental pathos into David's ears, he keeps angry silence. The only thing he insists I specify is whether Damira will last to see Heidert to his grave, not vice versa (I can't be entirely sure why this rather formal bit of information is so critical to my green-eyed minstrel, but so it is). The rest leaves David skeptical.

He has not—and will not ever—forgive me Damira's martyrdom or those whom I "allowed" to parish at Guido Karp's hands.

This is, I suppose, what I most love in David. Though an ethereal elf he is, he does not compromise—either with fate or with conscience. A quality I sometimes wish I could give myself credit for.

*

Now that I am robbed of Damira and Mihai, my grateful listeners, David's importance for me has increased all the more. Come to think of it, I have never needed a good lover as much as I needed a good interlocutor. Or perhaps it just so seems to me, because I never encountered much difficulty finding the former, while the latter has proved a rarity to be chased and cherished.

David is a unique case of both, plus a collection of numerous other incredible traits, half of which I have not even yet had a chance to discover. I certainly relish the thought of a long journey together that will gradually reveal to me all the facets of this jewel I've been blessed to find and call my own.

Yet right now it is his speckled, curious eyes, attentive ears, and the glib tongue I desire more than anything else. I am hungry for telling him my stories. I am thirsty for hearing his. I find myself purposely challenging him to a battle, just so that we talk more.

Right now he is sulking at me again, so I seek to dissolve the tension and tell him another Christian Heidert anecdote (these seem to work unfailingly).

*

'You can be jealous all you want, honey, but I must confess to you again; I find our Doctor Heidert one of the most astounding human paradoxes one can hope to meet.'

'I'm sure you do,' David grunts with feigned indifference.

'His entire life is a self-contradiction. He gets inspired by what he despises; what is repulsive to him simultaneously fills him with longing; what he most passionately loves he also most vehemently condemns. The day when the love of his life, Indigo, left his all-time rival, it was Christian who felt the most punished.'

'Right, but that's because after leaving his rival, she did not rush into his arms either, did she? You've said that day was the last time he saw her?'

'Yes, in effect she dumped them both.'

'No wonder. She must've been sick and tired of their company. I would've been in her place.'

'She was, and she told them so in no uncertain terms. Not only told—showed as well. Pulled no punches.'

The story I tell David is one the late Mihai would've enjoyed most. Another *choribe* tale.

*

There was no telling if Indigo had planned it or improvised.

Christian's words.

This, he says, is the detail that pains him most—his inability to read the music of her mind. It saddens him even more than her deed itself, which, predictably, he found disgusting.

The disgruntled girl decided to have the reckoning coincide with her birthday.

Christian arrived at Indigo's aunt's early in the afternoon with a bottle of champagne. He brought no flowers. There was a tradition kept every Indigo's birthday; she would take her friends to the flower shop of her choice and herself select the flowers she was in the mood for, after which her companions would jointly pay for the bouquet the birthday girl wanted.

Indigo kissed Chris lightly on the cheek and thanked him for the champagne. She was dressed up, fragrant, and looked ready to go out "on the flower quest," as it was referred to between her and her closest circle.

Indigo's cousin Bernie was lolling about in a bathrobe. He was unshaven, disheveled, yawning, and lazily swapping jokes with his blue-eyed friend Peter.

Peter, on the other hand, had arrived at the place even earlier than Christian. He was looking a complete opposite of Bernie—uniformed, cologned, and alert. Every now and again he flashed a toothy smile at

Indigo, who responded with a coy twitch at one corner of her lips.

'All right, get ready, lazybones, you are the one everybody is waiting for!' Peter gave Bernie a slap on the back of the head. 'Lovely Fräulein Indigo needs her flowers; come on, hurry!'

'I'll be ready in five minutes,' Bernie meowed languidly. 'Don't rush me, you naughty creatures. By the way, cuz, have you yet made up your mind which flower shop we are going to this time?'

'Herr Shmoel's on Rethelstraße,' Indigo responded quickly. 'Herr Shmoel remembers my birthday and always orders fresh black and purple roses for me the day before.'

That had been her favorite florist for the years she lived with her aunt and cousin. In fact, she rarely wanted flowers from any other place. Both Christian and Bernie knew it. But they both also knew old Shmoel's shop didn't exist anymore—had been demolished during the recent Kristallnacht raids and now stood boarded up and abandoned.

'That shop is defunct though, isn't it?' Christian muttered in embarrassment. 'It is closed, Indie... Or am I mistaken?' He had been sure Indigo too was aware of the inconvenient circumstance.

At that moment some daemonic force prompted the blue-eyed Peter to interfere.

'Rethelstraße? I remember the place, I do! We got that little Jewish rat hole smashed up all right. The old usurer sold flowers grown on our Arian soil, to us, Arians, at three times the normal price! We don't need such poison on our land, Miss Indigo. I'll bring you the flowers my mother grows in her garden—I promise you've never seen such roses before!'

Indigo's eyes flashed, as if lighting struck from under her eyelashes; her body tensed. For a second, Christian feared she would pounce at Peter and tear into his rosy cheeks with her long fingernails. She, however, simply turned her back on the three young men and, without saying a word, retired to her room. She audibly locked the door from the inside.

'Come on, cuz, don't be a drag,' Bernie shouted. 'There are plenty of florists in this town; choose any other you like!'

There was silence in response.

No amount of Christian's cajoling and Peter's loud apologies cut any ice.

Eventually it was decided Peter would rush out and buy the best flowers in the nearest shop, along with some chocolates and liquor, to make amends for his tactless remark.

'I won't be fifteen minutes,' he declared, taking his wallet and leaving his big leather bag on the armchair in the hall, lest he drop something from it while shopping.

It must be noted that by the described period Peter had become a member of several activist organizations which frequently raised money for all manner of patriotic purposes. As a responsible young member, Peter was made treasurer, so he often carried substantial amounts of Reichsmarks in his big leather bag. Such was the case on Indigo's birthday.

As soon as the door behind Peter closed, Indigo's door opened.

Indigo came out of the room in her trench coat and high-heeled shoes, with her suitcase in one hand and a pet valise with her cat in the other. She proceeded to the telephone and called a taxi.

'I'm leaving,' she said. 'I'm going home. And then elsewhere, away from here. I've had enough of this place and this country. I'm grateful to you, my friends, for all the good times we shared, and I'm immensely sorry you both have espoused the Nazi filth.'

Trying to stop her would be to no avail; that much was clear.

Dejectedly, Christian looked out the window, expecting the cab which would take his love away from him—forever, as he now felt—fearing the imminent moment of the cab's arrival. For want of the right things to say or do, Bernie too joined Chris at the windowsill and lit a cigarette.

Both stood for a minute with their faces to the window and their backs to Indigo, to Peter's big leather bag and to Indigo's suitcase—which happened to be much bigger than Peter's bag—just the size to swallow it comfortably and swiftly.

Christian wept as he watched her getting into the taxi; Bernie still looked awkwardly lost for words.

By the time Peter returned with flowers and another bottle of champagne, Indigo was gone. Gone, too, was Peter's big brown bag with all the money.

*

Just as I, in anticipation of David's giggles, pronounce the last word "money," my narrative is interrupted. Something swift and painful occurs—like the proverbial bolt from the blue.

The bolt is in fact quite literate—and it strikes directly at my midriff.

Wind momentarily knocked out of me; I fell on my back to have the nose of a hobnailed boot pressed against my left side at once.

A wheezy, whiny voice threatens to break my ribs one by one and have each one of them pierce my heart a thousand times, until it is torn to pieces in my chest, unless I tell where I am hiding the money.

The voice is instantly recognizable; it belongs to poor Moshe. The hobnailed boot is his too—he makes his boots himself, as he is actually a shoemaker.

Moshe's story is a dismal one; Moshe has gone insane. Apart from the minor and major misfortunes of the camp's day-to-day reality, what made Moshe crack was the knowledge of the successful Guido Karp scheme. The news of our systematically milking Guido got circulated a lot, and those tidings stole Moshe's sleep, appetite—and eventually his mind.

I have been told Moshe had it in for me and David and might get bellicose.

Apparently he has found a moment which seemed suitable to him.

'Money, money, where are you hiding the money? Tell me where the money is?' he whimpers as David pulls him off and I get back to my feet.

What a second ago was a bloodthirsty aggressor is now just a forlorn, tearful human being.

We sit him down (thankfully no eyes from the side witnessed the incident) and pat him on the back. I ask David to give him a smoke.

Moshe's teeth chatter as I light a match, and he tries to take a drag. David and I wait for him to finish as David dabs at the cuts on my left flanc with a piece of cloth (they are nothing serious, but my love won't rest while I'm bleeding), and then I gently ask Moshe to go back to the works, which he does.

Moshe doesn't attempt to attack or ask about the money anymore. His tears stop too, little by little.

It suddenly reveals itself to me that David's cigarette, which Moshe has smoked, is going to be the last one today and in his life. The despondent shoemaker will not make it until tomorrow, for at night the inner voice in his inflamed mind will instruct him to suicide himself by throwing his weight on the electric wire fence, which Moshe will waste no time in accomplishing.

'The wretched sufferer is going to finish himself tonight,' I voice my vision of Moshe's future to David. 'Shall we try and stop him?'

'Can you play him out of it?'

'No chance. A broken soul cannot be unbroken. The best we can do is physically prevent him from harming himself.'

'But if it cannot cure his soul, what good shall it be?' David muses quietly. 'Just prolong his suffering? Let him go ahead with what he wants to do; this might at least relieve him.'

Sometimes, though not very often, a bit of my non-interference philosophy does seem to infiltrate my love's idealistic mind.

So we leave Moshe to his free will.

XIX
1st Violin

The black snake twisted and wriggled.

It coiled its agile body around me, grappling me in multiple deadly steel hoops. It hissed in my ear.

'Sins against me have to be washed down with cash.'

I clenched my fists, sank my upper teeth into the flesh of my lower lip, shook my head with all the might I was able to summon, and forced myself into wakefulness.

I sat up in the bed—drenched in sweat, heart pounding, hands clammy, and shaking.

With horror and revulsion, I realized the snake in my dream was Indigo.

*

Indigo's stealing the money from that ill-starred boy Peter entailed a tragedy. Peter was murdered.

The amount stolen had been substantial enough, and belonged to the leaders of a pseudo-occult clone of the Ahnenerbe, which Peter had been using as a stepping stone to membership in the actual association. The poor candid soul faced his bosses, took the blame for having lost the money due to negligence, and promised to repay within a month. His words were never believed; he was never forgiven. His dead body was found in his rented flat some weeks after Indigo's birthday. He had been strangled.

Bernie cursed his cousin after she'd caused his friend's death but was too fearful to testify against her. Not sure which thing he was more afraid of—me (I said I'd kill him if he harmed Indigo) or her "witchcraft." The superstitious namby-pamby got it fixed in his head that by stealing from Peter, Indigo had also somehow jinxed him and programmed the murder. Bernie seriously suspected that if provoked further, his vengeful "cuz" might turn her spells against him, Bernie, this time.'

Naturally, I didn't bother to assuage the coward's fears.

I repeatedly tried ringing her up and talking to her. I tried to arrange a meeting—at her place in Prenzlauer Berg or anywhere else outside.

She point-blank refused.

'This young man was killed, Indigo,' I told her over the phone. 'Your revenge, as you choose to call it, cost him his life. Are you sure you hated Peter so much, or he did to you something so bad that he deserved a death sentence?'

'Serves him right,' was the inevitable answer to my reproaches. 'One Nazi scumbag less.'

*

Sometimes I wonder why she didn't pick my, or Bernie's, or her aunt's pockets as well. By that time we, all of us, must've amounted to approximately the same quantity of "Nazi filth" for her.

Did love—once felt by her or for her—continue to matter in some way, perhaps? It did, I believe, and this circumstance excused her in my eyes. To an extent. Not completely—otherwise, why would I be seeing her in my dreams as a snake who wants to strangle me?

Those last several weeks before her fateful birthday that she'd been largely spending locked up in her room with Tino the cat—Indigo, in fact, talked to me a lot—both over the phone and vis-à-vis when I visited. She mostly talked about the art of pretense and propounded the theory of masterful deception as an optimal means of dealing with the majority of human beings. She became completely obsessed with the subject.

'Do you know what you should do if you don't like yourself?' she asked me as she lay on her black silk-covered bed, chain-smoking into the ceiling, tapping her ash out into a blue crystal, mermaid-shaped ashtray. 'If you are not one bit the person you want to be? You should act like that person for the others' benefit! You should project yourself on other people, and the image they see will reflect back on you... rub off, as they say... Thus, by pretending to be something, you will, step by step, bit by bit, eventually become it.'

She expounded her "good lying strategy."

'If you want your lies to pass effortlessly for the truth, recall how you reacted to a similar situation in the past. Your voice, facial expression, breathing, and heart rate. Then learn to imitate it as close as possible...'

'I'll serve them my delicious lies generously sprinkled with colorful truth,' each such monologue of hers ended, while I listened silently—bewildered, aghast—terrified of what might be happening to her sanity.

After finishing half a bottle of French or Italian wine (which she at that period rather overdid on), Indigo would switch from her proclamations of lying as a living strategy to harangues against the Reich and The Cause. She said Germany was a rotting corpse devoured by maggots, and the maggots were the German people themselves.

'The only relief is Dad and Gina (talking of her mother; she always referred to her by her first name) did not live to see this mayhem. Dad would've not been able to bear it; he would've protested and got himself killed.'

At that point she'd usually break into semi-drunken tears and cry herself to sleep while I patted her on the head, muttering inarticulate consolations only because I was completely at a loss for what else to do or say.

There were moments—and those were numerous—when she demonstrated undisguised aversion to me and my tender gestures. Screwed up her face at the sound of my voice and shuddered at my touch. Every time this caused me agonizing internal pain, as though my intestines were scalded with boiling water. Unable to bear her revulsion, I failed to contain myself and feebly pleaded with her to reassure me—tell me she didn't loathe me.

'I know you cannot, and never could, love me. Please say at least you do not hate me.'

Her features would soften, though sometimes it took her an effort.

'No, Chris. Of course not. Whatever our differences, I will never hate you. You are my friend. The only one that remains. All the things you've done for me... I would be an ingrate and a traitor to hate you.'

Yet often her rage against me and the values I represented got the better of her, and then she did little to hide it.

It is the look in her eyes at those moments—pure, living, unconfined poison—that trickled into my brain, slithered into it like a snake.

It is this snake that now creeps out at night, hisses in my ear, and wants to squeeze the life out of me.

It has just been waiting for its hour.

The hour has come.

*

These days I find myself wondering: was it just Indigo with her warped mind and perverted soul, or do women in general not appreciate being loved?

She said to me (not in that sore last period—much earlier—on one of our lilac-infused walks in Treptower).

'I find a man in love with a woman—especially chasing a woman—an entirely un-erotic show. Love and chase are the woman's realm. The man is about exploring, discovering, and creating. If anything, a man should be in love with himself and with what he does—not pine for some apron strings!'

She cited the insane electricity trickster Nicola Tesla as an example of "impeccable male eroticism."

'Just take a moment to consider the world's arguably most ingenious inventor—tall, exquisitely slim, extremely well-groomed, and devilishly handsome. Also, according to the relatively reliable press, he was exceptionally well-mannered and gallant with the ladies. And this remarkable man stays celibate throughout his life, claiming his only true love is science!' Here she drew a shuddery breath and licked her lips. 'Serves this passion of his ravenously—and the fruit his love for science bears illuminates the world. Both literally and figuratively. And it will shine ever brighter—you mark my words, Chris—as humanity will come to more and more appreciate its value.'

All I could feel then was jealousy toward the eccentric scientist and delight at the sound of her voice.

Only now have I come to fully realize the true and terrible meaning of her philosophy. Not just realize. I am physically poisoned by it. The snake's venom took years to reach its target, but it finally struck. It is murdering me.

Indigo despised and denied the very core of life—the sacred love of a man for a woman; of a child for a mother; a citizen for his motherland.

She saw the institution of family as "a vestige of the cave-dwelling past, only second in its retardation to patriotism." Quoted Plato even (though she generally preferred Aristotle and Socrates), who considered the complete abolition of the family in the upper classes a desirable aim.

We used to argue about this a lot.

I explained to her that Plato's view only reflected the major fallacy of the Greeks—the weak position of the family in their society, which resulted in their inferiority in matters of law as compared to the Romans. Indigo, as was her wont, responded that law was a straight jacket necessary to contain the brutal passions of cave dwellers—and something entirely redundant and chocking in a society of civilized living beings.

Those were the discussions we held on our outings, in the blessed era when she did not detest me yet.

The last weeks at her aunt's Indigo spoke less of the Antiquity and more of today. When she was not vilifying the Reich, she was eulogizing America. "The land of the free, the land that has people like my mother in it," she'd call it. She was making plans of going there to live in a small apartment in Manhattan, all alone with her cat Tino.

The corrupted country with its perfidious politics, the rotten system, became Indigo's dream haven; the Negroes, to whom, as she said, "the white world owed the future as a recompense for the past of slavery," became her heroes.

The only music she wanted to listen to in the insane period was jazz—not the well-known records, but some obscure, hard to find, and particularly disharmonious howling.

Those barbarian sounds she'd play for hours and they tore at my ears almost as painfully as her disdain lacerated my soul.

*

This was the creature to whom I have dedicated the musical work of my life.

The masterpiece, which is now complete. My jewel, which is destined to forever change people's perception of sound and the role of music in human life, throning it alongside love, health, and enlightenment.

Indigo Mind, ready to conquer the world.

I am blissed.

Am I blissed?

Why am I not confident?

Is it because I have devoted it to a snake who comes to me in my nightmares to squeeze the life out of me? Is this the reason?

Or because my musical diamond does not feel quite like my own anymore?

Because, every time Siegfried strikes and Cosima blasts into her furiously obstinate dance, it is now the vision of the Gypsy that instantaneously flashes in my consciousness, setting my mind ablaze.

All I can see and hear while I play my music is Jassengro playing something he claims to have composed recently on the daemonic instrument of his, which he lovingly calls by that ugly name ('just the Romani word for "violin,"' he explains).

The more I compare the Gypsy's creation with my own, the better his sounds.

And then he unstoppably makes those hellish minute changes to mine.

Every time the Gypsy gives I. M. a "tweak" (another of his many obnoxious words), the diamond immediately adds a new facet, reveals a new dimension of splendidness.

The devil, they say, is in the details.

Now I understand the meaning of the expression all too well.

It is those haunting, taunting details that he so effortlessly throws on. That stardust I can never conjure and sprinkle on, no matter how I strain my creative forces.

So many times during our sessions, in the endless conversations we held, he mentioned he thought nothing of stealing. Spelt it out to me quite shamelessly.

Thieving is a gypsy thing; has always been it. No matter what their bloodline, they have practiced the execrable vice, unabashed, in all times, like Jews have usury.

It is now obvious the Gypsy has violated my mind and stolen my musical jewel. No question about it.

The question arises, however, why am I not able to take it back?

Do I not have the wherewithal to retrieve what's mine—sacredly mine—and punish the defiler?

Will I—a creator, an aesthetic man, and a Teutonic warrior—not make a reprisal against the thieving fiend?

*

And I know exactly what reprisal I will conduct.

The Idea will be my weapon—*Force vitale,* the force of life itself.

I have discovered it; now it is time to learn to harness its power and use it against my enemies.

In fact, why even *learn*?

However, insulted, robbed, or betrayed I feel; however scalding or righteous my wrath, what right do I have to interfere with nature's purposes? And, more importantly, what NEED is there to do it?

I have rediscovered and meticulously explored the principle of *Force vitale*. No one in the world knows or understands it better than I do. Proceeding from my extensive theoretical knowledge of the subject and basing my conclusions on the by now accumulated substantial practical evidence, I assert that the principle is true for all representatives of the Hominina subtribe, without exception. The *exitium sui* mechanism self-launches for every single specimen—it just gets enacted at different ages and via different types of affliction for each, depending on their individual living conditions and role in maintaining the natural balance within and beyond their species.

Why do some of them remain unaffected longer than others? Because somehow their existence brings other things into being or prevents something that should not happen, from happening. All beings—from the sublimest to the basest—come into the world for a reason; they all have a mission to carry out. My religious views might have always been rather reprehensibly under-shaped, but I can state with utmost certainty that thus far my faith in the divine is firm.

Why did Jassengro linger on? Why was he not afflicted with *cancrum oris* and self-neutralize when he was at the age of the objects under my observation? The answer is clear: because he was to become an instrument for the realization of a creative vision conceived by a superior being. His mission was to become my tool. Now that it is accomplished, he has to go.

I truly need not hate Jassengro or make any specific effort to deactivate him.

All my objects knew the exact moment when their self-deactivation should start. For all of them, that moment was the one at which the *exitium sui* mechanism took over. And, whereas *cancrum oris* is certainly the most representative—I would say, quintessential—expression of *exitium sui*, the mechanism can certainly be effectuated in a multitude of other forms, molded by the individual characteristics of the specimen.

A creature as highly developed for his species as Jassengro will know precisely when his time has come. His finely attuned system will register the signal and react to it.

I assume the *exitium sui* is already at work in him.

He will be gone in no time.

My prediction is—in several weeks.

Days.

*

The accuracy of my forecast for Jassengro is easy to validate.

I shall go to block 32 now.

I have been deliberately avoiding all contact with the objects for a week, lest my haste to see the desired result infiltrate the air and pollute the experiment. All the parameters have come into such a fine yet delicate configuration that even the slightest movement of the air might disturb the balance.

I have been postponing my visit to the ward till the time the objects are, all four of them, dead.

By my calculations, their respective four missions were to be exhausted, approximately by today. Ergo, today they should, all four, be extinct.

If this parameter conforms, then all doubt regarding Jassengro's case will be dissipated and the probability of cessation of all his vital functions within another week—two weeks at most—be estimated, according to my standard formula, at 95.4 percent.

Another sensational article to send to the Institute for Anthropology and an augmented copy to the Hygiene Institute.

I better start writing today. Time is precious—more so than ever before.

*

I've just realized I almost forgot how pretty she is.

How radiant her smile and melodic her voice. How shimmery the pale skin; how exuberant the autumnal hair.

Birgitte, my Freia.

My head has been all over the place lately; I have not been thinking about her often nor seeing her around much.

It is somewhat of a blinding experience to see her coming down the corridor now—that swift, airy yet confident gait of hers—in the company of the dashing-as-ever Anton Lauer.

With Anton, it seems, I've not been talking quite a while too. When was the last time we had a whiskey together, a coffee, or even exchanged a couple of words over a quick smoke in the yard? Maybe indeed not so long ago, but to me it feels like ages have elapsed. Obviously, the recent weeks I have been too occupied with my own thoughts and deeds to notice any of the world around. Anton's glow dazzles no less than Birgitte's as he is walking toward me, hand in hand with her, telling her some joke loudly, laughing at his own words, squinting and shaking his head with mirth, pressing her fingers, and making her laugh too—her crystalline laughter.

I forgot how funny Anton could be, how sparklingly charming.

I forgot so much.

'Chris! Hallo, hero, what are you up to, looking so serious? You'll work yourself into the grave with this obsessiveness of yours; you mark me; you need to relax!'

'Hello, Chris, dear—Anton is right, I tell you all the time you are overworking—you must rest.'

'Anyway, I've been sharing with Birgitte here something hilarious; just listen.'

While Anton retells me a rather convoluted anecdote about a possible big order we may receive from Naturechemie, and Birgitte chimes in in her melodic fashion, I find myself torpidly wondering what they were doing in my ward, because it was definitely there they've been coming from.

'Naturechemie's chief curiosity, Mittlerkopf—you know the fellow's a little cranky, don't you—had this bright idea to go to India, and there, rumor has it, he got in with some local *hashishins*.'

'Are they actually called that?' Birgitte jingles. 'I thought the *hashishins* were a poetic gathering in Paris in the middle of the last century?'

'Doesn't matter,' Anton dismisses her frivolously. 'Active and experienced local users of the stuff is what they are, anyway... So

Mittlerkopf got so much under their influence that upon return he commanded a complete company restructuring and concept overhaul. Naturechemie are currently phasing out all their programs to make way for this new "cannabis anesthesia" baby Mittlerkopf's smokey mind delivered. Long story short, if we here are lucky enough to land this gig, we may have the whole Reich legally—and massively—smoking hashish in less than half a year's time! An opportune move too—this angst-ridden country's going to need some exotic potion to bury its woes in, just about then...'

Too wordy, too noisy, too peacocky, talks mostly gibberish. Yet irresistible. Anton will be Anton.

And Birgitte, so cuddly and feminine, demurely smiling and laughing at his jokes.

They continue holding hands; each also holds a puffy folder full of paperwork under one arm.

WHAT were they doing in the ward?

What are they doing in block 32—especially Birgitte? Helping Anton with his fatigue study?

It doesn't look so to me.

*

They are gone finally.

It took them a good forty minutes to get their fast-talking done; I thought they were never going to leave.

Make an effort they did, but succeed they didn't. I saw right through their trickery.

In vain did Anton go out of his way to put me off the scent; in vain did he deliberately vex me, stretching and relishing every syllable of his treacherous speech, "Now that we had our asses kicked big time in Normandy—which is, believe me, the shape of things to come—hashish will be our only solace."

In vain did Birgitte play along to him, so subtly and artfully.

I did not listen to their nonsense. Instead, I watched them. I looked at them—both of them—closely and attentively. I looked them both straight in the eye.

The more they were trying to sidetrack me, the clearer I understood the purpose of their visit to this building.

A while ago (which now feels like an eternity), when Birgitte and I were close, I told her many things. Much of what I even then knew I shouldn't be discussing with her or anyone else. But I was too grateful for the help Birgitte had rendered me; too blinded by her charm. My infatuation got the better of me—I wanted to trust my Freia. I itched to confide in her. I felt ashamed of my suspicions; I pushed away my doubts; I banished my common sense.

I should've never done so.

I told her, for example, that I was keeping a diary of my observations of the children—some very detailed notes on *cancrum oris* and its development as a part of doing the will of the Vital Force. That I was going to base all my further theoretical work on this invaluable material, some of which I obtained thanks to her. That I never took the diary home for fear I may one day forget to bring it back to the block and then fail to register some significant detail. That I always kept it locked in my desk in the ward.

The reason why Birgitte and Anton came to my ward today is as plain as day, therefore.

Birgitte told Anton about the diary. Anton, who was always somewhat jealous of my scientific success and especially of The Idea, decided to steal my results and publish them as his own. He got intimate with Birgitte and talked her into complicity. Together they came to the block, broke into the ward, found the key to the desk drawer, took out the diary, and made copies of the notes (this explains the loads of paper they were carrying).

Plain as day.

A question that's more difficult to answer is: Why am I not infuriated? Why am I not chasing them, confronting them, and accusing them?

Why am I standing here in the corridor instead, staring at the door of the ward, feeling tearful and self-reproachful? Why am I hating myself instead of hating Anton for his theft and Birgitte for her betrayal?

Is it because I realize that what the two of them have done is perhaps for the best? That it works toward establishing the right order of things? Because at the end of the day, Anton is worthier of my results than I myself am. He deserves more to present them to the world, for he is in fact a much better scientist and a stronger man.

Birgitte, as a woman, feels it: she senses his overall superiority; this is why she agrees to assist him against me.

A woman, yes. A female. They sure have a keener instinct for success and failure than men.

*

Enough self-devouring!

For here I stand—a creator, an inventor, an aesthetic man—the hope of my country and the civilized world.

Here I stand—on the threshold of this ward with four dead objects—literally on the threshold of a new age of medical science, which I am about to launch. Knowing there are fiends keen to put a spanner in my works.

Knowing this and doing nothing to prevent it—moreover—facilitating their job with self-deprecation!

Enough!

I'm not committing this crime against myself and the world.

I am going to deal with my enemies—one by one.

First—Jassengro.

Jassengro has to go. I have to make sure of this before all else.

I mustn't forget my duty. My duty to myself and the world is to get rid of Jassengro.

If all four objects are dead, so will soon be Jassengro.

Very soon indeed.

Away with the fear.

Turn the key.

Step over the threshold.

Here we are.

The blessed smell of death.

The glorious sight of decay.

All four dead, of course. Maybe a day already. Maybe several hours.

Grisha.

Patrin.

Mara.

Extinguished. Devoured. Accounted for.

Damira.

Damira?

Breathing?

No, it cannot be.

Calling me?

Did I just hear "Onkel Heidert"?
Damira! Are you talking?
Are you alive?
She is.
Unbelievable.
Unbelievable.
Damira is still alive!
The little obstinate fiend. The poison.
She too!
Damira.
Is.
Still.
Alive.

XX
2nd Violin

It warms the heart to watch them, it truly does.

Baba Tanya and Vasil.

An endearing sight, and a perfect match. She needs a Vasil to remain what she is; he—a Baba Tanya to resist change, which he has instinctively shunned from the cradle and will grow increasingly wary of as he becomes older. It can even be said that with his fear of change, he takes after her. Does trace inheritance transcend the purely physiological then, perhaps? Can reactions and attitudes be handed down from an adoptive parent that will only appear in the child's life when the child is already an adult?

The two of them remind me of a myth the late Mihai used to love telling.

'My old *Bibi* Maya was a settler, did I tell you, son? She had *lové* too. Owned a house in Niš, a handsome affair... Those were the happiest days when we stopped over at Maya's—I imagined I was a rich *gospodar* and the house was all mine... But, happy as it made me, that house also scared the crap out of me—do you know why? Because it was haunted! Two *mulani* lived in the place—two!—and *Bibi* Maya knew each of them by name! They were, really, the reason why she chose to settle and bought that house. Those two *mulani*—she said she protected their peace, like a priestess.

'Sometimes I saw them with my own eyes—I did, believe or not, son!—chasing each other up and down the stairs, or through the doors and windows, as if playing tag. One had no shape; leastwise, I could never say what its shape was. The other looked like a *chavoro* about the same years I was then—only that kid was made of air, you could see right through him. *Bibi* Maya told me the one without shape was called Tyutya, and the other was Tyutya's boy. That's right, *bibi*'s words.

Tyutya and his boy.

'*Bibi* Maya said, there'd dwelt a tribe in the place many thousands of years before her house was built. That tribe had a God they prayed to, much like we pray to ours. They built a stone statue of the God on the local mountaintop and climbed up to that statue and sang their songs to it and asked it for harvests, rains, and all things one asks one's God for. That God of theirs was called some name no one in our times would know how to say—only the clevers like you, or Vano would, maybe! But it began with something like "tyee" or "tyoo."

'One day—so *bibi* told me—another tribe came, and attacked the settlement and killed most, and whom they didn't kill, they took slaves and drove away like cattle.

'Only one little boy happened to be playing on the mountaintop near the statue and then, when the fight began, hugged the God and hid in his shadow. That boy stayed alive and unhurt.

'Time passed; new tribes came to the land around the mountain; built new settlements; fought wars with neighbors; then others came in their place. And the little boy on the mountain still played around his stone god— no one saw him, and if they did, they didn't touch him. Years went by, and the boy didn't grow—he was always the same young kid. Talk, he could neither. The only word he knew how to say was his god's name, but say it properly he could not—what came off his tongue was some sounds akin to "tyuuutyaaa-tyuuuuutyaaa."

'Later, already in the Vlastimirovići rule, some wise monk from Byzantium noticed the weird goings-on and reasoned that the old, ungodly god kept himself being with the help of the boy. That God, so the monk wrote, only knew himself as long as there was a living soul who believed in him. But of those who prayed to the God, only the boy remained alive. The boy, the monk wrote, was Tyutya's only hold on the world of the living. But if the boy'd grown up, he might've left his native parts and forgotten to believe in Tyutya. That's why Tyutya did so that the boy would not grow.

'Thus they went on, one thanks to the other. Tyutya kept the boy alive, and the boy kept believing in Tyutya. As long as the boy believed in Tyutya, Tyutya was. And as long as Tyutya was, the boy lived but didn't grow.

'Later still, *bibi* told me, much good and ill alike came to pass—more wars and destructions, as well as peaceful times and great new buildings. Time didn't spare the stone statue; the mountain was razed to the ground. But Tutya did not leave those parts. Nor did his boy…'

So do Baba Tanya and her very own boy Vasil keep each other's essences intact, and so they will be doing until the boy discontinues believing in his *biryul'ky*-wielding goddess.

When placed before the choice between Baba Tanya and life, Vasil, though not without vacillating, will choose the latter.

'Come, come, come, boy,' Baba Tanya clucks, beckoning to Vasil. 'Move closer to Baba Tanya, and she will show you something neat. See this silver thimble? And this red thread doll which your Baba Tanya was given by her *daj* when she was a little girl? And now look, if you put the thimble on the doll's head, what happens? See? It fits her head so well and looks just like a tall silver hat!'

I find Baba Tanya's mention of a hat a funny coincidence, because, to the sound of her and Vasil's purring at their doll game, I'm also admiring "a hat" (learned this word first in France and later heard its equivalent in Russia from the memorable *Predsedatel* Georgyi—this is how the French and the Russians call an official letter heading).

I'm rereading the final letter to Guido Karp, I composed and typed on his own Olympia last time Christian and I met for music. I wanted this text, which was to mark the closure of our fruitful relationship, to look especially solemn, so I added "a hat."

To Obersturmführer Karp
From his Invisible Friends
With Great Trust and High Expectations.

Lower down the page comes the traditional request of Guido's services as a transporter, this time for Vasil, Baba Tanya, and little Dando.

The completion of my last order by Guido will be in progress when David and I are already far from AU. Nothing much will be different in the barrack then from what it is now, except for my absence, which no one will notice much, and Marusya's sickness. Dando's and Damira's mother will be dying of typhus by then, which circumstance shall place her toothy baby in Baba Tanya's care.

In those pudgy hands, Dando will safely remain until Guido comes to collect the three of them.

Despite her contemptuous attitude toward "karp-shmarp," Baba Tanya will have to follow the Obersturmführer quietly into his car; she will preserve her bewildered silence even when driven through the main gate, even when ordered out of the car in the middle of a dark alley, with the bundled Dando at her belly and Vasil clinging to her big shoulder. Even when picked up and led into the unknown by Chloya.

It is when the unknown becomes the known—namely in Chloya's flat—that Baba Tanya's booming protests will begin.

The *gicisvara* will plainly refuse to leave AU. She will insist on being transported back into the family camp. She will curse the sneaky bastard Karp for having, by deception, thrown her and the two poor children out of the camp's safety.

'He was always afraid of me, Karp, the dirty pig—always! Always knew what this old Zigeunerin could do to him if she wanted to! The old Tanya's curse—that's what he dreaded! That's why he got rid of me—at night, in the dark, so no one could see! Threw me out—me and the two innocent babies—all because he knows this old woman loves her two boys more than she loves her own life. All to hurt me more—because he fears me, the snake!'

No amount of reasoning on Chloya's part will cut any ice, nor timid, tearful cajoling on Vasil's. The only result their efforts will yield is convince the stubborn *gicisvara* that Chloya is in Karp's pay and her naive little Vasil—dangerously deceived.

'Silly, silly boy, don't you understand what they are doing to us? Think!' She will desperately knock herself on the forehead with her knuckles. 'Throwing us out of the place where we know all the rules. Where everyone who is someone respects us. The place where we are masters! The Jews are under us, the doctors listen to us, the officers fear us... And outside—what shall we do, where shall we go? Who will feed us? How will I raise you two? How will I provide for you?'

Baba Tanya's indignation will little by little be drowned in squelchy sobs, and eventually she will weep herself to sleep on the big sofa where Mihai found eternal rest.

When the Krajowa people come before daybreak, it will only be Vasil and little Dando they take along.

Chloya will softly pat Vasil on the shoulder to wake him. She will place the bundled baby in his arms.

Vasil will understand.

Though through tears and remorseful hesitation, he will, nevertheless, kiss the snoring Baba Tanya on the cheek and quietly take his leave of her.

*

Vasil will hide in the woods with the Home Army for some time and even, despite his bleating voice and crybaby disposition, distinguish himself as a fairly good partisan.

When the war ends, he will safely return to Bulgaria, his homeland. Although among the Polish resistance there will be friendly women willing to adopt the kid Dando and take him off young Vasil's inexperienced hands, Vasil will not want to part with his little "brother."

Dando will follow Vasil to his hometown of Varna (soon to be renamed "Stalin" for a while), and there they will be sharing a life as a family of two orphaned Romani siblings, survivors of the *Porreimos*.

The fraternal coexistence will be relatively cloudless for about a dozen years, until Vasil's mental health begins to deteriorate. Dando will by then be a rowdy yet bright and achieving school-leaver.

Contriving to place his adoptive elder brother in a privileged asylum reserved for the kin of the communist elite, Dando will conscientiously repay Vasil for the years of brotherly care. Though Vasil will spend most of his late life in a catatonic state, it will be, thanks to Dando's ongoing efforts, in the safety, satiety, and comfort of a hospital ward shared with some not so distant relation of general secretary.

As for young Dando, the toothy one will successfully gnaw his way through all imaginable obstacles right up the communist career ladder, gaining favor with all the who's who in Sofia, and eventually become one of them.

It is the toothy ones of the world that make good communists and capitalists.

When Baba Tanya wakes up at Chloya's after some ten hours of good sleep and finds Vasil and baby Dando gone, she will immediately conclude that the two little ingrates have disobeyed, betrayed, and abandoned her. Far from upsetting her, though, this notion will only reinforce her pride and strengthen her self-righteousness. The two ungrateful rapscallions will be without delay ejected from the *gicisvara's* memory as useless, foreign rubbish. Who refuses to hang on Baba Tanya's every word, follow in her footsteps, and admire the *biryul'ky* with her, is automatically relegated to the status of a complete stranger.

She will confront Chloya and demand to be returned to the family camp alone.

The *gicisvara's* wish shall be granted—this also will have been prearranged. In fact, her temporary exodus from the camp will only be needed to emotionally facilitate the rescue of Vasil and Dando, while within the confines of AU, Vasil may refuse freedom unless Baba Tanya be offered the same grace.

At dusk, Vatslav will take the curmudgeonly Baba to the same dark alley corner where Chloya picked her up with the boys the day before. There, a quarter of an hour later, she will be offered a seat in the already familiar "karp-shmarp"'s auto, which will safely deliver her back to the family camp. The details of this particular operation have been carefully specified in my last letter to Guido, which I am rereading. The important point is that the Obersturmführer must not answer a word to Baba Tanya's bitter scolding and vitriolic accusations, which he is going to hear on this final ride.

Once reunited with her prestigious seat in the corner of the barrack and her treasure box, the *gicisvara* will waste no time in finding herself another young male protégé. The boy will be Sergo, a brisk, dark-blue-eyed new arrival from Belarus. Sergo will spend the rest of his days entertaining Baba Tanya and enjoying her *biryul'ky* until, when the day comes, they both enter the gas chamber—she on his hand—like a venerable mother and her respectful adolescent offspring.

*

Like Tyutya-the-heathen-God that Mihai related me about, Baba Tanya will not leave the place where she is believed in. She will stay till the end and die in the oven, where the latest reincarnation of her "boy" shall dutifully follow.

Jedem das seine, as our fellows from BU are quoted to say.

Whom else would I be able to take care of?

Looks like that's it.

There's Rosa, but her path, for the nearest future, is inextricably entwined with Hauptsturmführer Lauer's.

The luscious maiden used to dream of Dr. Heidert, but she will be getting his best friend instead. Not a bad lot at all. Also a doctor. Also a dandy and a heartthrob—even more so than my lugubrious-faced Chris, methinks.

It is going to be Anton who breaks Rosa out—I needn't budge.

With Christian gone, the role of our barrack's curator will automatically pass to Dr. Lauer, who will soon end up smitten by Rosa's dusky-husky allure. Not only will Anton, at his own risk, free Rosa from AU and take her in to be his "housemaid." He will also successfully treat her epilepsy. Thus, the results of Anton's fatigue study will not altogether go down the drain.

It will be Rosa's testimony that, in its turn, will save Doctor Lauer from the gallows when his case is held up to scrutiny in Nuremberg.

She will, eventually, leave him, and be off to Paris, and break bad, but not before she plays her brass section part in Anton's life. I even wish I could stick around to watch the flamboyant spectacle.

Speaking of Anton—our Doctor Lauer, the pianist—he himself has already played a resonant part in the life (or, to be more precise, upcoming death) of his friend, colleague, and collaborating musician Christian Heidert. Did his bit, along with Birgitte and little Damira.

The shock of Damira still living when Christian had pinned all his hopes on finding her dead was grievous. The ensuing realization that I too may prove resistant to the force he'd believed omnipotent was horrible.

It wasn't, however, enough to kill Christian on the spot.

Instead of feeling immediately suicidal, Chris felt mawkish. He wanted consolation. He craved comfort.

And, for those, he went to me—to the one he desired dead.

Self-contradictory behavior, in the best tradition of my Young Werther, my (still) living oxymoron.

*

I met Christian outside the barrack.

I was standing up, eyes closed, and playing Le Storie when he approached.

Chris listened till the end. When I finished, he touched me on the shoulder. His hand was trembling.

I opened my eyes.

'Are you doing this on purpose?' he asked.

I greeted him and answered his question in the negative.

'Though I do often play with a practical purpose, this time it was exclusively for pleasure.'

'Have you been expecting me?'

'I always expect you, Chris. You know it.'

'Take a walk with me. Please, will you?'

'Sure.'

I followed him outside the gate, and we proceeded along the wire fence—he leading, me behind—against the playful breeze, toward the sunlit, fragrantly whispering birch copse.

For about a minute, my companion trod in silence, head tilted toward the sky, as though contemplating the nervous flow of the clouds.

Then, in his spontaneous manner, Chris stopped and faced me. His hair was tousled, cheeks blotched, and eyes glistening with boyish pain.

'Say, Jassengro. Tell me...'

He swallowed hard.

'Yes, go on. Tell you what, Chris?'

'Tell me what you think of Indigo Mind. As a musician. A composer. And a listener. Please, be honest.'

'I think it is a masterpiece. From all these points of view.'

He gritted his teeth and breathed noisily, as if hearing my voice was a physical trial.

'Say. Do you think it is my composition? Or is it yours, really?'

'It is yours, of course.'

'Mine. It is mine, isn't it? But would it have ever been embodied at all, without your participation? And—would it, just the same, be a masterpiece? Or would it be nothing but soppy, mediocre crap, with me alone as its creator?'

'Chris.'

I halted to let the meaning of my serious intonation sink in. Then I continued.

'You know it is the bottomless depth of your soul that conceived it and the vast expanse of your talent that materialized it. I've just been your humble assistant. Your obedient instrument.'

I took another pause to allow him to object.

He did not. Intently listening, he was now drinking my words like an elixir of life.

'There is no reason for you to question yourself. You have proof of your genius, which you should allow the world to hear. Indigo Mind is not your sole brilliant creation. You have composed Freia's Motherhood, a piece of no lesser greatness. Why don't you finally perform it to the one who inspired it?'

Our conversation was getting overly intense, even for me. It was time to send Young Werther to suffer his final sorrow—back to Birgitte and Anton.

Which I did.

*

Suggesting that the romantic soul should recite his translation of Ossian to his Lotte, I knew that, sadly, it would never happen. Birgitte is not destined to hear the sonata dedicated to her—at least not in the author's performance.

Christian, however, did take my advice. After I returned to the barrack he rushed home to fetch Cosima and went looking for Birgitte everywhere around the camp. In a new bout of self-belief ignited by the pep talk I gave him, Young Werther now hastened to unleash his genius on his muse. In fact, he was wondering what had kept him from doing it so long. Why the hell had he been hesitating? What on earth had he been afraid of?

Birgitte was nowhere to be found, and Christian concluded she must be at home, working on a new article. So he went to her building. He knocked on the door.

He came to the right place this time. Birgitte was at home. She was wearing her bathrobe, chirping merry songs to the sound of the piano, and laying the table for tea in the company of Vano, Grisha the dog, and—lo and behold!—Anton Lauer.

Anton, predictably, was the one responsible for the sound of the piano, which accompanied Birgitte's nightingaling.

'Wow, Maestro, it must be Apollo himself, the patron of arts and serendipity, that brings you here!' the gregarious pianist exclaimed at the sight of his colleague. 'Our diva hostess and I have just been rehearsing for the Naturechemie Evening, and we are at more than a bit of a loss here. We need your help desperately.'

Then Anton's voice turned a tone more serious, and he asked Christian whether he had some ideas for the mentioned evening.

'The party for Naturechemie—come on, Chris, don't look so dazed! The one that's planned next Saturday! I asked you to think of some sensational piano-vocal stuff; have you forgotten? I mean, we are all set with the violin pieces, given your magic and Cosima in your hands, but, for the piano—it has to be something new! Something timeless, flowing, and soulful—we'll be negotiating a hashish deal after all! Chris, for God's sake, what's going on? You look like you don't remember shit! Are you all right?'

Chris was, of course, the very opposite of all right. And, naturally, he didn't remember anything Anton was talking about. In fact, he could barely hear what Anton was saying. His ears were filled with a humming noise; in his eyes was darkness.

When Christian found Anton in Birgitte's flat, his last bastion of hope fell. He forgot what he himself had come there for. All he now saw was that there was an affair going on between Anton and Birgitte and a conspiracy against him.

It was, all over again, revealed to Christian that Anton had stolen his scientific work. It was again made obvious to him that Birgitte had assisted Anton.

Nothing could serve as stronger evidence than finding Anton and Birgitte together at her place just when Christian decided to seek her out.

'Can I have a word with you?' Chris confronted the pianist. 'As a man with a man? Shall we step outside?'

'Goodness, Maestro, what's this about now?'

Christian's wild stare and shaky voice astonished Anton, but, true to his jolly self, Anton kept trying to make all sound like an operetta.

'All right then. Birgitte, will you excuse us a moment?'

He stood up from the piano and followed Christian outside the flat into the murkiness of the stairwell landing.

*

Since our romantic hero had by then cast aside all doubt, there was to be no beating about the bush. He drew his sword and rushed straight to the attack.

'As you and I stand here, face to face, I accuse you, Anton Lauer. I declare you guilty of betrayal, theft, and murder. I denounce your betraying a friendship and murdering a love, but I consider it beneath myself to challenge you on these two accounts. May your conscience be your judge there. In regard to your attempt at intellectual property, however, I advise you of my intention to bring the matter to the People's Court. I am going to press charges against you and the woman behind this door who aided you. And, believe me, your deed will be deemed a crime against the Motherland, for, in your vanity, you obstructed the progress of science and, in your ignorance, attempted to misuse its discoveries.

If Christian hoped to get the wind up his former friend, he achieved the effect.

The jovial smile on Anton's face was fading with every new sentence Christian uttered. Anton's usually unbreakable sense of humor was failing against such drama.

'Chris... Maestro... Whoa whoa whoa, wait! I don't understand a word you're saying. If it's a joke, I'm not getting it. Please, explain. You are freaking me out.'

More reproaches followed in the same, partly jurisprudential, partly operatic style.

Anton listened, struggling to put two and two together. Little by little, he got the picture. Christian and Birgitte must've had a brief fling; Christian now thought that Birgitte was cheating on him with Anton; Christian convinced himself that Anton tried to plagiarize his noma opus and that Birgitte was somehow involved in it.

The picture was dismaying, but at least now it was clear.

The course Anton adopted with Christian was one of comforting, reassuring, and encouragement—the very banalities I'd used on him some time before.

'Chris, my dear friend...Look, you cannot be serious... Tell me you're joking... Birgitte is like a sister to me, and you are like a brother. Closer than a brother... and whatever on earth made you think Birgitte was attracted to me? For goodness sake, she thinks I'm an infantile clown! She'd be laughing out loud if she could hear us now—but we are telling her none of this, of course. And your noma thing—holy shit, Maestro! I understand you may not be of the highest opinion about my moral qualities—indeed that you can hold them in such a low regard as to suspect me capable of stealing from a friend. It hurts, yet, I suppose, I may deserve it. But you certainly must grossly overrate my intellectual abilities to assume I could ever get my head around your boffinry, brother. You forget you are a genius here—I am a mere mortal. Should I even want to attempt at something of yours, I would never be up to it. Your theories are way over my head, Chris.

Way over everybody else's head, but your own...'

Slowly but surely, Anton's approach extinguished the flames. Christian's mood was reduced from outright belligerence to stubborn peevishness, and lower still—down to tearful remorse.

A few times Birgitte's alarmed face appeared from behind the door, the eyes widened with questions, and every time Anton raised a calming hand and shook his head slightly, asking her not to interfere.

When Christian's tears came, Anton made the decision that Birgitte would not forgive him for years to come. He felt he could handle his friend's emotional crisis alone, without female participation.

Gently and resolutely, he told Chris to wait just a moment, went into the flat, and, asking Birgitte not to worry, explained that everybody was fine—just there was an issue which needed his and Christian's urgent attention. Added that it implied no danger to anyone. Promised he would give her detailed explanations later.

At this Anton excused himself, and, counting on Vano to calm down the entirely unsettled Birgitte, he took Christian home across the market square.

*

Back home, Chris completely mellowed out. There were no accusations anymore—only apologies.

'I am not myself, Anton. I don't know what I am anymore. Please forgive me for all the horrible nonsense I said to you. It was not me, it was a daemon inside me speaking. I am beginning to believe myself possessed. A fiend entered my soul and is scorching it. Or perhaps he has always been there. I am burning within, Anton. I am lost.'

As becomes a good friend and a genial person, Anton made Chris a cup of strong tea, rushed out, and returned with a bottle of whiskey.

'Let's chase those nasty demons of yours away, old-timer.'

While they were drinking and chain-smoking, Chris's spirits seemed to lift up. He got conversational. The conversation, however, kept circulating around his noma research—somehow Chris found it hard to depart from the subject. He started sharing his latest concerns. Now that his trust in Anton was restored, he got into the most delicate details.

'With those new findings of mine, I would right away break it to the institutes and call an urgent conference. They would nominate me for the Nobel Prize, Anton. But there is a snag. An unpleasant one. Something doesn't connect. A crucial link is missing.'

He went on to complain to Anton about Damira not dying when she was supposed to, and that meant I was not going to die at the right time either, and both those factors summed up to compromise the work of the *exitium sui* mechanism.

The whiskey by then relaxed Anton, and he partly forgot he was nursing a friend through a breakdown. Anton lost caution; his amused airs returned.

'That Jassengro dark and handsome violin bugger? I didn't know you had him in the lab! I thought you and him were thick as thieves and fiddling together after lights out!'

'He was never in the lab. I was observing him outside. But this is the whole point. *Exitium sui* must stand for all used-up subs and treat them equally; otherwise, the structure collapses.'

Anton blew out his cheeks, stuck out his underlip, and shrugged lazily.

'Well, change the parameters a bit, play around with the definitions, reformulate. Don't stick to the words much. *Exitium sui* is just a metaphor you came up with, so it's up to you to rephrase it. Think of another one that'll give you freer reign.'

Christian gulped.

'*Exitium sui* is not a metaphor, Anton. It is an unshakable principle, the very physical action and primary effect of *Force Vitale*...'

'Oh, and by the way, I always wanted to suggest you reword that last one too,' Anton interrupted with a yawn. 'It's hopelessly outdated and, in our rational times, will sound way too fantasy-like for a central thesis. The Pharma-Ko bunch swallowed it, but the Hygiene will cry "unscientific" the instant they hear this *Force* whatever. They are stuffy old bags there, don't forget.'

Christian gulped again and took a lungful to voice an argument, but he suddenly felt short of breath, and, at the same time, mortally tired. It was as if he were in a moment drained of all energy. The world condensed over him to press on his head and chest with its unbearable weight.

Christian said nothing in response to Anton's suggestion. Instead, he closed his eyes and sank partly into heavy somnolence, partly into hollowed-out stupor.

To Anton, his friend looked calmed, drink-lulled, and peacefully asleep on the armchair. Therefore, Anton counted his therapy successful and the duty of friendship fulfilled. He entrusted Christian to Morpheus and quietly left for another glass at U Barbary.

*

Christian Heidert woke up this morning at six o'clock on the dot.

Chris had always been an early riser and never a particularly good drinker. Today it was partly habit, partly hangover that jolted him into wakefulness.

The wakefulness was unpleasant: numb back and aching legs from the hours slumped on the armchair; heavy head, burning mouth, queasiness—the standard set. Chris, however, found a more expressive word to define his condition—shame.

His first, sickeningly loud thought upon awakening was, *Now I know what true shame feels like.*

It was shame that weighed on his being like an entire universe—the suffocating load from which he passed out yesterday.

Though hungover, his mind was singularly clear. The memory of Anton's last monologue blazed through it like an incised wound.

"This *Force* whatever…"

'Shame, shame, shame!' screamed Christian, pressing his hands to his eyes and shaking his head furiously. 'What excruciating, hideous, and murderous shame!'

Ashamed of the people he had befriended. The society for which he had lived, invented, and created. Of himself for having been that society's eager clown.

Then, out of the fire of shame which was devouring him, a revelation came.

If he could not enlighten the world with his science, art, and love—if, in short, the world refused to be convinced by his being—perhaps it could be convinced by his ceasing to be?

The ultimate solution. The soundest decision he's ever made.

Why did it take so long to dawn on him?

Now that he knew what to do, Christian found himself busier than ever. He prepared and took a long bath—meticulously washed off yesterday's grogginess. He painstakingly greased his hair; he took particular care styling it. He wanted to spray his neck and wrists with his favorite cologne, but then rejected the idea as it smacked of vaudeville.

He wanted to put on his dress uniform but rejected that also in favor of the field gray duty one.

Non pomp. No melodrama. May it be casual. His working, creating, inventing, loving, and living daily self.

He took out of the drawer and placed upon his desk the fair copy notations of Indigo Mind and Freia's Motherhood—first in two neat piles; then, on second thought, he scattered the dusty rose sheets around a bit. May the masterpieces look casual, like their creator.

On the opposite side of the desk, he threw his *Force Vitale* typing, also as loosely as possible. The main body of work was locked up in block 32, but they will surely search the ward after they find him dead. They will bring it out.

Christian checked himself in the mirror.

Never did he look more unpretentious and sleek at the same time.

He was pleased.

He then sat on the chair before the desk, put his violin Cosima on his lap, unholstered his silent Browning 640(b), pressed it tight to his temple, closed his eyes, and pulled the trigger.

*

It is Tuesday today.

A weekday like any other, only for Chris, it used to be his "library day." It meant that on a Tuesday Chris would work on his academic writing, mostly at home, and wasn't normally expected to show up in the office or the lab. It means that, until tomorrow, no one will be surprised not to see Doctor Heidert around. Until tomorrow, no one will go looking for him.

Until tomorrow is a hell of a long time—almost a life to be lived before David and I leave this place forever.

The plan for our last day in AU is as follows: While I tie up the loose ends inside, Vatslav will perform a rather delicate task outside. Namely, he will put on a pair of rubber gloves and inconspicuously enter Christian's apartment via the door; which Anton Lauer left unlocked last night. He will take Christian's dress uniform out of the wardrobe (for Chris has chosen the field one to die in).

Then, careful not to touch anything else, Vatslav will hide the black tunic, trousers, and jackboots in a large tarpaulin sac—one of those used for medium heavy supplies he carries in and out of AU as part of his daily job.

This sac he will bring to the Jewish camp the way he regularly does with the sac's numerous copies, and bury it in the supply block, right by the entrance, next to the left wall, deep under the other sacs.

This is where it will wait for me.

I, meanwhile, will busy myself with looking after my own. I have more or less combed through the family camp; now there are the Jews to take care of. The closest circle, at least: Marek, Shlomo-the-Bagel, Abi, Max, and the Greeks. Some of them are to get out, others not. Some will be transferred to BB and later liberated there; some will not make it. It is not my business to tell them about their future, nor is it within my power to intervene in it on any of these men's behalf. My task is to ensure they each fulfill their mission while still here in AU—and they each have got an important one. For that, they need things. Simple things, like extra food rations, shoes, clothes, tools, and stationery. All the same as usual. I have hitherto provided them with those necessities via Krayowa agents, and not without help out of Guido Karp's pocket. Now I'm going to make arrangements for the flow of commodities to continue even when I'm gone from here and even when Pharma-Ko's funds run out. Outside contacts are mostly David's specialization, but he's going to need a hand to round off some deals. My hand, preferably, with Lavuta in it.

So I say my last goodbye to the Gypsy family camp—I will not return here.

Off I go to the Jewish camp and run straight into Bushalo. More precisely, into a Bushalo situation. And, considering that today's our reckoning day, the situation couldn't be more convenient.

There is a usual hue and cry around the incident. The commotion this time has been caused by what's known as "AU special treat": *Durchfall*, or starvation diarrhea. An inmate hasn't been able to make it to the latrine, soiled his pants, and is, therefore, in for a reprisal.

Szymon, the wax-complexioned, skin-and-bones culprit, is writhing at Bushalo's feet. Sour One is not only too happy to mete out punishment for such transgressions—he also takes immense pleasure in causing them. Apart from punching, kicking, and whipping, one of Bushalo's special hobbies is holding up the unfortunates with weak intestines and forcing them to perform pointless tasks just at the moment when they badly need to relieve themselves. Then, after the inevitable accident happens, the offender is made to lick the traces of his wrongdoing, as well as the latrine where he couldn't go in time, off with his tongue.

This is, apparently, the lot awaiting Szymon. Bushalo has him firm by the collar. He is hauling him over to the latrine pit, which is relatively far, behind the blocks.

Perfect.

Unseen by Bushalo, I follow him and his groaning victim. I wave at the bystanders, inviting them to come along. They do—all of them—David, Yossi, Yonas, Marek, Shlomo, Isaak, and Konstantin. While the yet unknowing Bushalo relishes the thought of the pain he is going to inflict on Szymon, my witnesses likewise anticipate the show with Bushalo in the main role, which I have promised to give them on my last day in AU.

Bringing up the rear trots Petko-the-prominent. The opportunist that he is, Petko has an unmistakable instinct for a power shift.

Bringing the semiconscious Szymon to the very edge of the cement pit, Bushalo shakes him forcefully from side to side.

'Now, my limp rag, you stick your tongue out nice and long, and you give this toilet a good licking.'

My audience forms a tight semicircle, cutting the scene off from the rest of the camp.

I strike a string vigorously.

Bushalo Karl shudders. His grip on Szymon's collar is instantly loosened.

The next moment, Bushalo lets go of his victim. Suddenly released, Szymon nearly falls into the ditch, but David, who is ready for this, rushes forward, catches him by the arm, and pulls him back to safety.

As I watch Bushalo's beafy face turn from crimson to ashen, I find myself thinking I'd drive this bulldog's teeth up through the skull with my fist much rather than soil my violin with the dirty job.

But it so happens that Bushalo is too digestible a meal for Lavuta. Much like the Russian commissars, he belongs to the type that's completely in her power—she can positively squash him. A perfect match. It is thus her sacrosnact right to carry out Bushalo's sentence.

'The stage is ours, partner,' I announce to Bushalo. 'I'll play a merry polka, and you will dance. We shall steal the show.'

By now Bushalo himself is shaking more violently than he was shaking Szymon a minute ago. His teeth are audibly rattling. He is too terrified to beg—to produce any coherent word.

The first sounds of the lighthearted Capriccio make Karl loose his bowel control and suffer massive incontinence. The brown-yellow liquid not just soaks the bottom of his overalls—it starts dripping down, between his legs, on the narrow ledge over the latrine. The ledge, clammy as it is, gets clammier.

The Intrada section has Karl's one booted foot slip and lunge forward in an improvised chasse; the other foot lags behind—and, loosing his balance, our dancer slumps into the ditch brimming with feces.

The last beats coincide with Karl hitting his head against the cemented edge of the latrine.

By the time he lands flat on his face, Bushalo is partly out. His senses, however, are in—just enough to feel every second of the latrine's content entering his nose and mouth.

There's no music anymore except for Karl's bubbly oinks, wheezes, and squelches. In about two minutes, these too die down. The carcass in overalls arches convulsively and freezes stiff in the fetid brine.

I turn to my mesmerized audience and take a quick bow.

'Hope you enjoyed the music.'

Then I personally address our "prominent" Petko.

'Now everyone will disperse and go about their usual business. You will report this mishap to your superiors at the evening roll call—not before. Got it?'

Petko shudders and comes to attention, eyes bulging.

'*Jawohl. Verstanden.*'

I pat him on the shoulder.

'*Gut.*'

*

This day has been long one—longer than I wanted it to be. The odds and ends seemed to be forever odding and never ending.

Only after the roll call, when Bushalo Karl's tragic death in the latrine came to the knowledge of the authorities, did David and I get round to our own affairs. Bushalo-the-Fierce was a conspicuous figure; his demise has caused a stir and diverted attention—exactly what I counted on.

Here at AU, I saw many die of disease, emaciation, beatings, and overwork, but I witnessed more die of sheer deprivation of the possibility to urinate or defecate when they needed to. Let Bushalo's end be in their memory.

While everybody else hustled and bustled retrieving Bushalo's corps from the latrine, David and I, unhindered, went to the supply block and drew the sac Vatslav had left for us from underneath the others. Unhurriedly, we changed—David into my overalls, I—into Christian's uniform.

David struggled with his new attire a little more than I did with mine—the exertion got him a bit nervous.

'Shit, Jass! How do you get into this?' He raised his eyes and trailed off.

'God Almighty!'

For want of a mirror, I looked into his wide open green eyes to catch my reflection.

The resemblance, I had to admit, was indeed flabbergasting.

'Well, hello, Doctor Heidert,' David muttered uncomfortably. 'If only I didn't know exactly you are not you, but my friend Jass, I would get serious doubts about spending the rest of my life in your company.'

'Ain't it a dim prospect?' I took a lungful of air and sighed melancholically, like Chris would've. 'Come on now, doubting one, pull that cap down low, and let's be off.'

And off we went—Doctor Christian Heidert and his Gypsy violin boy (David had the cased Lavuta under his left arm—the way I usually carry her—but, as we walked under the watchtowers manned by vigilant Waffen veterans, he passed her to me so that I could, ever so slightly, touch a string for their keen ears' benefit).

Past the capos on duty, past the perimeter guards; along the barb wire fence, along the undergrowth and the railway. Through the gate.

Even if someone saw Christian Heidert taking his Gypsy fiddler somewhere, they would not be curious enough to ask questions.

The only old acquaintance we stumbled upon was Guido Karp. Guido was returning from U Barbary—scruffy, snuffling, and drunk as a skunk.

As soon as Guido saw me, he made a jerky movement, began

blubbering, and fell into my arms.

'Chris… There's so much I must tell you, brother… Only you can understand,' he whimpered. 'We have to get together, one of these days, for a long talk, brother. We have to…'

'We shall, we shall,' I promised, patting his back comfortingly. 'Tomorrow, I promise. Right after you've had a good sleep.'

'I know, I know… I will, I'm going to…'

I took the wallet from Guido's trousers while he was hanging on me—we could always use extra cash.

Coda

David and I are sitting in a small mud hut in Las Wolski, drinking mulled wine with honey prepared for us by charming Chloya. The hut is our home for some days to come, courtesy of The Home Army.

It is late July, high summer—and the forest, air, our hair, and skin—all smell of honey.

I touch my warm glass to David's bare back, and he rubs against it luxuriously, stretching his limbs.

'Hey, languorous creature. Let's drink to Damira. She passed away yesterday.'

David stiffens momentarily, moves away, and drinks in silence.

He still holds and will always hold Damira's fate against me.

'She died the very next day after Heidert. Correct?' he speaks at last.

'Yes, as promised.'

'And by the way, they have already found him, haven't they?'

'They have.'

'Look.' David suddenly stirs. 'Did he leave any suicide note? You never told me. He may have indicated you.'

'No, he didn't leave any. As he wanted it to look unpompous, he decided for eternal silence to play his final note. And I swear to you, I intended no cynical pun here.'

David smirks and sips his wine silently for a little while again.

'So where are we headed next when we get the papers?'

'First to England, I guess. Will show you my birthplace. Then we'll take a boat across the Atlantic. Explore some new world.'

'To the States, you mean?'

'Yup, what do you think?'

'That's a plan. Do you know what we will do there?'

'Hmm, not really; haven't thought of that yet.'

'Do we at least know anybody there?'

'Don't think so. But we will. There's a girl who is lonely and might welcome good company.'

'Do you mean Indigo?' he guesses instantly. 'Because you promised Chris?'

'Kind of, yes. He never asked for such a promise. But I feel responsible. If nothing else, someone must play her Indigo Mind. Besides, I have a feeling we may all become good friends. What's your thoughts?'

'I agree.' He smiles and rubs his bare back against my arm.

www.ingramcontent.com/pod-product-compliance
Lightning Source LLC
Chambersburg PA
CBHW060830270525
27285CB00010B/136